SAVED BY THE ALIEN CRIME BOSS

ALIENS AMONG US #4

TIFFANY ROBERTS

SAVED BY THE ALIEN CRIME BOSS

An alien criminal in hiding. An enticing female he can't ignore. But can he protect her from his violent past?

With her birthday just around the corner, Mina Walker has found herself reflecting on her life.

Thirty and still stuck in her tiny hometown.

Thirty and still clinging to the ghosts of people she lost years ago.

Thirty and still alone. Still a virgin.

She refuses to spend this birthday by herself. So when chance brings her face to face with the town's mysterious newcomer, she knows exactly who she wants to celebrate with.

Tall, intense, and sexy as sin, Viktor Novak clearly has dark, dangerous secrets. But she never could've guessed the truth of what he is—an alien with black horns, wicked claws, and fangs that make Mina wish he'd take a bite of her.

She should be frightened of him, of what he is, yet he saves her at every turn, and every time she looks into his burning eyes, she's drawn closer until she's finds herself yearning to be incinerated by their depths.

After years of loneliness, Mina's ready; she wants him. Except she wants so much more than pleasure. She wants his heart.

She wants forever.

Check the author's website for detailed content warnings.

There are over 120 million books in the world, but you're reading this one. And that means everything to us.

This is dedicated to you.

ONE

"Should've closed up earlier," Mina mumbled as she turned her car into Cornerstone's parking lot.

She should've known. Winter storms on the forecast always got people out for some last-minute shopping. But instead of taking that into consideration, she'd kept The Bookish Bean open until seven, like usual, and hadn't skipped even a single part of her closing routine afterward.

Now it was already seven thirty-five, and Cornerstone—the only grocery store within fifty miles—closed at eight.

Twenty-five minutes is plenty of time to get my groceries.

She rolled past the parking spots in front of the entrance, all of which were taken. Big snowflakes drifted lazily through the orange glow of the building's floodlights, adding to the layer of white that had already gathered on the ground. According to the weather forecast, the snowfall would worsen overnight.

She pulled into an empty spot at the far end of the row, just outside the building's light. The clock changed to seven thirty-six.

Though she knew they wouldn't shut off the lights and lock her in the store the instant the clock struck eight, she hated the thought of inconveniencing the employees by making them stay past closing. She could imagine the angry glares they'd give her, could imagine the sound of their feet impatiently tapping the floor, could imagine the things they would be thinking but not saying out loud.

But she wouldn't have to worry about that, right? Because twenty-four minutes was still more than enough time.

Mina switched off the headlights, killed the engine, and grabbed her purse and canvas grocery bags from the passenger seat before stepping out of her SUV.

Winter air swept in to replace the warmth of the car's heater. Her first inhalation stung her nose, making it feel like shards of ice formed in her lungs. If living her whole life in Alaska hadn't been enough to get her used to the cold, she probably never would be.

Mina looked up at the sky and smiled.

She wasn't a fan of the cold, but the snow... She loved watching it fall. Loved watching the flakes dance toward the ground, loved the way they sparkled, loved that each and every one of them was unique. And she loved how the snow transformed the landscape into something magical.

Groceries, Mina. Remember? Before the store closes.

"Right," she said, bumping the car door closed with her hip.

Shouldering her purse and tucking her tote bags under her arm, she hurried to the building. The ice melt on the concrete walkway crunched under her boots in a quick rhythm.

Strings of colorful lights illuminated the store's entrance. The air smelled of fresh pine from the wreaths on display and cinnamon from the bin of scented pinecones, and she gladly breathed it all in. Mina loved the holiday scents that were prevalent this time of year.

The automatic door slid open as she approached. Just as she was about to step inside, an older man turned the corner with a bag-filled cart, nearly colliding with her. They both drew to abrupt halts.

"Whoa!" the man said, shifting his cart aside. "Sorry, Mina. Didn't see you there."

Mina smiled at him as she crossed the threshold. "It's okay, Mr. Stevens."

"Well, you're such a tiny thing, and my eyes ain't what they used to be."

"Really, it's okay."

Before she could continue onward, Mr. Stevens asked, "Say, how's that little coffee shop of yours doing?"

Grinning, Mina unzipped her coat and shook off the bit of snow that had accumulated on it. "Busy enough that I'm still in business."

Mr. Stevens chuckled. "You do make a good cup of coffee."

"I'm glad you enjoy it."

"I'll have to drop by soon. The missus loves your Danishes. Would be a nice treat for her."

Mina nodded and took a step deeper into the store, just as eager to escape this conversation as she was anxious to get her shopping done before closing. "Make sure you come in early to get them fresh."

He glanced around before he lowered his voice. "Don't tell no one, but yours are better than Randy's."

She chuckled. "Well, I learned from the best."

"You did, you did. Your mother made a fine baker, too. Too bad it wasn't enough for her to avoid all that...other business."

Mina's smile faded, and she curled her hands into fists.

Steady breaths. Stay calm.

Clenching her jaw, Mina drew in a deep breath. "Mr. Stevens, I—"

"I miss that old man though. Randy was a pillar of this community. Guess I understand him going somewhere warmer and all, but I can't imagine living anywhere but here." Mr. Stevens reached out and patted her shoulder. "But listen to me, jaw-jacking over here. I'll let you get going. You take care now, Mina."

Mina ducked out of his touch and stepped back, offering another, albeit forced, smile. "You too, Mr. Stevens. Drive safe." She turned away but paused to look back at him. "Oh, and could you let Mrs. Stevens know that a couple more of the romance books she requested came in?"

The way the old man's face reddened and fell was almost

satisfying after his comment about her mother. *Almost*. Mr. Stevens stammered a reply and rushed out into the cold.

Mina exhaled.

Suddenly quite exhausted, she walked to the carts, tugged one free, and dropped her bags into the top basket. Opening her purse, she pulled out her phone.

Twenty-one minutes until closing.

"Shouldn't be a problem," she muttered, unlocking the phone to bring up her grocery list.

Her confidence in those words was sorely tested when she glanced over to see only a single register open with a long line of people waiting. Cornerstone's owner must've loved this time of year.

Quietly humming along to the holiday music playing on the overhead speakers, Mina moved through the aisles, placing items into her cart. As she did so, she couldn't stop her thoughts from returning to her conversation with Daniel Stevens.

Mina had opened her coffee shop and bookstore, The Bookish Bean, seven years ago. Before she'd owned it, the place had been the Thomas Bakery, owned by Randy Thomas. Mina's mother had worked there for years before Mina joined the staff at fifteen.

That time of her life had produced some of Mina's favorite memories. Some of her best memories. Randy had always been supportive, basically filling the role of grandfather for Mina, but working there had only brought them all closer together. He'd taken her and her mom fishing in the summer, baked them personal birthday cakes every year, and would close the bakery early for private little celebrations. It had been the first time in a long while that she'd felt secure, safe, happy...

But that had been so long ago. Now, it was just her. Randy had retired, sold Mina the shop, and moved to Arizona. Her mother had passed almost twelve years ago, and her father...

It would be twenty years next year.

Everyone Mina loved had been gone for years. She'd be thirty in six days. Thirty years old, and just as alone as she'd been at twenty-two.

Thirty years old and still a virgin.

How sad was that?

Well, that's quite a turn in my train of thought.

More like a derailment.

Mina wrinkled her nose as she turned down the pasta aisle. There were...reasons for her celibacy, but the main one had been the fact that she'd never felt that spark, that ember of desire, for anyone. Not once.

As much as she loved reading romance books, she'd never met someone who'd made her feel even the slightest hint of the yearning those stories described. She knew those books were fictional, that her expectations were probably too high, but she was supposed to at least feel something, right?

And it wasn't that Mina had no interest in sex. She did. She really, *really* did, especially more recently as it seemed her libido had kicked into overdrive. But her own fingers and the toys tucked away in her bedroom drawer weren't enough. Self-pleasure dulled the urges, but afterward, when the high wore off, there was always an emptiness. A deep, ever-expanding loneliness. She longed to feel another person's arms wrapped around her in a tender embrace, to feel their warmth, their breath on her skin, the beat of their heart beneath her palm.

She longed to simply feel...loved and wanted.

The few guys she'd dated had been physically appealing, but there'd been nothing more there—no chemistry, no substance. A bit of attraction simply hadn't been adequate to sustain anything lasting.

There just hadn't been enough to make Mina want to open herself to anything physical. Especially sex.

It didn't help that most of the townsfolk were so judgmental when it came to Mina's mother, even all this time after her death. Sullford was a small town filled with people who did nothing but gossip and whisper behind each other's backs. The only thing Hannah Walker's passing had changed was that the judgment more often came with pity rather than disdain.

Anger simmered in Mina as she dropped a couple boxes of spaghetti into her cart.

Let it go, Mina. Don't let them get to you.

She released a heavy exhalation as she continued down the aisle to the sauces, where she looked up and groaned. Not only was her favorite sauce on the top shelf, but the jars were pushed toward the back, barely within sight and completely out of her reach.

She hopped in place, catching a glimpse of three remaining jars.

"Dang it."

Mina glanced around. There was no one in sight, and given how short-staffed this place always seemed to be and how close it was to closing time, she doubted she'd find an employee to help.

She sighed, faced the shelves, and pursed her lips to the side.

Looks like I'm on my own.

Nothing she wasn't already used to.

It wasn't like this was the first time she'd have to scale the shelves to get something she needed.

Taking hold of a higher shelf, she stepped onto the bottom one. "They seriously need to provide step ladders if they're going to stock things so high."

Mina released the shelf with one hand and reached for the jars. They were still too far back. Flattening her palm on the top shelf, she climbed up onto the edge of the next, pulling herself higher. She stretched her arm. The tips of her fingers brushed the side of a jar.

"Just a little more..." Determined, Mina pressed her lips together and stood on her toes, extending her reach.

Her wet boot slipped.

She gasped, and her heart stopped. Mina flailed for purchase, but she'd already lost her grip, was already falling backward.

Her back hit something solid but yielding, and a pair of strong arms wrapped around her waist from behind, fingers gripping her tight.

Fall successfully halted by the stranger, Mina looked down to find herself hanging in his arms, the toes of her boots inches above the polished concrete floor. Only those arms and the big body they were attached to supported her.

Somehow, she felt more secure and stable than she had with her feet on the ground.

I must've lost my mind, because this is kind of...nice.

The rich, woodsy scent of teakwood enveloped Mina. It was accompanied by leather and cloves, and something earthy, smoky, and musky. She inhaled, drawing that masculine fragrance in deep. It spread through her languidly, heating her, *arousing* her.

Had any man ever smelled so divine?

Mariah Carey's *All I Want For Christmas Is You* blasted over the store's sound system.

Warmth suffused Mina's face.

"Umm, thanks," she said, offering the man's arm an awkward pat.

His chest rumbled with a grunt, and he gently set her onto her feet, let her go, and stepped back.

Mina steadied herself, tugged her coat back into place, and took in another deep breath, once more filling her lungs with that heady fragrance.

Nope. No man has ever smelled this good.

Smiling, she turned, intending to thank the stranger again for saving her from what would've been, at best, a bruised backside. At worst, they would've needed to call for a cleanup on aisle three for her brains being spattered across the floor.

She froze.

Her eyes settled on the broad expanse of his chest and shoulders, which were covered in a long-sleeved black shirt that didn't do much to hide the muscles beneath. She dragged her gaze upward. He was tall enough that she had to tip her head back to fully see him.

His black hair was drawn into a thick bun atop his head, with long wisps dangling to either side of his face and behind his ears. His features were sharp—a chiseled jaw, high cheekbones, and a straight, narrow, pointed nose that led up to thick, arched eyebrows. But it was his silver eyes that held her captive. They were so ethereal, so mesmerizing, that she wondered if they were even human.

Mina's heart quickened.

Viktor Novak.

He was the most beautiful man she'd ever seen.

Not that this was her first glimpse of him. Mina had seen him around town a few times since he'd moved to Sullford a year ago, whether in a fleeting glance as he walked past her shop or the occasional sighting here at Cornerstone. She'd thought him handsome from afar. But this close, he was utterly breathtaking.

And everything within her body was reacting to him.

"Are you all right?" Viktor asked, his deep, gravelly voice bearing a thick accent she couldn't quite place.

Mina started. "Oh! Um, yes."

Smooth, Mina. Real smooth. Just keep staring, because that's totally normal.

"I...don't normally make a habit of falling for men—er, I mean, *onto* men..." Mina cringed. "Okay, that didn't sound any better."

The corner of his mouth ticked up, adding a wicked edge to his features.

Oh God...

Mina cleared her throat and shifted on her feet. "What I'm trying to say is thank you for saving me. They, uh"—she gestured to the shelves—"don't make it easy for shorter people."

His gaze flicked to the shelf. He stepped closer, and that masculine scent wafted over her anew as he reached up and effortlessly plucked down one of the jars of sauce. He held it out to her.

Mina stared at his hand. Why was she only now realizing how sexy hands could be? Was it simply because it was Viktor's hand? Its size, its long fingers, its defined knuckles and tendons. There was strength in it, undeniable strength.

"This is what you want, isn't it?" he asked.

Oh, it was definitely what she wanted. Those hands all over her, caressing her flesh, those fingers slipping between her—

Viktor chuckled. It was a low sound, rumbling and gritty like his voice, with a dark allure that teased at unspoken promises. She watched, unable to process what was happening, as he took her wrist and lifted her arm.

His big hand completely encircled her wrist, even with the padding of her coat. She yearned for him to slide that hand under the cuff of her sleeve and...

He placed the jar on her upturned palm.

The touch of the cold glass snapped her out of her trance.

Were you really just standing there staring at his hand that whole time? What is wrong *with you?*

"Oh! Yes, thank you." She snatched her arm out of his hold. Clutching the jar to her chest, she looked down at it and let her short, curly hair fall forward to hide her blush from him. "I guess I could've picked one of the others, but it's not the first time I've had to do that. Climb the shelves, I mean. I've never fallen before. I just... I hate to trouble the employees and feel like a burden when there are twenty other sauces within reach just because this one's my fav—"

Mina snapped her mouth shut and wrinkled her nose. "I'm sorry, I'm rambling."

"Do not apologize," he said. "There's no shame in taking what you want."

What if I want you?

Her cheeks burned hotter.

She peeked up at Viktor to find him staring at her. "Could you...get another for me? If you don't mind? I probably shouldn't try climbing again."

Those otherworldly silver eyes lingered on her for a moment, his expression unreadable, before he took another jar down for her. As she turned to place the sauces in her cart, she willed herself to calm.

Chill, Mina. Just be chill.

You live in Alaska. When are you not chill?

When I'm speaking to an insanely attractive man, apparently.

Straightening, Mina faced Viktor. "So...you're the new guy, right? The one who bought the cabin out on the lake?"

He narrowed his eyes and slowly tilted his head. "Yes."

"People have been talking about you since the day you moved in. You're kind of a mystery around here." Mina clasped her fingers against her belly. "Sorry if that comes off a little creepy? I own the coffee shop bookstore, and people come in all the time with gossip, so I just hear things."

"The Bookish Bean."

"That's the one!" Lips stretching into a sheepish smile, she gave him a little wave before extending her hand. "Hi! I'm Mina Walker. Usually I start with the 'hi' part, but I was a bit busy falling for—*when*, I mean falling when—you showed up, so..."

His gaze fixed on her mouth, and he remained unmoving.

Mina leaned closer and playfully lowered her voice. "You're supposed to take my hand, shake it, and tell me your name."

Viktor drew in a breath, and his pupils expanded. His eyes only grew more focused, more intense, and something sparked in their depths. That spark caused heat to curl low in her belly and made her sex clench.

Is this *what real attraction feels like?*

Viktor's hand engulfed hers. His skin was rough and warm, and his hold was firm yet gentle. And that touch, that skin-to-skin contact, sent a rush through Mina that made her flesh prickle in awareness and her heart pound wildly.

He shook her hand—not up and down, but side to side. "You already know who I am, Mina."

How could a name be said so seductively? How could *her* name be said that way?

Mina chuckled a little breathlessly. "It's nice to finally officially meet you, Viktor."

He dipped his chin in a shallow nod. When she withdrew her hand, he released it, though she sensed a slight reluctance from him. The air felt colder in the absence of his touch.

Mina curled her fingers against her palm, sorely tempted to take his hand again. "So, what brought you to Sullford?"

"The quiet."

"It is pretty quiet here. I'm sure it's even more so at your cabin.

I've never been there personally, but I saw pictures of it on the flyer board right here in Cornerstone when it went up for sale. It's a beautiful place, and the scenery is gorgeous. Though the pictures were taken in summer, when everything was bright and green. I bet it's—"

Mina pulled her lips in and bit them as she thrust her hands into her coat pockets. "Sorry. You were just helping me get something down and here I am babbling away, taking up your time."

"It is," he said, his eyes again on her mouth.

"It is...what?"

Viktor met her gaze. "Beautiful."

Heat swept through Mina. "Oh."

The cabin. He's talking about his cabin, Mina. Not you.

Static crackled over the PA system before an employee, voice muddied by the speakers, announced, "Attention Cornerstone shoppers, we will be closing in five minutes. Please bring your items to the front now so we can get you checked out."

Mina's eyes widened. "Shoot!" She grabbed her cart with one hand, her phone with the other, and quickly unlocked the screen. "I still have some things to grab. I'm so sorry!"

"Find me if there's anything else you can't reach," Viktor replied. "But it might cost you next time."

Mina chuckled. "You should come by the café. I'd love to give you a coffee, or a pastry, or even a book to thank you."

Viktor offered another small nod, and it made her belly flutter when the corner of his lips again curled upward.

As she walked away, pushing her cart ahead of her, she felt his gaze upon her back like it was a physical touch. Though the sensation faded when she rounded the corner, it took a few more steps for that fluttery feeling to pass, and even then, she still felt like he was close.

Mina rushed through the store, tossing the rest of her groceries in the cart. The deli was already closed, so she settled on prepackaged cold cuts before making her way to the front.

The line at the register had dwindled to only two people. Mina drew her cart to a stop behind them.

It took everything inside her to keep from looking around for Viktor. Was he still shopping, or had he already checked out? Had he left?

Would he actually visit her café?

He came for the quiet, but you stood there yapping his ear off.

But...he listened to me. Smiled at me.

That's called being polite. You should be able to recognize it, you have to do it every day.

Her mouth fell into a frown as a new realization struck her. Viktor wasn't local, but he'd been in town for a year, and he knew of Mina and her café. What had he heard about her and her family?

She tightened her grip on the cart's handle.

Let it go, Mina. Just let it go.

When she reached the conveyor belt, she stacked her items atop it. By the time she was done, the person in front of her had finished paying, allowing Mina to step up the keypad.

The cashier, an elderly woman, glanced at her and asked her about her day. The conversation was awkward but thankfully brief as the woman rang everything up.

Once Mina had paid, she returned her cart to the front of the store and grabbed her bags and purse. She offered a smile to the employee at the door before stepping outside.

The cold struck her immediately. She shivered, wishing she'd zipped her coat.

"Just need to make it to the car and then you can be nice and toasty with the heater again."

A lock clicked behind her. Mina glanced back to see the employee walking away through the glass doors. A moment later, the interior lights dimmed.

Snow drifted down around Mina as she walked to her car. The parking lot was much emptier and eerier than it had been when she'd arrived. Every sound was muffled by the snowfall, even that of the ice melt breaking under her boots and the rasping of her coat's material. The world was preternaturally quiet.

Upon reaching her car, she slid the handles of the bags higher up her arm so she could reach into her purse.

Her brow furrowed as she searched for her keys. "How do they always disappear when there's hardly anything in here?"

Down in the deepest, farthest corner of the purse, her fingers touched the metal of her keys. She felt for the key fob and pressed the button to unlock the car. It beeped, and the lights flashed.

Mina opened the rear driver's side door, deposited her bags on the seat, and shut the door.

Snow crunched behind her.

Before she could turn, something heavy collided with her, violently shoving her forward. She slammed into the side of the SUV. Her bare hands struck the frigid metal, the air burst from her lungs, and her purse was crushed between her body and the door. Snow fell from the roof, dusting the top of Mina's head.

A gloved hand roughly covered her mouth, and something sharp pressed into her side. Mina whimpered, trying to shift away from it, but the hard point dug deeper into her skin through her sweater. She cried out, but the hand muffled her voice.

"Not a sound," the man growled into her ear as he pinned her against the car with his body. "Don't you make a fucking sound."

Terror flooded her as she stared, wide-eyed, at the reflection on the car window before her. She could vaguely make out the shadow of the man behind her, but nothing more. The image became distorted as tears welled in her eyes. Her breath sawed in and out through her nose, and her heart raced. With this side of her car facing away from the store's entrance, toward the blank brick wall of the neighboring building, no one would see them.

The man squeezed her face, crushing her cheeks against her teeth. "Did you hear me?"

Trembling, Mina nodded as much as he allowed her to.

He removed his hand from her mouth and held it out to the side. "Give me your purse."

She turned her wrist. Her knuckles scraped the side of the car as she curled her fingers around the handles of her purse. She tried tugging her arm free, but it was tightly wedged between her and the vehicle.

"I said give me your fucking purse!" The man dug the knife more firmly into her side. The tip broke her skin with a flaring sting that was followed by a bloom of heat.

Mina clamped her lips together to hold in a cry of pain as her tears spilled.

"I-I can't," she whispered raggedly.

With a curse, he withdrew the blade, grabbed a fistful of her hair, and bashed her head against the window.

Pain exploded through Mina's skull, and the world went fuzzy. The man thrust his hand between her and the car and grabbed the strap of her purse, ripping it from her grasp.

Something growled—not quite human, not quite animal, but wholly unsettling.

The man withdrew so abruptly that Mina staggered backward. Her head was spinning, her legs were wobbly, and her backward steps somehow turned her around. Just as her legs gave out, her back hit the side of her car. She slumped down onto the cold, snowy pavement.

The pressure in her head increased, and her sight dimmed around the edges. Two men struggled before her—one lying on his back, the other straddling him. Though they were only feet away from her, their shadowy forms were indistinct amidst the falling snow. Their snarls, grunts, and curses were so faint, so distant...

She strained to bring the men into focus, but the harder she tried, the more the darkness encroached on her vision.

Her eyelids fell shut. As her body grew heavier and colder, her head felt lighter, and her mind grew oddly detached, as though her consciousness were floating away. The quiet around her expanded. She felt the delicate, icy kisses of snowflakes lighting upon her cheeks and nose, and she caught a hint of the most delightful smell—teakwood and cloves.

Then she succumbed to the serene embrace of darkness.

TWO

He harmed Mina.

That thought blazed through Sevik's head anew with each thump of his heart, flooding him with waves of roiling heat. He felt his control over his holoshroud wavering, felt its projected disguise threatening to flicker, threatening to expose him.

The male human struggled beneath him like a wild animal, desperate and reeking of terror. He flailed, writhed, kicked, and clawed, but Sevik would not be dislodged.

He. Harmed. Mina.

Sevik hammered his fists into the man's face again and again, setting a brutal rhythm. The human curled his arms around his head to shield himself; Sevik only rained blows upon the man harder, faster.

Each punch landed with a dull, meaty *thwap*. He'd heard such sounds countless times throughout his life. They were especially insignificant and unsatisfying now after hearing the hollow thud of Mina's head striking her vehicle's window. Sevik needed more—more volume, more impact, more damage inflicted.

He needed more to drown out the memory of that sound, of the quavering fear in her voice, of how wrong this all was.

Zekt'al, none of that should matter to me!

But it was Mina. *Mina.*

A growl tore out of his chest, and he bared his fangs, further quickening his blows, punishing anything within the path of his fists. Pain and warmth radiated in his knuckles, but the sensations were muted.

The smell of human blood, with its iron tang, filled Sevik's nose, tainting the crisp night air and Mina's clean, sweet, alluring fragrance. His nostrils flared. Something within him reveled in that blood scent—a dark, ferocious, ravenous thing in the pit of his being, the primal part of Sevik that had carried him through a life of struggle and strife.

A life he was supposed to be hiding from.

Snarling a curse, Sevik stilled his hands. The human's black knitted facemask glistened with blood and condensation, the flesh around his eyes was swollen, his lips were split, and his teeth, at least those not missing, were stained red. His ragged breaths drifted into the night in small, fleeting clouds, and his limbs lay unmoving in the snow.

He harmed Mina.

Sevik clenched his fists so tightly they shook. He had every reason to kill this human...and only one reason not to.

Fuck.

The male groaned, and his head lolled. Droplets of his blood were scattered across the snow, coloring it pink and red. Mina's purse lay to the man's left, while the knife, its blade partially covered by the snow, lay to his right.

Gritting his teeth, Sevik shoved himself to his feet, lifted his gaze, and swept it around the lot.

The only remaining vehicles were Mina's SUV and Sevik's truck, which was parked closer to the store's entrance. Any tire tracks left by the recently departed cars were already filling in with snow. Cornerstone's interior lights were dimmed, and the employees, who usually parked behind the building, seemed to have gone home for the night.

Yet even with this spot being beyond the reach of the store's exterior lighting, it was only a matter of time before someone drove by on Main Street and saw something.

Witnesses were complications, and complications were to be avoided.

Sevik snatched up the fallen knife, tucked it under his belt, and strode to Mina. She lay on her side next to her vehicle with her eyes closed, her coat open, and a light dusting of snow atop her, breathing but unaware.

She looked so small there, so pale and vulnerable. And even now, so fucking beautiful.

He'd seen this scenario before. He'd been the aggressor, and he'd taken from people who'd already had so little. Innocents were caught in the crossfire all the time. What made her different? Why the fuck did he care at all?

Why does my route always take me past her café when I'm in town?

Why do I always glance through her window as I walk by?

Why do I always glance through her window as I go by, and why do my eyes always find her instantly no matter how many humans are inside?

Growling, Sevik knelt, scooped up some snow, and scrubbed his bloody hands clean. After wiping them dry on the sides of his shirt, he slipped a hand under the female's neck. "Mina?"

She didn't respond. Her pulse was slow and faint against his palm, and her skin was cool.

Keeping her neck supported, Sevik carefully lifted her into a sitting position and checked her for wounds.

The red flesh on her forehead was swollen, pulled tight over a lump forming beneath. Her mouth and the skin around it were also reddened, though not as severely. A shallow puncture wound on her side had stained her sweater with blood.

Sevik gritted his teeth and somehow resisted the violent urge to return to her attacker.

"Mina," he repeated, patting her cheek. "Wake up."

Again, she did not react.

Each beat of Sevik's heart was a distant boom. His knowledge of humans was lacking, but he knew head trauma was a serious risk to them. Who could say what damage had been done under the surface?

"This isn't easy to get on this planet," he muttered as he lowered a hand to the small case on his belt and glanced around the lot again. He already had his med injector in hand when he returned his attention to Mina. Angling her head aside, he pressed the tool to her neck and activated it. "You owe me, female."

With a *click-hiss*, the tool injected her with the serum that had saved Sevik's life many, many times. He could only hope it would have the same amplified healing properties for a human as it did for most other species.

Mina still did not stir.

Headlights from the street cut across the parking lot.

Sevik pressed his shoulder against Mina's vehicle and curled over her, shielding her with his body. He quickly returned the injector to its case and grasped the pistol hidden under his waistband at his back. Tension rippled through him as he watched the lights glide across the ground; the vehicle was turning onto Main Street, which ran parallel to the front of Cornerstone. It would drive right past this little scene.

For an instant, the headlight beams hit the back of Mina's SUV, spilling bright light across the snow only feet away from Sevik. Then the vehicle straightened, and the beams swung away.

Sevik didn't draw his weapon, but neither did he release it.

Snow crunched beneath the vehicle's wheels, and the engine rumbled. Sevik flattened himself against Mina's car as much as he could without crushing her.

The vehicle rolled past. It was another SUV, with *SULL-FORD POLICE* written on the side in gold and black letters.

Cyr orkaal. Nine hundred people in this town, yet it had to be one of the three fucking cops who drove past now?

He glimpsed the face of an older human male in the glow of the dashboard instruments within the cab—likely the police chief, Dick Harrigan—before the vehicle moved out of sight.

Sevik didn't ease until he couldn't hear it anymore.

Releasing the weapon, Sevik glanced at the male who'd attacked Mina. He knew how this would look to the local authorities. Two injured, unconscious humans in a dark parking lot after the store had closed, one of them severely beaten...and only the town's gossiped-about outsider, Viktor Novak, left standing.

Suspicion would fall on him. Blame would fall on him. And whatever the truth, the authorities would draw their own conclusions, would create their own narrative.

He was supposed to be hiding, was supposed to be... What was the human term? Lying down? Lying...low?

This was anything but that.

Yet whether on Vabos or here on Earth, the instincts Sevik had honed over the years would serve him well.

He eased Mina down again, rose, and stepped away from her. Something tried to pull him back to her immediately; denying that urge was far more difficult than he could've anticipated.

How had he managed to stay away from her before now? He'd been drawn to Mina from the moment he'd seen her through the front window of her shop a year ago, when he'd first arrived in Sullford. How had he resisted? *Why* had he resisted?

Because things couldn't have gone far before she noticed some differences in our anatomies. Aggaan sin thar!

Sevik tugged his gloves from his pocket and slipped them on. His claws, rendered invisible by his holoshroud, slipped through the cuts at the ends of the fingers. He grabbed the male human by the coat and hauled him off the ground, tossing him over his shoulder. The man groaned with the pain and confusion of the not-quite-conscious.

With long strides, Sevik carried the man toward the store's entrance, activating his neural transceiver as he walked. The readout flashed into his field of view, highlighting the building's various computer and electronic systems.

If for nothing else, he was grateful that he'd already hacked into so many of the town's systems. It would save precious time now.

Neural commands set the implanted transceiver to work.

Before he'd even reached the entrance, the cameras were deactivated with their recordings for the day wiped, the alarm was disarmed, and the automatic lock on the entry door was disengaged.

Cornerstone's door slid open as Sevik neared. Without slowing, he stepped inside and dumped the human on the floor.

The man grunted and curled onto his side, grating out what must've been a curse.

Sevik continued deeper into the store. He grabbed a bottle of wine from a shelf on his way to the coolers, where he collected six cans of beer connected by plastic rings. Alcohol in hand, he returned to the front of the store, where he paused to kick the man in the stomach.

The man doubled over with another groan.

"Hurt?" Sevik asked.

A strained sound of assent emerged from the man's throat.

With his thumb claw, Sevik sliced away the foil around the wine bottle's spout before prying the cork out. A firm shove from his foot rolled the human onto his back. Sevik planted his boot on the man's chest, pinning him in place.

"Touch what's mine again, and I'll cut off your fingers one by one and shove them down your fucking throat."

He tilted the bottle and poured the red liquid onto the man's face. Some of it fell into the human's mouth, but his sputtering and writhing splashed much more onto the floor.

Sevik dropped the bottle beside the man. It landed with a *clang*, but the thick glass remained intact. He tore a beer can from the bunch, popped the tab, and poured that onto the man next. The empty can soon joined the bottle on the floor.

As he opened another beer, Sevik leaned down, putting more weight on the man's chest. The wheezing human weakly grasped Sevik's leg.

Growling, Sevik caught the man's cheeks and squeezed, forcing his mouth open. He poured the amber liquid directly into the man's mouth.

The human choked and squirmed, spraying beer and spittle

over his own face as he struggled to swallow. Part of Sevik wanted to see this fucker drown, though it would be an easier death than he deserved.

Sevik poured faster, watching the man struggle until the can was empty.

Still breathing. Too bad.

Need to get back to Mina. Wasting too much time on this esklaat.

Opening a third beer, Sevik pried one of the man's hands loose and pressed the can into it.

The human coughed and retched.

"Drink." Sevik dropped the remaining beers atop the man's chest before slapping his cheek. "Might help with the pain."

Not sparing the man another moment, Sevik exited the store, removing his gloves and stuffing them back in his pocket. The door closed behind him, and the lock engaged. Scanning his surroundings ceaselessly, he hurried to his truck, climbed in, and started it. He pulled up beside Mina's vehicle, turned off the engine, and hopped out.

Mina remained just as he'd left her—tiny, pale, and dusted with snow. He pressed his fingers to her neck. Her pulse was a bit faster and stronger. A minor improvement, but it was something.

Delicately as he could, Sevik brushed the snow from her coat and pants. He gathered her in his arms, holding her against his chest, and brought her to his truck. Somehow, she looked even smaller once he'd laid her on the back seat. Sevik leaned into the cab and folded one of his spare coats, tucking it under her head for support.

Closing the door, he returned to her vehicle and collected her purse from the ground. He pried it open and peered inside. Her keys were at the bottom, beneath her wallet, her phone, an electronic tablet, a pack of tissues, and a few other strange human items.

Sevik sighed. "Not how I'm supposed to be spending my evening."

He tugged open the driver's door of her car and climbed in.

His knees bumped the bottom and sides of the steering wheel, which also pressed against his chest. With a growled curse, he tossed Mina's purse onto the passenger seat, reached down between his legs, and blindly felt for the release. The wheel dug into the side of his arm, and his cheek came dangerously close to pressing the horn.

It felt like the space was getting tighter with each moment.

Finally, his fingers hooked the bar. He tugged it up and shoved back with his legs. The seat jolted backward and slammed against the ends of its rails, shaking the whole vehicle.

Zekt'al, but she was a tiny thing.

Oddly, that thought diffused his annoyance.

He shut the door even as he pressed the button to start the engine. A flick of a lever cleared most of the snow from the windshield with the wipers; he wasted no time shifting into gear and pulling out of the parking lot.

Reaching Mina's home was simple enough—it wasn't even half a mile away, straight down Main Street. Thankfully, most of the town's other businesses were closed, and the road was all but deserted. He pulled into her driveway and parked behind the building, where she usually kept her car.

Sevik grabbed her purse, killed the engine, and pulled himself out of the vehicle. His steady heartbeat marked each passing moment.

It was only a matter of time before someone would pass Cornerstone and notice his truck in the parking lot. It was only a matter of time before the masked human regained his senses and created a commotion inside the store. It was only a matter of time before the serum either healed whatever damage had been done to Mina...

Or before it killed her because it was incompatible with humans.

That possibility made his stomach twist. He clenched his jaw and shook away the alien feeling.

Death was nothing new. People died all the time, and he'd

done plenty of killing himself. Why feel grief now, when she was still alive? Why feel it for her at all?

Because it's Mina.

Get fucking moving.

Only as he was turning away from her car did he notice the bags on the back seat—the groceries she'd just bought, including the jars of sauce he'd taken down for her. His fingers tingled with the memory of their hands touching when he'd handed a jar to her. That delicate brush of skin had awoken something hot within Sevik, something with a fierce yearning.

After retrieving the bags, he locked her car and returned to Cornerstone. Though the snow and bright streetlights counter- acted the night's darkness, the snowfall was heavy enough to reduce visibility and provide him with some cover as he moved. He kept out of sight as much as possible and used his neural trans- ceiver to erase his presence from any surveillance devices he passed.

His heart rate had quickened by the time he reached his truck. Using the side of his boot, he kicked the bloody snow nearby, breaking up the crimson stains until they were unnoticeable. Then he tugged open the driver's side door, climbed into the cab, and placed Mina's belongings on the passenger seat.

Grasping the back of the seat, he twisted to check on her.

Mina Anastasia Walker was unmoving but for her breathing.

He closed the door, started the engine, and drove. Just before exiting the lot, he sent a neural command to reactivate the store's alarm system.

Sevik had no doubt the alarm would be tripped soon enough, but there'd be no evidence of either himself or Mina having been anywhere near Cornerstone when it happened.

The town remained unsettlingly peaceful, like all the people of Sullford, many of whom had been out only an hour ago, had vanished simultaneously. Yet there was no peace to be found inside Sevik's truck.

Mina's scent dominated the air. It was layered, a blend of

smells for which he'd learned the names largely by sampling scented candles at the grocery store. A hint of coffee—lingering on her from the café—with raspberry, lavender, and something clean and crisp, reminiscent of snowfall. That fragrance built a heady fog in his mind and flowed into his blood on growing waves of warmth.

His gums ached, and he clenched his teeth as he fought back primal instincts to bite her, to mark her, to mate with her.

To imprint upon her.

Sevik growled. His hands tightened around the steering wheel, making it creak. Heat coalesced low in his belly.

Only one thing made it possible to resist the lure of that scent, to deny the insistent impulses. The faint smell of blood—Mina's blood.

He latched onto that scent and held it at the forefront of his mind.

She's hurt. I will not harm her further.

She's hurt.

And I'm not human.

Sevik slowed as he approached Mina's café. He'd sometimes watched her through its front window—watched her smile brightly to customers, watched her wipe her brow and catch her breath after a busy afternoon, watched the longing looks that sometimes crept onto her face when no one else was around, especially while she was reading. He'd seen her around town too. He'd seen her grin as snowflakes tumbled through the air, had seen her stick out her tongue to catch them upon it. He'd seen the warm summer sunlight play upon her dark brown curls.

Mina was vibrant, kind, and alluring. He had never been drawn to a female like her.

Never *wanted* a female like her.

It would've been easy enough to stop and bring her up to her apartment, which was over the shop. Would've been easy to lay her in her own bed. But to think it would've been easy to leave afterward, to cease his involvement in this, would've been foolish.

He still had no idea what the serum would do to her, and he couldn't leave her to the unknown.

And part of him still insisted that he take what he wanted. That he take what was his.

Because even if he couldn't have her, Mina was fucking his.

So he kept driving, heading for the only secure place he knew—his residence.

Sullford's soft lights and brick and wood buildings gave way to dark woodland as he followed the road out of town. Tall, white-crusted trees loomed on either side, offering glimpses of rugged terrain between their trunks.

Sevik made his turns with little conscious thought. He'd been sure to familiarize himself with the land upon arriving here, making navigation second nature.

Maybe one day it'll be second nature to stay out of situations that don't involve me.

He squeezed the steering wheel again. Things were different. *Everything* was different. This wasn't Vabos, he didn't have connections here, didn't have the power and influence he'd once commanded. The smart thing to do was keep quiet, avoid attention, and bide his time.

But what was the point of such an existence? Without risks, without struggle, without rewards, why bother? He would create an opportunity to return to Vabos, kill that traitorous fucking coward, Brekker, and take back what was his. Yet why deny himself pleasure until then? Why stop living while his heart was still beating?

He knew better than to underestimate anyone, even these relatively unadvanced humans, but he refused to cower in hiding.

Grasping the rearview mirror, he angled it down sharply. He couldn't see Mina's face in it, but he could see her chest, slowly rising and falling, and one of her dainty hands, its pale skin contrasted by the dark gray paint on her blunt claws.

The only way he could've left her behind tonight was by never having been there in the first place. He was neither arrogant nor delusional enough to believe that he would've been able to witness her get attacked, shrug, and leave without a second thought.

Not Mina.

After several turns onto increasingly narrower roads, Sevik reached his property. The trees opened to reveal his cabin and the serene lake beyond. It had already frozen over, and the wind had blown most of the snow to the shoreline, leaving the ice bare.

He pulled in under the carport, turned off the truck, and slipped out. After checking her pulse again, he carefully lifted Mina from the back seat and carried her into the cabin. In the entry room, he slid off his boots before he removed hers, along with her coat, setting them aside to dry.

The automated interior lights came on, and the holo-shades he'd installed adjusted the tint of the windows, preserving his view while making it impossible to look in from outside.

Not quite realizing what he was doing, he walked through the kitchen and climbed the stairs to his loft bedroom. The vaulted ceiling and floor-to-ceiling windows overlooking the snowy forest on the other side of the bed made the room feel spacious.

He swept the covers aside and laid Mina on the bed. Again, he couldn't help noticing just how small and delicate she was, just how lovely. Something warm stirred in his chest at the sight of her there, in his bed, surrounded by his scent and adding hers to the air.

She seemed to...fit here. And something deep inside Sevik urged him to lie beside her and hold her, to share his warmth with her, to experience her softness, to shield her from the universe with his body, to—

Vazk, *what the fuck is wrong with me?*

The only reason he'd ever had a female in his bed had been to rut. There'd been no affection involved, no cuddling, no comfort. They'd use each other for sexual release, and he'd send them on their way. He had no desire to share his bed beyond that.

But with Mina...

Sevik forced himself into motion again. Her sweater and pants were wet, the former stained by blood. Barely keeping his hands steady, he removed the damp garments. Every bit of pale, smooth flesh revealed in the process was a test of his willpower, especially when his skin met hers.

It was soft. So fucking soft.

Mina's heady scent only made it harder, overcoming all others to cloud his mind. He raked his gaze over her body; those slender, shapely legs, the little flare of her hips, that narrow waist, the smooth plane of her belly, the swell of her breasts, her elegant neck...

Sevik once more filled his lungs with her fragrance. His gums itched, and his fangs ached to mark her flesh, to leave a sign for all to see that she was his.

With a claw, he hooked the material connecting the cups of her bra and lifted it away from her skin. The only things hiding her cunt and her small, pert breasts from him were a few scraps of white, lacy fabric.

His cocks strained behind his slit. He wanted to rut her, *needed* to imprint upon her. To make her his in every way.

Take.

Take.

Take.

A flick of his claw would slice the material, and the bra would fall away...

No!

He shook his head sharply.

Aggaan sin thar, she's wounded and fucking unconscious.

Sevik forced his gaze to her side. He lightly touched his fingers to the skin around her wound as he tried to ignore the effects of her scent, nearness, and feel. The puncture wound was no longer bleeding. It seemed to be closing, albeit slower than it would've for Sevik's kind.

"Fuck," he rasped as fire blazed through his veins and his confined cocks twitched. He held his breath and clenched his jaw, but the pressure only worsened the ache in his fangs and deepened his desire.

Lungs burning, Sevik pushed away from the bed, caught hold

of the blanket, and drew it over Mina's body, tucking it up to her chin. Slowly, he exhaled.

This would be difficult, but he welcomed the challenge. Welcomed the chance at conquest.

Mina let out a heavy breath that ended in a soft moan and turned her head to the side.

Sevik's tension eased against a wave of soothing warmth. He moved a hand to her face and stroked her cheek with the backs of his fingers. Was her forehead a little less red, a little less swollen?

He traced her delicate features with his fingertips. Her skin was losing its chill, another hopeful sign. When his hand encountered a coiled lock of her short brown hair, he swept it behind her rounded ear.

Canting his head, he gently combed his fingers through that hair. It was soft, and the curly strands clung to his fingers and bounced back into shape in such an endearing fashion.

He'd never been so fascinated by hair.

Sevik withdrew his hand. There were still important matters to attend, and he'd learned long ago not to put pleasure before such business.

Though she was tempting enough to make him want to forget that lesson.

Gathering her wet clothes, he descended the stairs. This would be a long night, and it'd be much, much warmer than he was accustomed to.

Sevik couldn't stop the grin that spread across his lips.

THREE

A savory, garlicy aroma lured Mina from the land of dreams.

Spaghetti sauce?

"Mmm..." She smiled and stretched as she inhaled, bowing her back and reaching her arms over her head. The exhalation that followed came out in a rush.

When was the last time Mina woke up to spaghetti for breakfast? She'd loved those Saturday mornings during her childhood when she'd walked into the kitchen, still rubbing sleep from her eyes, to find her mom boiling pasta and heating up sauce. It was so out of the norm. Most kids had pancakes, bacon, eggs, or sugary cereal. But Mina? She got to have dinner for breakfast. Ha, take that!

It wasn't until she was a little older that she'd realized the true reason behind it. Mina's mom had barely been making ends meet. Spaghetti was inexpensive, and the two of them could make a pot last for days. But Hannah had always made it fun, and she and Mina would laugh as they slurped their noodles, leaving their mouths and cheeks splattered with tomato sauce.

Even after they'd gotten back on their feet, they'd kept up the tradition.

Wait. *Why* was Mina waking up to the smell of spaghetti? Her mom had passed away years ago, and Mina lived alone.

She blinked her eyes open and stared up at the rafters of a vaulted ceiling. A wholly unfamiliar ceiling. Dim golden light filled the room, casting deep shadows.

Mina bolted upright. The blanket covering her flipped and landed on her lap. Cool air touched her bare skin, sending a chill through her. She looked down, gasped, and crossed her arms over her chest.

She wasn't sure if it was a good sign that she was still wearing her bra and panties. On the one hand, she wasn't entirely naked. On the other...

I'm in my underwear!

Releasing the blanket, Mina squeezed her breasts before slipping a hand between her thighs to cup herself. Nothing felt off or tender, and there was no pain. She felt...normal.

Closing her eyes, Mina bowed her head, slid a hand into her hair, and clenched the strands as she racked her brain. "What happened last night?"

She was guilty of drinking on special occasions, but she was sure she hadn't touched any alcohol yesterday. All she could recall was closing the café and going to Cornerstone. Just a normal day. Everything had been fine. She'd run into the store, grabbed her groceries, checked out, and then...

The assault.

Her eyes snapped open. "Oh God."

She straightened and dropped a hand to feel her side. But there was no sign that she'd been stabbed. No broken skin, no scab, not even a scratch. Nothing at all. Yet Mina remembered the pain. She touched her forehead, which her attacker had slammed against her car window. There wasn't even the slightest bump, wasn't even a hint of soreness.

Mina's brow creased. Had it all just been a bad dream?

"No," she said quietly, drawing the blanket up to cover her chest. It had been real. There was no way the absolute terror she'd felt had been a figment of her imagination.

So where was she? Her memory was fuzzy after hitting her head, but she remembered it had been snowing, and everything had been so eerily quiet except...

She'd heard a deep, inhuman growl, had heard grunts and cries and the sounds of flesh striking flesh. There had been someone else. It was all hazy, but Mina had seen a second shadowy figure.

Someone had come to help her.

But where were they? Who were they? And why hadn't they taken her to the police or the clinic?

Why was she lying nearly naked in their bed?

Mina frowned as she looked around the room. One wall followed the roof to its peak and was made up entirely of windows, granting an unhindered view of the snow-covered pines in the gloom outside. To the other side of the bed was a railing and stairs leading down from this loft.

Everything was made of beautiful wood—the walls and slanted ceiling, the floorboards, the bed frame, the nightstands, the mounted shelves, and the long dresser against the wall in front of her. Brass electric lanterns stood on the nightstands, creating that golden glow. Old books, small antlers, pinecones, and an assortment of trinkets filled the shelves. The warm, dark red of the rug and the sage green of the bedding fit perfectly with the cabin aesthetic.

But there were no pictures to give any clues as to who lived here.

Mina tossed the covers aside and scooted to the edge of the bed until her sock-covered feet touched the floor. The chill of the air made her skin prickle, sending a shiver through her. Crossing her arms, she rubbed them with her palms as she padded to the dresser. Her clothes lay atop it in a neatly folded pile.

"Oh, thank you, thank you, thank you," she muttered as she pulled on her jeans and sweater.

Grasping the hem of her top, she stretched it out and looked down at her side—where the knife had pressed into her. There wasn't even a speck of blood. Brow furrowing, Mina ran her fingers over the knitted material. Some of the stitches were large enough that a knife might've slipped through without causing damage, but what were the odds of that?

"I know it happened," she whispered.

Hadn't it?

With a sigh, she glanced around the room. Her purse was nowhere to be seen.

Mina made her way toward the stairs and looked down into a wide-open living space. A pair of sofas and a coffee table stood at the center, perpendicular to the large stone fireplace, with another red area rug beneath them. The windows and glass door along the wall looked out over a deck and the snowy landscape beyond it, which dipped to a wide, flat area beneath the dark sky. It took her a moment to realize she was looking at a frozen lake.

The smell of tomato sauce intensified as Mina descended the steps, and when she reached the bottom, she could hear the gentle bubbling of boiling water. Both the sound and the smell came from her left, where an open doorway beneath the loft led into a kitchen.

Flooded with unease, she paused before reaching the opening.

Who was in the kitchen? Who had brought her here, undressed her, and was now cooking pasta of all things? She caught her bottom lip between her teeth and clutched her hands against her belly, struggling to quiet her growing anxiety and fear.

Calm down, Mina. Whoever they are, they helped you, right? So why would they hurt you now? It's not like you woke up locked in some creepy basement or chained to the bed.

Taking in a deep, fortifying breath, Mina quietly approached the opening, curled her fingers around the doorframe, and peered inside. Her eyes widened.

A man stood in profile in front of the counter to the left. But he wasn't just any man.

He was Viktor Novak.

Viktor turned his head toward Mina, and his silver eyes locked with hers.

"It's you," Mina breathed.

I am in Viktor's house. Viktor's *house.*

I was in his bed.

She tightened her fingers on the doorframe. What had happened? Why was she here?

Dark blue jeans hugged his legs, and his black T-shirt molded to his chest. His black hair hung loose down his back. And it was long. So, so long. She had a sudden urge to comb her fingers through it, to smooth her palms over it, to feel the strands brush across her bare skin.

"How do you feel, Mina?" he asked as he looked her over.

"How do I..." Mina blinked and shook her head. "What's going on? Why was I in your...your bed? Why am I in your house? Something happened, but I... It's all very fuzzy, but I know I was attacked last night."

So why was there no evidence of the assault?

"That's a lot of questions." He turned away and plucked up an empty spaghetti box from the counter, turning it so the instructions faced him. After a moment, he glanced at the digital clock on the stovetop, which read eight thirty-five.

He set the box down, moved to the stove, and switched off the burner. Wrapping a dishtowel around the handle, he carried the pot of steaming water to the sink and poured its contents out into a waiting colander.

Why wasn't he answering her? Why was he acting like everything was perfectly normal?

With steam wafting around his face, Viktor glanced at Mina. "These go together, yes? The spaghetti and the sauce?"

Mina's brow furrowed. "Yes... What is going on, Viktor?"

"I'm feeding you. You said this sauce is your favorite."

Okay, that's...sweet?

Focus, Mina! Back to the many, many questions at hand.

She stepped into the kitchen. "But why am I even here to begin with?"

He raised the colander to shake out the remaining water before returning the pasta to the pot. "Because you were attacked last night." Placing the colander in the sink, he removed the lid from a small pot on the stove and curled his fingers around the handle. "Do I pour the sauce onto the spaghetti?"

Mina approached him and placed her hand over his, guiding the pot back to the stove. "Viktor."

Viktor stilled, and again his eyes fixed on her. They were intimidating, mesmerizing, piercing, and completely unreadable.

"Why am I here and not in the hospital?" she asked. "I mean, not that I feel any pain, which is really weird considering I swore I was stabbed, and my head should be killing me. Actually, I should have a concussion. But...no hospital, no police?"

Releasing the pot, he took hold of Mina's hand and turned toward her. His hand was so warm, and though he towered over her, his size didn't make her feel threatened. His nearness, his touch, his very presence, made her feel...safe.

"I've taken care of all that," he said. "That male will not harm you further."

That male? Who talks like that?

Not important.

There was someone. I was attacked.

"He was arrested? They got him?"

"Doesn't matter. He received the message."

"I...don't understand. What do you mean?"

Again, he glanced at the clock. "The police have probably collected him by now, but he'll need medical attention before they do much with him."

The growl, the sounds of a fight...

Mina gaped up at him. "You beat him up?"

Neither his expression nor the indecipherable light in his eyes changed. "He's fortunate that he's still breathing."

Oh God. Did that mean that Viktor had nearly killed the man? Because of her?

A burst of anxiety had her pulse racing and her chest rising and falling with rapid breaths. Her hand trembled. "Viktor you... The police..."

He placed his free hand over her heart, and a low rumble rose from his chest. "Easy, Mina. You're safe."

"B-But what about you? Won't they be looking for you after—"

Viktor's hand darted up, catching her jaw. Mina's breath hitched, and her eyes widened.

"I was not there. You were not there. Understand?" His low, commanding voice bristled with menace barely held in check, and his hold on her jaw, while not painful, remained firm. She felt something else beside the press of his fingers—sharp pricks against her skin. Like...claws?

But that couldn't be right.

"Are you going to hurt me?" she asked softly.

Slowly, he dipped his head, moving his face closer to hers. When their noses were nearly touching, he drew in a deep breath and hummed. "That would be a shame."

Despite everything, she couldn't bring herself to try to break away; she could only stare into his eyes as he held her there. Mina should've been terrified of this man and the way he was touching her, the way he was talking.

But her body reacted in a very different way. Arousal flickered low in her belly, and her nipples hardened into aching points. With him being this close, his rich, spicy scent clouded her senses, beckoning her to lean closer still, to bury her nose against his throat and breathe him in.

What is wrong with me?

Viktor lifted his fingers away, one by one, until only his thumb remained. It slid to her chin and teased her lower lip before he withdrew it too. "Go sit. You need to eat."

Mina took a step back, relieved to put some distance between them. Her lower lip tingled in the aftermath of his touch.

Anyone with an ounce of self-preservation would be seeking an escape. Viktor had basically admitted to beating a man nearly to death. Not that the man hadn't deserved a beating, but that was beside the point!

It was in Viktor's eyes, in his body language—violence was not new for him. He'd done it before.

He might've even done worse.

Except he did it to save you, Mina. You weren't murdered and buried in a shallow grave somewhere in the woods, you woke up safe and warm in his bed. And now he's cooking you a meal.

But she also knew that him being nice so far didn't mean he'd be nice forever.

So Mina did the only thing she could. She obeyed him.

Her gaze lingered upon Viktor before she turned, rounded the island counter, and walked to the dining table on the opposite side of the room. Her attention flicked to the closed door on her left as she pulled out a chair.

What did it lead to? A bedroom, a bathroom? A garage? Outside?

She plopped down onto the chair a little harder than she'd meant to, making it scrape on the wood floor.

Her hands slapped down on the table in startlement, and her eyes flew to him. "Sorry."

"For what?" Viktor asked without looking back at her as he took two plates down from a cupboard. He set both on the counter, picked up the spaghetti pot, and dumped a pile of pasta onto each plate.

"Nothing." Mina worried at her bottom lip as she dragged her gaze away from him to look around the room.

While it was lit only by a single antler chandelier, which cast a warm glow over everything while leaving the edges of the room dim, the kitchen was still...inviting? Homey even. A long butcher block counter ran the length of the wall in front of Viktor, ending with the fridge tucked in the corner. There were all sorts of knick-knacks, old kitchen gadgets, cast iron pans, and rustic kettles on display atop the cupboards. Pictures of wildlife and landscapes hung on the walls, and mason jars filled with vegetables and dried beans decorated the shelves.

She shifted her attention to the windows on the other side of the table. Though the overhead light should've reflected on the glass and made it difficult to see through, the dark, snowy world beyond was clearly visible—a gradual slope leading down to a dense fir forest.

Mina looked at the door again.

As if you could outrun him. Forget about it.

I wasn't thinking about it!

Mina's inner voice snorted.

And where would I go? We're in the middle of nowhere, and I don't even have my boots!

"You wouldn't get far," Viktor said, jarring Mina from her thoughts.

Her eyes snapped toward Viktor to find him carrying the plates to the table, each mountain of spaghetti now topped with a *very* generous helping of sauce.

Mina's cheeks flushed, and she hunched her shoulders. "I wasn't thinking about running."

He set the plates down, along with a pair of forks, before sitting across from her. "I know the look, Mina. If you want to fool me, learn to hide it better."

She stared down at the spaghetti as her fingers fidgeted on her lap. "Do you kill people?"

Viktor slid his plate closer to himself and picked up his fork. "Eat, Mina. I'll drive you home after you're done."

Eyes flaring in surprise, Mina looked at him. "You're...you're not keeping me captive for knowing too much? Not throwing me in the basement and locking me away? Wait, do you have a basement?"

He jabbed his fork into the mound of pasta before him. "I don't think basement is the word. It's more...a big hole?"

"You mean a crawlspace?"

"Sure," he replied with a shrug.

"So you're just letting me go?"

"Eat, Mina."

He still hadn't said whether he killed people...

Maybe it's best I don't know.

Mina tentatively picked up her fork. There was at least half a box of pasta piled on her plate, with more than half the jar of sauce, but she didn't have an appetite. Still, she twirled her fork through the noodles, leaned forward, and took a bite.

The instant the sweet, savory flavor hit her tongue, a wave of nostalgia swept over her. She had a fleeting sense of sitting at her mom's kitchen table in her pajamas, giggling over who could slurp up the longest noodle the fastest.

But it wasn't Hannah Walker sitting across from Mina. It was Viktor Novak. A man who was far more dangerous than she or anyone in town had suspected.

Still, it was nice, in a way, to be sharing a meal with someone. To not feel so alone after years of eating by herself.

Sure, Mina. Just eating a spaghetti breakfast with a possible killer. Nothing wrong with that.

Totally freaking normal.

Mina peeked up. Viktor was watching her—or, more specifically, her mouth.

Brow furrowing, she wiped the back of her hand across her lips. "Do I have sauce on my face?"

"No," he replied, eyes unmoving.

Her lip tingled with the memory of his thumb stroking it.

She dropped her gaze to his sculpted mouth. His lower lip was just a little fuller than his upper, and they looked so inviting...

What would it feel like to have his lips upon hers? Would they be hard or soft? What would he taste like?

Seriously, Mina?

She bit her lip, hoping the slight pain would quell the tingling and distract her from thoughts of kissing, and forced her attention to her plate.

For a time, Mina shifted the food around with her fork, unable to bring herself to take another bite. Apart from the scrape of metal on porcelain and the soft squelching of the pasta, the room was silent, and that silence quickly became too much for her to take.

And even though she knew she shouldn't have pried, knew she should've just had a few more bites, claimed she was full, and asked him to take her home, she couldn't resist her own curiosity. He was like a wild tiger—dangerous and unpredictable, but all the more beautiful and intriguing for it.

She had to know more about him. Having spent a whole year

wondering about Sullford's newest arrival certainly didn't help curtail that desire.

"So...what do you do when you're not, you know, beating people up?" she asked.

Though Viktor had speared his spaghetti as though he'd intended to shovel half of it into his mouth in one go, he hadn't actually eaten any yet. "Either threaten people with beatings or think about beating them up."

Mina blinked at him. He stared back, the corner of his mouth quirked.

She huffed a little laugh. "You're joking."

He didn't answer.

Mina's smile faded. "That *was* a joke, right?"

That hint of a smirk remained on his lips.

Maybe he wasn't joking...

"Okaaay... What do you do for a living?" she asked.

"I am..." He lifted a hand, palm up, fingers loosely curled as though grasping at something. "Retired."

Mina side-eyed him. "You're pretty young to be retired."

Viktor snickered. "I was very good at what I did."

"Maybe it's best I don't know what you did." She looked down at her food and tried not to let her imagination run wild and fill in the extremely large blanks he'd left open.

"It was business. Just business."

Mina picked up her fork and pointed the saucy utensil at him. "Says every shady person with something to hide."

That smirk of his widened, and something sparked in his eyes —not that they became any easier to read. "I have many things to hide. But everyone has something to hide, don't they? Even you, Mina."

Warmth spread across her cheeks, and she absently twirled her utensil through the noodles. "I don't have anything to hide."

"Says every shady person with something to hide."

"You're the one deflecting."

She hated that his chuckle was so sexy, hated that it made her feel things low down in her belly.

He propped an elbow on the table and leaned toward her. "You didn't answer my question earlier, Mina. How do you feel?"

Her brow creased. "I feel...good." Releasing the fork, Mina sat back in her chair. "It doesn't make sense."

Viktor canted his head. Strands of his long, dark hair shifted, falling over his shoulder. "You prefer to feel bad?"

"No, but after what happened..." She shook her head, recalling the pain of the knife sinking into her side. "He stabbed me. I felt it. I *remember* it. But there's...nothing there."

Mina pressed her fingers to her forehead. "There's not even a bruise where my head hit the window. It's like...like it never happened at all. But I know it did."

"It happened."

The unexpected gentleness in his voice caught Mina off guard. It was almost like he was trying to comfort her. Almost.

"Then where are my wounds?"

"You're just tougher than you think."

"Viktor, that doesn't—"

"Eat, Mina." He nodded toward her plate.

Mina glanced at the heaping pile of spaghetti. As good as it tasted, she just couldn't stomach more. "I'm not hungry. But... thank you. For making it."

Viktor's gaze lingered on her, giving her the sense that he saw through her, that he already knew everything about her.

Which made her suddenly realize something.

Viktor had been the one who undressed her while she was unconscious.

An embarrassed flush spread over her skin.

He abruptly pushed away from the table and rose. "Let's go."

As Mina watched him stride toward the fridge, her stomach twisted into knots. Had she angered him? She hadn't meant to seem ungrateful. She was thankful that Viktor had been there to help her last night, thankful that he'd taken care of her, that he'd cooked her breakfast. But this was all so...strange. Something was off. Something wasn't right.

Well, besides the fact that Viktor seemed to have a very dark, morally questionable past.

As she pushed her chair back and stood, Viktor opened the fridge and pulled out a few canvas bags.

Mina's bags.

Her eyes widened. "You brought my groceries?"

Viktor paused, glanced at the bags, and arched a thick, dark eyebrow.

"It's just thoughtful, is all," Mina said.

He offered a shallow nod, shifted the bags into one hand, and moved to a small console table beside the closed door. After collecting his keys from a tray atop the table, he opened the drawer and retrieved another familiar bag from within—Mina's purse.

A tidal wave of relief washed over her.

She rounded the dining table and walked to Sevik, taking her purse and clutching it to her chest when he held it out to her. "Thank you."

Opening the door, he stepped through into a small, dark room. Mina followed him, blinking at the sudden brightness when he flicked on the lights. A washer and dryer stood against the wall to the right. There was another door to the left, this one with a window that looked out at a black pickup truck parked in the shelter of a carport. Straight ahead, coats hung from a wall-mounted coat rack that had a bench beneath it. Several pairs of boots and shoes were tucked away under the bench.

Thankfully, Mina's coat and boots were there.

Mina sat on the bench as they put on their boots. Once she was done, she rose and pulled on her coat, barely getting it over her shoulders before he opened the door.

Frigid air swept into the room. Shivering, Mina quickly zipped her coat. However chilly the inside of his house felt, it was nothing compared to the temperature outside.

And Viktor didn't so much as flinch at the cold. He walked out, descended a couple steps, and opened the back door of the truck.

"Do you, uh, want to grab a coat?" she asked, hesitating at the threshold.

"No." He placed her groceries on the back seat, closed the door, and entered the vehicle on the driver's side.

"Okay then," she muttered as she slipped the handles of her purse to the crook of her elbow. "He can freeze his tush off. That's his choice. Won't bother me."

The truck rumbled to life.

The freezing air stung her nose and throat as she hurried to the vehicle. She climbed into the cab, and his scent enveloped her the instant she shut the door. No other smell diluted it now; there was only Viktor's pure, intoxicating, spicy fragrance.

The things that scent did to her body...

How was that possible? It was an aphrodisiac, a drug, and Mina just wanted to breathe it in deeper. She'd never been addicted to anything in her life, but this? She was already hooked.

Mina drew in shallow breaths through her mouth as she buckled her seatbelt, but there was no escape, not even when she tucked her nose behind the collar of her coat.

As the truck rolled along the driveway, she kept her gaze averted from Viktor, trying to focus on the dark, snowy world outside. Trying to tell herself that her coat hadn't picked up some of his scent.

But of course it had.

I'll just run it through the wash later.

Sure you will, Mina. Sure.

Trying to distract herself, she looked at Viktor. "Where did you move from?"

"Far away."

"Do you have family here?"

"No."

"Any friends? Business partners? A significant other?"

"No."

Mina wrinkled her nose. "You're bad at this."

His eyes flicked toward her, their silver oddly reflective in the instrument panel's glow. "Where I'm from, people don't ask so many questions."

Mina tilted her head. "Sounds like a very lonely, very unhappy place."

There was a subtle shift in his brows as he stretched his fingers and curled them tighter around the steering wheel. "Probably."

She studied him quietly. His accent definitely wasn't American or Canadian. Sometimes he sounded Russian or Eastern European, but she knew that wasn't quite right either. Wherever he'd come from, his refusal to answer questions about his past suggested that he was trying to get away from it.

There'd been many times when Mina had longed to do the same. Sullford was where she'd been born, where she'd grown up. It held all her happy memories of her parents. The hills where they'd gone sledding, the forest where they'd searched for their Christmas tree every year, the diner where they'd had breakfast every Sunday morning, the river where they'd gone fishing.

All that had changed when her father died.

Those memories were all she had left of her parents, and Sullford was filled with little reminders of them. Leaving this town would've been like saying goodbye to her parents forever. Without these places, how long would it be before her memories faded? How long would it be before she forgot their smiles, their love, before she forgot them? That was the main reason she'd stayed.

Because what had Sullford done for her since? It was a town full of people who, seeing Hannah Walker and her daughter devastated and impoverished by loss, had chosen to judge, gossip, and harass. A town full of people who had taken advantage of Hannah's desperation and then turned around and called her a whore. When they came to Mina's shop, they acted like they'd always been friendly and supportive, and they offered her their pity and backhanded compliments like she should've been grateful for them.

The only person who'd actually cared through that long, difficult time, the only person who'd actually helped, had left town years ago.

Mina settled back against the seat and looked out the side window. "It's lonely here for me too."

Only the sound of snow crunching beneath the truck's tires filled the silence as they drove. Mina stared out the window, looking at the landscape but not really seeing it. Sometimes, she felt Viktor's gaze upon her, felt its weight, its intensity. But she didn't turn his way.

It was only when the truck came to a stop and Viktor shifted it into park that she realized where they were—her driveway. Her brow furrowed as she stared at her SUV, which was parked in her usual spot and covered in a layer of snow.

Like it had been there all night.

She looked at Viktor. "How…"

"I told you, Mina"—he turned his head to meet her gaze, his face again unreadable—"I took care of everything."

He had told her, but Mina couldn't have guessed how thorough he'd been.

I was not there. You were not there. Understand?

What kind of life had Viktor led before coming here?

Mina nodded. Whatever he'd done, he'd saved her life last night, and she was grateful for that.

Unbuckling her seatbelt, Mina opened the door and slipped out of the truck. Her boots sank into the snow. Shouldering her purse, she retrieved her grocery bags from the back seat and looked up at Viktor. He was watching her.

"Thank you," she said. "For helping me and, well, not being some creepy murderer who chained me up in his basement."

He chuckled. "Only because it's a hole, not a basement."

Mina's brow arched. "Not sure if that makes me feel better, but I guess I'll take it. Tying me to the bed would have been another option."

Did I seriously just say that out loud?

A slow, sultry grin spread across his lips, and his eyes gleamed.

"*Okaythanksbye!*" Mina slammed the door and rushed to the back entrance of her building. Her face burned so hot that she wondered how the snow around her hadn't melted.

FOUR

"Mommy, I want a chocolate muffin," six-year-old Trinity said with her hands and face pressed against the pastry display case glass.

Mina grinned. The little girl was absolutely adorable in her puffy, bright pink coat, tutu skirt, and snow boots. The beads within her little braids even matched. But seeing her smush her nose and forehead against the glass as though she could push through it to reach the muffin on the other side made her all the cuter.

Naomi gently took her daughter by the hand and guided her back. "Let's not touch the glass and make it all dirty."

"Sorry." Trinity pointed at the muffin that had caught her interest. "Can I?"

"Yes, you can." Naomi turned her head to her son, who was three years older than his sister. "Jake?"

The boy looked at Mina. "Can I have one too?"

Mina nodded, picking up a brown sheet of tissue paper, and opened the case. "Yep, you can. And you're both in luck, because those are my last two chocolate muffins of the day."

"Thanks, Mina," Naomi said.

"Of course." Mina picked up the muffins and deposited them in a pastry box. "Anything for you?"

"Hmm…" The woman tilted her head back and surveyed the blackboard menu on the wall behind the counter.

Trinity hurried to the kid's play corner, plopped down on one of the kiddy chairs, and immediately began coloring a page in a coloring book that had been left unfinished by another child earlier in the day. Her brother wandered off to check out the small selection of graphic novels.

"Can I get a medium caramel macchiato with extra caramel?" Naomi asked.

"Oh, that's my favorite!" Mina set the box on the counter, plucked up a medium cup, and turned to the back counter. She pumped the caramel and vanilla syrup into the cup and started the expresso machine. Taking a jug of milk from the mini fridge beneath the counter, she poured it into a small metal pitcher before slipping it under the steamer.

"How's Elijah?" she asked.

Naomi Harris and her family were regulars. They'd been coming to Mina's café for five years—since Trinity was a baby and Jake was barely a preschooler. Mina had delighted in watching the kids grow, and Naomi and Ellijah were always so kind, friendly, and genuine.

"He's doing good, but he's tired," Naomi said. "He's been working overtime with the power outages in Fairbanks."

"How long will he be gone?"

"They're sending him back on Monday if nothing else goes wrong." With a chuckle, Naomi added, "So hopefully only three more days of 'Mom, is daddy almost home?'"

Elijah was a lineman for the power company, which meant he was especially busy during the winter when storms brought down powerlines. Mina shuddered at the thought of working out in this weather—the freezing temperatures, the wind, ice, and snow. As a logger, her father had also worked through similar conditions.

Mina wouldn't have lasted a day.

But people did what was necessary to get by, and someone had to do those jobs so everyone could survive the winters.

"How have you been, Mina?" Naomi asked.

Mina turned off the steamer. "I've been great. Business has been pretty steady, and there have been some great new books released lately."

"Did you hear about the incident at Cornerstone?"

"What incident?" Mina poured the milk into the cup.

"Kevin Williams was arrested for breaking into the store three days ago. They found him covered in blood and alcohol. Apparently, he was pretty beat up."

Mina froze, unable even to draw breath.

Kevin Williams.

A wave of vertigo swept through her, and she grabbed the counter to keep herself steady.

She knew Kevin. They'd gone to school together. He hadn't been kind, not to Mina or any of the other kids he used to pick on. His father was just as much of a brute.

She didn't know what was worse—her assaulter being a nameless, faceless entity, or someone she'd grown up with.

Mina forced herself to take in slow, measured breaths as she carefully added the espresso to the cup. "Did...did the police say what happened?"

"That's the weird thing. Apparently, the store's security system was down that day. Their cameras are missing like a whole twenty-four hours, and the alarm didn't go off until he'd been in there for who knows how long. They're pretty sure that he must've hidden inside until the store closed and then drowned himself in booze. But as far as I heard, he refuses to say what actually happened. Claims he fell down, but the cops don't buy it."

Hand trembling, Mina set the empty espresso glass in the sink. How had Viktor done it? She didn't believe it was a coincidence that the security system had been down that night, that there had been no evidence at all of what had truly happened.

"Mom, can I get this?" Jake asked, shaking Mina from her thoughts.

She glanced back to see the boy holding up a graphic novel with two dragons on the cover.

"Hmm..." Naomi tapped her chin. "What do you think, Mina? Is it a good one?"

Mina topped the macchiato with caramel sauce, covered the cup with a plastic dome lid, and carried it to the front counter, where she set it beside the box of muffins. "I think you'll love it. Lots of action, adventure, and dragon riding."

"Please, please, please?" Jake made his brown eyes as big as possible as he clutched the book to his chest.

Naomi chuckled. "Oh, okay. But I expect some extra help around the house tomorrow."

"Okay!"

"Anything else?" Mina asked as she rang up the items.

"Hmmm..." Naomi raised a finger. "One second."

She jogged to the romance section. After perusing the books, she plucked one off the shelf and brought it back to the counter. It was thick and heavy enough that it made a small *thump* when she set it down. It had a gorgeous cover—a woman standing in front of a monster that had horns and a deer skull face. The title read *A Soul to Keep, Duskwalker Brides Book 1*.

It was the start of one of Mina's favorite series.

"I've been eyeing this one for a while now," Naomi said with a sheepish smile.

Mina grinned. "It's amazing, and you're totally in for a ride." She leaned in closer and lowered her voice to a whisper. "It's pretty spicy too."

"I can't wait! I just finished reading Regine Abel's latest Prime Mating Agency book. I've loved every single one."

"Oh, that's such an amazing series too!"

"Monster romance is so addicting."

After Mina added the new book to the total, Naomi paid and passed Trinity the muffins to carry.

"Tell Elijah that the next time he comes in, his favorite coffee will be waiting," Mina said. "It'll be on the house."

"That's so sweet of you. He'll be in for sure." Naomi picked up her drink and book. "Have a good evening, Mina!"

"You too!"

Trinity waved. "Bye bye, Mina."

Mina smiled wide and gave her a wave. "See you later. Enjoy that muffin!"

Jake followed them, reading as he walked. He was already several pages into his comic.

Once the Harrises were out the door, Mina checked the clock. Twenty minutes to seven. The café was slow enough that she could begin her closing routine.

She cleaned up the machines and counters, placed the dishes in the dishwasher in the kitchen, packaged the remaining pastries to sell at a discount tomorrow, and swept the floor.

Thankfully no one entered while she was cleaning up. She always hated turning people away, even if they came in right at closing.

Reaching behind her back, she untied her apron, lifted it over her head, and tossed it into the small laundry basket along with the towels and rags she'd used through the day. She'd bring them upstairs to wash once everything was locked up.

Mina ran a hand through her hair. The roots were damp, and her forehead felt sticky from sweat. She couldn't wait to take a shower.

Rounding the counter, she walked to the entrance, flipped the sign to *CLOSED*, and glanced out the window just as the door to the hardware store across the street swung open. Viktor stepped out into the glow of the streetlight, holding a paper bag in hand. His hair was pulled back into a messy bun atop his head, and his black jacket was unbuttoned. The shadows cast on his face by the light sharpened his features, granting him an almost inhuman visage.

He's so gorgeous.

Mina pressed her palm to the glass.

Viktor turned his head toward her shop, and his eyes locked with hers.

She gasped. Her skin warmed, her belly fluttered, and her heart quickened.

They hardly knew each other, and what little Mina did know of him didn't exactly make him seem like a knight in shining armor. At best, he was a morally gray antihero. Was it healthy to be obsessed with such a man?

Yes.

No.

Maybe?

I'm not obsessed!

Sure, keep telling yourself that. Like you haven't been thinking about him nonstop for the last three days.

Mina couldn't deny that. And now, here she was, staring at him from inside her café.

Before she could talk herself out of it, before she could convince herself to lock up, turn around, and race upstairs, she grasped the handle, opened the door, and stepped outside.

The cold struck her with all the force of a charging moose, and her long-sleeved cotton dress offered about as much protection from the chill as it would have from a set of massive antlers.

She shivered and let out a shaky breath, which briefly fogged the air.

I won't be long. I can stand the cold for a little while.

I just...need to talk to him.

Shutting the door behind her, she folded her arms across her chest, tucked her hands beneath them, and made her way across the street toward Viktor.

He remained where he was, looking ethereal in the streetlamp's glow, and tilted his head as he watched her. Only as she neared did she notice the little crease between his eyebrows.

She grinned as she stopped in front of him. "Hello, stranger."

Viktor's eyes dipped to take her in. "Hello, Mina."

"Buying some chains for your not-basement?"

Her cheeks flushed as soon as those words left her mouth.

Really, Mina?

It just came out!

"No chains." He eased closer and stroked the backs of his fingers down her cheek, sending a shiver through her that had nothing to do with the cold. "Leather bindings would be gentler against your skin."

Mina's eyes flared, her lips parted, and her blush deepened.

Her imagination ran wild. She could see herself tied to his bed, stripped bare, vulnerable, her chest heaving and heart racing with anticipation. Could see him wearing that devilish smirk as he crawled onto the bed, could see the muscles playing under his skin as he advanced like a predator that knew its prey was helpless.

An ache blossomed in her core, intensifying that inner heat and making her nipples tighten.

She could picture the hunger in Viktor's silver eyes as he lowered his face—

"At least your mother kept it private," a man said as he passed, drawing a laugh from the other man walking beside him.

With a gasp, Mina withdrew from Viktor's touch. As she swung her gaze toward the men, her embarrassment turned into anger. She clenched her hands, hugged herself tighter, and narrowed her eyes in a glare.

Of course, she knew both men—Mike Jacobson and Trevor Rydell. They'd been two grades ahead of her in school, but they knew all about Mina and her mother. She'd avoided them as much as possible in the halls, knowing they'd always had some lewd comment to throw her way.

Some people never changed.

"Mina?" Viktor asked, calling her attention back to him.

His eyebrows had fallen low, and the dark shadows over his eyes turned his irises into reflective silver orbs, like a pair of alien moons. He looked exactly like the predator from her imagination.

She shook her head. "It's... I'm fine. It was nothing."

He scowled. Seeing those sculpted lips curl downward was just as tempting as it was intimidating. His head turned toward the men, who were talking in hushed voices, laughing, and glancing over their shoulder at Mina.

Trevor grinned. "If you're getting into the family business"—he cupped his groin—"how much?"

Mina gritted her teeth as tears welled in her eyes.

I am not going to cry in front of those assholes.

"Sorry, Viktor," she said, voice tight with emotion. "I'd better go."

But Viktor was already stalking toward them, his heavy boots thumping on the sidewalk. The men stopped and turned to face him.

"Got a problem, buddy?" asked Mike.

"Fuck off, man," said Trevor.

Viktor growled. "Apologize."

Mina chased him, grabbing his hand to bring him to a halt. "Viktor don't."

She knew at least in part what he was capable of, and could only guess the extent to which he'd go. But they were standing in the middle of town, out in the open, where anyone could see.

Mike guffawed. "She got you on a leash? Isn't it supposed to be the other way around?"

That triggered fresh laughter from Trevor. "Bitch walking its master. Power of the pussy, huh?"

She felt the tension in Viktor's hand, felt the strength just waiting to be unleashed. He turned his face toward her. "They disrespect you."

"They're just words," she said softly. The tears spilled down her cheeks. "It's not worth you getting in trouble. I'm...I'm used to it."

"You shouldn't be."

Mina knew that. She'd always known it. But nobody had ever said it to her out loud. No one except for Randy had ever stood up for her. Most people didn't like confrontation and didn't want to get involved, so they'd always turn their heads and pretend they hadn't seen or heard anything.

And how could she have spoken up when most of the town already believed what they wanted to believe? What did Mina's voice matter?

Viktor grasped her jaw and angled her face more directly toward his, leaning closer. He narrowed his eyes as he searched hers, brushing his thumb over her cheek to wipe away her tears. "I do not like this water in your eyes. I'd rather see fire, Mina."

"Better be careful, man," Mike said. "If she's anything like her whore mother, she'll be spreading her legs for any guy who waves a dollar at her."

Mina's heart pounded hard against her ribs, and her pulse thrummed in her ears.

Whore.

Whore.

Whore.

How many times had her mother suffered in silence when someone called her that to her face, whispered it behind her back, or communicated it through a judgmental stare?

Mina clenched her jaw. Her breath sawed in and out of her as more tears gathered in her eyes. But these were not simply tears of hurt; they were tears of rage.

She yanked out of Viktor's grasp and strode up to the two men.

Mike's mocking grin widened, only spurring her anger.

"Aw, Mina," Mike said, "you ready to—"

Her palm cracked across his face. The sound seemed to echo along the quiet street, amplifying the stunned silence that followed.

Mike's head snapped to the side, and he stumbled back, his hand flying up to cover his cheek.

"What the fuck?" Trevor glared at Mina.

Ignoring the sharp sting in her palm, which was only worsened by the cold, Mina took a step closer and curled her hands into fists. "No, fuck *you!* My mother did what she had to do to survive because *no one* cared, no one offered to help. She lost her husband. I lost my father. We were going to lose our home, and we had nothing else. The people of this town used her to get what they wanted, and then they looked down on her for it. There is no shame in what my mother did. She survived and took care of her child."

Her body trembled, thrumming with adrenaline and twenty years of pent-up anger. "It wasn't her fault your fathers couldn't keep their dicks in their pants."

"You fucking cunt," Mike spat, shoving her hard.

Mina jolted backward, certain she was going to meet the pavement. But something familiar halted her—a pair of big, strong arms that drew her against a warm, solid chest. She felt Viktor's snarl vibrate into her before the sound actually emerged from him.

He swept her aside and lunged at the men. His paper bag fell to the ground with a jangle of metal hardware. Trevor and Mike both said something, but their words were so quick and panicked that they jumbled together.

Viktor caught Mike and Trevor by their throats. Mina's eyes rounded as he turned, lifting the men—each of whom had to weigh over two hundred pounds—off the ground.

He slammed both men against the hardware store's brick wall and held them there with their boots hanging a foot above the sidewalk.

It was surreal seeing him holding two full-grown men like that. Mike and Trevor had been football players in high school, and they still had muscular, stocky builds. But their struggles seemed to trouble Viktor no more than those of an infant might have.

"*Do. Not. Touch. Her*," Viktor grated through his teeth. The tendons on the backs of his hands stood out in sharp relief. "Touch her again and I remove your hands. Speak of her again, I remove your tongues."

He tightened his grip on their throats. Choking, Mike and Trevor clawed at Viktor's forearms.

"Do you understand?" Viktor's voice was so low and gravelly that it hardly sounded human.

Mina could only watch in shock.

"What's happening?" someone asked from behind her.

"Mike shoved Mina," someone else replied. "This guy stepped in."

"Anyone call the cops?"

Their voices shook Mina out of her daze. She turned her head to see several people gathered on the sidewalk, including Trish and Barry, who both worked at the hardware store.

No. The authorities could not get involved. She would not have Viktor get in trouble, not for her, especially not when she was the one who'd escalated the situation.

She rushed forward, ducked under his arm, and stood between Viktor and the men, facing him. Reaching up, she took his face in her hands and forced him to look at her. His lips were drawn back, and his eyes were alight with fury.

"Viktor, stop," she said softly, but firmly. "Let them go."

His nostrils flared with a deep inhalation, and his pupils shrank nearly to pinpricks. It was Viktor's eyes staring at her, but there was something primal in them now, something bestial.

Something...ravenous.

Mina stroked her thumbs over his cheeks. "Please. You need to stop. They're not worth it."

"But you are."

Mina's heart leapt, and something sparked low in her belly. Those three little words held far more weight and meaning than they had any right to.

"Then let them go and come with me," she said.

Viktor held her gaze for another heartbeat, then two, three, before the wildness in his eyes faded. He released Mike and Trevor, both of whom fell to the ground clutching their throats and gasping for breath.

Mina didn't hesitate to entwine her fingers with Viktor's and lead him toward the café.

"I don't think you're supposed to leave, Mina," said Trish.

"The police know where to find me," Mina replied, snatching Viktor's brown bag off the sidewalk before stepping into the street.

FIVE

THE BELL JINGLED as the door shut behind Sevik. The café's lights were dimmed, and the chairs had been put up on the tables.

Heat coursed through his limbs, and his muscles ached with unspent rage. With fury and bloodlust having seized his mind, he'd felt his control over his neural transceiver wavering, and even knowing that his holoshroud had been in danger of faltering, he'd not relented. Only Mina's intervention had stopped him. His every instinct still demanded that he act, that he rend flesh, that he destroy.

Or that he rut.

He raked his gaze over Mina. She wore a long, flowing dress with a belt cinched around her waist, but he knew what hid beneath it—soft skin, small breasts, flaring hips.

His cocks pushed against his slit, held in only by his jeans. It would've been so easy to bend her over a table, flip up her skirt, tear away the scrap of cloth covering her cunt, and thrust into her. To release the energy burning him from within.

But this was Mina. Sweet, gentle Mina.

She wasn't a thing to be used and cast aside, wasn't an outlet for his lust, his stress, his animalistic urges.

"Sorry. I was just closing up when I saw you. Just a sec." Mina released his hand, hurried behind the counter, and flicked a set of light switches.

Sevik slitted his eyes against the sudden brightness, angling his face down. He balled his fists.

A little more pressure, and he would've crushed the human males' throats. A little more pressure and he would've eliminated a source of Mina's suffering.

He drew in a deep breath. The air was laden with scents; coffee was foremost, rivaled by sharp chemical odors that had likely been created by cleaning solutions. But he could smell food beneath those—yeasty, sugary, fruity—as well as the earthy scent of books.

Yet none of it could mask Mina's scent. It was everywhere here. He didn't doubt that he would find traces of it in every corner, on every object.

Mina returned to him. She set his bag on a nearby table before taking down a couple chairs from the tabletop. Her fingers curled around the top rail of one chair, squeezing tight enough that her knuckles went white. "Please sit."

Sevik lifted his gaze to her face. Her brow was pinched, her expression was strained, and there were frantic blotches of color on her cheeks. Seeing her like that cut through some of the turmoil in him, granting him a semblance of control. "Breathe, Mina."

Letting out a short laugh, she shook her head. "I am breathing. Because of *you*, I'm still breathing." She ran her fingers through her hair, mussing the curls. "I can't believe everything that just happened. I can't believe I slapped Mike!"

Mina pointed at her chest. "*Me.* I'm never violent. I've never hit anyone. But I hit him! I've just had enough. I'm so tired of my mom's name still getting dragged, even after she's been gone for so long. And I'd hit him again if I could. He deserved it. Has for years."

Her eyes rounded. "But hitting someone is assault. It's a crime. I...I committed a crime. I'm a criminal!"

Sevik chuckled. Though it had been so long ago, he remembered when he'd first joined a gang, when he'd first broken the law. Remembered the rush, the high, the plummet back to the ground. Remembered the fear...and the freedom he'd felt when his fears hadn't come to fruition.

But Mina wasn't like him.

Despite the steaming plate of shit this town had served her, she was a good person. A kind person. She was a ray of brightness and warmth in a lonely, frozen wasteland.

Mina directly countered Sevik's cold and darkness. She was his opposite. Innocent, selfless, compassionate, patient...

A strange feeling sparked in Sevik's chest—desire like he'd never experienced, hunger like he'd never known. A yearning beyond lust.

And what if I extinguish her light? What if I leech her warmth?

What if I corrupt everything that sets her apart from me, everything that makes her...Mina?

He could not answer those questions directly, but a response resonated from deep within him, nonetheless.

She was his, no matter the consequences.

Gritting his teeth, he clenched his fists. The pain of his claws pressing into his palms sharpened his focus. He'd nearly lost control with the human males, had nearly made a mistake from which there would've been no return. He could not afford to lose control again. Every time he did, he risked being discovered.

Every time he did, he put her in danger.

"You are not a criminal, Mina," Sevik said.

"But what I did was illegal." She rounded the chair and dropped onto it. "I could get arrested." Leaning forward on her elbows, Mina propped her chin on her hands.

Sevik tilted his head. The way she cradled her face with her fingers, the lingering crease between her eyebrows, the way her bottom lip stuck out a little more than usual... It was all so endearing. So...adorable.

He should've taken that as his signal to leave. These feelings were almost as foreign to him as this planet and its people, and they were dangerously disarming. Sevik couldn't let his guard down, but Mina made him want to do so.

"Most people break the law at some point," he said, lowering himself onto the other chair.

She looked up at him with those large, beautiful brown eyes. "They arrested him. The man from the other night."

Sevik remained silent, holding her gaze.

"They said there was no security footage. Not for the entire day."

He dipped his chin in a nod. "Fortunate for us."

"You did that, though, didn't you?" Mina sat up but kept her voice low. "You did something to it."

Some small part of him, long buried, envied her for her naivety, for her innocence. He'd never had the luxury of either.

He rested an arm on the table. "And what do you think I did?"

"I...don't know."

"And that bothers you."

"You said you took care of it. Of everything. So when I hear that the police found him inside a locked store with no recordings of how he got in there, reeking of booze and beaten to a pulp, yes. I have questions."

Mina groaned, burying her face in her hands again. Voice muffled, she said, "And I know I shouldn't ask those questions, but I can't help wondering what happened. How it happened. How you...how you did it without getting caught."

"Mina..."

She lowered her hands just enough to peek at him over the tips of her fingers.

Even if he'd been willing to tell her, she wouldn't have believed him. Not unless he showed her.

And that was *not* going to happen.

He stared into her expressive, captivating eyes. They held emotions that he recognized, that he related to, but there was so much more in them he did not understand. So much he could not identify. Though it made him a hypocrite, he couldn't deny his own curiosity, his own need to know more about her.

He *wanted* her.

But he could not have her. At least...not fully.

Why not take what he could? If nothing else, it would be a distraction for them both. And Mina very much needed her thoughts deflected from their current path.

Sevik grasped the seat of her chair to either side of her legs and dragged her closer, trapping her knees between his.

Mina started, hands flying to his chest as she stared at him with wide eyes. "Viktor, what—"

He caught her jaw and slowly lowered his face toward hers. She stiffened her arms to keep him at bay, but she couldn't stop him; soon enough, she wasn't even trying.

With his mouth beside her ear, he said in a low, husky voice, "I can tell you anything, Mina. Any story I choose."

He brushed his lips across the soft, smooth skin of her cheek, nearly shuddering at the feel. Mina curled her fingers against his chest, gripping his shirt.

"And no matter what I say"—he trailed his mouth down to her jaw—"there will always be that voice in your mind whispering doubts. Insisting that you don't know the truth."

Her scent filled his nose, suffusing him and fogging his mind with a lustful haze.

As he continued down, trailing kisses along her neck, Sevik's heart pounded, pumping fire through his veins. His cocks throbbed with need, demanding release from their confinement, and his fangs ached with an instinctual drive to bite her, to mark her, to make his claim.

"Viktor," she whispered.

Zekt'al, but he wanted to hear his true name from her lips.

He settled a hand on her knee and slid it upward, gathering her skirt and pushing it higher. "That voice will urge you closer and closer to me."

Mina's breath quickened when he reached her upper thigh, and she whimpered as he dipped his thumb lower to trace slow, sensual circles so, so close to her cunt.

"You will wonder. You will ask your questions." Sevik grazed her throat with his fangs. His overflowing venom glands forced drops of sweet mating venom onto his tongue, and his muscles tensed as he fought the need to sink his teeth into her tender flesh.

She let out a soft moan, arching her neck as she pulled him closer. Her scent changed; a new, intoxicating layer wove into it, straining his control and transforming his desire into agony.

Mina's arousal.

Her body trembled with her need.

Sevik's next words came out in a half-rasp, half-growl. "But it's not the truth you desire, Mina. You want something else. Something more primal..."

His thumb shifted lower and caressed the top of her slit through the fabric of her skirt.

Mina gasped his name. Her thighs strained against his legs, and she tilted her pelvis, pressing her slit more firmly against his thumb, which slipped between the folds of her cunt.

Sevik groaned. She was so fucking hot. He could feel the wetness of her arousal seeping through her underwear, could feel the heat radiating from her core. He wedged his thumb deeper until it encountered a small, firm nub at the apex of her slit.

A soft, needy moan escaped her, and she whispered, "I want y—"

The bell over the door jingled again, shattering the café's quiet.

Fuck.

Mina jerked away from his touch and shoved hard against his chest. Her eyes widened with panic before her chair tipped backward.

Sevik leapt up, knocking his own seat away, and thrust out his hand, catching the top rail of her chair and halting its fall.

Mina stared up at him, and he stared down at her. She blinked.

Laughter burst from her.

Something warmed within Sevik, something separate from his desire, from his lust. That lively, lyrical sound melted away the weight that had been bearing down upon him for so long, making him feel lighter, making him feel less alone.

Mina smiled. "You're always saving me."

The corner of his mouth ticked up. "You're always falling for me."

A male cleared his throat at the café's entrance.

Mina started, cheeks flaring pink, and scrambled atop the chair in an attempt to right herself. "Sorry!"

Barely holding in a chuckle, Sevik set her chair down on all four legs and stepped back, allowing her to stand. She adjusted the skirt of her dress, smoothing her palms down it before she turned and approached the newcomer.

Still smelling of desire, she goes to another male.

Unmarked, unclaimed.

All humor fled Sevik.

Sevik moved behind Mina and placed his hands on her shoulders. He clenched his jaw, worsening the ache in his teeth.

"Mina," said Chief Dick Harrigan, flicking his gaze between her and Sevik. He was a tall, thin human, with weathered skin, short cropped gray hair, and a bushy moustache. His brown coat was lined with wool and bore the insignia of the Sullford Police Department. "And Novak, isn't it?"

"I'm sorry," Mina said quickly. "I know I hi—"

Sevik squeezed Mina's shoulders. She looked up at him questioningly.

He gave her what he hoped was a meaningful look. When he returned his attention to Chief Harrigan, the man was staring at Sevik with narrowed eyes.

"Everything okay here, Mina?" Harrigan asked.

"Just...nerves," Sevik said.

"I asked her."

Mina furrowed her brow and glanced between Sevik and Harrigan. "I'm fine. Just a bit shaken."

"Uh huh." With his gaze lingering on Sevik, Chief Harrigan hooked his thumbs behind his belt, positioning one hand not far from the pistol holstered at his hip. "Want to ask your friend to step out so we can chat?"

Somehow, Sevik kept himself from lunging at the man, but the urge to attack was almost too strong to deny. He would not be separated from this female. He would not leave her alone with another male. Would not—

Get a fucking hold of yourself, Sevik.

"It's okay," Mina said, placing a hand over one of Sevik's. "Viktor can stay."

Harrigan's eyes finally shifted to her. "You sure?"

"He's the only reason I didn't get hurt."

"Suit yourself." The chief stepped deeper into the café, nonchalantly studying his surroundings. He was the top authority in this small town, and he carried himself as such. Sevik knew his type.

"Now typically, we'd separate the two of you for individual questioning," Harrigan said as he reached the counter. He tapped the glass display case thoughtfully. "See if your stories line up. Those two jackasses claim you slapped Mike, Mina. Said you provoked them."

Mina tensed against Sevik. "I didn't provoke them! I was having a conversation with Viktor, and they started...started..." She went quiet, and her hand tightened over his. "They were harassing me. They were saying horrible things about me, about m-my mom."

Emotion saturated her voice, making her words thick and heavy. She carried such pain in her heart...

Sevik shouldn't have stopped—he should've crushed Mike and Trevor's throats, should've ripped out their vocal cords so they could never insult Mina or her mother again.

"How'd that escalate into your friend almost choking the two of them out?" Harrigan asked.

"Because I...I slapped Mike," Mina confessed.

Shit.

She rushed to add, "I didn't mean to, but it just happened. I was just so angry, and after so many years of their verbal abuse, I just... I snapped." She dropped her hands to her belly. "And after I hit Mike, he came at me."

Jaw clenched, Sevik watched the chief. He would not allow Mina to be taken. Would not allow her to suffer consequences for this. His pistol was hidden at his back, and he knew he could draw it and fire before the chief could react, but the complications that would cause...

If he touches Mina, fuck the complications.

Harrigan continued his leisurely stroll, acting as though everything in the café was more interesting than what Mina had just told him.

It was all blatant posturing from a man who thought himself in control of the situation, a man whose whim could decide the fates of those involved. But Harrigan had no idea who he was dealing with.

"I didn't believe them when they told me," the chief said. "All anyone else saw was Mike shove you something fierce. Little Mina, slapping someone? Never in a million years." He chuckled and shook his head. "Of course, their behavior doesn't really justify your friend killing them in retaliation..."

Mina thrust a finger in the air with a smile. "But he *didn't* kill them. Just throwing that little detail out there. Well, it's not a little detail since they're, well, you know, still alive. So maybe it's a big one? Let's just say that it's an important one."

Chief Harrigan turned to face Mina and Sevik. Smile fading, she slowly lowered her hand.

"Attempted murder is still a crime," the chief said.

There it is.

Apparently, the threat of overblown charges was common to law enforcement officials on both Earth and Vabos. An intergalactic fear tactic meant to intimidate and coerce confessions.

Had Sevik's hands not been on Mina's shoulders, they would've been around Harrigan's throat. He drew in a deep breath through his nostrils. How was it that Mina's scent could simultaneously calm him and fan the flames within his chest?

Harrigan stepped closer, holding Sevik's gaze, scrutinizing him. Looking for a tell, for a weakness. "You're a hard one, aren't you?"

Sevik stared back at the human, unflinching, allowing none of his rage to show on his face. "Not sure what you mean."

"I think you know, son."

"I am a law-abiding citizen," Sevik replied evenly. "I acted in defense of a woman who was accosted by two males twice her size, as is my right under this state's self-defense statutes."

The chief ran his tongue along his teeth. "Familiar with the laws of the great state of Alaska, are you?"

"Yes."

"Hmm..." Harrigan's eyes ran up and down Sevik. "In my experience, there's only two kinds of people who study up on laws. Honest, hardworking folks who want to uphold them, and opportunistic scumbags who want to break them."

"Any other questions, Harrigan, or are we done?"

After a few more moments of scrutiny, the chief shook his head. "The two of you happen to be in luck. Those boys aren't pressing charges, and frankly, they wouldn't have a leg to stand on even if they wanted to. I'd rather not deal with all the paperwork, anyway."

All the tension bled from Mina's body, and she sagged against Sevik.

"But Mina, do me a favor..." Harrigan moved closer still, forcing Mina to tip her head back to maintain eye contact with him. "Let this stuff go. Your mother made her choices, and people have a right to talk about it. You're going to have to learn to take in stride eventually."

Her tension returned as swiftly as it had vanished. Mina clenched her skirt in her hands, pressed her lips together, and gave a stiff nod.

Sevik tightened his grip on her shoulders. It was all he could do not to hammer his fist into the chief's face and knock a few of those flat human teeth down the man's throat.

"And you, Novak"—Chief Harrigan lifted his gaze to Sevik

and leveled a finger at him—"keep your hands to your damned self. You're getting off this time, but I swear to God, you start any more trouble in my town, and you will regret it."

In the life he'd left behind, Sevik never would've let words like that go unanswered and unpunished. Police Chief Richard Harrigan's head would've been torn from his body, leaving no questions as to who held the true power.

Keeping his face expressionless, Sevik replied, "I'll use my best judgment."

"See that you do, son." The chief offered a nod. "Have a good night, Mina."

"Good night," she said quietly.

Breathe.

Sevik watched the man exit the café. Only when the chief was no longer in sight through the front windows did Sevik exhale. The air was like fire, blazing out of his lungs, scorching his throat.

Mina spun around and looked up at him. "I am so, so, *so* sorry. I never meant for you to get involved in...in"—she waved her hands at herself—"the messed-up drama that is my life."

She dropped her gaze to the floor, but not before tears glistened in her eyes. "I'll understand if you don't want to talk to me anymore. You've put yourself at risk for me twice now, and that's not fair to you."

Sevik had seen the spark in her. He'd glimpsed the solid, unyielding metal at her core. He knew it was there still, and he hated that a pompous shit stain like Harrigan had driven that part of Mina back into hiding. He hated that she thought this was how she had to be—meek, submissive, apologetic.

Fuck the risk. He wanted to see her burn again. Wanted to *feel* it.

He cupped the back of her head, fisted her hair, and forced her face up toward his. Before Mina's shock could fully register in her expression, he crushed his mouth against hers. She gasped, and Sevik took advantage of her parted lips to thrust his tongue between them.

Zekt'al, Mina tasted even sweeter than she smelled.

Fierce hunger roared through him. He wanted more, craved more.

Slipping an arm around her waist, Sevik pulled her against him. She came willingly. Her little body was so soft, so pliant, molding to his perfectly. She slid her hands up his chest, took hold of his shirt, and tugged him closer still.

He ravaged her mouth, his tongue moving ruthlessly to twine around hers. And when she shyly brushed her tongue over his, pure, overwhelming lust seized him. He wanted to tear her clothes from her body, push her to the floor, and thrust his cocks deep inside her. To take her, claim her, possess her.

To make her his mate.

A new heat blossomed within him, coalescing at his neck and his groin. It was pulsing, thrumming, nearly as heady as the kiss itself, and as it strengthened, so too did his drive to claim her.

Sevik drew in a breath, again drinking in her fragrance, and realized something had changed. His own scent had shifted. It was thicker, stronger. Fuller.

No. Aggaan sin thar, no!

He was starting to imprint on her. His fucking traitorous body was initiating the process against his will, and his glands were secreting chemicals that would alter his whole fucking brain.

And he was still kissing her. Still letting it happen.

Even after the events on Vabos, where he'd seen the disastrous effects of a one-sided imprinting, he was standing here like a fool.

Sevik tore his mouth from hers and sucked in a ragged breath. Her cheeks were flushed, her lips red and swollen from his kiss. He nearly succumbed to their invitation and took her mouth again.

Mina's lashes fluttered open. Her eyes shone with desire.

Leave. Now.

But that was hard. So fucking hard. It went against his every instinct, his every want.

He lowered his face until their lips were but a breath apart. "In the future, *val'syra,* do not blurt out confessions to the chief of fucking police."

Using every shred of willpower in his possession, Sevik broke away from her. She stumbled as her hands fell from his chest; he nearly reached out to steady her.

I called her val'syra. *Of all the korasi words that could've fallen out of my mouth...*

It was only another sign that he wasn't thinking clearly, that he was letting desire blind him, letting his cocks take the lead.

Go. Now!

Not allowing himself another glance at her, he stalked to the door, tugged it open, and stepped out into the night. The cool air only served as a mocking reminder of the heat their bodies had shared a moment before.

SIX

Mina removed the empty tray from the display case and replaced it with a fresh batch of cream cheese Danishes.

Viktor kissed me.

She turned and added the empty tray to the stack on the back counter.

Viktor kissed me.

That thought had been on replay in her mind since he'd left last night.

Viktor kissed *me.*

Barely paying attention to what she was doing, Mina closed the back of the display case, wandered down the hall and into the kitchen, and retrieved a bag of freshly ground coffee.

Phantom sensations haunted her—the hard press of his mouth, the bold sweep of his tongue, the savageness and intensity that had left her reeling.

Mina had been kissed before. Some of those kisses had been sloppy enough to make her cringe, a few had been almost decent, but they'd all left her...empty. Cold. Not one came anywhere close to what she'd experienced with Viktor.

When his lips had been upon hers, heat had erupted in her core, and her clit had thrummed with desire, craving more of his touch. He had consumed Mina and drunk from her like a man dying of thirst.

She'd been aware only of Viktor—the press of his fingers and his grip on her hair, the feel of his mouth and tongue, his taste, his scent. Oh God, his scent. Spicy cinnamon and cloves, growing stronger and sweeter with each breath, wrapping her in an intoxicating cocoon.

And when he'd pulled away, her lips had tingled with the aftermath of his fiery claim.

It wasn't until he had gone, and Mina had reflected upon that kiss over and over and over again, that she'd registered a few... strange details from her encounter with Viktor last night.

The touch of his fingers had been accompanied by sharp pricks, like claws against her skin. Which wasn't possible, because she'd seen the neatly trimmed nails at the ends of his long, sexy fingers. His tongue had seemed preternaturally dexterous and long, leaving no part of her mouth unexplored. And when his teeth had grazed her throat, his canines had felt sharper and longer than what seemed normal.

But those sensations had been fleeting, and her mind had been caught in a lustful haze. Could she really trust what she'd felt during those heated moments?

Returning to the main room, Mina popped open the lid of a nearly empty coffee canister and slowly poured in the fresh grounds. She blushed as she recalled just how hot she'd been, starting from the instant he'd dragged her chair toward him. That heat had only intensified when he'd leaned close, and his warm breath had whispered over her skin, when his lips had grazed her throat.

And when he'd stroked between her thighs, pressing his thumb against her clit...

That was the most thrilling, erotic moment of my life.

Pleasure and need had unfurled within her, and her pussy had grown wet and achy. If only she'd been able to spread her legs farther, if only Viktor had pushed his thumb just a little deeper, pressed a little harder. But he'd only teased her.

Mina had never realized how touch starved she'd been until last night. She'd arched into his touch, wordlessly begging for more. Had Chief Harrigan not walked in...

I want you, Viktor.

She'd almost spoken those words aloud, and they were true. Mina wanted him. Wanted him like she'd never wanted anything in her life.

Someone loudly cleared their throat behind her.

Mina started, spilling coffee grounds onto the counter as her hand jerked. She blinked away the remnants of her reverie and surveyed the mess she'd just made. The canister was overflowing, and there was no way she'd be able to replace the lid without scooping out some coffee first.

"What is wrong with me?" she whispered.

Touch starved, sex starved, desperately lonely.

Take your pick! It's likely all three.

It is definitely all three.

Letting out a sigh, she set the bag of coffee down, plastered a smile on her face, and turned toward the front counter. Daniel and Linda Stevens stood on the other side. The elderly couple were bundled in thick coats, hats, and scarves. Their clothing glistened with melting snow under the warm overhead lights.

Mina brushed her hands down her apron, wiping away the coffee grounds. "Good morning, Mister and Misses Stevens!"

Linda smiled. "Good morning, Mina."

Mr. Stevens nodded. "Mornin'."

"What can I get you today?" Mina asked. "Oh, that's right! I have the books you ordered, Linda."

Mr. Stevens's face reddened, and he turned away, occupying himself by studying the snacks displayed atop the counter. Mina took delight in his discomfort as she crouched and opened the cabinet where she kept her book orders.

"Oh, thank you." Linda chuckled as she glanced at her husband.

Mina sorted through the twine-bundled stacks until she found Linda's. She rose and set the two books on the counter. Both were older, with old-fashioned, painted clinch covers depicting the couples in passionate embraces. Those were Mina's favorite style of cover.

Are you imagining yourself and Viktor in similar embraces?

Hush!

"Don't know why they can't be more discreet," Mr. Stevens grumbled.

Linda leaned over the counter toward Mina and lowered her voice. "Don't you mind him. These books helped us get that spark back, if you know what I mean. He's not complaining about that."

Mr. Stevens's cheeks darkened further. "Linda! Don't go telling people about our private lives."

His wife waved him off. "Could I also get four of those delicious Danishes, Mina?"

With a grin, Mina nodded. "Of course. I just put out a fresh batch too. Anything else?"

"I'll take another of those chai lattes you had me try. Daniel?"

"Just black coffee."

"Mediums?" Mina asked as she totaled their order.

Linda smiled. "Mmhmm."

After Mr. Stevens paid, Mina stepped behind the display case and placed the Danishes neatly into a pastry box. Just as she'd picked up the last pastry, the bell over the door rang.

"I'll be with you in just a—" She looked up and froze.

Viktor stood just inside the doorway. Snowflakes clung to his long, loose hair and dusted his black jacket. Their eyes met and held.

Viktor kissed me.

Everything came rushing back to her again, and her cheeks warmed. The darkening of his silver eyes as they dipped to Mina's mouth hinted at his thoughts being in the same place as hers.

She wanted him to kiss her again, and again, and again. Wanted that mouth to move down her throat like it had before, but she didn't want it to stop there. Mina wanted his kisses on her breasts. She wanted to experience him taking her nipples into his hot mouth, wanted to feel his tongue rasping over them, wanted him to go lower, and lower, and lower, until that tongue slipped between her thighs.

Mina's pussy clenched with an onslaught of desire.

The pastry fell from her grasp and landed on the tray with a soft *thump*, snapping her back to reality. Mina's cheeks flamed even hotter as she hurriedly picked up a different Danish and placed it in the box with the rest. Surely everyone must've seen her standing there, staring at Viktor and practically salivating.

"Mina?" Linda asked gently. "Is everything okay?"

Mina heard Viktor's heavy boots on the floor as he walked deeper into the café.

"Y-Yes, sorry." Mina straightened and closed the pastry box, setting it on the counter. "I, uh, just got a little distracted."

Mr. Stevens glanced from Mina to Viktor, who had taken a seat at one of the small round tables in the back, near the bookcases. "Heard there was a bit of a situation across the street last night."

She turned to the back counter and grabbed two medium cups. "Oh?"

Because of course gossip moves at the speed of light in Sullford.

"People talk, Mina," Mr. Stevens said, casting another glance at Viktor. "Just think about what it looks like for you to be cavorting around with certain types, given your family history."

Mina gritted her teeth as she poured coffee into one cup and got to work on the chai latte. She inwardly cursed the moisture stinging her eyes. She hated that her emotions could be so overwhelming, hated that anger always brought her to tears, but she held them at bay.

Linda slapped him on the chest with her purse, making the man jump. "Leave the girl be, Dan! I swear, you're the worst gossip in town."

Mr. Stevens scoffed. "Just trying to give the girl some advice, Linda."

"Did she *ask* for advice?"

He sputtered a response too broken and mumbled for Mina to make out.

"I'll have your drinks ready in a moment," Mina said over her shoulder, trying to keep her tone pleasant, but anger simmered beneath the surface.

She was grateful for Linda's intervention, but it wouldn't stop Mr. Stevens. He saw the world through his own ignorant lens, and he was determined to judge Mina for her mother's actions, never stopping to consider that he had no right to judge anyone.

She turned her head slightly to peek at Viktor. He was leaning back in his chair with an elbow on the table, exuding all the confidence and indifference of a king among peasants—like everyone in the room was beneath him.

Except for Mina.

His gaze was intent upon her, almost expectant.

Mina's heart raced.

She looked down at steaming cups in front of her.

I want him.

It didn't matter what anyone thought of her and Viktor, didn't matter what anyone thought was going on between them. It was no one else's damn business—not Mr. Stevens's, not Dick Harrigan's, not Mike's or Trevor's or anyone else's in this town.

Mina placed lids upon the cups, picked them up, and set them in front of the Stevenses. The old man had a sour expression on his face.

She smiled at him and said in her best customer service tone, "Respectfully, Mr. Stevens, you don't know anything about me, my mother, or what we went through, and I don't appreciate the constant remarks and implications. If you can't keep your comments and your unsolicited advice to yourself in the future, I'm going to have to ask you to get your coffee elsewhere from now on."

His eyes widened, his brushy brows rose, and his cheeks once more turned ruddy. "I...I... T-that's not fair, Mina. I was just—"

"Dan, I've told you a thousand times that it's not helpful"—Linda collected her books, pastry box, and latte—"so don't you dare tell her that you're only trying to help." She looked at Mina. "Have a good day, dear."

Mr. Stevens glanced back and forth between his wife and Mina, bewildered. "That isn't... But I—"

"I'm sorry." Linda opened the door. "Those are the two simple words you're looking for, Daniel."

With his head bowed, Daniel picked up his coffee and took two packets of sugar from the nearby holder. He muttered, "Sorry, Mina. Didn't mean no harm."

Mina nodded. "I hope you both have a wonderful day."

She waited until the door closed behind them before turning her attention to Viktor. He was wearing that sultry half smirk again.

God, that man has the most beautiful lips...

And there was a new gleam in his gaze—a prideful gleam.

It hit her then what had just occurred.

She'd spoken up for herself. She'd stood up to Daniel Stevens.

Maybe nothing would change, but she hoped she wouldn't have to hear his opinions about herself or her mother ever again. At the very least, she'd taught herself an important lesson—even if he kept it up, she didn't have to take it.

All that anger faded, and the little surge of adrenaline triggered by the confrontation wore off, leaving her a bit unsteady.

Mina turned around, closed her eyes, and took in a deep, calming breath as she ran her palms down her apron.

It was over. She didn't have to dwell on it. Instead, she could focus on Viktor.

Viktor and his sensual lips.

Viktor and his soul-searing kisses.

Get a grip, Mina!

Opening her eyes, she glanced around the café. Her other customers were sitting with their breakfast as they worked, read, or scrolled through social media.

Mina grabbed a fresh cup and made her favorite drink—a caramel macchiato—making sure to add extra caramel because that was the best part. When she was finished, she placed a Danish on a small plate, rounded the counter, and made her way to Viktor.

Since the moment she'd first seen him, she'd felt a pull, like some invisible force was drawing her toward him. But she'd always been so busy, and her sightings of Viktor had often been so fleeting—catching him out of the corner of her eye as he strode past the café, seeing him pull up to the grocery store just as she was leaving. There'd been no way to naturally initiate a conversation.

Not that she really would've known how. It'd been so long since she'd tried, and he was unlike anyone she'd ever met. So she'd just let herself want him from afar.

But since she'd literally fallen into his arms, that pull had strengthened tenfold. The closer she got to him, the harder it was to resist.

And she knew it wouldn't be long before resistance was impossible.

Viktor didn't take his eyes off her as she approached. That unwavering stare made her belly flutter with whispers of desire.

Mina smiled and stopped next to his table. Now that she was here, so close to him, nervousness flooded her. "Hi."

His smirk widened. "Hello, Mina."

Mina stared at his lips, tempted to lick her own as though his taste still lingered upon them. Why did his mouth have to be so sinfully alluring?

"I, uh...believe I owe you these." She set the coffee and pastry on the table in front of him.

He looked down at the plate and arched a brow.

"Oh! There's one more thing." Mina moved to the nearby bookcases and scanned the spines. Her lips stretched into a grin. Romance. Absolutely perfect. His reaction would tell her a lot about the kind of person he was, and it would help her determine whether whatever it was she felt about him could become something real and lasting.

Getting a little ahead of yourself, aren't you Mina?

She selected a book that she'd particularly enjoyed, which featured a purple-haired, plus-sized heroine and a wickedly sexy incubus hero. Hugging it to her chest, she returned to Viktor. "I promised you a coffee, a pastry, or a book on me. But since you've saved me three times, here's one of each."

Mina placed the book beside Viktor's plate. She watched his hand slide over the table, watched the subtle play of muscle and tendons as he slipped his fingers beneath the book and lifted it.

After studying the front cover, he turned the book over and read the back. Mina clasped her hands in front of her and bit the inside of her lip. He hadn't sneered, hadn't tossed the book down in disgust, hadn't given her a judgmental, disapproving glare. That was a good start.

Viktor released a deep, thoughtful hum. "This book is about mating?"

Mating? Why would he word it like that?

It was strange, but perhaps it was because English wasn't his first language?

Warmth spread over her cheeks and down her neck. "It's a romance. But yes, it does have...explicit sex scenes."

He nodded slowly and flipped through the pages, giving away nothing in his expression.

Mina shifted her weight from foot to foot as Viktor opened to the middle of the book and began reading. His head tilted, and a long strand of hair fell over his shoulder.

"You've read this?" he asked, glancing up at her.

"It's one of my favorites."

There was still no change in his expression as he continued reading.

Mina reached for the book. "If you're not interested, I can pick something—"

He snatched it out of her reach and closed the pages around his finger, brows falling low. "You gave it to me. It's mine now."

Her eyes rounded in surprise, and she dropped her arm. "Oh. Okay."

Then the absurdity of the situation struck Mina—he reminded her of a child unwilling to give up their favorite new toy. She couldn't help laughing. Tall, strong, handsome, dangerous, mysterious Viktor...acting like a toddler over a book she'd just handed him.

"What is funny?" he asked.

Mina shook her head. "Nothing."

He regarded her with narrowed, skeptical eyes before he opened the book and resumed reading. The corner of his mouth ticked up ever so slightly. "I think I will enjoy this."

He's reading a sex scene. Right in front of me.

And based on where he was in the book, Mina knew exactly which scene it was. She imagined herself lying in front of Viktor, feeling his solid, muscular body and the hard length of his cock at her back as he stroked her between her thighs. Desire flickered in her core, and her clit twitched.

So often, he was guarded, controlled, revealing none of what was happening in his head. He was capable of such gentleness with her, but she'd seen the savagery running beneath his self-control, had seen the aggression he barely held in check. She'd felt it in the strength and firmness of his touch, which always reminded her that he was in command, that pleasure and pain would come at his whim.

And when it came to sex, she knew that fierce, passionate, dominant side of him would come out.

Viktor's nostrils flared as he drew in a deep breath, and a low growl rumbled in his chest. His gaze met hers. The way his silver eyes shone...

They really put the lust in luster.

Okay, that was corny...but not wrong.

"Mina..."

The bell over the door rang. Face flaming, Mina turned her head to see a woman step inside.

"Back to work for me!" Mina said as she retreated from Viktor. "Enjoy!"

Saved by the bell.

SEVEN

Seeing Mina hurry away awakened something bestial in Sevik. His instincts clawed to the forefront of his mind, insisting that Mina wasn't trying to escape him.

No, she was issuing a challenge, a test.

Catch me to prove yourself a worthy mate.

Mina left a trail of fragrance behind her, flavored by the aroma of her arousal. She might as well have been dragging him along by the nose.

Sevik clamped a hand on the edge of the table, digging his claws into its underside. His slit strained against the pressure of his hardening cocks. His fangs ached to their roots, but the discomfort had already spread, pulsing through his gums, his jaw, his neck, his skull, even into his horns. His muscles tensed, preparing to propel him off the chair and across the widening distance between him and Mina.

Difficult was far too mild a word to describe how hard it was for him to remain in place.

He'd gone too long without release. True as that was, it didn't explain the magnetic pull this little female had on him.

He watched as she took her place behind the counter to help her new customer. Watched her put on that warm and welcoming smile. Watched as she filled the other woman's order, doing everything she could to avoid looking in his direction again.

Sevik understood his own reasons for resisting. Revealing himself would only bring trouble for him. But even as detached as he was from the culture of his people, he knew the korasi did not shy away from sex and desire. What shame was there in mutual pleasure?

Mina desired him. If she'd been trying to hide it, she'd done a poor job. Why did she fight that desire so strongly?

He finally pried his gaze away from her, dropping it to the table. Food, drink, and a book. Simple gifts—at least based on the way she'd treated them.

Sevik's claws sank deeper into the table's underside. He told himself that Mina didn't know, couldn't have known, that such gifts would have a deep meaning for a korasi. Though his mother had rarely talked about her homeworld and their people, she had passed on a few korasi values to Sevik before she'd died.

Offering food was meaningful. Powerfully so. It was seen as placing the needs of another over one's own. When parents offered food to children, it was a display of parental love and care. When friends offered food to one another, it was a display of affection and respect, and it had been the same when Sevik and his brother had given food to their ailing mother. The tradition had held particular meaning in his family given their poverty.

Food wasn't always easy to come by, and it was no small gesture to give it freely to another, keeping it from your own belly.

And when a prospective mate offered food...

It was a sign of interest in something more than the casual rutting so prevalent amongst his kind. It was a sign of commitment, of a deeper desire.

When he'd cooked for her, it hadn't been the same. The food had been hers to begin with; there'd been no sacrifice on his part. Yet what she'd given him now came from her business, from her profits—it came at a cost to her, however small.

He told himself again that Mina's gift was merely one of gratitude, that it didn't hold any other meaning. And yet...

Willing his hand to relax, he released the table and plucked up the pastry between the claws of his forefinger and thumb.

The soft crust was golden and flaky, drizzled with a white garnish, and had a glob of something creamy in the middle. Though he'd lived on Earth for a year, his diet had consisted primarily of meat. He remained unfamiliar with most other human food.

After another glance at Mina, who was now very intently mixing a drink, he lifted the pastry to his mouth and took a bite.

The buttery crust had a hint of saltiness to it; on its own, he might've found it enjoyable. But when that white topping and the creamy glob in the center hit his taste buds, he was assaulted by overwhelming sweetness.

The muscles of his neck and jaw twitched, and his tongue recoiled as though it could somehow escape the saccharine wave. Sevik pressed his lips together and fought back a shudder.

How the fuck could humans eat food like this without retching?

Mina gave this to me.

And he would eat it and be grateful, because he refused to insult her by rejecting this gift.

He exhaled heavily and forced himself to chew. Even after he choked down the bite, the sweetness lingered, coating the inside of his mouth. Returning the pastry to the plate, he sucked the crumbs from his fingers, hoping the slight saltiness would counteract the sweet.

Mina happened to look his way as he did so. Her eyes rounded, pink spread across her cheeks, and she froze, as though she'd forgotten she was carrying a drink to a customer. She shook herself and turned away from him abruptly.

But fuck if that hadn't started him up again despite the persistence of that foul sweetness. His cocks strained for freedom with new insistence.

Vazk. *I shouldn't have come here.*

Yesterday, he'd come dangerously close to rutting her right here in the café. That would've led to a very long night of explanations he didn't want to give, of trying to calm a panicked female, of...

Of silencing her, if necessary.

But the tightness in his chest told Sevik that was something he couldn't do, whether it became necessary or not. He couldn't bring himself to harm her. Sevik, who'd taken so many lives without a second thought, would rather turn his weapons on himself than on Mina.

She was a risk. And being with him put her at risk, because she burned away his self-control.

Yet he couldn't stay away.

Last night's sensations refused to fade. He still felt echoes of her lips against his, of her skin under his fingertips, of the heat radiating from her sex. He still felt her hands on his shirt, pulling him closer.

Instinct drove him to be near her, to see her, to touch her, to... protect her.

Time to move to a different part of Earth.

Yet he knew it wouldn't matter where he went, whether here on Earth or anywhere else in the universe. No distance would disrupt his thoughts of her.

With her face very firmly directed forward and her spine stiff, Mina raced into the back hallway, leaving his sight.

Again, Sevik battled the urge to go after her. He muttered a curse to himself, picked up the cup, and sniffed the steam rising from the opening on the lid.

It had that coffee smell, which was prevalent in almost any place humans gathered in any number, but there was more to it. He knew that other smell...

What was it called? Caramel? Another sweet thing, if he wasn't mistaken. But based on the heat seeping through the cup, he risked burning away all sense of taste if he drank now.

He set it back down and opened the book to the first page.

Sevik's cabin didn't have direct access to what seemed to be humanity's preferred sources of entertainment—television and the internet. He could get onto the latter via the aetherkey he'd brought with him, which functioned similarly to a human computer, but he limited his usage of the device for fear that it could be tracked from Vabos.

So, he'd turned to books—of which there'd been many in the fully furnished cabin—to occupy his time. The English letters had seemed bizarre to him at first. He'd understood them only due to his neural transceiver's translation function. But practice over the months had made reading the language second nature, and he could do so now without need for the transceiver's aid.

Books provided fascinating insight into humans, their experiences, and their minds. For all the differences between them and other species, there were even more similarities. So many common emotions and motivations.

Reading this book, which Mina had said was one of her favorites, would teach him about her. And based on the bit he'd sampled earlier...

This certainly wouldn't make it any fucking easier to resist her.

Sevik read slowly, giving every word the time and respect it deserved. His gaze occasionally flicked toward Mina after she emerged from the back. She continued working as though he wasn't there.

That amused him as much as it irritated him.

He forced himself to eat the pastry one bite at a time. The sweetness only compounded, not diminishing no matter how long he waited between mouthfuls. But the more overwhelming the taste became, the more determined Sevik became to finish it.

Sevik nearly gagged when he attempted to wash away the pastry's taste with a swig of the coffee, only keeping the liquid in his mouth by pressing the back of a hand over his lips. The blend of overly sweet and overly bitter was almost more than he could handle. Though he could almost appreciate the smell of coffee, its taste made his facial muscles threaten to twitch with every sip.

He drank it all regardless. His female had gifted him the food and drink, and he would not spurn her by discarding either.

Not far into the book, the main characters agreed to something with which Sevik was quite familiar—sex with no attachments, merely for the pleasure of it.

Fuck, it has *been a long time...*

Even though Sevik and Mina weren't anything like the book's main characters, his mind inserted them into the roles.

He pictured himself taking off Mina's clothes. Pictured himself stroking her slit, sliding his fingers into her. He pictured her lips parted and her face flushed, and it was the scent of her arousal rising from his memory as he imagined himself licking her slick from his fingers.

Sevik couldn't keep his eyes on the page; they continuously sought Mina, and every time they settled upon her, his imagination strengthened. Molten heat flowed through his veins, clouding his mind with lust, dulling his resistance to his instincts.

Mina was right there. So close, so eager. If he moved now, if he took her, she wouldn't fight. She'd be more than willing.

His slit parted against the press of his bulging cocks. Only his jeans kept them from extruding. He shifted upon his seat in an attempt to relieve the ache at his core, but nothing helped. One hand curled atop the table, nearly burying his claws in the wood.

Somehow, he kept reading, though each new word only intensified his yearning and made it harder to focus on the page.

This is what she enjoys. This is what she craves.

Had she gifted him this book as a message? As an invitation? As a...challenge?

Was she showing Sevik exactly what she wanted him to do to her?

Zekt'al, this was torture. The best fucking torture of his life. He'd never wanted anyone like this, had never had so immense an interest, so consuming a need. And he never would've imagined himself feeling this for a human, of all things.

He'd pleasured many females, and he had received pleasure from many females. But there was no part of him that was not desperate to have Mina. Not even Enthi, the korasi female to whom he'd been closer than anyone, had made him feel even a tiny sliver of what Mina had ignited in him.

Sevik wanted to see Mina's hunger, wanted to feel it. Wanted to hear her beg. He wanted to drink her passion and wrap himself in her pleasure, and he wanted to take his own pleasure from it.

It wasn't until Mina made eye contact with him again that Sevik realized he'd closed the book and had been staring at her for some time. His heartbeat quickened. He'd tried not to reveal anything in this little game between them. He'd tried to hide the depth of his desire while stoking the flames of hers.

Surely, he'd exposed himself now. Surely, she'd seen him staring, had seen the heat in his gaze.

But the smile she offered him was so pure, so sweet, so warm, that its radiance withered away his worry.

He knew in that instant that he wouldn't hesitate to kill just to see that smile again.

EIGHT

SOMETHING IS WRONG.

Sevik squeezed the steering wheel and clenched his jaw.

Nothing was wrong. He was fine, he was calm, he was in control.

Yet each beat of his heart came quicker than the last, and the restlessness coursing through his limbs grew stronger as the distance between him and The Bookish Bean increased.

As the distance between him and Mina increased.

Enough of this. Enough!

But that sense of wrongness only intensified. He shifted his weight on the seat and eased his grip, hardly noticing that he immediately began drumming his fingers on the wheel.

His chest fluttered, brimming with anticipation, as he glanced in the rearview mirror.

In the reflection, he saw only a snowy, forested road, cloaked in the shadows created by the still-rising sun.

That fluttering became a heaviness that sank into his gut, pooling there—cold, dense, and unsettling.

"*Leskahn tor lesk*, what did I expect?"

Expectation was one thing, desire another. He'd wanted to see

The Bookish Bean behind him, with Mina out front, smiling and waving. But she was long behind him.

Sevik's heartbeat only continued to quicken. It echoed through his body, steadily gaining volume and force.

He pressed down on the accelerator pedal. The truck roared and lurched forward, carrying him toward his residence that much faster.

Leaving the café—leaving Mina—had been a test of his willpower, but he'd met the challenge. He'd walked out of his own accord not long after choking down the last of the drink she'd given him. The cloying taste of the coffee still clung to his tongue, fouling his every inhalation.

He'd chosen to leave. So why this reaction?

Sevik had dealt with danger throughout his life, had looked his own potential death in the eyes more times than he could count, and had faced the deepest betrayal and loss, all without flinching.

Why was leaving Mina causing this escalating physical response in him when nothing else had? All the nervousness and anxiety he'd never felt was piling atop him now, burying him.

You have a lifetime of pain behind you, Sevik. And now that you're stuck here with nothing else to do, it's all catching up to you...

No. He refused to believe that, just as he refused to believe this was merely the result of being separated from Mina. He hadn't imprinted on her, and though she was more tempting than any female he'd ever encountered, this reaction wasn't natural. This was entirely unlike Sevik.

As he turned onto the long driveway leading to his cabin, his mind raced with theories, each more outlandish than the last—and all interspersed with intrusive thoughts of Mina.

Was Earth's atmosphere adversely affecting him?

Why now, after he'd been here for so long?

Would Mina tremble as he undressed her? Would her eyes smolder with lust?

Was another nonhuman being hacking into his neural transceiver, disrupting his mind?

But his holoshroud remained active, and the interface had remained hidden all morning. Plus, given the nature of his particular implant, someone would have had to get pretty damned close to even attempt accessing it.

Would the sounds of Mina's pleasure be as enthralling as her laughter?

Would her moans be light and airy, or would they be breathy, husky, primal?

Was his body revolting after a year with no sexual release?

That seemed more likely than the rest, but some part of him recognized it as untrue. No, this was something more recent, something he was overlooking...

He pulled in under the carport, turned off the truck, and reached for the romance book lying on the passenger seat. His hand shook in the air.

He felt like a fucking inexperienced youngling on the comedown after the adrenaline rush of his first brawl.

Sevik snatched up the book and exited the truck, pausing on his way to the cabin's entrance when the coffee flavor struck him anew. Wincing, he muttered a curse, turned his head, and spat into the snow.

Sevik froze, brow furrowing.

From what he'd seen, he wouldn't have been surprised to learn that some humans drank their own body weight in coffee every week. He'd thought it a cultural tradition, a morning ritual, but there was another bit of information rattling around in his mind, drifting amidst the things he'd learned about these alien people and their world during his time here...

Caffeine.

That was why they drank that bitter sludge. Caffeine woke them up, got their minds moving, chased away the grogginess of sleep.

And like any other drug, there was no telling how caffeine would affect nonhumans.

No telling how it would affect a korasi.

Sevik held up his free hand, palm down. Tremors coursed

through it and along his arm as though it were overloaded with energy that had no outlet.

"The fucking coffee," he growled.

He stomped into the cabin, tore off his boots and coat in the laundry room, and stormed into the kitchen.

"Had to drink it all, didn't you?"

Asking himself that question out loud only fueled his anger; he already knew the answer.

Yes. Every fucking drop.

Gritting his teeth, he moved to the living room, sat on the couch, and opened the book. His eyes roved over the page. But the words seemed skittery, evading his understanding like vermin fleeing a beam of light.

Heat coursed both under his skin and over its surface. The fireplace was dark, but the cabin was almost unbearably hot.

Mina had said this book was one of her favorites. What else did she enjoy? Did she have favorite music, a favorite food, drink, or color?

He forced his attention back to the top of the page and tried to read again.

What was her favorite scene in this book?

Images again flashed through his imagination—Mina in place of the book's female character, being undressed by Sevik's hands, being pleasured by his mouth and tongue, his fingers, his cocks.

With a frustrated grunt, he snapped the book shut and tipped his head back onto the couch's rear cushion. It was only then that he realized he'd been bouncing his leg incessantly since he'd sat down.

Shouldn't have gone there today.

And yet he couldn't find any regret for having done so. Not even a sliver.

Their encounter today replayed in his mind's eye, over and over, and a smile crept onto his face. Mina was his opposite in so many ways. Even had she lived on Vabos, their paths never would've crossed due to his old life. She was that rare sort—honest and innocent.

Without someone to look out for her, someone to protect her, Sevik's homeworld would've devoured Mina. Alone...she would've had to sacrifice all of who and what she was to survive.

Sevik bared his teeth and growled, irritated by his own dismissal of her strength and perseverance. That steel at her core was part of what drew him to her; how could he have forgotten it?

It's not like she's unfamiliar with hardship. She's suffered. She's struggled.

Giving in to his body's need to move, he shoved himself up off the couch and walked to the bathroom.

He brushed his teeth and tongue, finally ridding himself of the coffee flavor, and then set about cleaning the bathroom. Seeking relief from the stifling heat, he tore off his shirt and tossed it aside. Once done, he moved on to the rest of the cabin, scrubbing, dusting, sweeping, and wiping everything down. Before long, he'd also removed his pants, socks, and underwear.

Even naked, sweat beaded on his skin, and he was only more aware of the heat.

And all the while, Mina dominated his thoughts.

His body moved of its own accord, still jittery, still off, desperate for relief from the unending restlessness. More than once, he had to press a hand firmly over his slit to keep his throbbing cocks from emerging as his thoughts turned to rutting Mina.

That ache low in his belly grew deeper and stronger each time.

The day wore on that way, sometimes dragging, sometimes blazing past. He paced throughout the cabin, convinced he'd soon wear the rugs down to threads or erode grooves in the hardwood floor.

He knew there were other things to occupy him, other topics to consider, but he could not turn his thoughts away from Mina. A few times, he felt compelled to grab his keys and drive back to town. Fortunately, he convinced himself not to do so for a multitude of reasons—not the least of which being that he was still wholly unclothed.

No task could hold his interest for long before he moved on.

When snow began to fall late in the afternoon, part of him envied the big, slow-falling flakes, which seemed completely unbothered by anything.

What did Mina think of snow? Based on what he'd seen, humans weren't particularly tolerant of the cold, insulating themselves against it with heavy coats, hats, and gloves. She seemed especially sensitive to it. Did that mean she hated the cold, hated the snow, or could she find beauty and wonder in it?

Sevik had never seen it before coming to Earth. Vabos's urban centers were highly industrialized, and though there was seasonal cold, it was never cold enough to produce ice and snow. But the korasi came from a world where both had been prevalent. He'd always enjoyed the cold. It was in his blood, an ancestral tie to his people that hadn't been taken away by circumstance.

In an odd way, that made this place—a remote lake in the mountains on a remote planet—feel more like home than Vabos ever had.

He watched the snow fall from the living room, walking back and forth along the windows like a beast trapped in a zoo display. Once he couldn't bear watching any longer, he pulled on his pants and stepped out the back door to shovel snow off the deck.

Snowflakes lighted upon him and melted, and the droplets ran down his bare flesh, sharpening the bite of the cold. Yet though the chill was refreshing against his heated skin, it couldn't cool the fires raging inside him.

Thanks to the fresh layer of snow blanketing the land, it was even quieter outside the cabin than it had been within, making Sevik's thoughts louder in comparison.

He continued working as the gray sky darkened, plowing a path around the side of the cabin, knocking icicles from the eaves, and clearing snow from the driveway.

Despite the cold, he was only sweating more when he was done. Tremors still coursed through him, his heart still beat too fast, and he was still overly warm. The ache behind his slit was constant now, flaring and fading in rolling waves but never going away.

By then, the sun had been down for some time, and the frozen lake was like a mirror beneath the night sky, striated with veinlike snowdrifts created by the wind.

Sevik scanned the shoreline. There were only a few other residences around the lake—of which only two were occupied—and they were out of sight of his cabin.

He allowed himself no time for further consideration. Tugging off his pants, he tossed them onto the floor mat just inside the back door before walking down to the water's edge.

The ice groaned beneath his feet as he stepped onto it. He knelt, closed his fist, and hammered at the surface until it cracked and broke away. With hands and claws, he expanded the hole so it was more than wide enough for him to fit through.

Sevik dove in.

The frigid jolt awoke his every nerve, making his skin hypersensitive.

Zekt'al, what he wouldn't give to have Mina's lithe little hands running over him right now. What he wouldn't give to have her warmth contrasting the cold, to have her soft, smooth skin caressing his, to feel every tiny movement, every faint brush, every wicked stroke.

His cocks pushed against his slit, parting it. The chill of the water only increased the uncomfortable pressure in his shafts, only heightened his need for friction, for release.

He ignored them for a long while, focusing on the water and the motions of his body as he swam, surfacing when he needed air and ensuring his opening didn't freeze back over. He had no idea how long he stayed in the lake. Much longer than it would've taken for a human to be killed by the cold, most likely.

But not nearly long enough to freeze that inner heat.

Only when his muscles burned with exertion did he pull himself out of the water. His ragged breaths emerged in clouds of steam as he trudged back to the cabin.

"Should've set out a fucking towel," he muttered before entering through the back door. Even with his body radiating heat, the moisture on his skin had begun to frost.

He walked to the bathroom and showered, again finding himself battling the primal urge for release as he imagined Mina in the stall with him. He imagined her naked form, lathered with soap, pictured their hands upon each other's bodies, cleaning, teasing, soothing, pleasuring...

The water very quickly became too hot for him. He finished washing himself, dried off, and wrapped a towel around his waist —primarily so he didn't have to see his cocks poking out through his slit.

Sevik mopped up the water he'd trailed from the back door with another towel, collected his discarded clothing, and tossed it in the washing machine.

Without bothering to get dressed, he went into the kitchen to cook a couple steaks. Despite the long swim, he couldn't stand still; his legs demanded movement, his fingers tapped and fidgeted, and his tongue swept back and forth over the points of his fangs.

He grabbed a glass and filled it with water from the faucet. "Never fucking drinking coffee again."

Tossing his head back, he drank quickly and deeply.

And if Mina were to offer me more?

He slammed the empty glass down hard enough to nearly shatter it. "*Fuck.*"

If she were to offer him more coffee, he'd drink every drop— but he would ensure she was there with him, so he could use her delectable little body to rut this energy out of himself. Consequences be damned.

Sevik devoured the steaks and guzzled more water, hoping it would leave him less time to think. Less time to dwell on Mina.

That night was a restless one. He spent most of it tossing and turning in his bed, kicking off the covers, dragging them back on, turning from his back to his side to his front until he scarcely knew which was which. Every time he found a comfortable position, some part of his body would soon protest—a twitch of his leg, an involuntary jerk of his hand, a twinge in his back or a kink in his neck. Comfort became an impossible to obtain dream.

Not that any dreams were fucking possible, since sleep refused to take him.

Whenever Sevik closed his eyes, he saw her. Whenever he inhaled, he *smelled* her. Her scent lingered on his bedding, which he'd refused to wash after she'd slept here.

When he glanced at the clock, it read 5:47 AM.

Sevik groaned and turned onto his stomach, burying his face against his pillow.

His next inhalation was more laden with Mina's scent than any since he'd entered his bed, and his memory was more than happy to fill in what was missing—the allure of her arousal.

She'd wanted him. The proof had perfumed the air of her café the other evening. Had he chosen to pursue her then, they'd have rutted. He'd have filled his nose with that sweet, sensual scent, would've lapped up her essence with his tongue, would've worn it on his cocks.

And so many of his questions about Mina, those wonderings to which his imagination could not do justice, would've been answered.

He would've learned the expressions and noises she made in the throes of passion. Would've learned all the places to touch, kiss, and lick to make her cry out in pleasure. Would've known the tight grip of her cunt, the softness of her flesh in his firm grasp as he drove into her again and again...

Sevik lifted his hips from the bed, slid a hand down his abdomen, and pressed his splayed fingers over his slit, parting it. His cocks emerged readily, one gliding between his thumb and forefinger, the other between his forefinger and middle finger.

He curled his fingers around the oil-coated shafts and pumped his fist.

A shudder racked Sevik. He turned his cheek onto the pillow and let out a harsh groan as he moved his hand again. Pleasure swept through him with each slide, making his hips buck and his breath hitch.

Behind his eyelids, he saw Mina. Mina in his bed, clad only in her undergarments, just as she'd been when he'd brought her here.

Mina looking at him with that spark in her brown eyes, that hint of fire, that lustful ember. Mina with that warm smile turned sultry.

Mina with her hand on his cocks, squeezing just right as she pumped up and down.

"Ah, *val'syra*," he rasped, tightening his grip and quickening his strokes.

He wanted to run his fingers through those short, dark curls. Wanted those full, pink lips against his. He wanted not just her scent to fill his lungs, but her breath, her essence. Wanted that body tucked against him, moving, pulsing, grinding.

That inner pressure built, deepening to pleasure-laced pain, to delicious agony. It echoed throughout his body, consuming him.

In his mind's eye, he dragged Mina close, pushed her face down on the bed, and climbed atop her. He pictured a flick of his claws tearing away her underwear, baring her dripping cunt to him.

The smell of her arousal flowed from his memory, flooding his brain. He saw himself draw back his hips and drive into her waiting heat.

Sevik's free hand closed on the bedding, claws ripping the sheet and digging into the mattress beneath. He spread his knees for support and gyrated his hips, making his strokes harder, faster, deeper, trying to match the speed of his racing heart.

A strained growl tore from his throat as his cocks thickened, jerked, and spurted thick ropes of seed. His mind went black against the burst of pleasure.

Sevik's hips bucked wildly, driving his hand and his shafts down onto the bed. He kept them moving along with his fist, using the added friction to coax everything out of himself.

When his motions finally slowed to a stop, the bedding and his hand, belly, and thighs were sticky with seed, and the ache had moved down into his bones, pulsing from his core.

Forcing his body to relax, he breathed deep and slow, ignoring the burning in his lungs. He squeezed his throbbing cocks to combat the lingering pressure.

"*Vazk.*"

He'd never come so much in his fucking life.

And it still wasn't enough. Were Mina here now, he'd rut her —again, and again, and again. This had only slightly eased his craving. What he wanted, what he needed, he would never get from his hand.

He needed his female. His mate. Mina.

Sevik had always been practical. He knew he couldn't resist for long, knew he'd succumb soon. When that happened, when he inevitably crumbled...

Well, he'd figure out what the fuck to do when the time came.

He chuckled at the thought, though he shouldn't have found humor in it.

I should clean up...

Sevik scowled. He was loath to wash her scent from his bedding, and he would mourn its loss.

With no small difficulty, he pushed himself up on shaky arms. His legs were unsteady as he slipped off the bed and onto his feet. Of course, now that he *had* to clean up, he was exhausted.

After pulling off the soiled bedding, he walked downstairs, leaning on the banister to steady himself. The walk to the washing machine felt like the longest of his life. Once it was running, he made the equally taxing trek to the bathroom.

Somehow, Sevik stayed on his feet as he washed himself off in the shower. His body was heavy now, sluggish, spent. He barely kept himself from falling over as he dried off and exited the bathroom.

But he didn't make it to the stairs. As he collapsed onto the couch, he couldn't recall if he'd fallen there accidentally or if he'd chosen to do so—not that it made any difference.

Sleep seized him before he could even try to rise, and he gladly sank into that abyss, where his thoughts of Mina would meet no resistance from his conscious mind.

NINE

It had been a languorous day. A day during which Mina had slept well past her usual wake up time of six o'clock, had eaten lunch without feeling rushed, and had served not one single customer. She'd just turned on ambient rain sounds, curled up with a thick blanket on her cozy, oversized chaise, and read.

It was the day she turned thirty years old.

Yet as much as she'd wanted to lose herself in the fantastical world of her book and get swept away by the passionate, swoon-worthy romance, it kept reminding her of just how alone she was.

Mina had no one to wake up alongside, no one to caress her cheek and kiss her good morning, no one to hold her as she lounged in bed. She had no one to share meals with, no one to talk and laugh with.

She was so damned lonely it hurt.

So when the characters in the story finally professed their love for one another, Mina closed the book and cried. The fact that she had no one to comfort her only made her cry harder.

When her sobs ebbed, she wiped her eyes and looked out the nearby window to watch the big snowflakes fall. The wind's howl rose over the rain sounds playing on her speaker. The sun had set a couple hours ago, around two-thirty—not that there'd been much sunlight today with the dark storm clouds dominating the sky.

She didn't even have someone to cuddle and watch the snowstorm with.

Tears again filled her eyes, blurring her vision.

Stop. Just stop. Feeling sorry for yourself isn't going to change anything.

No, it wouldn't.

But it was her birthday, and she could cry if she wanted to.

Mina sighed, unraveled herself from her blanket, and scooted off the chaise. There was no way she could bring herself to read anymore. Picking up her phone, she swapped the rain sounds for something more upbeat. Dancing and singing along to the pop music, she made her way to the kitchen and fixed a quick, easy, nostalgic dinner—boxed macaroni and cheese.

She stood bent over the island counter, rocking her body to the beat, as she ate spoonful after spoonful of delicious, creamy, cheesy pasta.

Her music was abruptly interrupted by her ringtone.

Mina looked at her phone and grinned. Setting her spoon down in her bowl, she snatched up her phone, disconnected the Bluetooth, and accepted the call. "Hi Randy!"

"Happy birthday to you, happy birthday to you," Randy sang loudly, exaggerating every word dramatically. "Happy birthday dear Mina... Haaaaaaappy Birrrrrrrthdaaaaaay toooooo youuuuuuuuu."

"Thank you," Mina said, laughing. She hadn't realized how long it had been since they'd last spoken until now—a month, at least. It was so good to hear his voice. "You remembered."

Randy scoffed. "Of course I remembered! I'd never forget. How does it feel now that you're thirty years old?"

Lonely. Sad. Pitiful.

"The same," Mina replied, keeping her true feelings out of her voice. "How have you been? Enjoying the sunny desert life?"

"Sure am. I've never been so tan in my life. I actually just got back from a Caribbean cruise—with my girlfriend."

Mina gasped. "What?" That ache in her heart intensified. "Girlfriend? When? How?"

"What do you mean how?" he asked with feigned offense. "I'm a good-looking man who knows how to cook."

"Oh, you know I didn't mean it like that. I've just never seen you with anyone in all the time I've known you. When did this happen?"

"Over the summer. I wanted to tell you sooner, but it felt like it was *too* soon, I guess. Sorry, Mina."

"You don't need to apologize. I'm so excited for you! So, tell me about her. Tell me how you two met!" She took another bite of her mac and cheese.

Randy chuckled. "I was in Las Vegas for a weekend, and while I was getting a drink from the bar by the hotel pool, I heard a beautiful laugh behind me. I turned around, and there Katy was, wearing this bright pink and white polka dot bikini. The way she smiled at me... I felt like I'd been struck by lightning.

"Of course, I stood there staring at her like a fool. But damn, Mina. She was beautiful. And I told her so, right there, out loud, in front of everyone. Her eyes went so wide. I didn't care if she was married or not, I just had to tell her."

Mina smiled as she picked up her bowl and brought it to the sink. "I guess she wasn't married, considering she's now your girlfriend."

"Divorced thirteen years ago," Randy said. "It was mutual, and they're both happier for it. Now, she's all mine. And it just so happens that she lives in Arizona too, only twenty minutes away from me."

"Well?" She set her bowl down before walking the sofa. "Tell me more about Katy and your cruise!"

Sitting with her legs curled to the side, Mina listened as Randy explained that he and Katy had started off as friends for those first few weeks, but their connection had been so strong that they couldn't deny it. They'd leapt in headfirst. He excitedly described their first date, and he gushed about meeting Katy's kids and grandkids.

Pure joy radiated from his every word.

Randy had opened the Thomas Bakery with his wife, Amanda, and the two had run it together for years. But she'd passed away from a stroke in her thirties. There one day, gone the next.

Mina understood that all too well.

From what people said, Randy had struggled terribly in the years following his wife's death. He'd been alone and devastated, withdrawn, pouring everything of himself into the bakery. By the time Mina had met him, Amanda had been gone for longer than they'd been married, but he still hadn't moved on.

Mina didn't doubt that Randy had seen his own grief and loss reflected in her and her mother—and that, knowing such suffering firsthand, he'd done everything he could to ensure they didn't have to endure it without support. To ensure they didn't have to feel as alone as he had.

She knew he'd always wanted a family. It had been apparent in the way he'd helped Mina and Hannah during their time of need—especially when he found out what Hannah had been doing to earn extra income. It had been in the way he'd spent time with them, taught them, cared for them. The way he'd made them feel like they were still important even though their world had crumbled beneath their feet, made them feel loved. He'd treated them like the daughter and granddaughter he'd never had.

Selling the bakery had been his way of finally finding closure, of finally allowing himself to move on from his first love, who'd been gone for nearly three decades by the time The Thomas Bakery became The Bookish Bean.

Now, he was living his best life and making the most out of every minute, and Mina was thrilled for him.

"What about you, Mina?" Randy asked. "How are you doing?"

"I'm...good," she said carefully. "The café's doing great, and it's been keeping me busy."

"I'm not worried about the café. I'm worried about you."

Mina let out a little chuckle. "Oh, you don't need to worry about me. I'm fiiiine."

Randy sighed. "I know how it is there. Know how *they* are."

She closed her eyes and held her phone just a little tighter.

"The offer still stands, Mina. You could sell the building and move down here. You'll always have a place with me." He softened his voice. "You need to let them go."

But Mina wasn't thinking about her parents; she was thinking of Viktor. Had Randy brought this up a week ago, she might've been tempted. She knew it wasn't healthy to hold onto this place simply because it was where her parents were buried and where her memories of them had been made.

Yet...she still wasn't ready to let go. And now...

Now there was Viktor.

"I...met someone," Mina said, opening her eyes.

"What?" Randy asked, the word coming quickly in his shock. "Who?"

"Do you remember the mystery man I told you about who moved into that cabin out on the lake? The one everyone in town was gossiping about?"

"Well, who is he then? Can't be much of a mystery now."

Except Viktor *was* a mystery. Mina knew his name, knew that his accent was foreign, and that he'd had shady dealings in the past, but nothing more. She had no idea where he was born, what he'd been like as a child, his favorite color, or what his hobbies were. She didn't even know what he did for a living.

"His name is Viktor. And when I say I met him," Mina said, "I really do mean that I just met him."

"Mina..."

"But he's...he's been good to me, Randy. He's not like the others. He stands up for me, and he's helped give me the confidence to stand up for myself."

She recalled the pride that had been in Viktor's eyes after she'd confronted Daniel Stevens. Even now, it made something in her belly flutter. But even more powerful was the pride she felt in herself.

Mina stood up from the sofa. "You know how you said it felt like you were struck by lightning the moment you saw Katy?"

"Yeah."

"That's what it felt like for me with Viktor. My whole world just lit up. We just...need more time to get to know each other."

If he lets me know him at all.

"Just be careful, Mina," Randy said. "I don't want to see you hurt. You have a big heart, but there are too many people who'd take advantage of that without a second thought."

"Viktor won't."

"Good. Because if I have to haul my sun-bronzed ass back to that frozen—"

"Oh gross! You did *not* just say that about your ass."

Randy laughed.

They talked for a little while longer before finally saying their goodbyes and hanging up.

Mina smiled down at the phone. "I miss you, old man."

But she was so happy for him.

After washing her bowl and setting it in the drying rack, Mina showered, taking her time to relish the hot water. When she was done, she pulled on some cozy pajamas to prepare for a night of cake, champagne, and a movie.

She opened the fridge and took out the expensive bottle of champagne she'd saved for the occasion. Mina didn't drink often, but you only turned thirty once! She also grabbed the cake she'd baked for herself yesterday, placing the box on the counter. When she opened the lid, the rich, enticing fragrance of chocolate and raspberries filled her nose and made her mouth water.

Retrieving a lighter and a single candle from the counter drawer, she stuck the latter in the center of the cake and lit it.

Mina stared at the flame.

A lone flame on a lone candle, jabbed into the top of a cake she was about to eat alone.

She was stricken by another horrible wave of isolation. Here she was, thirty years old, and she had no one to celebrate with. No friends, no family. No one.

The conversation she'd had with Viktor as he'd driven her home the other morning came back to her.

Where I'm from, people don't ask so many questions.

Sounds like a very lonely, very unhappy place.

Probably.

In all his time in Sullford, no one had bothered to get to know him. No one had braved even approaching him. Most people kept their distance and speculated about him from afar.

Except for her.

Mina didn't know what Viktor had left behind, but from what she'd gathered, he'd been just as lonely then as he was now.

She turned her head and looked out the window. Despite the light reflecting on the inside of the glass, she could see the snow falling out there.

Viktor was probably by himself in his cabin right now. Was he watching the snow? Was he sitting in front of a crackling fire, reading the book she gave him?

Was he... Was he thinking of Mina?

A sudden yearning to see him flooded her.

Go to him.

Mina shook her head. "No, I shouldn't."

Go to him.

"The roads are horrible. It'd be stupid to drive in this storm."

Go to him.

She bit down on her bottom lip as she looked back at the cake.

Make a wish.

What did she want?

You're a thirty-year-old virgin, Mina. You know what you want.

Wax dripped down the candle to pool on the chocolate frosting. She closed her eyes.

She felt the phantom press of Viktor's lips upon hers, recalled the possessiveness of his mouth, his taste. He'd claimed her, consumed her. He'd branded her with his fiery, passionate kiss.

Mina curled her fingers around the edge of the table as desire sparked within her core.

I want him.

Opening her eyes, she drew in a deep breath and blew out the candle.

She wouldn't spend another birthday alone.

TEN

SEVIK STARED at the holographic display projected from the aetherkey on the coffee table. The message onscreen stared back at him tauntingly—*Seeking Connection.*

Seeking fucking connection.

How long had it been? Twenty minutes? Thirty?

He rested his elbows on his knees, ground his teeth together, and bowed his head. He knew there were complex processes at play right now. The aetherkey was trying to link to a network on Vabos, a universe away, through hundreds, maybe thousands, of proxies across galaxies to obscure the origin of the signal. And he knew the universe was a big place.

He'd crossed it while recovering from the injuries he'd suffered at the hands of that coward Brekker, and he'd felt every inch of the journey.

But that knowledge didn't ease his impatience.

"Fucking storm," Sevik growled, glancing out the living room window.

An endless torrent of huge snowflakes dominated the view, whipping wildly through the air. Wind battered the cabin's exterior and howled across the lake. Not that he could see the lake through the heavy snow.

He couldn't even make out the deck railing that stood ten feet past the window.

Last night's quiet flurries had escalated into a blizzard while Sevik slept the day away. Though he'd shoveled off the deck since waking this afternoon, several inches of fresh snow had already accumulated atop it.

The weather must've had something to do with the delay in connection.

He couldn't know that for sure, but having something to blame made the inconvenience just a tiny bit easier to tolerate.

Unwilling to let this ruin his night, he picked up the book from beside the aetherkey and opened it to the marked page. The book's scent filled his nose when he inhaled—paper and roasted coffee, with just a hint of Mina's sweetness.

Heat coiled low in his belly. The smallest trace of her fragrance was enough to rouse his hunger, the intensity of which could distract him from almost anything.

Distraction or fucking obsession?

He refused to answer that question.

Keeping the aetherkey's display at the edge of his vision, Sevik resumed reading about the incubus and his mate. He couldn't help but see some of the differences between korasi and humans echoed in the differences between incubi and humans.

Sevik traced the helix of his ear to its point, then swept his hand along the hard, curved length of his horn. He felt faint vibrations through the appendage as his fingertips brushed over its ridges.

What would Mina's hands feel like on his horns? Would she be unsettled by them, or intrigued? How would she react to his fangs, his claws, his pale skin and white hair? What would she make of his *lyros*, the bold black markings on his neck, back, and hips?

On Vabos, Sevik had dealt with many alien species. People of all shapes, sizes, and colors. People with skin, fur, or scales, with feathers or carapaces. He'd done business with some, had fought a good few, and had rutted his fair share. He'd seen the differences —and the similarities—between alien species.

He didn't know if incubi were real or a fantasy, nor did he care. The incubus in Mina's book was teaching Sevik a great deal, particularly about how to pleasure human females.

He intended to discover firsthand whether that information was factual. The list of things he wanted to try with Mina was growing longer and longer... And he hadn't even finished the book yet.

"*Zekt'al*." Leaning back on the couch, he slid a hand up his thigh to cover his groin, pressing down on his sweatpants as his cocks bulged and throbbed behind his slit.

What scant preparation he'd undertaken for living on Earth had come during the journey here, while he'd still been limited by his injuries. But he'd made sure to study basic human anatomy as he'd traveled; it was essential to know the differences between his kind and humans if he was to hide amongst them. He'd garnered enough knowledge to make him believe that he would be compatible with female humans despite the two-to-one cock-to-cunt ratio.

This book confirmed that belief beyond what he'd imagined.

Human females only had one cunt, but their asses could also be used for pleasure.

Would Mina enjoy that? Would she enjoy him filling her that way, with both his shafts buried as deep inside her as they could go? Would she delight in the feel of his hands on her body, firm and unyielding, guiding her every movement, even as they worshipped her soft skin?

Would she beg him to caress that little nub at the apex of her slit? Her *clit*?

His cocks pushed forward, parting his slit to hit the barrier of his pants and the hard palm atop them. Sevik groaned, tipped his head back onto the headrest, and set the book on the cushion beside him. Heat roiled through his veins.

His free hand settled on his belly, and his claws grazed the bare skin of his abdomen.

Stroking himself early this morning to thoughts of Mina must've dulled his appetite far less than he'd thought.

Control. Maintain control.

But his body didn't seem keen on obedience. What harm would it do? He was alone, isolated, cut off from Sullford—from Mina—by this blizzard.

The clit fascinated him. To have the source of Mina's pleasure so easily accessible...

Korasi females had no such part; their pleasure came entirely from within, from the slide of a male's ridged shafts. Only because of this book had he realized that his thumb must've brushed over her clit that night in the café, when he'd teased her cunt through her dress.

He'd seen the reaction that small touch had elicited. A little more pressure might've been enough to make her come undone. He wanted to touch her there again, wanted to see the pleasure on her face, wanted to make her lose control with a few strokes of his fingers.

Or his tongue.

How hot would she burn for him? How brightly would she shine?

Had his thoughts continued along that path for even a moment longer, Sevik may well have shoved his pants down, taken his shafts in hand, and brought himself to another climax right there on the couch.

But an alert tone sounded from the aetherkey, quiet but demanding, and called his attention back to the display.

Connection established. Data acquisition in progress.

He drew in a ragged breath through his gritted teeth. The program was automated; he didn't have to stop what he was doing, didn't have to restrain himself. The aetherkey would disconnect when it was done, and it would sort through the data it obtained to present anything worth his attention.

But the alert reminded Sevik of what the program was doing and why.

It reminded him of Brekker.

That reminder fanned the flames of his passion into an inferno of anger.

Every time Sevik ran this program, he risked detection. Even if Brekker had convinced everyone that Sevik was dead, he didn't believe it himself, and he was still searching. Were these intrusions ever discovered, it would only be a matter of time before they led straight back to Earth.

Part of Sevik welcomed that. Let Brekker come to finish what he'd started.

Sevik would not hesitate to stain the Alaskan snow with korasi blood.

Regardless, the risk was necessary. Brekker had seized control of Sevik's organization, the Kanthor Syndicate. Anyone else who'd held any sort of power within the syndicate had already been replaced by people loyal to Brekker.

Sevik needed to know what Brekker was doing, needed to know if Brekker had picked up his trail, needed to know when it was the right time to return and strike. The aetherkey was his only way to gather that information.

Because whatever the risk, Sevik would have vengeance. He would reclaim what was his.

All of it.

The couch's wooden frame creaked as Sevik sat forward. He fixed his eyes on the display and waited. Outside, the wind continued wailing, the snow continued falling in dizzying swirls, and countless lightyears away, Brekker continued leading the organization Sevik had built...

Sevik's neural transceiver injected a silent alarm message into his view. The security system he'd installed on the property had been triggered.

His heart quickened, and fresh fury flooded his muscles. If the time had come, if he'd been found, Sevik would make Brekker wish their business had ended on Vabos.

Sevik was already on his feet and striding into the kitchen as he accessed the holo recorder feeds through his transceiver.

A car was rolling down his driveway, toward the cabin. The

heavy snowfall and bright headlights made it difficult to determine the color and shape of the vehicle.

Brekker wouldn't drive up to my front door so directly. He'll know I'm watching…

But Sevik knew better now than to put anything past his old friend, didn't he?

Still, this was probably just a human from town. Not that Sevik could guess why anyone would be coming here, after dark, during a blizzard.

He tugged open one of the kitchen drawers and retrieved the plasma pistol hidden in the false bottom before moving to the laundry room doorway, where he pressed himself against the wall. The car continued its approach in the security feeds.

Snow crunched beneath tires outside as the vehicle stopped behind his truck, its rear end jutting past the car port roof.

Back in the living room, the aetherkey chimed another alert. Probably stating that had acquired the data and disconnected.

Sevik raised the pistol, watching through the transceiver as the vehicle's door opened…

And Mina emerged.

Sevik's heart stopped. For an instant, everything was silent. Then another thunderous beat of his heart shattered the preternatural quiet.

"*Shit,*" he growled, eyebrows angling down. He clenched his jaw and squeezed the grip of his weapon.

What the fuck is she doing here?

She could've gotten into an accident. Could've gotten stuck out there, freezing, in the middle of a storm.

She could've been harmed…or worse.

That last thought sank into Sevik's gut and coiled around his insides, pulling them tight. Death had been a regular occurrence in his life. He'd known it from a young age. But very few of the deaths he had witnessed—or been involved in—had affected him.

Just the thought of Mina's death made his throat constrict, his chest burn, and his fangs ache.

As Mina trudged through the snow toward the cabin door,

Sevik shoved away from the wall. He returned the pistol to the drawer, then rushed into the living room to grab the aetherkey, glimpsing only one word on the screen before he powered it off.

...aborted...

Storm interference had probably broken the connection.

No time to speculate. Worry about it later.

Sevik pulled up the loose floorboard near the fireplace, stuffed the aetherkey in the hole beside his small cache of spare weapons and security devices, and dropped the floorboard into place. He kicked the rug over the spot and stalked back toward the cabin's entrance.

His muscles were tense, his movements were stiff, and opposing instincts warred within him.

He'd yearned to see Mina again, to smell her, to touch her. And now she was here. She had come to him, as if in answer to his silent yearning.

But she'd endangered herself in doing so.

Anger and desire swirled inside him to create something fierier and more intense than either.

Good luck maintaining self-control now, Sevik.

Just before he dismissed the holo feed from outside, he saw Mina on the doorstep, lifting a fist.

A quick, soft knock sounded from the door, followed by another that was louder but more hesitant.

His cocks twitched behind his slit.

Pressing his hand over his pelvis, Sevik took a deep breath. If nothing else, at least he was wearing pants. He reactivated his holoshroud and padded into the laundry room.

Mina was visible through the door window, looking over her shoulder at the torrential snowfall. She was holding a cardboard box in her arms and had the straps of a canvas bag hooked over her shoulder. Despite the shelter of the carport, the wind swept away the little puffs of breath emerging from her nose and whipped through the short, curly locks sticking out from under her hat, making them brush her pinkened cheeks.

Foolish female.

Sevik turned on the light and opened the door. Though he was only half dressed, the frigid air that blew into the cabin did not cool him.

Mina jerked her face toward him and smiled wide. "Surprise!" When her gaze dipped to his chest, those big brown eyes widened, and her smile faltered. "Oh..."

Oh? What the fuck was he supposed to do with *oh?* Did that mean she liked what she saw, or that she was unimpressed?

How could that tiny fucking word trigger a thousand questions in Sevik's mind?

Barely holding back a frustrated growl, Sevik asked, "Why are you here, Mina?"

Her eyes snapped back up to his. "Um, well, I..."

A strong gust of wind battered Mina with snow and cold. She squinted and turned her face away from it, shivering as she clutched the box tighter to her chest.

Ah, fuck. Fucking...fuck.

Sevik grabbed her shoulder and dragged her into the house. Mina gasped but didn't resist. Once she was clear of the door, he forced it shut, battling surprising resistance from the wind.

Surprising? It's a fucking blizzard out there.

He clenched his jaw, drew in another deep breath through his nostrils, and turned to face her. "Why are you here?"

"Hold this," she said as she pushed the box against his chest. "Careful with it."

Sevik's hands came up reflexively, catching the box just before she let it go. He blinked down at the unmarked brown cardboard. "Mina..."

"It's freezing out there. I swear it feels colder every winter." She unzipped her coat and shrugged it off her shoulders, passing her bag from one hand to the other as she tugged her arms from the sleeves.

Reaching up, she hung her coat on one of the empty hooks on the walls before toeing off her boots. She wore a thin, light brown, off-the-shoulder sweater, tucked into a darker, semi-transparent skirt adorned with lacy floral patterns.

Sevik stared at her exposed shoulder. His teeth ached with the memory of her delicate skin against his lips, of its pliancy beneath his fangs, ached with the need to bite her. "Mina, what are you doing?"

Mina unwound her scarf and pulled off her hat, stuffing them into her coat pocket. She shook out her curls as she stepped into the kitchen. "It smells great in here."

Smells much better now that you're here.

He followed her, transfixed by the subtle bounce of her hair, the skirt swishing around her legs, and the gentle sway of her hips as she walked. An ache in his pelvis echoed the one in his fangs.

Mina stopped beside the dining table and placed her bag atop it. "I'm not interrupting anything, am I?"

Before he could respond, she took the box from him and set it next to her bag.

Brow knitting, Sevik tilted his head. "Yes."

She cast him an innocent, apologetic look. "Sorry! But I have just the thing to make up for it."

Slipping her hand into the tote, she pulled out a bottle and handed it to him with a bright smile. "You open this. I'll get the cups."

The instant he accepted the bottle, Mina walked to the cabinets, opening one after another.

What the fuck is happening here?

Sevik looked down at the bottle. It was green glass, with golden foil around the neck and a label that marked it as *champagne*. An alcoholic beverage. Earth seemed to have an endless variety of them.

"Where are your— Oh!" Mina pulled two mugs down from the cupboard. "These will do."

Enough of this.

He put the bottle down hard on the table and stalked toward her. She flinched when he snatched the mugs away and set them on the countertop. Catching her wrists in his hands, he backed her against the counter and pinned her with his body.

"What the fuck were you thinking?" he demanded, glaring

down at her. "This is a blizzard, Mina. A fucking blizzard. If anything had happened, if you had slid off the road or taken a wrong turn, you could've frozen to death before anyone found you."

Mina stared up at him, searching his eyes as her own glistened with gathering tears.

Sevik's heart lurched, and his chest constricted.

"I know," she said, voice cracking. Tears spilled down her cheeks, and she bowed her head.

No, don't do that. No tears, val'syra...

That tightness crept down into his belly and up through his neck, tensing his jaw and making him grit his teeth. The bestial instinct at his core snarled and lashed against the walls of its flimsy cage, demanding freedom. Demanding to rip this world to shreds until the sources of Mina's pain were destroyed and those tears ceased flowing.

"I drove slowly, and I was careful, but I...I know it was stupid," she continued quietly. "I just..."

"Why are you here?" he growled through his fangs.

"It's my birthday." Mina shook her head and laughed humorlessly. "That's even more stupid a reason to risk driving in this storm, huh?"

"I don't understand."

"I turned thirty today. And after spending the last seven birthdays alone, I..." She pressed her lips together and sniffled. More tears ran down her cheeks, gathering at her chin before falling. "I thought that since you were alone too, I could celebrate it with you, and then...then neither of us has to spend tonight feeling so lonely."

Mina's emotional pain struck Sevik like little else ever had, and it fueled an impotent rage within him that only exacerbated his existing anger.

He was angry at her for risking the storm. Angry at himself for feeling her sorrow. Angry at his instincts for demanding even now that he take her, rut her, drown the two of them in pleasure so they could snuff out their loneliness for a little while.

Her analysis had been right—he was lonely.

But Sevik knew one time would never be enough when it came to Mina, because his instincts weren't merely urging him to fuck her and move on. Why would it be that simple? No, his instincts demanded that he imprint on her.

And he would not do that. For his sake...and for hers.

Sevik released her arm, took hold of her chin, and tipped her face up toward his. "It was stupid to come here."

Her lips quivered as fresh moisture welled in her eyes. "I'm sorry. I didn't mean to—"

He pressed his thumb over her mouth, silencing her. "No. No more apologies. No more crying."

Mina quietly held his gaze.

Sevik moved his face closer to hers. Her tears smelled of salt, a subtle but unmistakable scent that made something deep within him stir. He parted his lips and extended his tongue, catching a teardrop falling down her cheek. Mina sucked in a sharp breath.

That saltiness blended with the sweetness of her skin, stoking his craving.

His tongue trailed along her jaw until his mouth was beside her ear. "Do you understand?"

"Yes," Mina whispered against his thumb.

"Good," he rumbled. Straightening, he let go of Mina, stepped back, and picked up the mugs. He handed them to her. "Go sit."

Mina brought the mugs to her chest and stared at him with wide eyes. "I—"

"Sit."

Biting her bottom lip, she hurried to the table.

Sevik nearly groaned. He wanted to be the one to bite that lip. For years, he'd simply reached out and taken whatever he wanted. Having the object of his desire right in front of him but being unable to seize it was torturous.

He turned away from her and braced his hands on the counter, squeezing his eyes shut. Though his life wasn't in immediate danger, he was playing a dangerous game with this female.

Where the fuck is your control, Sevik?

He'd maintained control the first time she was here. Even having stripped off most of her clothing with his own hands, he'd resisted temptation. All through that arduous night, he'd been painfully aware that she was right upstairs in his bed, yet he had not succumbed.

And he wasn't going to now.

After everything he'd seen and done, the challenges he'd overcome, the blood he'd spilled and sacrificed, keeping his fucking cocks in his slit should've been effortless.

He couldn't make her his.

No matter how much he longed for her.

Dismissing those thoughts, Sevik opened his eyes, pushed away from the counter, and walked to the table.

He snatched up the champagne bottle and tore off the foil seal, revealing a cork held in place by thin wire that wrapped around the neck. His attention flicked to Mina. She was intently watching his hands.

Ah, the things I would do to you with these hands, val'syra.

Mentally cursing himself, he turned the bottle to find a loop where the wire had been twisted together.

"Where I am from," he said as he pinched the end of the loop and began unwinding it, "we do not celebrate...birthdays."

"You don't?" Mina cocked her head. "Where *are* you from?"

When his gaze met hers, she smiled widely. A glimmer of mischievousness in her eyes belied the innocence of her expression.

"Far away from here."

Her smile dropped, and Mina wrinkled her nose. "So secretive. Even if you don't celebrate birthdays, when were you born?"

With the wire loosened, Sevik braced his thumb on the side of the cork. "Thirty-two years ago."

"You're only two years older than me! What day? What month?"

"Always with the questions."

"I'm just trying to get to know you."

"Is it really possible to know anyone, Mina?" Sevik pushed on the cork. After a brief resistance, it burst free with a loud *pop*. The cork launched across the table, passing only inches above Mina's head, and struck a decorative plate on a shelf over the counter. The plate fell, bouncing off the counter's edge before shattering on the floor.

Mina jumped and turned on her chair to look at the porcelain shards.

Brows low, Sevik stared down at the bottle. Fizzy liquid bubbled from the opening, running over his hand and dripping on the table.

The cork had nearly hit Mina. It could've hurt her. *He* could've hurt her.

Why the fuck did humans seem so determined to make everything dangerous?

Would I care if it was anyone else?

He lifted his gaze to Mina. She'd turned back to him, her rounded eyes locking with his. He'd almost fucking hurt her, and now—

Mina laughed.

It was soft, brief, but that laughter pierced the tension in the air and deflated it.

"I didn't realize how dangerous you are with a bottle of champagne," she said. "Remind me to stand behind you next time."

Just like that, she'd laughed it off.

A ball of heat coalesced in the center of his chest, making his heart stutter and his breath falter.

I could fall in love with this female.

Where the fuck had that come from?

He set the bottle down in front of her. "Pour."

Sevik walked away without allowing her to respond. His thumping pulse echoed throughout his body, impossibly strong, impossibly loud. He tried to ignore it as he washed his hands at the sink. Tried to ignore the deep ache in his groin as he scrubbed away the moisture with a hand towel. Tried to ignore her scent pervading his senses as he moved to the entry room to retrieve a broom.

But he couldn't ignore the press of his cocks against his slit. All he could do was will them to remain inside.

He didn't allow himself to look at her as he swept up the broken plate. The clinking of porcelain shards only emphasized the silence—which in turn made the noise inside Sevik seem all the louder.

She's mine.

But I can't have her.

Just need to take her...

Aggaan sin thar, *fucking control!*

Control... If he did take her, he'd have no chance of controlling himself. Especially now, with this new feeling roiling within him, with this new layer to his desire.

Sevik dumped the shards in the trash and returned the broom to its place. He stepped back into the kitchen to find Mina standing next to the table, waiting for him with a drink in each of her hands.

Mina offered him a mug. "I...hope that wasn't something important to you?"

As he accepted the offering, his fingers brushed hers, adding even more weight to her gesture. A wild urge sparked at his core—he would offer her the fucking world. "The plate?"

She nodded.

"No. This place was furnished when I bought it. The plate was already here."

"Oh, wow. That must've saved a lot of trouble. It's not always easy getting new furniture out here."

His eyes dipped to her slender neck, following it to her bare shoulder. That delicate skin begged for a caress, for the graze of his claws, begged to be marked by his fangs...

Sevik's tongue slipped out, trailing over his lips before he forced his gaze back up. Mina was staring at his mouth. Was she thinking back on their kiss? Because he was, and he wanted nothing more in that moment than to capture that pretty mouth again and ravish it.

Fuck.

Needing something else, anything else, to focus upon, he raised the mug and drained the contents in a single large gulp.

Fuuuuck.

He wasn't sure what he'd expected, and he was less sure of what he was tasting. There was a sweetness to the champagne, but it was overpowered by wince-inducing sourness, the two flavors compounded by stinging bubbles that made his nose burn. None of that hid the distinct taste of alcohol.

Sevik turned his face away from Mina and coughed; even the air he expelled stung his throat.

There were drinks from hundreds of worlds and cultures on Vabos—drinks to alter the mind, to take off the edge, to plunge into blissful oblivion. Not all alcohol, but similar enough.

He'd never had anything this...confusing. This unpleasant.

These humans enjoy suffering.

Mina placed a hand on his arm. "Are you okay?"

Not even the champagne's lingering effects could diminish the power of that soft, warm touch. He inhaled, wiped his mouth with the back of his hand, and nodded. "It is...not like the drinks I am used to."

She chuckled. "It's kind of meant to be more sipped than chugged."

Mina picked up the bottle and refilled his mug.

It was no different than her offering him another drink.

Zekt'al.

As the golden liquid poured, he swore the fizzing bubbles were laughing at him.

"Thank you," he said through his teeth.

"I ordered this months ago and saved it just for today. I'm glad I won't be drinking the whole thing all by myself." She set the bottle back down and raised her mug with a smile. "A toast?"

Sevik tilted his head. "Don't have any bread."

Mina laughed and shook her head. "No, no. Not that kind of toast. The kind of toast where people drink together in honor of something."

"What are we honoring?"

She grinned. "How about we toast to you not kicking me back out into the storm?"

He frowned and raised his mug. "Or...to your birthday."

Her grin softened. "To my birthday, and to not being alone tonight."

She clinked her mug against his, brought it to her mouth, and drank.

Sevik took a sip of the champagne. In a smaller amount, it was more tolerable, though the flavors were still overbearing and the bubbles still made him cringe. Bad enough that he could smell the stuff so strongly, but now that taste was lingering too.

Yet a glance at Mina made her enjoyment clear. This was special for her, something she'd bought in advance, something she'd saved for months. That tempered the champagne for him, if only a little.

Mina peeked at him over the rim of her mug and quickly looked away, her cheeks pinkening.

"What must we do to celebrate your birthday, Mina?" he asked.

She lowered the mug, grasping it between both hands. "Are you sure this isn't too much of an inconvenience? I know it's late, and I just popped in on you out of nowhere..."

He hooked a finger under her chin, guiding her face back toward his. The words emerged before he could fully consider them, but he didn't regret saying them aloud. "You were already in my thoughts, Mina. Now you're here."

Her blush deepened. "You were thinking of me?"

Sevik slid his thumb up and brushed it beneath her lower lip. "Hard to think of anything else lately."

Her lips parted, and it took every bit of Sevik's restraint to prevent himself from claiming that mouth, from doing something from which there'd be no return.

But the temptation remained...

He dropped his arm, needing to sever physical contact with her. "You didn't answer me."

ELEVEN

ANSWER HIM? Answer about what?

Mina couldn't think. Her heart was racing, and her belly was aflutter.

Viktor was thinking about me.

And he'd looked like he'd been about to kiss her.

Kiss me. Please kiss me.

She wanted to feel his mouth on hers again so badly it hurt. Wanted to feel the press of his body against hers, to feel those arms around her, to feel the strength of his hands as he held her tight.

But instead of pulling her close, he'd let her go, breaking that contact and turning the small distance separating them into an insurmountable barrier.

My birthday. Viktor wants to know how to celebrate my birthday. Right.

Mina took another drink of champagne, this one much deeper despite her advice to him. The carbonation tickled her mouth as the sweet, cool liquid ran down her throat.

It did nothing to stave off the desire simmering in her belly.

She clutched the mug more firmly to keep her hands from trembling.

When it came to Viktor, she was too weak to resist.

Birthday, Mina. Focus.

Walking around the table, she set her mug down and opened her tote bag. "I, uh, noticed you didn't have a TV the last time I was here." She withdrew her tablet. "The screen isn't very big, but I thought we could maybe watch a movie together?"

His silver eyes, almost as unsettling as they were alluring, followed her movements intently. "That's the celebration? Watching a movie?"

"It can be anything. Sometimes parents throw big parties for their kids, with games followed by cake and presents. I never had anything big though. Just a few friends over for sleepovers where we always tried to stay awake all night. But after my dad died..."

Mina carefully laid the tablet on the table. "I...didn't have many friends after we lost him. So birthdays were just me, my mom, and Randy. Every year, they baked me a cake and cooked my favorite dinner. After we ate, we'd each take a slice of cake into the living room with some popcorn and watch a movie. But now..." She dragged the cardboard box closer and opened it, looking down at the cake and the sad looking, slightly melted candle on top. "Now it's just me."

Viktor placed his mug on the table and stepped up beside Mina. His scent enveloped her, and heat radiated from him, beckoning her closer. It was all she could do not to press herself against him.

"Now it's us." He leaned forward to study the cake. A long lock of his black hair fell over his shoulder, brushing the tabletop. "Why is there a candle sticking out of it?"

"Another tradition. You light the candles, and the birthday person makes a wish and blows them out."

He shifted his gaze to Mina. How could his eyes be equally piercing and curious, as though he could see right through her but didn't understand what he saw?

His eyes narrowed. "You already did so."

Mina ducked her head, an embarrassed blush creeping over her skin. "I did before I came."

His attention lingered on her a little longer. Then, wordlessly, he walked to the counter, opened a drawer, and returned with a lighter. He flicked it on. The tiny flame sparked to life, and he touched it to the candle's wick. When he withdrew the lighter, the candle was burning.

"New celebration," Viktor said. "New wish."

Mina looked up at him in surprise as warmth flooded her chest and tears burned her eyes. When she'd shown up at his door earlier, he would've had every right to turn her away. She'd come uninvited, had barged into his home, and had thrust her birthday woes onto him.

But Viktor hadn't turned her away. In his own way, he was comforting her, he was listening to her, he was doing these little things to make her happy. He had no obligation to Mina, yet he'd already done so much for her.

And here he was, doing even more.

Mina curled her fingers into her palms and pressed them against the tabletop as she stared down at the flame.

A new celebration. A new wish.

But Mina didn't want to make a new wish. What she wanted was still the same. Except now, she yearned even harder, with every part of herself, for it to come true.

I wish Viktor was mine.

Mina blew out the candle.

Please, please, please make him mine.

The wick glowed orange as smoke curled from it.

"You didn't make a wish," Viktor said.

Mina smiled at him. "I did."

His brow furrowed. "What was it?"

"I can't tell you or it won't come true."

Viktor leaned closer, positioning his mouth beside her ear. His breath stirred her hair and tickled her skin as he whispered, "How can I make it come true if you won't tell me?"

Mina's heart quickened, and heat flared in her core. The air felt electrified. Viktor was so close, and his presence was overwhelming, dangerous, sensual. He was a predator, and she was his prey. But she'd never once felt as though he were a threat to her; she had no impulse to run.

She turned her face toward him and met his gaze. Their mouths were only a breath away. Softly, she replied, "Maybe I'll tell you later."

Viktor smirked. He lifted a hand and, slowly, teasingly, swept back the loose strands of hair from her face. His nails—which she swore still felt like claws—grazed Mina's sensitive skin as he tucked her hair behind her ear.

Mina shivered, wanting more. She wanted to feel those nails trail down her neck, over her shoulder, wanted them to follow the curve of her breast to the peak of her nipple, wanted them to rake down her belly and up her thighs...

"I look forward to it," he purred.

Kiss me.

His eyes dipped as though in response to her thought, and his smirk took on a rakish slant. Just as she was about to lean forward, to take the initiative and bridge that gap between them, Viktor withdrew.

Mina swayed on her feet at the abruptness of his departure; he'd moved so quickly that it was like the space he'd left behind almost sucked her in. She blinked as he walked to the cupboards. Heat crept over her face.

Did he know that she was trying to kiss him? Had he purposely pulled away to prevent it? Or had that moment just been in her head, entirely one-sided?

I look forward to it.

No. The way he'd said those words, the way he'd been looking at her... It definitely hadn't been one-sided. She'd felt his passion when he'd kissed her in the café, so why would he pull away now?

Mina picked up her mug and took another hearty drink of champagne as utensils rattled behind her. Once the cup was drained, she set it down and refilled it.

"We're supposed to eat the cake, yes?" he asked, drawing her attention to him. He stood beside the counter with plates in one hand and forks and a knife in the other.

But Mina's gaze moved past those hands, taking in his broad shoulders and bare chest before straying down his chiseled, oh-so-lickable abs to the teasing V of his adonis belt, which disappeared under the waistband of his low-slung gray sweatpants.

Because of course he was wearing nothing but gray sweatpants.

Is that drool Mina?

Maybe.

Viktor stepped toward her with a chuckle, his movements bearing all the effortless grace and power of a stalking tiger. "Mina?"

She snapped her gaze back up to his. There was a knowing, mischievous glint in his eyes, tinged with a spark of hunger.

And she was sure it wasn't for cake.

"Uh, yes. We're supposed to eat," Mina said, quickly facing the table. "The cake, I mean. We're supposed to eat the cake."

Well, what else were you going to eat?

No! No. Don't answer that, Mina. Don't you dare.

As she lowered the front of the box to better access the cake, she most definitely was not thinking about how much she would've preferred a bite of him. She wanted to run her tongue over every delicious, ridged muscle.

Viktor stopped next to her and arranged the plates and utensils on the table. Her skin prickled with awareness. He was so close that she could once more feel his body heat, and her every breath was infused with his spicy scent. Her core clenched, as much in reaction to his nearness as to the path her thoughts had taken.

"So what kind of movies do you like?" she asked, picking up the knife and cutting into the chocolate and raspberry confection, struggling to ignore what his proximity was doing to her.

"I don't know."

Mina arched a brow after placing the first slice of cake on a plate. "You don't know?"

He offered a shallow nod. "Don't watch many movies."

Considering how many people were glued to screens all the

time, his answer should've been surprising. But again, Mina hadn't seen a television in his house, and now that she thought about it, she'd never seen him with a phone. That was odd. Who didn't have a cell phone these days?

She glanced around the kitchen. There was a phone jack on the wall near the counter, but nothing was plugged in to it.

Did he really have no phone at all?

Yet another thing that should've concerned her, except...it didn't. Whatever he had been in the past, whatever he had done, she knew in her soul that he wouldn't hurt her. And that probably should've scared her too.

Mina's brow pinched as she plated a second slice of cake and handed it to Viktor. "Do...you even have Wi-Fi?"

He held the plate on his palm, studying the cake as though he'd never seen anything like it before. "No."

"Okay then. The movie idea is out." She slipped onto her chair and picked up her fork. "Maybe we could...play a game?" Mina took a bite of the cake and nearly moaned. The bold, decadent dark chocolate was complimented perfectly by the sweet raspberry filling.

Viktor put down his plate, pulled out his own chair, and sat down, keeping his eyes on her all the while. "A game?"

"It's called 'Never Have I Ever'. It's a fun way to get to know someone. I would say something like, 'never have I ever built a snowman.' Each person who's done that thing takes a drink, and anyone who hasn't doesn't drink. So, for the snowman, I'd take a sip. And you would..."

"What's a snowman?"

Mina gaped at him. "You've never built a snowman? It's when you roll out big balls of snow, stack them on top of each other, and then use sticks and rocks to— You know what, when the storm passes, I'll just show you."

He tilted his head and narrowed his eyes as he studied her. He seemed intrigued, but it was impossible to tell with him. "How do you win?"

"There's not really a winner."

"Games have winners and losers. Life has winners and losers."

"Some games are just for fun. There doesn't always have to be a winner." She gave him a droll look. "You *do* know how to have fun, don't you?"

The corner of his mouth quirked up. "Never have I ever had fun."

Without breaking eye contact, he lifted his mug and drank.

Mina laughed and took a sip from her own mug. The champagne went perfectly with the chocolate cake. "You'll have to show me just how fun you can be."

"Ah, *val'syra*," Viktor purred, "you have no idea what you're asking for."

Those words, combined with the deep rumble in his voice, flooded Mina with heat. She tried to keep her hand steady as she set her cup down, but there was definitely a noticeable tremor in it. She hadn't realized how easily her words could be twisted, how wickedly he could interpret them, and now she was wondering what sort of *fun* he intended to have with her.

"What...what does *val'syra* mean?" she asked.

Viktor picked up his fork and used it to break off a chunk of cake. "It means I like you, Mina. Despite all your questions."

She could only watch as he brought the fork to his mouth and slipped the bite between his sensual lips. And the whole time, he watched her right back, his silver eyes blazing.

He withdrew the fork and abruptly broke eye contact with her, turning his face down. The muscles of his jaw worked as he slowly chewed, and the cords of his neck briefly stood out.

"Are you okay?" she asked, leaning toward him.

Raising a hand to ward her from moving any closer, Viktor nodded and grated, "Fine."

With a frown, she eased back, dropping a hand to her lap to grasp the fabric of her skirt. "Do you not like the cake?"

"It's..." Viktor swallowed thickly and ran his tongue across his teeth, giving his head a shake before raising it again. "Sweet. Very, very sweet."

"Oh! I'm sorry. You don't have to—"

"You like it?"

"Yes."

"Then don't apologize," he said firmly. "My taste is my problem, not yours."

Mina looked down, absently brushing aside some of the crumbs on her plate with the tines of her fork. "So you're just...not big on sweet?"

Viktor's chair creaked, calling her attention to him again. He'd leaned back, and now sat with one arm casually propped on the table, the other resting on his thigh, and his head cocked to the side. His gaze roamed over her slowly. It was so hungry, so intense, that she suddenly felt as though the table didn't shield her from it at all.

Voice low, raspy, sultry, he said, "I prefer a different kind of sweet, *val'syra.*"

She pressed her thighs together. Viktor's words flowed right into her, coiling with that desirous ache at her core.

"Now"—he tapped his fingers on the table—"it's your turn."

Her turn? Her turn for...

Oh. Right.

She could already feel the effects of the alcohol; she'd forgotten how quickly champagne usually hit her, especially since she rarely drank.

"Never have I ever..." Mina flicked her gaze to the ceiling before returning it to him. "Stolen something."

Viktor plucked up his mug and took a slow sip. She couldn't say she was surprised. Theft was nothing compared to the other things he'd probably done.

Holding his gaze, Mina reached for her own mug and took a drink.

He smirked. "Innocent Mina committed a crime?"

"I was fourteen," she exclaimed with a laugh. "And it was one time."

Mina sat back and ran her hand through her hair, wincing when one of her fingers snagged on a curl. She wrinkled her nose as she withdrew her hand. "My mom asked me to pick up a few things from the grocery store after school. We only had so much money, and I knew I couldn't stray from the list she'd made. I walked by this little rotating stand that had a bunch of CDs. They had Lady Gaga. I loved her music, but it wasn't something we could afford to get.

"I knew it was wrong. Even as I slipped the CD into my bag, I had this horrible feeling that I was committing the worst crime. I hurried away from the stand and grabbed the rest of the items on the list for my mom, knowing that at any moment, the police were going to show up and arrest me. I felt like everyone was watching me. That they knew what I'd done.

"I didn't even open it when I got home. I hid it away under my mattress, afraid my mom would see it and ask questions. The guilt was eating me alive. So I...returned it a week later."

Viktor laughed—not the smug yet seductive snicker she'd heard from him before, but actual laughter that sparked a new light in his eyes. It was deep and rolling, making his lips stretch wide and the corners of his eyes crinkle.

Mina's heart skipped a beat; he was *gorgeous*.

"I guess that's the difference between us, Mina." He reached out and grasped her chair, dragging it closer to his, just like he'd done at the café that night. "When I take what I want, I don't let it go."

Mina stared up at him, her pulse racing at the implication of his words. He...he couldn't have meant it that way. Couldn't have meant that she was his.

Right?

But I want to be.

She curled her fingers, grasping her skirt atop her thighs. "It's your turn."

His grin faded as he again leaned back in his chair and returned one arm to the table, keeping her legs trapped between his. "Never have I ever had a mate."

"A...mate? Oh! Do you mean a friend? I know some people in Europe and Australia use mate in reference to a friend."

"No, Mina. I do not mean a friend."

Mina's brow knitted. "A partner then? Like a girlfriend or boyfriend?"

Gaze unwavering, he nodded. Neither of his hands moved toward his mug. Not even the slightest twitch.

Stunned with disbelief, Mina stared at him. How? How could this man never have had a partner before? "Was it because of your...job?"

A thoughtful hum rumbled from his chest.

Mina pursed her lips to the side and cocked her head. "That dangerous, huh?"

Viktor's fingers curled, and his nails scraped the table's surface. Mina's eyes flicked toward them and widened. There were tiny grooves in the wood, following the short path his fingers had just taken.

"More dangerous than you can imagine," he said.

"Oh."

Again, Mina wondered what kind of life he'd led, wondered what had brought him to the middle of nowhere in Alaska. No Wi-Fi, no computer, no TV, no phone. What was he running from? *Who* was he running from?

Mina picked up her mug and looked at him over the rim as she took a long drink.

The physical changes to his face were subtle—a slight angling down of his eyebrows, a tightening of his lips, a bulging of his jaw —but the effect was staggering. She saw the real him in that moment—the darkness, the danger, the threat, the power and fury that he normally hid just beneath the surface.

And he still didn't frighten her.

He growled, "Who?"

"It was a long time ago, and nothing came of them. It doesn't matter. They don't matter."

"They?"

She heard his nails scrape the table again, but she didn't look this time. She was too focused on his face.

Something changed. *He* changed. She saw a flash of something, of someone, like Viktor was only an image projected over another person. It was a glimpse of pale alabaster skin with dark markings at the neck, of long white hair, black horns, and glowing white-on-black eyes. Of sharp features and pointed ears.

Of something utterly inhuman...and utterly entrancing.

Mina blinked, and he was just Viktor again.

She shook her head and glanced at the champagne bottle. How strong was this stuff?

Mina had never experienced anything like this while drinking, and she wasn't even drunk yet. With her second cup almost empty, she was feeling a little tipsy, but it was way too soon for hallucinations.

"I had two boyfriends," Mina said, holding her mug on her lap and staring down at it. "One only lasted for three months, but he was pushing for too much too fast. Thankfully, I found out that he had a job he was leaving the state for and realized he was just trying to use me for sex before he left. It was a pretty nasty break up, and he hurled all kinds of vulgar words my way. He'd heard about my mom, and thought I'd be an easy lay.

"My other ex's name is Lee. We were together for a little more than six months, but I... Nothing felt right with him. I think he felt the distance between us too. So we parted ways, and he ended up moving to Anchorage for college not long after. His mother comes into the café sometimes, and last I heard from her, he's still in Anchorage, now happily married."

When Mina looked back at Viktor, he was glowering. His jaw remained clenched, its muscles ticking, and his entire body was tense, like a beast about to pounce.

Was he...jealous?

When I take what I want, I don't let it go.

Don't think too deeply into his words, Mina.

But why else would he react this way to Mina talking about her exes? Wouldn't she behave similarly if she knew he'd been close to someone?

Even just the thought of him being with another person made her chest tighten.

Viktor said he never had a partner.

That didn't mean he'd never been intimate with anyone. That he'd never had sex.

Her chest constricted further. She'd never done anything more than kiss, had never wanted to do anything more.

Until Viktor.

"I, uh…guess it's my turn," Mina said, offering him a nervous smile. Tightening her grip on her mug, she drew in a deep, fortifying breath. "Never have I ever had sex."

Viktor's attention lingered on her until he raised his mug. He brought it to his lips, tilted his head back, and drank, and drank, and drank. Given that he'd only sipped champagne during the game so far, she wasn't quite sure how to interpret this. Was he trying to ease his discomfort and tension?

Mina's heart twisted. Or was he implying he'd had a lot of sex?

He slammed the now empty mug on the table and drew in a shuddering breath, lips pulling back in a snarl. Strands of his dark hair fell around his face and shoulders. His free hand was curled into a white-knuckled fist, and his muscles were in sharper relief than when she'd arrived. Again, the cords of his neck stood out, and he let out an unhappy grunt.

Then he turned his attention to Mina.

They stared at one another. When his eyes dipped briefly to her mug, a crease formed between his brows, and blossoming confusion did what the alcohol had not—it eased the tension on his face.

Mina placed her mug on the table. "Do you want to know what I wished for?"

"Tell me."

She felt her face flushing, felt that old embarrassment bubbling up, felt her courage wavering, but she refused to stand in her own way. Before she could think about she was doing, Mina stood up, lifted her skirt, and straddled Viktor's lap.

His hands immediately grasped her hips.

"Mina?" he rasped.

She reached up to cradle his face. Viktor caught her wrists, halting her arms before they could even get past his shoulders.

He drew in a deep breath through his nose, making his chest swell, and a low, ravenous growl vibrated from him. Those silver eyes, now half-lidded, searched hers.

Lowering her face until their noses nearly touched, Mina whispered, "I wished for you."

She closed her eyes and pressed her mouth to his.

TWELVE

Viktor was rigid and unmoving beneath Mina. Not even his lips yielded, despite her caressing them with her own. He didn't make a sound, didn't breathe, just sat like a statue.

Please. Please kiss me back.

His grip on her wrists strengthened infinitesimally, and a barely perceptible tremor ran through his body.

Mina touched her forehead to his. "Viktor..."

With a snarl, he crushed his mouth against hers. She rocked back at the suddenness and force of it, but his hold on her arms didn't let her move far—and he didn't allow the kiss to break. His mouth was hungry, savage, and punishing, claiming her with merciless intensity.

Fire erupted within Mina. It blazed between her legs and licked at her every nerve, leaving no part of her unaffected.

He guided her arms down and behind her back, where he locked her wrists together with one big hand.

Mina pressed against him and returned the kiss with reckless abandon. Her hardened nipples grazed his chest through her sweater. The sensation made her clit twitch, but it wasn't enough. She wanted to feel his skin on hers, wanted to feel his heat, his touch. Wanted no barriers between them.

Viktor's free hand rose, and his fingers delved into her hair at the nape of her neck, grasping a fistful of curls as he deepened the kiss. His tongue swept into her mouth and curled around hers, claiming it as thoroughly as he had her lips. She didn't care about the strain in her shoulders or the slight sting on her scalp. All that mattered was him, this kiss, this moment.

Her core felt heavy and achy, and her pussy, slick with arousal, was swollen with need. Mina ground her pelvis against him and whimpered at the friction on her clit.

Viktor shuddered and growled, tightening his grip on her hair and breaking the kiss. "*Zekt'al, val'syra.*"

"Please," she rasped, opening her eyes. She tugged her arms, wanting to touch him, longing for him to touch her. "I need you."

He bared his teeth. His chest heaved with his ragged breaths, and his eyes were pools of molten silver, blazing with fervent hunger. They reflected her desire, her need, amplifying it tenfold.

"Hands on my shoulders," he commanded, releasing her wrists, "and keep them there."

"But I—"

"*Now*, Mina."

Mina's core clenched in response to the authority in his voice as she obeyed. His powerful muscles flexed beneath her palms, and heat radiated from his skin.

Grasping her ass, Viktor lifted her against his body as he stood. Mina's legs instinctually wrapped around his waist. As he carried her toward the living room, he buried his face against her neck and shoulder and inhaled.

"You smell so fucking good." His husky voice was hot against her sensitive skin, punctuated by the touch of his lips and the teasing scrape of his teeth.

Shivering, Mina squeezed his shoulders and tilted her head, allowing him more access to her. She gasped when she felt the wet glide of his tongue along her throat.

His groan vibrated into her. "Taste even better."

When they reached the couch, he laid her upon it and followed her down. Kneeling between her thighs, he grasped the hem of her shirt and drew it up over her head, forcing her to let go of his shoulders. Cool air touched her bare skin. Her nipples, already hard, tightened further, but it was Viktor's gaze upon her now exposed breasts that made them ache.

Rather than cover herself—as would've been her instinct were he anyone else—Mina let her arms fall to either side of her head. There was no shame in this. No shame in their primal, burning passion.

Viktor tossed her shirt aside without looking away from her. He flattened his hands on her belly, sliding them up until his calloused palms glided over her breasts and brushed her nipples. Mina's breath hitched, and her skin prickled.

"You're so soft." He cupped her breasts, kneading and caressing as he stroked her nipples with his thumbs, tracing little circles around the budded peaks.

Mina's brow creased as pleasure tingled through her body. When she touched her breasts, it never felt like this—it was no more sensual or pleasing than touching her own arm or leg. But the sensations Viktor's hands elicited were potent, pervading, and maddeningly erotic. He wasn't just touching her, he was worshipping her.

Eyelids growing heavy, she sighed and arched into his touch, wanting more. *Needing* more.

He rolled her nipples between his fingers and thumbs, heightening the ache between Mina's thighs and making her whimper. If he continued, she would come from this alone.

And then he pinched.

Pain-coated pleasure zipped through her, straight to her clit. She cried out and slapped her hands over his.

Viktor chuckled. "So fucking responsive."

"Viktor, please," Mina pleaded. She was so aroused that it hurt.

He turned his hands to take hold of Mina's, guided her arms over her head, and pinned them on the armrest. As he leaned over her and lowered his face, his long hair fell forward to brush her skin. His mouth came so close to hers that his words tickled her lips. "I like hearing you beg, *val'syra*."

Mina stared up into his eyes. His heat washed over her body, and his spicy scent suffused her senses, growing stronger and more intoxicating by the moment.

Viktor flicked his tongue over her lips. Mina tilted her face up for a kiss, but he remained just out of reach.

"Tell me what you need, Mina."

She tightened her thighs around his hips and tugged her hands. He didn't budge, keeping her wrists firmly trapped above her head. She wanted to touch him, wanted to feel his warm skin beneath her palms. "I need you."

His lips curled into grin as he switched his hold on her arms to a single hand, which was still too strong for her to overcome. "Do you want my hand?" Gaze locked with hers, he slowly moved down Mina's body as his free palm trailed along her arm and side. "Or my mouth?"

Viktor dragged his tongue over her nipple.

Mina drew in a sharp breath. "Viktor..."

"Which is it, Mina? Hand..." His hand descended, gliding over her hips and along her outer thigh. "Or mouth..." He licked the hard peak of her nipple again before nipping it with his teeth.

The jolt of pleasure made her pelvis buck and forced out her answer in a gasp. "Both!"

"Ah, *val'syra*..." Viktor changed the direction of his hand, pushing her skirt up the rest of the way as his fingers shifted to her inner thigh. "Good answer."

He closed his lips around her nipple and sucked it into his mouth.

Mina moaned, closing her eyes and arching her back. She again tugged against his hold, but it was to no avail. He kept her wrists prisoner. His mouth was scalding, the suction sublime, and each pull on her nipple sent a pulse to her core. His warm breath fanned over her skin as he sucked, and sucked, and sucked until she was panting and writhing, uncertain of whether she wanted to beg him to stop or beg him for more.

Her clit thrummed, and she couldn't even close her legs in an attempt the relieve it. She was close to coming, so close, just from the feel of his mouth on her breast.

But he did relent, releasing her nipple to twirl his tongue around the sensitive bud while his fingertips skimmed her pussy through her underwear. He hummed appreciatively. "So wet for me."

She opened her eyes to look down at him.

"I can smell you, *val'syra*." Viktor slipped a finger under the fabric. He curled that finger, and a soft moan escaped her as his knuckle grazed her sex. He hooked her panties and drew them away from her damp flesh. "I can smell your desire."

God, his words, spoken in that deep, sultry voice, combined with his touch to send ripples of excitement through her.

He pulled on the fabric. The band of her panties dug into her skin briefly before the material gave way with a *rip*.

Viktor's gaze fixated on her pussy.

"Ah, Mina." He trailed his fingertips through her pubic hair. "Your cunt is prettier than I imagined."

And then his fingers delved between her folds. He growled through his teeth as his eyes bored into hers. "So fucking hot and wet."

Those fingers explored, tracing her labia, her entrance, and Mina tensed in anticipation, clenching her hands, undulating her hips, needing him, wanting him to—

Mina cried out, her entire body twitching, when he brushed her clit.

Viktor's lips curled into a sinful smile. "Ah, there it is."

Had her mind not been so clouded by desire, had her body not been on edge with the need for release, she might've questioned those words. But all her focus was on his touch.

He stroked her clit again.

Mina whimpered, shivering at the sensation that swept through her, and undulated her hips. "Viktor... Please. Please, don't stop. It feels so good."

Something flashed in his eyes, and all humor faded from his

expression. He didn't look away from her as his fingertips circled the throbbing nub. His touch was unhurried but reverent as he watched her, seemingly transfixed by her every reaction.

The pleasure within Mina coiled tighter and tighter. Her breaths came quick and shallow, and her hips rolled, desperate for the pace to increase, for him to press harder and alleviate that growing pressure inside.

Until it became too much.

Mina closed her eyes and spread her thighs wider. Her breasts bounced as she rocked against his fingers, reduced to a wanton, wild thing yearning for release. Flames curled in her belly, growing hotter and hotter with each circle he traced. She was so wet that it was dripping down her ass. Her shoulders ached from the strain created by his hold on her wrists, but she didn't care. The whole universe was narrowed down to his touch, to the pleasure it provided her.

"So beautiful," Viktor rumbled.

Mina forced her eyes open to look at him. His gaze burned, hot and possessive. His spicy, delirious scent filled her senses, stronger than ever, thickening the lustful fog in her mind. She breathed it in greedily.

A tremor swept through her, making her thighs quiver.

That was her only warning.

Mina's body tensed. She threw her head back as a wave of sensation took hold of her. Her lips parted with a silent cry, voice stolen by the pleasure, and light burst behind her eyelids like an exploding star. Her core contracted, and finally, *finally*, a cry tore from her throat.

She snapped her thighs closed, unable to withstand the force, but they were halted by Viktor's body between them.

And he didn't stop. He was merciless, tightening his grip on her wrists as he applied more pressure to her clit and quickened his strokes.

"Yes, *val'syra*," Viktor growled. "More. Give me more."

Moaning, Mina twisted and thrashed. Viktor kept her caged

in, but she didn't want to escape. Never wanted to. She wanted this moment to last forever.

"Fuck, your pretty cunt is soaking," Viktor grated. "That's it, Mina. Look at how passionate you are. Come from my hand again."

His command was like magic, leaving her body no choice but to obey. Another orgasm struck Mina, almost too painful to endure, seizing her every muscle as liquid heat gushed from her. That flow went on and on and on, wrenching a ragged cry from her.

Mina gasped, her eyes flying open in shock to look at Viktor. *Did I just...*

His fingers stilled, and his nostrils flared with a deep inhalation. She felt his chest rumble with a growl as he cocked his head and brought his hand up. It glistened, dripping with her essence.

Humiliation flooded her. "Oh God. I-I didn't... I never—"

Viktor brought his hand to his mouth.

Stunned, Mina watched as he ran his tongue up his palm before slipping his fingers into his mouth. His eyes met hers. Their silver seemed almost reflective, but it shrank rapidly as his pupils expanded, turning his gaze into a ravenous void.

He drew himself up and lowered his face toward hers, not breaking eye contact with her for even a fraction of a second. "Keep your hands right fucking here, or I'll stop. Understand?"

Mina's brow knitted. "What—"

"Do. You. Understand?"

She nodded quickly, still uncertain but trusting him.

Viktor kissed her roughly, the sort of kiss that left no question of his claim on her. She tasted herself on his lips; it only turned her on more. When he broke the kiss, he also released her wrists.

Sinking to his knees on the floor, he threw her legs over his shoulders, dropped his head, and dragged his tongue along her pussy.

"Viktor!" Mina's eyes rolled back, and her toes dug into the backs of his shoulders.

THIRTEEN

MINA DOMINATED SEVIK'S SENSES. No sight had ever been as beautiful as she was now, with her hair disheveled and her skin flushed, writhing in passion. No sound had ever been as satisfying as her cries of pleasure. Nothing had ever felt as good under his palms as her warm, soft, yielding skin. No scent in existence was as tempting and intoxicating as hers.

But Mina's taste…

Fuck, her taste was the most powerful of all, more potent and addictive than any drug on Earth, Vabos, or anywhere else. Salty, sweet, feminine, *her*. He'd never encountered anything like it.

He lapped at her cunt like a thirsty beast at a watering hole, leaving no part of her delicious slit ignored. Every drop of her essence upon his tongue amplified his want—his need—for more. He wouldn't merely lick up her essence, he would drink it from the source.

And that sweet, sweet essence was fuel poured onto the fire at his core. Those flames would consume him if left unchecked.

Strengthening his hold on her legs, he spread her thighs farther and plunged his tongue into her cunt.

"Viktor!"

He snarled against her, hating that name more and more every time she spoke it. He wanted to hear his true name from her lips, wanted it to be the only word she could utter in the throes of ecstasy, wanted her to cry out for *Sevik*. For the real him.

The scent of her arousal perfumed the air, and he took it in as hungrily as he did her slick. He barely noticed his smell mingling with hers, and he didn't register the new hint of spice it bore, nor its heightened musk.

Mina left no space within him for thought.

Her breathy cries came with another flood of essence. Sevik groaned and pressed his mouth to her sex, sucking up every bit. His hips gyrated involuntarily, grinding his throbbing, extruding cocks against the couch. That pressure, that friction, only deepened the pervading ache.

Take her.

Claim her.

Mine. Mine. Mine!

Every curse he knew roared through his mind. Need grasped Sevik with merciless claws and pulled him in every direction simultaneously, threatening to tear apart his mind and body alike.

He had to drive his cocks into her heat, had to sink his fangs into her tender skin.

Sevik drove his tongue deeper into her tight cunt instead, curling and twisting it within her channel, coaxing more, more, more from her. She undulated her hips, and her moans escalated. She was close again.

His nose brushed her clit.

Mina gasped, and her hands swiftly fell upon his head.

Upon his horns.

Sevik growled, yanking his head back and forcing her hands away.

"No!" she cried, her dark, desperate eyes meeting his. "Don't stop! Please, don't stop!"

"*Hands up,*" he grated.

Mina threw her hands back over her head, grasping the armrest. Her chest rose and fell with her rapid breaths. One of her nipples was bright red thanks to his earlier attentions.

Zekt'al, he wished she could grab his horns and ride his face as she came. Wished he could palm her ass and prick her with his claws as he lifted her off the couch to drink from her.

Wished she was looking into *his* eyes with such passion rather than at the mask he was forced to wear.

"Good female." He dropped his face and latched his mouth onto her clit.

Mina moaned, her thighs trembling beneath his palms.

Sevik sucked hard on that little nub, lashing it with his tongue.

She sucked in a sharp breath as she bowed her back, lifting her hips off the couch to press her cunt more firmly against his face. Her whole body shuddered an instant before more essence poured from her.

"Oh God!" Mina's cries were ragged.

Though she tried to close her legs, Sevik held them splayed as he feasted. He drank until she lay limp beneath him and the only sounds she made were soft whimpers when he flicked his tongue over her swollen clit.

Sevik emitted a low growl. To have her pleasure at his finger-tips, his tongue... His painfully engorged cocks twitched, and seed seeped from their tips. He could only imagine how she'd react to his ridges dragging over her clit, to the slide of his cocks inside her, could only imagine how her cunt would feel gripping his shaft.

Sevik gritted his teeth, pressing his forehead to Mina's lower belly, his breaths ragged as he battled for control.

He was about to come himself. Just a little more friction, a little more pressure, and he'd spill his seed. Fuck, he needed to be inside her. He needed to fill her with—

No!

Sevik dropped a hand to the couch cushion and curled his fingers, burying his claws in the upholstery.

Mina hummed softly, dreamily; it was the sweet, contented sound of a well-pleasured female.

Pride swelled in his chest, but it was accompanied by bitter regret. No matter how much more he wanted to do, needed to do, he could go no further than this.

Sevik pressed a kiss to her clit. He resisted the urge to lavish that delectable little bud with more attention, satisfying himself instead by breathing in more of her scent.

His brow furrowed. Mina's fragrance was stronger than ever, beyond what could be explained by her essence still coating his lips. He'd never smelled anything so clearly. It was as though no other scent could clash with it, as though it existed apart from all else.

And it had changed.

The added spice and musk of his scent was present within hers, a distinct part of the whole.

Sevik's heartbeat pounded in his ears.

I imprinted on her.

Fuck!

He jerked his head up and looked upon her. She lay lax on the sofa with her face turned to the side, her cheeks flushed, and her eyes closed. Asleep.

And she was fucking radiant.

She's mine.

Mine.

Mine.

Mine.

"*Leskahn tor lesk,*" he rasped, running a hand over his face.

What had he done? How was this any better than Brekker imprinting upon Enthi without her consent? The very event that had led Sevik, injured and hunted, to Earth, that had taken everything from him in a single night.

Not the same. This is not the same.

But how the fuck was it not the same? How could it be any different?

"Because I want Mina."

Oh, and Brekker didn't want Enthi?

"I'd never hurt Mina. Never."

What makes her any different than all the other people you've hurt? Your existence puts her in danger. You will hurt her.

Just a matter of time…

"Fuck," he snarled, shoving away from the couch and standing up. His hands rose, grasping his horns, as he paced around the small space between the couches and coffee table. He couldn't stop his eyes from returning to Mina over and over.

She looked so soft and sweet, so alluring. So serene.

So fragile and...human.

So...

Mine.

Despite his inner turmoil, his cocks throbbed with undiminished desire, and the heat in his blood had only intensified. He stared at her cunt, which was bare and glistening with her essence.

His inner conflict only worsened.

He turned to walk away only to stop himself. Was he really going to leave her there, practically naked and covered in her own drying slick, like the females he'd used in the past? Was he really going to let her wake up like that—like he'd simply forgotten about her after they'd finished?

With another muttered curse, he forced himself to the bathroom, where he dampened a cloth with warm water. He returned to the couch and knelt beside her.

Were her scent to fill his nostrils again, Sevik wouldn't be able to trust himself. He held his breath as he quickly but gently wiped the essence from her thighs and cunt. When the washcloth brushed her clit, she moaned softly and stirred, but Sevik didn't stop. Every moment of restraint was a precious resource, an extremely limited commodity.

Still, he couldn't ignore what he was doing.

I'm cleaning her. Nothing more.

You're touching her tight little cunt. Might as well have another taste. She's yours.

He retreated with a hiss, dropping a hand to his cocks and clutching them through his pants as he stalked to the kitchen.

His eyes settled on the green bottle on the table. He snatched it up, tipped back his head, and drank deep, barely noticing the sting of the bubbles or the clashing sweetness and sourness.

"Vazk!" He threw the wadded washcloth into the laundry room, splashed water on his face at the sink, and—after another swig of champagne—returned to the living room with the bottle in hand.

Mina remained just as he'd left her.

Unsteadiness crept into his stride as he walked back to her. Clenching his teeth, he stared down at her and the temptation she presented.

"Fuck."

He set the bottle on the coffee table, shifted her legs up onto the cushion, and draped the blanket that had been on the back of the sofa over Mina, leaving only her head exposed.

That will lessen the temptation.

He immediately knew that thought for what it was—a load of shit.

Plucking up the bottle again, he lowered himself onto the floor beside the couch. He knew he should've gone somewhere else, anywhere else. The other sofa, the loft, the bathroom, out onto the fucking deck...but he couldn't.

He didn't want to leave her. Would not leave her.

Sevik leaned his head back against the armrest, gulped down another mouthful of alcohol, and closed his eyes. The floor beneath him wobbled ever so slightly, and his head felt oddly light, in contrast to the heaviness settling over the rest of his body.

"Fucking imprinted on a human," he said. The words came out slow, slurred, nearly in a jumble.

Mina shifted on the couch behind him. He heard the blanket rustle, heard a contented sigh escape her. He wanted nothing more than to join her, to be cocooned in that warmth, holding her little body against him.

Sevik tried to get up—or at least he thought he did. Only his arm moved, bringing the mouth of the bottle back to his lips.

She's mine.

Mine, mine, all fucking mine.

His next sip brought only carbonated oblivion, dragging Sevik into silent, impenetrable darkness.

FOURTEEN

Mina smiled as she awoke. Her dream was already fading, but memories of what she'd experienced with Viktor rose to fill her mind with vivid images and tease her body with echoes of sensation—the feel of his hands on her breasts, his fingers on her clit, and his mouth...

God, the way his tongue had felt on her pussy.

She might not have lost her virginity by penetration, but what Viktor had done... It was beyond anything she ever could've imagined. She'd read hundreds of romance novels, had read countless erotic scenes, but she'd always thought them exaggerated. How could anything possibly feel so good?

Now Mina knew it didn't feel that good; it felt *better*. And she wanted to do it all again. She wanted more, and she wanted to give him pleasure in return.

With a deep inhalation, she stretched, reaching her arms over her head. Her breath hitched as the rough material of the blanket rasped over her nipples, particularly the one Viktor had sucked. Mina opened her eyes and cupped her breasts beneath the blanket. That nipple was still raw and tender, and the press of her palm over it elicited pain bordering on pleasure. It was like he'd marked her, leaving a reminder of what they'd shared.

She tucked her bottom lip between her teeth as she grinned.

And he apparently sent me into an orgasm-induced sleep.

Though Mina was sure the champagne was partly responsible.

She glanced at the windows. It was still dark outside, and the snowfall hadn't slowed. She had no idea what time it was, and at that moment, she didn't care. The café wouldn't be opening today.

Mina sat up. The blanket fell to her lap, baring her chest, and she shivered at the cold. She crossed her arms, rubbing them with her palms. Now that she was sitting, she could see outside more clearly. The snow had piled up overnight, high enough to partially block the windows—at least two feet, likely more. And the storm showed no signs of letting up.

Her café definitely wouldn't be opening, not for a few days.

She inwardly winced.

I hope Viktor doesn't get sick of me, because it looks like I'll be staying for a little while.

But where was Viktor?

Intending to grab her sweater and find him, Mina turned and lowered her feet to the floor.

She froze.

Someone—some*thing*—lay upon the floor, sprawled out between the coffee table and the other sofa. He was wearing gray sweatpants just like Viktor's, but this...this was certainly *not* Viktor. It couldn't be.

Not-Viktor had one arm resting across his belly, the other on the floor over his head, and long, silken white hair spread around him. Mina clutched the blanket as her gaze traced the black horns curving up and back from his temples. His skin was pale, closer to alabaster than any flesh she'd ever seen, with solid black tattoos hugging his hips and covering his neck.

His toes and fingertips were also a deep black that faded as it neared his feet and hands, and she couldn't help but notice the menacing black claws at their tips.

His eyebrows and lashes were the same white as his hair, and his features were sharp, almost elfin, a resemblance only enhanced by his pointed ears. But those features had a familiarity to them.

This isn't Viktor. It can't be him.

But hadn't she'd glimpsed this before? Just last night in his kitchen?

I was drinking. It was the alcohol playing tricks with my mind.

No, it hadn't been a trick. She'd seen this. She'd seen *him.*

Terror seized Mina, and she frantically shook her head as her heart and breath quickened. She squeezed her eyes shut.

This isn't real. I'm dreaming. I'll wake up and Viktor will be there.

But when Mina opened her eyes, the Not-Viktor creature was still there.

A whimper escaped her, and she slapped a hand over her mouth. She quickly searched the floor. Her shirt lay on the other side of him, next to the empty champagne bottle.

For a moment, she considered abandoning the sweater and running out of there half naked.

He's sleeping, and it's just right there. You can do this. Just grab it and go. Easy.

Lifting the blanket aside, she slowly rose from the sofa and tiptoed around him. When she reached her top, she crouched, casting Not-Viktor a fearful glance before snatching up the garment and standing. She swiftly tugged it on, jamming her arms through the sleeves and pulling the hem down.

But as she turned and stepped away, she realized she'd forgotten a very important detail.

The bottle.

Her foot struck it, knocking it against one of the coffee table legs with a loud *clank.*

Not-Viktor bolted upright, fangs bared in a snarl. She glimpsed ethereal white irises against inky black sclera just before he grabbed her leg and pulled it out from beneath her.

Mina cried out, throwing her arms forward to catch herself as she fell. She hit the floor hard, and the air whooshed from her lungs, stunning her.

A rough hand grabbed her arm and flipped her over. Not-Viktor loomed over her and caught her throat, silencing the scream that had built in her chest. Those claws bit into her skin, and she felt blood trickling from the wounds.

Mina grabbed his wrist with both hands as her wide eyes met his.

His nostrils flared with a ragged inhalation. He stilled. Some of the hardness eased from his expression, and his slit pupils expanded as he stared down at her. "Mina?"

A crease formed between his brows when his gaze dipped to his hand. Growling, he released her neck, pulling his arm back like he'd been burned.

As she drew in a gasping breath, Mina swung her arm upward. Her forearm struck the side of his head hard enough to throw him off balance. Without waiting to see how quickly he'd recover, Mina scrambled out from beneath him, got to her feet, and ran toward the kitchen.

Sevik braced an arm on the sofa to steady himself. Dull pain pulsed across his cheek, echoed and overshadowed by the preexisting throbbing in his skull. His mouth and throat were as dry as sun-scorched sand, his tongue was swollen and rough, and his limbs were heavy, filled with lead.

But he could only pay attention to his hand. To the crimson droplets clinging to his claws.

Fuck.

That word wasn't strong enough, not nearly. Sevik didn't know any words that could properly express his shock and anguish.

I imprinted on her.

Imprinted on her and harmed her. Hand around her throat, skin broken, blood drawn...

Not even a full fucking day since he'd imprinted on Mina, and he'd already hurt her.

The constriction in his chest made it a struggle to breathe, and the ice in his veins made every thunderous beat of his heart a new agony. He'd harmed many people. He'd spilled blood, dealt wounds, ended lives. But nothing had ever made him feel like this.

He turned his hand. The droplets shifted only slightly, too small to fall.

Everything inside him froze when he realized what he was looking at—black fingertips, sharp claws, and pale, pale skin. He dropped his gaze to find that same skin on his torso, and black *lyros* flowing down around his waist.

His holoshroud was deactivated.

And Mina had just fled.

"*Cyr* fucking *orkaal!*" Sevik leapt up, shoving the couch askew and bumping aside the coffee table. "*Mina!*"

Fuck, why was his own voice so loud?

His legs protested the sudden movement, and his head spun. He pressed a hand to his forehead, gritted his teeth, and stumbled across the living room, only regaining his balance when he finally reached the entrance to the kitchen and braced his shoulder against the doorframe.

Cold wind howled through the laundry room doorway.

She'll die out there.

She's seen me.

Those thoughts stemmed from two different instincts, one a need to protect his mate, the other a need to protect himself. But both led to the same conclusion—he needed to get her. Now.

His pounding heart pumped adrenaline through his veins as he raced across the kitchen and into the laundry room. The front door stood open, and large snowflakes drifted in on the wind. His eyes immediately fixed on Mina.

She was beside her car, digging through knee-deep snow with her bare hands to unbury the driver's side door.

"Mina," Sevik said as he approached her.

Her head snapped up. Her eyes met his, and she stilled, terror straining her features. Seeing it was like a knife to Sevik's heart.

Spinning away from him, she frantically trudged through the snow.

With a growled curse, Sevik gave chase, his longer legs devouring the distance between them. He wrapped his arms around her from behind, pinning her arms against her sides and lifting her against his chest.

Mina kicked and screamed. "Let me go!"

He clenched his jaw as that scream amplified the ache in his head.

"Where the fuck would you go?" he bit out, carrying her toward the house.

She wriggled in his arms and flailed her legs. Despite her size, she was deceptively strong, and he nearly lost his grip on her. She reared her head back, forcing Sevik to cock his head to avoid catching her skull with his chin. When her bootheel struck his shin, he snarled and tightened his hold on her.

He stomped into the house, kicked the door closed behind him, and brought her back to the living room. All the while, she fought fiercely.

Sevik shoved her face-down onto the couch. Catching her wrists, he forced them behind her back and held them with one hand as he yanked off her boots. Once her wet footwear had been tossed in the direction of the back door, he climbed atop her, straddling her legs to trap them against the cushions.

Mina screamed again, thrashing and tugging her arms. "Please! Don't hurt me."

Her desperate, pleading tone twisted that blade in his chest. Instinct demanded he eliminate the threat to her, demanded he destroy the source of her fear.

How the fuck was he supposed to do that when *he* was both?

Sevik leaned forward, lowering his head. Long white hair fell to the sides of his face. "Mina."

She shrank from him. "Let me go. Just let me go. Please don't hurt me."

Sevik growled. "I'm not going to fucking hurt you!"

Already did.

Mina whimpered, and her struggles waned as she turned her

cheek onto the cushion. She looked up at him with one wide, frightened, watery eye.

Fuck.

Drawing in a deep breath, Sevik gentled his voice. "Listen to me, Mina. There is nowhere for you to go. You are safest right here. Do you understand?"

She pressed her lips together and nodded.

"I'm going to let you up," he continued. "If you scream, I will gag you. If you run, I will tie you to a chair. I don't want to do those things. So, you're going to be nice and calm once I let go, yes?"

"Yes," she whispered.

"Good girl." Sevik slowly lifted himself off her legs before releasing her arms.

Mina scurried out from beneath him.

Sevik tensed, ready to grab her if she tried to strike him and flee again. But she turned, pressed her back to the armrest, and hugged her legs to her chest, watching him warily.

She looked so small and timid. If it had been anyone else cowering before him, he would've reveled in their fear and discomfort. All he felt now was a dense, foreboding weight sinking in his gut.

But he knew her trembling was due to more than fear. Those tremors shaking her shoulders, quivering her chin, shaking her curls... She was freezing.

Slowly, he picked up the blanket she'd discarded on the sofa and spread it between his hands. Mina tensed as he moved it closer to her. He draped it over her gently before backing away. Keeping his eyes locked with hers, he lowered himself onto the opposite end of the couch, bending a leg atop the cushion to keep his body toward hers.

She relaxed slightly, curling her fingers around the blanket and tugging it to her chest.

They sat like that in silence, Mina's gaze occasionally shifting to a different part of his body before returning to his.

"No questions now?" Sevik asked. "Usually they don't stop."

"Who are you?" The words burst from her, quickly followed by, "*What* are you?"

Sevik ran his claws through his hair. Deflection would've been the best tactic. Avoid giving any real answers, withhold information for his safety—and for hers. Nothing good could come from sharing the truth.

But it was too late. She'd already seen him, and he was already too involved.

And killing her to protect his identity was out of the fucking question.

Foolish as it was, he still yearned to hear his real name in her voice, breathy and lustful, suffused with passion and desire.

He wanted to keep her.

Sevik knew he couldn't do so without endangering her life. If Brekker ever found him, or if the human authorities discovered his true nature, she'd get swept up in it. She could get hurt or worse...

She deserves to know.

Sevik owed her that much, at least. She deserved to know what she was involved with. Who she was involved with.

"Anything I tell you, Mina, is never to be repeated to anyone," he said. "You hold these secrets until death. Am I clear?"

Mina nodded.

"Say it."

"Yes. I...I won't say anything to anyone. I promise."

He shouldn't have believed her. Sevik knew better than to take anyone at their word, knew better than to let his guard down. Even being careful and vigilant, he'd been betrayed by one of the people closest to him.

But he believed Mina down to his very core.

"My name is Sevik kol Talris. I'm a korasi."

Mina furrowed her brow. "A...korasi?" Her gaze flicked to his horns. "Are you a demon?"

Were it not for the reading he'd done here on Earth, Sevik wouldn't have had any understanding of the word. "I don't know if demons exist, but I'm not one of them. I'm what you would call an alien."

FIFTEEN

An alien. An *alien*.

Mina could only stare at Viktor—Sevik—in shock.

How many times had she wondered if aliens really existed? Given how vast the universe was, she'd always believed there was life beyond Earth. She'd read about monsters and aliens in romance novels, had fantasized about those heroes, yearning for one of her own. All the while knowing that the same vastness of space that all but guaranteed the existence of alien lifeforms also guaranteed she'd never encounter one.

Now, one was sitting right in front of her.

Mina quietly studied him. With her initial terror having faded, she could recognize the face of the man she'd known. His features were sharper, deadlier, more inhuman, but it was still him.

And it would've been a lie to say she didn't find this version even more devastatingly beautiful.

"How did you disguise yourself as a human?" she asked.

Something flickered across his skin—a fine, hexagonal pattern that enveloped him like a net. It was gone as quickly as it had formed. Mina's eyes widened.

He was Viktor again. No horns, no claws, no dark markings or preternaturally pale skin, no black sclera or shimmering white hair. He was human.

"Holographic projection. Hides everything but doesn't change it." Sevik lifted a hand, examining his long fingers and their blunt nails. "Usually doesn't require conscious thought to keep it up. But strong emotions—or too much alcohol—and control can slip."

"But those...parts of you are not actually gone?"

"They're not."

It made sense now. She hadn't imagined the scrape of fangs or the prick of claws against her skin. They'd been there all along. Invisible, but still part of him. How many times had he stopped her from touching his face or his hair? Like last night, when he'd forced her hands over her head and had commanded her to keep them there as he'd pleasured her with his fingers and mouth. Sevik hadn't wanted her to discover his horns.

But his efforts hadn't hidden everything from her. She'd definitely noticed his long, incredibly agile tongue. And it had delved so, so deep into her pussy.

She curled her freezing toes into the couch cushion and hugged her legs tighter beneath the blanket, trying to ignore the desire ignited in her core by the memory of what they'd shared.

Wasn't that memory tainted now? Hadn't the whole experience been built upon deception? This human version of him was what she'd known, what she should've wanted. But it seemed wrong now.

"Change back," she said.

Sevik snickered, the corner of his mouth rising. "That a request or a command, *val'syra?*"

"A command."

"Why should I obey?"

Mina averted her gaze as warmth flooded her cheeks. "Because this isn't you. It's... a lie."

He hummed low. From the corner of her eye, she saw those hexes shimmer again, and they called her attention right back to him. As the pattern faded, it revealed the real Sevik. The alien Sevik.

"What does *val'syra* really mean?" Mina asked.

"Say my name."

Mina furrowed her brow. "What?"

He leaned forward, those bright, otherworldly white eyes intent upon hers. "Say my name, Mina."

The low timber in his voice made her belly flutter and her heart patter wildly against her ribs.

Mina licked her lips. "If I say it, will you tell me what *val'syra* means?"

He stared at her before nodding once.

"Sevik," she said softly.

A slow, sultry smirk spread across his lips, offering her a glimpse of his pointed white fangs and black gums. "Perfect."

That desire in Mina's belly flared, spreading warmth through her that chased away the chill. His smile had always been sinfully alluring in the past. But throw in the fangs? Now it made her weak in the knees.

Mina fidgeted on the sofa, suddenly very aware of her torn underwear, which provided no protection as slick gathered in her pussy.

Stupid, stupid body. Now is not the time.

Sevik drew in a deep breath, closing his eyes briefly. When he opened them, his chest rumbled, and his smirk stretched into a predatory grin. "Suddenly you don't seem so afraid, Mina."

"How would you—"

Wait. Oh God, can he smell me?

"Maybe I'm not." Though her cheeks burned in mortification as she reflexively squeezed her thighs together, Mina lifted her chin. She refused to hide. "Well?"

"Well what?"

"You said you'd tell me what *val'syra* means."

"I lied."

"You..." Mina glared at him. She released her legs, letting the blanket fall to her lap as she leaned back and crossed her arms over her chest. "That's not nice."

Sevik's grin faded, but the hungry glint in his eyes remained. "Never said I was nice."

"No, but you're usually nice to me."

"Never said I was without flaws either."

"Jerk," Mina muttered.

He hooked an arm over the backrest of the couch and cocked his head. "Where I'm from, nice gets you killed."

Her gaze dipped, running over the markings on his throat and collarbone, following the thin lines of pale skin that broke up the solid black. "Are you finally going to tell me where you're actually from?"

"Far away from here," he said with a hint of that smirk.

Mina wrinkled her nose and pursed her lips at him.

Sevik chuckled. "Ah, Mina, you are adorable when you're riled."

She blinked at him, taken aback by how much that light-hearted chuckle transformed his face. And then she realized what he'd said, and that warmth within her strengthened, filling her with secret delight.

"Hestryn," he said. "A city on a planet called Vabos."

"What's it like?"

"It's...the opposite of this place. A particularly huge, filthy, overcrowded city in a world of huge, filthy, overcrowded cities. Everything is metal and glass, machinery and glaring lights that don't touch all the dark places where most people are forced to live. The kind of place where you can always see the best of what life can offer while endless suffering is shoveled into your face. But if you have money, you can do anything you want."

"And did you have the money to do anything you wanted?"

"Not always, but I never let that stop me. Decided when I was young that I'd do what I wanted regardless. The money... That didn't come until later."

She regarded him anew. His demeanor, right down to his usual posture, body language, and tone of voice, were those of a man in control—whether by force of will, personality, or muscle. It didn't surprise her to hear that he'd been like that before having any means to back it up.

Fake it until you make it, right?

But she couldn't settle for vague notions, for his airy allusions. She needed to know more about him.

"Will you tell me about your life there?" Mina shifted, crossing her legs in front of her and folding her hands on her lap. "Will you tell me more about...you?"

"It doesn't matter."

"It matters to me."

He narrowed his eyes. Their eerie white was piercing, but she didn't look away.

"Why not ask what I've done?" He demanded. "How many people I've hurt, how many I've killed?"

Mina was used to evasiveness from him, was used to him putting up impenetrable, indifferent walls. But this felt different. This was almost defensive. Almost...vulnerable.

"Because I want to know you, Sevik. The things you've done are part of you, but they aren't *you*."

"This *is* me," Sevik snarled, baring his fangs. "Do not mistake me for a good male, Mina. You know nothing of who or what I am."

"Then tell me."

A crease formed between his eyebrows as he stared at her, assessing, searching. Though she couldn't know for sure, she sensed that he sought a reason to distrust her. A reason to refuse to answer.

Swallowing thickly, she clutched the blanket in her fists and braced herself for the inevitable rejection. For his dismissiveness, for his irritation. She'd discovered one of his secrets—a massive, mind-blowing secret—and only had more questions than ever.

When he spoke, he did so quickly, like he was just trying to get through the words without feeling them. "I grew up in the slums. My brother brought me into a gang when I was six. My mother died when I was eleven. Brother didn't last much longer than her. When the first gang fell apart, I was recruited with a friend into a criminal organization. We rose in the ranks until we broke off and started our own operation."

She studied him closely, looking past those alien features to the man behind them. He'd been tightlipped since they met, offering scant information about himself, even when pressed, but there'd often been a hint of playfulness to it.

This was different. Though he hadn't given much away, he seemed uncomfortable. Seemed...self-conscious.

Keeping her voice gentle, she said, "I'd like to know more. About you, your family, your people. Anything you'd like to share."

Sevik held her gaze for a long, long while, dragging out the silence between them. The soft thumping of Mina's heart and the howling wind outside were the only sounds.

One of Sevik's hands rested atop his thigh. His index finger twitched, rising and falling once, twice, thrice, before stilling again.

"There's a lot I don't know," he finally said, shattering the silence with his low, measured voice. "Don't know why my mother left the korasi homeworld to live on Vabos. Don't know if she immigrated alone, don't know if she had any family or friends. I don't know my father. My mother never said if he died, if he abandoned us, if she left him. Never even told us his name. She...didn't really talk about anything she considered personal."

Mina frowned as something coiled in her chest and squeezed her heart. "I'm so sorry. That must've been hard, especially as a child."

He flicked his wrist in a dismissive wave. "Just the way it was. The way she was. Learned a bit about my people from her, but she wasn't very invested in korasi culture. I think she was on Vabos to disconnect...or forget. Maybe to hide. But why doesn't matter. She was there; we were there."

"You mentioned a brother. Did you have any other siblings?"

"Just Zoren."

"I always wanted a sibling. I never had many friends, so it

would've been nice to have a brother or sister. A best friend for life..."

"He was five years older than me. We were never close. The only thing he did for me was bring me into a gang. Told me I had to figure out everything else on my own, because he wouldn't have a stupid youngling dragging him down."

Mina shook her head. "That's cruel! You were just a little boy."

"It's normal on Vabos. Being alone and unaffiliated means you're weak. Vulnerable. An easy target. And since being in a gang can bring in a little money, it's hard to resist joining one. I knew we were poor. My mother tried to hide it, and she never complained, but I knew she struggled to keep us fed and sheltered. I noticed the days she didn't eat anything because there wasn't enough for all of us. Zoren used his earnings for himself. I used mine to help our mother."

That tightness in Mina's chest strengthened, but a gentle warmth now suffused it. How could a little kid trying to help his struggling single mother not be heartwarming?

And how could she not relate when she'd seen her own mother struggle in silence the same way?

"See, Sevik? There's good in you."

He snickered, amusement gleaming in his eyes. Yet those eyes remained just as intense, just as penetrating, just as dangerous.

She held his gaze, refusing to let that stare win—no matter how much it made her skin heat and her belly flutter. "What does a six-year-old even do in a gang?"

"Whatever the fuck the older members tell them to do. Create distractions, beg, help in simple cons. Sometimes run messages, sometimes pick pockets or steal small items. Watch out for author-ities and suspicious people."

"I...didn't realize the list would be so long."

"Only gets longer as you get deeper in," he said flatly. "But I thought it was exciting, and I was helping. Even made a friend, another korasi my age named Brekker. We had fun with it, even when we had the shit kicked out of us. Found creative ways to get revenge."

Mina's frown deepened. A six-year-old was supposed to be starting first grade, learning how to read and write, playing on the playground. Not stealing, begging, or fighting. And then to be abused on top of it?

"Then my mother got sick when I was ten." Sevik shoved himself off the couch, rising to pace across the floor. Tension rippled through his muscles as he moved. "She told me not to worry. But I saw the changes. Every day, her skin was grayer, her hair thinner, her eyes hollower. She could barely keep any food down. She was dying before my fucking eyes. The spark inside her...just gone."

"I finally convinced her to go to a clinic, and the doctor said she had some kind of wasting illness. She needed medication. The meds he prescribed...they weren't priced for people like us to afford. She said it was okay, that she'd be fine. But it wasn't fucking okay with me."

Mina had heard anger in his voice before, but this was unique —it was primal, soul-deep rage, raw and impotent, an insatiable fire with no way to vent the heat. And she couldn't blame him for that anger. She felt it for him.

People on Earth died every day because they couldn't afford healthcare, because they couldn't access the medicines and treatments they needed to survive. She didn't understand how it wasn't criminal for people to be denied lifesaving care when the tools and technology were readily available.

"Our gang couldn't source the meds. Too high profile, they said." Sevik laughed bitterly, and his hands curled into fists as he halted before the fireplace with his back toward her. That long white hair of his hung all the way to his waist, covering his back completely. "So I did everything I could to make extra money. Fucking gang took a cut of everything. Zoren put some of his own money in too, but he refused to do what he called 'shit work for tit-sucking younglings'. Even Brekker helped.

"It took months. Months of watching her waste away, watching…" His fists drew tighter still, making his already pale knuckles impossibly white, and the muscles of his arms and shoulders flexed. "We finally got what she needed. I was so proud, so excited, so relieved when me and my brother brought her those meds. By then she was so frail. But she smiled and embraced us, both rare things from her, and said, 'My sons will be okay'. I told her she would be okay too. She just held me tighter."

Mina's lungs burned with her held breath. She knew what was coming, but she couldn't accept it, couldn't stop herself from wishing it would be different.

Sevik opened his hands slowly, stiffly, as though doing so required great effort. She swore she glimpsed spots of crimson on his palms before he folded his arms across his chest, hiding his hands from sight.

"Found her dead three days later. We were out on jobs, and she just died. Alone."

Tears stung Mina's eyes and blurred her vision. She tried to hold them back, but it was impossible.

"I was ten when my father was killed in a logging accident," she said softly. "I know what it's like to feel that pain, that heavy grief that just feels so big while you feel so small and helpless."

He turned his head, peering at her over his shoulder with one ethereal eye. "It is big. Heavy. And I had to hold it all inside, because if I let myself look sad, my brother would rage. Because if I let any of it show, I would look weak."

"That's horrible. I don't care how old you are, no one should have to bottle all that up. No one should have to carry that burden alone."

After releasing a heavy breath, Sevik turned to face her. "No one was going to carry it for me. Zoren left before our mother was even cold. I followed him. Didn't want to be alone then, especially not with her. Couldn't bear the thought of it. He went to the clinic, found the doctor, and beat him nearly to death. Then we smashed the place up, took whatever meds we could carry, and ran. The only place left for us to go was the warehouse the gang operated out of. That was our only home.

"Most of the way there, Zoren berated me. Kept mentioning all the things he could've done with the money if I hadn't wasted it on meds that didn't work. If I hadn't been a fucking *esklaat*, a useless fool."

Mina gaped at him. "That's...that's horrible!"

Though she'd heard plenty of stories about family members being cruel and callous toward each other, she struggled to understand how a brother could treat their sibling like that after their parent's death, how a son could say the efforts made to save his dying mother had been pointless and wasteful.

"He was weak," Sevik said. "Within a few months, he was dead too."

"Did he..."

"Kill himself? Not directly. My brother was too self-absorbed for that. Fighting was part of life for all of us, but he became especially violent after our mother died. Volatile. Most of his money started going toward drugs that kept him amped up. He went looking for fights, and he instigated them when he couldn't find any. One day, he started a brawl with a rival gang. His friends dragged him back to the warehouse afterward. He was bleeding from a few dozen stab wounds. He was conscious until the drugs wore off. Then he was just dead."

"I'm so sorry, Sevik."

He ran his hand through his hair, between his horns. "He brought it upon himself."

"I...I know. I'm not just sorry for the loss of your brother, but for you not having a healthy way to deal with your grief after losing your mother and your brother so close together, and so young. You must've felt so alone."

"I had Brekker. He was more of a brother to me than Zoren ever was."

"When my mother died, I was lucky to still have Randy," Mina said softly. "Even with him there to comfort and support me, it was hard. Everyone was so cruel to her when she was alive, and then pretended to pity her when she was gone. Like she was this tragic figure, and they all cared so much, and it was a shame what happened. And it was all...fake. So fake and so sickening.

"But they never stopped being cruel to me. Some of them changed the way they presented it, acting almost like...like they were doing it for my own good. Like they were doing me a service I never wanted, never asked for. They acted like she was this horrible woman, and they were watching me close, waiting for me to slip up and show that she'd corrupted me too."

She looked down, absently fiddling with the material of her skirt. "I'm not sure if I would've made it without Randy."

"*Zekt'al, val'syra*," Sevik growled, calling her eyes back to him. His brows were slanted sharply down, and his lips were curled into a scowl. "You would've fucking made it. Maybe you don't know how, but you would have."

She shook her head and laughed without amusement. "You don't know that. You barely know me."

"I'm not fucking blind, Mina." He stalked over to her and seized her chin, angling her face up toward him. Those blazing white eyes held her captive, sparking sensations inside her that shouldn't have been possible from mere looks. "I see you, female."

Those words had been spoken with such confidence, such conviction, such firmness. Warmth bloomed within Mina; her mouth was suddenly dry, her breath short, her heartbeat rapid. She craved him more than ever in that moment. She wished he would tear off her sweater, lean over her, and cage her in with his body. Wished his long white hair would fall like a silky curtain around them, reducing her whole world to his face, to his eyes and their vibrant glow.

Mina wished he would touch her again, kiss her again, taste her again. Wished he would claim her just like the heroes in the books she so adored claimed their mates.

She wanted him to make her feel alive, to remind them both that they were still here despite the tragedy they'd endured.

There were no barriers between them now. There was no hiding what he was. He was Sevik. Not Viktor, not a mask, but an inhuman, otherworldly being.

And God, he was so dangerously *beautiful*.

His nostrils flared, and he hummed, gravelly and low.

Eyes widening, Mina withdrew her chin from his hold. "So! You, uh... You said that gang fell apart, didn't you?"

Sevik's pupils narrowed to razor-thin slits before expanding slightly. He blinked and huffed. Returning to his place on the opposite end of the couch, he sat with his back against the armrest. "It didn't fall apart. It ceased to exist."

"What happened?"

"The same stupid fuckers who told me the meds for my mother were too high profile somehow got their hands on a shipment of faloran arms. And everyone knows the falorans don't fuck around."

Mina tilted her head, flattening her palms on her thighs. "Are the falorans another gang?"

He laughed, flashing his fangs. "Might as well be. They're a species. A military power fallen on hard times after a virus killed most of their females generations ago. It's only made them more aggressive, and they really don't appreciate it when people steal their toys. They raided our warehouse with an elite special forces team.

"We tried to fight back, but it was a...a massacre. That the right word?" When Mina nodded, he continued. "Somehow, me and Brekker dragged each other out of there. Somehow, we survived."

"That must've been terrifying," Mina said. "Were you hurt?"

Sevik gestured to his bared torso, and only then did she notice the pale scars on his skin. A few looked like they'd been left by blades and varied in length. But between his chest and abdomen, she counted five that were more uniform, each with a center ring surrounded by slightly raised tissue that faded outward like sunbursts. They looked like bullet wounds encircled by small burn scars. Two of them were just over the place where a human's heart would've been, only inches apart from each other. The one on the left was darker, more jagged...newer.

He brushed a finger over a bullet scar on his abdomen before lifting his hand to touch another on his chest—the one beside the freshest mark. "These two. Both plasma bolts."

"I'm sorry, Sevik."

"Don't be. It's life. It's not fair, and it hurts. A lot. That day was when I decided I would take what I wanted, because life sure as fuck wasn't going to give me anything but pain."

She frowned, brow furrowing. "How old were you?"

"Fourteen."

"No one should have to go through anything like that, especially not someone so young."

Sevik turned his palms up in a very human gesture, as if to say the situation was what it was. Mina could only guess that the scars he carried inside, in his mind, on his heart and soul, were much more severe than the physical marks.

"It taught me a great deal about the universe," he said. "Taught me that the authorities are just like gangs, just with better funding and the law to wield or ignore as it suits them."

"Like Chief Harrigan," she muttered.

Sevik's mouth stretched into a full, sharp-fanged smile. "Like Chief Harrigan. But he's nothing. A small man in a small town who's fooled himself into thinking he's in control."

"And who enforces or ignores the law at his whim."

"His kind is a universal infestation."

"Some might say the same of criminals. That you're the bane of civilization."

"That's the difference between me and Harrigan, Mina." Sevik's chin dipped, giving his face a wicked cast. "I don't pretend."

Now Mina smirked, folding her arms across her chest. "What's that about not pretending, *Viktor?*"

"Never claimed to be honest, *val'syra.*"

"So, should I believe anything you've told me today?"

"You should." His expression sobered, the hint of playfulness that had brightened it vanishing. "Believe and remember, because I'm telling you exactly who I am."

Mina hummed, biting her lower lip as she studied him. "And if that doesn't scare me away?"

His eyes dipped and fixated on her mouth. "Then I should question your judgment as much as I've been questioning my own lately."

"Why have you been questioning your judgment?"

"You," he rasped. "You're a fucking fog in my mind, obscuring every other thought. Blurring everything."

Mina's heart fluttered as desire smoldered in her core. She did that to him?

Her gaze dropped and traced the line of his mouth. How could a scowl be so sexy? She wanted to kiss the corners of his lips, wanted to feel them soften beneath hers, wanted them to kiss her back.

Somehow, Mina forced her eyes back up. She met Sevik's gaze; it was fiery, electric, bristling with a primal force barely held in check. Everything about this situation, about him, should've urged her to run.

But the only direction she wanted to go was toward him.

"You said you were recruited into another gang?" she asked.

Sevik nodded. "Me and Brekker."

"What'd you do there?"

"We became enforcers."

"What does that mean?"

He ran his tongue across his fangs. "We enforced the rules. Kept people in line. When someone needed to be hurt, we hurt them. When someone needed to disappear, we assisted them in getting lost."

Those eerie eyes were unwavering, almost cold. He'd just admitted to killing people, and not a shred of remorse—or any emotion—had been visible on his face.

Mina drew in a shaky breath. She was awed by how quickly his intensity could go from hunger and lust to icy menace.

"So...even criminals have rules?" she asked.

"Successful criminals. This was an organization, run more like a company than a gang. Intricate operations hidden behind legitimate businesses, protected by bribes, threats, and the capability for swift, precise, brutal violence."

Mina's attention flicked to his clawed hands—hands that had felt so good against her skin. Hands that had inflicted untold damage, that had dealt death. "How'd you go from being the guy who hurts people to your own boss?"

"I was determined to take what I wanted. To live on my own terms. Hard to do that when you're just a beast on someone else's leash."

"So you're a beast then. A wild animal."

"We're all beasts, Mina," he said, devouring her with those eyes. "Even adorable little humans. Some people try to deny it. Some hide it better than others."

Unbidden, her tongue slipped out to wet her lips. "And you?"

He grinned; those fangs were just one of many features reminding her that he was very much not human. "I embrace it."

She barely suppressed the shiver threatening to course along her spine. She told herself it was due to fear, but she knew that wasn't true. No, it was a thrill, sparked by a single, superheated thought.

I want him to let his beast out of its cage.

"That's *why* you went on your own," she said. "But it doesn't tell me how."

Did she really want to know? Given all he'd told her so far, his path to the top had probably been awash with blood and violence.

"The boss took a liking to us. She had another korasi, Enthi, act as our handler early on. Enthi was one of the favored, only a few years older than us but very experienced. She was intelligent, clever, driven, professional, and fucking tough. Beautiful too. We'd never known anyone like her."

A female korasi took shape in Mina's imagination. Tall and lithe, strong yet elegant, with flawless porcelain skin, haunting eyes, perfectly curved horns, and long, shimmering white hair.

How could any human compare to that?

How could Mina compare?

And Sevik had called Enthi beautiful.

Jealously ignited in Mina's chest. She had no right to feel it, but feel it she did.

"She taught us how things were done, and we worked well together," Sevik continued. "Became quite a team. We...complemented each other. Challenged each other."

That jealousy wound through Mina, hot and heavy, tangling her insides.

Don't ask, Mina. It doesn't matter.

But the words tumbled out anyway. "Did you two... Did you..."

"Fuck?"

That word had never sounded as harsh and vulgar as it did at that moment. Mina could only answer with a tight, shallow nod before dropping her gaze.

"Yes. She rutted Brekker too. And we all fucked other people."

Gritting her teeth, Mina squeezed the blanket and willed her face not to redden. It was ridiculous to be jealous of a woman from his past. It wasn't like Mina and Sevik were even dating; flirting a few times and fooling around a little didn't make a relationship.

Mina had no claim on him.

"Is my little *val'syra* jealous?" Sevik asked.

"No," Mina replied quickly. Too quickly. "Why would I be jealous? It has nothing to do with me." She twisted the blanket, and her heart only thumped louder and faster. She felt his eyes on her, but she couldn't bring herself to look up at him, didn't want to.

"It was about pleasure," he said. "About release. We respected each other too much to ever pretend otherwise. Neither of us wanted a mate. We wanted to ascend. Wanted money, power, influence."

"So you..." Mina managed to open a fist, but could only wave her hand ineffectively as she failed to produce the words. "But never developed any feelings? Never felt anything but gratification?"

"No. The positions we were in...there's no lowering your guard. Sex with Enthi was never about deeper feelings. It was satisfying an urge, releasing our aggressions. But even as much as we trusted each other, we never truly knew each other. I didn't know what it felt like to be myself. Until now."

There was something in his voice, something raw and vulnerable, that called Mina's gaze back up to him. All the menace his face was capable of displaying was gone. There was still heat in his eyes, but it had softened, and the way he was looking at her now...

Mina swallowed and took in a slow, steadying breath. "Go on. I'd like to know more."

The corners of his mouth fell into the slightest of frowns; somehow, that subtle change was more expressive than anything she'd ever seen from him.

"Enthi was on her way up already," he said. "I was determined to claim my place. She was brought into the leadership, and I followed not long after. We were lieutenants, reporting directly to the boss."

"What about Brekker?"

Sevik shook his head, and a faint line formed between his brows. "I took him as my second, but... They wanted people who could pair vision and business sense with ruthlessness and ambition. People who could find new ways to bring in money, or who could make the current operations more efficient and profitable.

"Brekker is the best enforcer I've ever known. His instincts are sharp, and he's good at predicting what people will do under pressure. His targets don't evade him for long. But his talents don't suit what they were looking for in leadership."

"How did it make him feel to have his friends promoted around him?"

"Things would've been different if I had known the answer to that." Now it was Sevik who dropped his gaze, watching his hand as he pinched the fabric of his sweatpants. "Me and Enthi were planning. We saw holes to fill, needs to meet, money to be made. Power and influence waiting to be seized."

"So you became the boss by...by overthrowing the old one?"

He laughed, and some of the tension faded from his features. "No. I'm not afraid of death, but that doesn't mean I welcome it. That would've triggered a war that would've collapsed the whole organization. Countless rival groups would've swept in to carve up what was left. We wanted to start our own organization. A... brokerage, I think is the term you would use. To mediate dealings between Vabos's criminal organizations and prevent the betrayals that were so rampant.

"If those organizations could make transactions with one another without all the distrust, it would be better for everyone's business. We went to the boss, asked permission to break off and go independent. She agreed after we assured her that she would receive a percentage of our profits.

"We brought in Brekker as an equal partner. Needed him to head enforcement and security, because we knew there'd be challenges early on. Attempts at making us look incapable, incompetent. And no one did that work better than him.

"First couple years were rough. Fulfilled a lot of contracts in blood. But we were successful. Very, very successful. Soon enough, we were bringing in more money than any of us had ever dreamed."

Mina studied him, looking for any more clues in his expression, in his posture, in his voice, but she couldn't find anything definitive. "And now you're here?"

"Now I'm here." Sevik sighed and tilted his head back, looking up toward the ceiling. "I thought Brekker was dissatisfied. That he was envious of me and Enthi because we were running most everything. That he wanted more; more say, more power, more money, that he objected to the way we did business. But I've had a long time to consider it, to look back at everything. And it's so much simpler than that."

Lifting his head, he nodded to himself. "He wanted her. From the beginning, he wanted her. First as a conquest because she was beautiful. But when he realized she would not be conquered, something shifted in him. It became about proving himself her equal. About showing her that he was worthy to be her mate, to stand beside her, evenly matched, like no one else was. Enthi wasn't interested.

"Her ambition had no space for him. She wouldn't play mate to anyone, and didn't need a mate to feel complete. When they rutted, she saw it as casual sex. He saw it as much, much more. And his desire became an obsession. He grew jealous of anyone else she fucked, even me. Especially me. Started disagreeing with me more and more, questioned my decisions in front of others. I had to put him in his place a few times. I didn't realize until it was much too late that he imprinted on her.

"One night, Enthi came to my place. She didn't say anything. Just took off her clothes. We fucked, and afterward she mentioned Brekker had lost his mind. And like speaking his name fucking summoned him, he burst in, saw us together, and started screaming that Enthi had betrayed him. That she'd tainted their mating bond. She never took shit from anyone, especially not him, so she shouted right back.

"I was getting out of bed to get between them when he noticed my clothes on a chair nearby. My clothes and my gun. He pulled it free and shot her."

Mina gasped, eyes rounding.

Something new was creeping into Sevik's voice now, something she recognized from earlier. That deep, seething anger, that rage, boiling under the surface. "He looked just as shocked as she did. Like neither of them could believe what he'd just done. She fell dead on my bedroom floor. He stared down at her in silence. And I knew what was coming. Probably had enough time to do something about it, if I'd acted.

"But despite everything I'd seen, every betrayal I'd witnessed in my life, part of me didn't want to believe it. We were fucking brothers. We'd saved each other's lives. He looked at me like he'd just realized I was there. Told me this was my fault. That I'd made him do it. And then he shot me."

Sevik lifted his hand and tapped the newest scar on his chest, over his breastbone, producing small, hollow *thuds*. "Not sure if he charged at me or I charged at him. It all blurs. But we wound up grappling with each other, me trying to get the pistol from him. Felt my strength fading with every heartbeat. Somehow got the gun away from him, and he kicked me hard in the gut. All the air burst from my lungs. Then he threw me through the window."

Mina slapped a hand over her mouth. "Oh, Sevik…"

"No idea how I survived the fall," he said. "Probably should've died before ever hitting the ground. Just remember pain everywhere, and dragging myself out of a trash pile, along an alley. Stole medical supplies from one of our safehouses. Only stopped long enough to inject myself with drugs. I knew he'd be looking for me.

"I called in a favor, and left Vabos before the next sunrise. Only thing keeping me going were the drugs in my body. Came here to recover."

"Why here?" Mina asked, lowering her hand. "Why Earth, and especially why the middle of Alaska?"

"Because it's Earth. Small. Out of the way. Intergalactic laws say it's off limits, so only local authorities to deal with, and none of the other aliens here want to be revealed. And Alaska… What's the phrase? Middle of nowhere? This is a middle of nowhere town, in a middle of nowhere state, on a middle of nowhere planet. Where better to disappear?"

"Are you safe now, then? Brekker thinks you're dead, so you don't have to worry?"

"He knows I'm not dead. He also knows I'm a threat as long as I'm breathing. He's looking for me."

Alarm flooded Mina. "Will he find you here?"

"Eventually. I didn't plan to stay long enough for that to happen."

"Oh." A heaviness settled in her chest. "You're…leaving?" She shook her head and let out a small, humorless laugh. "Of course you'll be leaving. You're an alien. You can't stay. If people discovered you, you'd be in danger here too, because we all know how horrible humans can be."

"Humans don't seem any better or worse than any other species I've dealt with. You are people trying to survive. Just like anyone else."

"Haven't you seen what humans do to aliens in the movies?" she asked, worry tinging her voice. "If they discovered an alien, if they discovered you, they'd torture you and cut you open in the name of science."

"They're not going to find me."

"But what if they do?"

"They'll regret it. But they won't find me, Mina."

"I did."

"You're different."

Mina's brow creased as she canted her head. "How am I different?"

Sevik stared at her, long and hard, and so much meaning flashed through his eyes—frustratingly indecipherable meaning. As that silence stretched, she knew he wasn't going to answer her question. Knew that somehow, his stare *was* the answer.

Why was she so different from anyone else? Why had Sevik approached her in Cornerstone when he'd kept entirely to himself, speaking to no one, for the year he'd lived in Sullford?

Mina was...nobody. Why would he risk being discovered because of her? Why would he fight for her, even when he didn't know her? Why would—

Another thought suddenly occurred to her, a question that had haunted her for days. A mystery that had made her feel like she was losing her mind.

"Wait," Mina said. "The night I was attacked, I know that man stabbed me. I felt it. Right before he slammed my head against my car. But when I woke up here, I didn't have any wounds. Not even a bruise on my head, when I probably should've had a concussion. You did something to me, didn't you?"

"I saved you," he replied. When she just stared at him, he scrubbed hand down his face. "I injected you with a serum, hoping it would heal you."

"What do you mean, hoping?"

"The serum works for korasi. For most other species I'm familiar with too. But I didn't know what it would do to a human. There was a chance that it wouldn't do anything, or that it would cause more harm."

Expression strained, she studied him, searching his eyes for some indication of his feelings—even as she struggled to decide what she felt. This was...complicated. He'd saved her, but being injected with mystery drugs while unconscious...

"So you put that stuff into my body without knowing what it would do?" she asked quietly.

"Mina..." He exhaled heavily and shook his head. "There are moments when you must act. When you can't stop and analyze everything, can't calculate every possible outcome. Many people fall apart in those moments. I don't. I acted based on the information I had at the time.

"You were injured. The stab wound was shallow, and I could've stitched it up if necessary. But the head wound... I didn't know what that would do to a human, didn't know how severe it was. All I knew was that your kind can be fragile. I also knew that we weren't anywhere near a hospital if it was something serious. So I acted—and I hoped."

"Oh." It felt like a foolish response, but it was all she could manage.

"That's the main reason I brought you back here that night. Didn't know what the serum would do, so I kept you close. I... checked on you through the night."

"You did?"

"Often."

Something about the way he'd said that word made her think it was an understatement.

When she'd woken that morning to find Sevik in the kitchen, cooking for her, the first thing he'd said, as he looked her over, had been '*How do you feel, Mina?*'

"Sevik, I..." She let out a shaky breath.

He'd had no obligation to help Mina against her attacker. He'd had no reason to endanger himself, to risk exposing his true identity. Yet he had. And he'd done the best he could, which was far, far more than she could ever have asked of him.

There was only one thing for Mina to say to that. "Thank you. Really."

A tiny, prideful glint appeared in his eyes, and he nodded.

"So...there were other reasons you brought me here?" she asked.

"Just one. I wasn't ready to let go of you."

Again, she couldn't get anything out of her mouth but, "Oh."

There was too much heat building inside Mina for her to form any other words. The possessiveness in his voice did things to her, wonderful, frightening, thrilling things.

She ran her gaze over his alien features. This man wasn't at all what he seemed, and that extended well beyond the sci-fi disguise he usually donned. And the way he'd talked about himself, the way he'd told his story, made Mina wonder if Sevik even saw his true self.

Her eyes drifted up to his horns. She'd always found horns appealing, ever since seeing *Legend* for the first time, but now that there was a man before her who had an actual set of horns on his head, she couldn't help having a thousand more questions. "Are those heavy?"

"My horns? I don't really notice their weight."

"Can I...touch them?"

His brows drew down sharply.

"Well, it's not everyday someone you know suddenly sprouts horns. I'm just...curious. About what they feel like."

He smirked and beckoned her with a clawed finger. "Come then, *val'syra*."

Mina blushed. He'd just twisted her innocent curiosity into a seduction, and she...she was here for it.

Leaning forward, she placed her hands on the cushion and crawled toward him. His eyes remained on her, unwavering, stirring the embers of desire in her core.

His spicy scent filled her senses once she was before him. She rose on her knees, lifted a hand, and lightly ran her fingers along one of his horns. It was hard but surprisingly smooth despite the ridges ringing it. She traced her finger all the way to the curved tip and pressed on the point. It wasn't sharp enough to break her skin like this, but it would definitely cause damage with a little force behind it.

"Can you feel me touching it?" she asked.

"No."

"Nothing at all?" Mina eased a little closer, spreading her thighs to either side of his slightly bent knee to maintain her balance, and wrapped both her hands around his horns. She rubbed them with her thumbs. "What about this?"

"No," he rasped, his warm breath teasing her collarbone.

Her skin prickled in awareness, and her nipples hardened.

Wait. Why am I feeling his breath on my chest?

Mina's cheeks burned hotter as realization set in. She was kneeling in front Sevik, straddling his leg, with her breasts directly in his face.

Mina looked down. Sevik's eyes were fixated on the outlines of her nipples, which were pressing against her sweater.

She dropped her arms with a gasp and leaned back. "Sorry. I shouldn't have—"

He caught her jaw in his hand, halting her retreat. Mina's hands instinctively flew to his shoulders. She could feel the press of his claws against the side of her neck, could feel the strength in those fingers, the roughness of his palm. When he tilted her head aside, she didn't resist.

His nostrils flared as his gaze shifted to her neck. Those pupils again shrank to slits, and he released a low, ragged growl. He slid his hand down her throat and brushed his thumb ever so lightly over one of the spots where his claws had cut her earlier.

Mina winced at the slight sting.

"Didn't mean to hurt you," he rumbled.

There was true regret in his eyes and his voice, and it made Mina's chest constrict. When Mina had run from him, she'd fought as hard as she could, had kicked and thrashed and hit him several times. Yet though Sevik had been rough and firm in his handling of her, he hadn't hurt her, hadn't even threatened to do so.

Well, he *had* said he would gag her and tie her up if she kept struggling. But he hadn't threatened to harm her. All he'd done since meeting her was keep her safe.

"I know," she said softly.

He met her gaze again, and she saw that hint of vulnerability in his eyes once more, saw him searching, questioning.

Finally, he released her. His hands dropped to her hips, and he lifted her off the couch effortlessly, setting her on her feet before he stood up.

Sevik stepped away, turning his head toward the windows. The snow was piled a little higher against the glass than before. "Storm hasn't let up yet. Probably won't for a while."

"Guess you're stuck with me for a while." Mina cast him a sheepish smile. "Sorry. I...didn't plan to get snowed in while celebrating my birthday with an alien." She ran her fingers through her hair, wincing when they snagged in the curls.

He clasped her wrist and gently extricated her fingers from her tangled hair. "Stop apologizing."

Mina looked up at him. He hadn't said those words harshly, hadn't said them with annoyance or impatience. His tone had been almost...endearing.

When Sevik let go of her, he turned and crouched, picking up the empty champagne bottle. "Make yourself comfortable. I don't have much, but you don't have any other choice, do you?"

"Thank you." She brought her hand to her chest and stared at his back.

His long white hair had parted, revealing the black tattoos on his neck, which circled it entirely. Those marks ran down his spine in three narrow, closely packed lines before flaring wide at his lower back, where they disappeared under his sweats. But the lines wrapping his hips weren't hidden. She knew they followed his Adonis belt, flowing directly toward his pelvis...

Mina curled her hand into a fist, battling the urge to reach out and trail her fingers over those markings. To trace their path down, down, down, across his hips, right to his—

She inhaled unsteadily and pressed her thighs together as arousal pulsed low in her belly.

"Could I, uh...take a shower?" she asked, a little breathlessly.

He pointed toward the entryway beside the stairs. "Just in there."

Mina couldn't escape fast enough.

SIXTEEN

MINA STEPPED INTO THE SHOWER. The hot water felt so good against her chilled flesh, which prickled in goosebumps. She caught the water in her cupped hands, letting the overflow cascade down her breasts and belly to splash on the stone floor.

You weren't so cold while you were ogling a nearly naked alien.

No, she hadn't been. She'd been positively burning up. She still was. Mina had never really had much of an opinion when it came to tattoos, but seeing those black markings on Sevik, so stark against his white skin...

Mina wanted to not only run her hands over them, but her tongue.

"Stop it," she whispered, closing her eyes.

But the words were useless. She couldn't stop thinking about him. Couldn't stop thinking about his hands on her body, about his mouth and tongue between her thighs as he made her come again and again. Except now, she wasn't picturing the dark-haired man she'd known as Viktor. It was the white-haired alien, Sevik, keeping her thighs spread with those clawed hands as his long black tongue licked and thrust into her pussy.

"Oh God..." Mina groaned, pressing one hand against the cold tile wall and flattening the other over her lower belly. Even though he wasn't in the room, she could smell him. It was as though his scent had suffused her being; it lingered around her, upon her, a relentless reminder, an unending temptation.

Her sex was achy, hollow, desperate for more of his touch. For him to take her, to—

To fuck her.

Mina tipped her head forward, opened her eyes, and stared down at the floor. Water fell over her hair.

Despite all she'd learned, she wanted him. Wanted him even more than before. Everything inside Mina yearned for him.

Did...did that make her a horrible person?

"No," she whispered.

Was she simply desperate for companionship, for a scrap of kindness? So desperate that she'd throw morals to the wind and fuck a man—an alien—who'd killed and tortured people for a living?

No. It wasn't fair to Sevik to view him that way...and it wasn't fair to view herself that way either.

It didn't matter that he was an alien, didn't matter that he had a dark, violent past. Sevik had shown her a side of himself capable of compassion and thoughtfulness. A side with more humanity than many of the humans she'd known.

And she still wanted him.

Mina smiled. This revelation didn't change a damn thing.

She was going to have him.

Straightening, she plucked up a bottle of bodywash, opened it, and gave it a sniff. The fragrance was spicy and earthy, exactly what she'd expect from a man's bath product, but it was neither as prominent nor as alluring as Sevik's natural scent.

She scrubbed her body and gently washed the dried blood away from her neck. The cuts were tiny, but the skin around them was tender, having likely bruised. After she washed her hair and rinsed off, she turned off the water and grabbed the towel hanging outside the stall. It didn't take long for the freezing air to chase away the steam's warmth. Chills ran through her as she briskly dried herself.

Wrapping the towel around herself, she stepped out of the shower.

At the sink, Mina cleared some of the fog from the mirror and examined the marks on her neck. Yep, there were definitely bruises forming. She leaned forward and lightly touched them. Oddly—or maybe disturbingly—she *liked* them.

"What is wrong with me?" she muttered.

Okay, so maybe the way she'd received those marks had been terrifying. But under different circumstances, were Sevik to wrap his hand around her throat, pin her down, and viciously thrust into her body...

Mina gripped the sink as her core clenched in need.

Yes! Yes, I want that.

She wanted him to shed his restraints. To lose control, to free himself, to show her the beast he'd claimed to be. To...*rut* her.

Get a hold of yourself, Mina. You're a virgin. Maybe take it slow the first time...

Mina drew in a slow, deep breath, and released it in a soft chuckle as she shook her head. "This is years of abstinence catching up to me all at once."

She picked up Sevik's brush and combed out her hair. Without her usual haircare products, her curls would dry frizzy, but there was nothing she could do about that now. When she finished with her hair, she squeezed some toothpaste onto her finger and scrubbed her teeth as best she could, grateful to at least rid her mouth of the nasty combination of morning breath and alcohol aftertaste.

"Now to find my alien."

Clutching the top of the towel where she'd tucked it in, Mina opened the bathroom door and stepped out. The familiar, comforting scent of burning wood and the soothing crackling of a fire greeted her. The light from the fireplace cast a gentle orange glow over the living room.

The empty living room.

Where was he?

"Sevik?" Mina called.

She heard a whisper of movement from the kitchen—Sevik's steps. He emerged through the doorway, scrubbing a towel over his damp hair. Droplets of water glistened on his chest and shoulders, and her eyes followed the path of one as it slid down his abdomen. He must've washed up at the sink while she'd showered.

Sevik looked up at her and froze. His gaze flicked down to her towel, and his pupils expanded, their darkness nearly eclipsing the white of his irises. "Mina, what are you doing?"

She shuffled her feet. "I...would think it was obvious. I was looking for you."

He clenched his jaw, and tension sharpened the definition of his muscles as he draped his towel over his shoulder. "Get dressed."

Mina shook her head. "No."

"Mina..."

There was warning in his tone, and a hint of anger, but it was colored by desperation. By feral want. He was on the verge of losing control, and that was exactly what she wanted. She just needed to push him a little more.

Keeping her eyes locked with his, Mina untucked her towel, letting it fall to pool on the floor around her feet.

Sevik's lips peeled back, baring his fangs. It was her only warning before he threw his towel down and stalked toward her. The distance between them vanished in an instant, and his hand was suddenly around her throat, pushing her back against the wall, pinning her there. He slammed his other hand on the wall above her head. Though he kept his body angled away from hers, heat emanated from him.

"Do not fuck with me, female," he grated through his teeth. His blazing eyes, almost entirely black, held her just as firmly as his hand. "I'm a criminal. A killer. Remorseless, merciless."

Mina placed her hands upon his chest; his heart hammered against her palms.

"I'm not afraid of you, Sevik."

"You should be."

She held his gaze. With one squeeze, with one slash of those wicked claws, he could end her. But she knew he wouldn't.

Sevik leaned closer, lowering his face until their mouths were a hair's breadth apart. He was all she could see, feel, smell.

"Once I take you, Mina, there is no going back. I will keep you. You'll be *mine*."

Desire, restless and ravenous, unfurled inside her. Her core was aching, eager, needy. She wanted this. She wanted him.

She smoothed her hands up his chest until they rested upon his shoulders. "I'm already yours."

"Mina..." he growled, and his fingers tensed, pressing those claws against her skin. His eyes burned, dark and forbidding.

Then he slanted his mouth over hers, claiming her lips, claiming her breath, claiming her.

Mina parted her lips, succumbing to the savagery of his kiss and returning it in kind. That inferno of desire roared to life within her, blasting through her in a fiery wave, incinerating every thought except for one.

She needed more, needed to be closer, needed to feel him against her, around her, *inside* her.

"Sevik," she rasped against his mouth.

As though he'd heard her thoughts, he dropped his hands to her ass and lifted her. Mina's arms and legs instinctively wound around him as he turned and strode toward the stairs.

SEVENTEEN

MINA MOANED against Sevik's mouth as he raced up to his bedroom. Her hard nipples rubbed against his chest, and her slick pussy ground against his lower abdomen with every step. He gripped her ass tighter, pricking her skin with his claws. Those flickers of pain only heightened the pleasure building within her.

His delicious, spicy scent filled the air. She tasted it with every stroke of his tongue. It was intoxicating, potent, addictive. And she wanted more, more, more.

Except Sevik broke the kiss, and Mina's world pitched as he laid her atop the bed. He came down over her, his hands planted on either side of her head, his body cradled between her thighs. His long hair fell like a white curtain around them. It blocked out the rest of the world, creating an intimate space just for them. His ethereal, glowing eyes flashed with a predatory glint as he stared down at her. Their passionate intensity made her heart race.

"Mine," he growled before his head descended to her neck.

He caressed her there with his lips, teased her with his tongue, grazed her flesh with his fangs.

Mina gasped and thrust her fingers into his hair, closing her eyes and tilting her head to give him more access. Shivers of delight whispered through her. His tongue swiped across her pulse, once, twice, and then he sucked her skin in a way that left her shaking.

"Sevik..." Mina clutched his hair as slick pooled in her core.

He only sucked harder. She knew he'd leave a mark there, and she didn't care. She wanted it.

When he finally released her, he flicked his tongue over the sensitive, cooling spot before moving down her body, trailing kisses along her collarbone and chest as he made his way toward one of her breasts. She was burning up from the inside, had been for so, so long, and every touch of his mouth branded her, leaving a searing path.

"I love the little sounds you make," he rumbled, kissing the small mound of her breast. "Every breathy sigh"—he bit her nipple, causing Mina to jolt—"every whimper."

After soothing her nipple with his tongue, he took it into his mouth, lifted a hand to cup her other breast, and kneaded her flesh. He caressed the soft mound in big strokes, pinching the hard peak, tugging and twisting. Every pull was like a direct link to her clit. Mina arched her back, tightening her legs around his sides.

"Oh God," she breathed, opening her eyes to look at him. "Sevik... I... I need you."

He grinned. "Ah, *val'syra*. Soon."

Sevik released her breast and skimmed his claws down her belly. Her skin prickled with goosebumps as the sharp points rasped over it. "I love how your body reacts to my every touch."

He moved his fingers farther down, brushing them through the dark curls on her mons, and finally, *finally* slipped them between her thighs and through the slick gathered there.

Sevik groaned, spreading her arousal as he traced her sex. "And I love how fucking wet you are for me. So fucking needy."

Those fingers dragged up to her clit. Pleasure zipped through Mina, and she gasped, bucking her hips.

Sevik chuckled. "But this convenient little thing, your *clit*... I think I love this most of all."

Two of his fingers parted, pressing down on either side of the nub. She watched him, breath short, brows drawn.

"Your pleasure, at my fingertips. At my whim." His fingers circled her clit and teased it, building the sensations with torturous, deliberate slowness. "A little push"—the tip of his finger flicked across the bud, exerting just a tiny bit of pressure—"and you'll come undone for me."

Mina cried out, pressing her toes into the bedding as her pussy clenched. But there was nothing for it to grip, nothing to fill her, just this vast emptiness that only left her wanting.

Sevik didn't stop. He lavished her clit with leisurely strokes, his eyes intent upon not her pussy, but her face. And Mina couldn't look away from him. As much as her lashes wanted to drift closed, she couldn't look away.

Soon, she was writhing beneath him, clutching the bedding, and wantonly undulating against his hand. Her breath came in short, shallow pants and her body trembled as he edged her closer and closer to that peak. Slick dripped down her ass, and perspiration coated her heated skin. Her clit thrummed.

She was right there. *Right there.*

"Sevik," she begged, voice cracking. "Please."

He hummed, but didn't quicken his touch. "*Zekt'al*, you're so fucking beautiful. That fire in your eyes, the pink on your cheeks, those little tits bouncing. And all fucking mine. You want to come, *val'syra?* Need to?"

"Yes," Mina whimpered. "I want to come. Please make me come."

The pleasure inside her was ready to burst, coiled so tight it hurt. With one hand, she reached down to touch herself, seeking relief.

He abruptly withdrew his fingers from her pussy and caught her wrist in a viselike grip. "No."

"No, no, no!" Mina sobbed, pelvis rolling, clit pulsing, needing his touch. "Don't stop!"

"Your release is *mine.*" Sevik tossed her hand aside and eased farther down her body. "And it will be on my tongue."

Grasping her thighs, he shoved them wide open, dropped his face to her sex, and thrust his tongue deep inside her pussy.

Mina cried out, hands flying out to grasp his horns. His long, thick tongue filled her. She felt it twisting as he thrust it in and out in short strokes. When it curled against her G-spot, she let out a deep moan, tilted her pelvis up, and pulled his head down. The vibration from his hungry growl only heightened her pleasure.

She moved against him without inhibition, using his tongue like a cock, fucking his face as much as the hands imprisoning her thighs allowed. All that mattered was one thing, one single thing—an end to this torment. The release she so desperately needed.

She was close. So—

Sevik suddenly withdrew his tongue, latched his mouth onto her clit, and sucked.

"Oh fuck!" Mina rasped as her body seized with rapture so powerful that it stole her breath. Her back bowed, and her eyes rolled back before she squeezed them shut.

Sevik just kept on sucking, and sucking, and sucking, lashing her clit with his tongue.

Her entire body erupted with sensation. Mina gripped his horns harder and spread her legs wider. A ragged cry tore from her throat, and liquid heat sprayed from her as a tidal wave of pleasure crashed through her.

Releasing her clit, Sevik returned his mouth to her entrance. He slipped his tongue deep inside her contracting pussy before withdrawing it again and dragging it along her sex from bottom to top.

A low growl rumbled from him. "You taste so fucking good, *val'syra.*"

He sucked and lapped her folds as Mina trembled in the aftermath of her orgasm. Each time he grazed her clit, she whimpered and bucked against his face, making him chuckle.

"I will never tire of this," he said, pressing a chaste kiss to her clit. He pressed another to the inside of her right thigh, followed by one more on her left, stroking her legs with his thumbs. "You're so fucking beautiful."

Chest rising and falling with heavy breaths, Mina let her hands fall from his horns and looked down at Sevik. He stared at her with reverence in his otherworldly eyes as he rose onto his knees. But there was something more in them, amplified by the pools of infinite blackness rimmed in thin slivers of white that were his pupils. Something darker, more primal, more thrilling.

Possessiveness.

Sevik was looking at Mina like she was the only thing he'd ever wanted in all the universe, and he was finally, after a lifetime of waiting, about to take her. About to take what had been his all along.

His tongue slipped out to lick her essence from his lips. With that look in his eyes, she felt like prey, and the predator had just tasted her blood.

She knew he wouldn't stop until he'd had more.

Muscles flexed beneath Sevik's pale skin as he ran his hands down to the waistband of his sweatpants. The fabric stretched over the huge bulge at his groin was damp, but it only hinted at what was hidden beneath.

She bit her lip. Anticipation stilled her heart and trapped her breath in her lungs as she watched.

He pushed his pants and underwear down.

The air rushed from her in a *whoosh*.

Extruding from a vertical slit at his pelvis was not one, but *two* cocks.

They were long and thick, as black as his markings, with one positioned below the other. Ridges ran along the tops and bottoms of the thick shafts, and their heads narrowed to pointed tips. They glistened with their own secretions—were near dripping.

Mina's wide eyes shot to his as she propped herself onto her elbows. "You have two?"

Sevik smirked, kicking off his clothing. "The better to pleasure you with."

"But...but... How do you..."

Alien. Sevik was an *alien*. Did she really think that stopped at horns, claws, and fangs?

Holy shit, my pussy did not just clench at the thought of taking both his cocks inside me.

But it had. It *so* had.

"How?" He curled his fingers around the bases of both shafts, separating them slightly. They twitched. "I read the book you gave me, Mina. You know exactly how."

She stared at his cocks, transfixed, as his hand stroked up and down. White seed seeped from their tips.

Mina licked her lips. What would he taste like?

His other hand moved to her ass, and the pad of his thumb brushed across her rosette, making her start with a gasp.

"That book was a gift in many ways, *val'syra*. There are so many things I can do to you." His other fingers curled around her ass cheek, and his claws grazed her skin. "So many ways to pleasure you."

He leaned down, his voice falling into a husky rasp. "And I will claim every part of you, Mina. Every. Fucking. Part."

Oh God. Oh God. Oh God.

Mina's heart raced. The intensity of his stare, the promise in his words...

He smiled roguishly as he teased her rosette. "Even here."

His thumb dipped, applying enough pressure to breach her hole. Mina's breath hitched, and everything inside her clenched. The sensation was foreign, strange, but it didn't hurt.

"Yes," she whispered, unable to look away from him.

He pulled his thumb away. "But not yet."

Sevik moved over her, once more nestling between her thighs, and Mina lay back with her hands on his chest. His heart thumped against her palms.

Bracing one hand atop the bed, he used the other to guide the tip of his lower cock toward her pussy. He nudged the head into her as the underside of his upper shaft rested over her clit.

A soft sound escaped her throat. Sevik's cocks radiated heat, and it was all she could do not to squirm in anticipation.

"I've wanted you for so long, Mina. Waited too long. But now..." He curled his lips into a fanged grin that poured fire into Mina's core. "Now you're all fucking mine, *val'syra*."

Sevik pressed into her slowly, easing back only to push

deeper. Mina's lips parted with a shuddering inhalation as his girth stretched her wider and wider. The sting was nothing compared to the pleasure wrought by his fullness.

He continued his slow, deliberate entry, his bared fangs and drawn brow belying the control he demonstrated in his movements. And he made her feel *everything*—the slickness of the natural lubrication coating his cock, the stretch, the burn. Ridge after thickening ridge. With every shallow pump, with every flex of his hips, the ridges on his upper cock stroked her clit, sending little bursts of pleasure through her.

Mina curled her fingers against his chest and moaned.

"You're so tight," Sevik growled. "So fucking tight."

She knew he was holding back. Knew he was taking it slow for her. But she'd waited too long for this, too long for him. She wanted him inside her, filling her, pounding into her. She wanted him at his most primal, wanted him wild. Wanted the beast.

And she wanted him now.

Wrapping her legs around his hips, Mina cradled his face between her hands and stared into his eyes. "Fuck me, Sevik."

Then she pulled his head down and captured his mouth with a searing kiss.

EIGHTEEN

Sevik stilled his hips. Everything inside him froze for a heartbeat.

Fuck Me, Sevik.

He'd intended to go slow with Mina's untried body, to ease her into this. To avoid harming her. But her slick heat, her tight cunt, and her tempting scent compelled him. It had taken everything within him to not succumb to instinct and plunge deep into her body.

But Mina's words and her soft mouth moving against his, caressing, nipping, sucking, shattered whatever good intentions he might've had.

Need surged within him, and he returned the kiss, crushing his mouth to hers.

She wrapped her arms around his neck, pulling him closer. Those delectable nipples grazed his chest as she arched into him, and Sevik groaned when her cunt clenched around his lower shaft, adding to the already unbearable pressure within it. His upper shaft was tortured by extremes—the heat of her flesh below, the comparatively frigid air above.

Fuck her. Claim her.

His fingers bent, burying his claws in the bedding.

A year. A single human year. That was how long he'd wanted her, how long he'd craved her, how long he'd denied himself. It had felt like an eternity.

No more denial, no more restraint. With Mina, he didn't need to hide, didn't have to hold back. She wanted *him.*

He slid his hand up her body—over her belly, between her breasts, along her slender neck—and cradled the underside of her jaw. When he broke their kiss by lifting his head, she attempted to follow, but he held her down and met her lustful, half-lidded gaze.

"*Ornyr valaas duun,* you're so fucking beautiful." He trailed a claw across her cheek and slid his cock back, dragging it along her inner walls. He barely suppressed a shudder at the pleasure. "Is this what you want, female?"

Before she could answer, Sevik slammed his hips forward, burying his cock deep in her heat.

Mina gasped, head falling back and legs flexing around his hips. Her blunt nails dug into the backs of his shoulders.

Sevik snarled, battling to hold himself up against the wave of bliss sweeping through him. She was so hot, so wet, so tight, so *perfect.* She enveloped his entire length, fitting so snugly that he could feel the rapid rhythm of her pulse from within.

The pressure in him was near to bursting. His cocks twitched, seeping cum, and he gritted his teeth as his whole body tensed. He refused to spill his seed already. He planned to make this last, to revel in her.

His mate.

His Mina.

"You feel it, *val'syra?* How we fit?" He lowered his forehead to hers. "You were made for me. To be mine."

"Yes," she whispered, tangling her fingers in his hair. "I am yours."

He pulled back again. Her inner muscles squeezed his shaft, fighting his withdrawal, desperately trying to draw him back in. Sevik grinned and obliged. He drove into her again, hard enough to jolt Mina backward and coax another breathy sound from her.

Pleasure spiraled through him, coiling low in his belly, where it built that fire. Exhaling heavily, he drew his hips back slowly and hammered into her, over and over. Her body pulled him deeper and deeper—but never deep enough.

Mina's whimpers and moans matched the deliberate pace of his thrusts. Combined with his ragged breaths and the wet sounds of their bodies sliding together, coming together, *fucking*, they became music unlike any he'd ever heard. Music that could only have been created by Sevik and Mina.

Her brow was drawn, and her brown eyes remained locked with his. He felt her heartbeat against his fingers, a delicate flutter; a life so fragile, so easily taken, so precious.

His to protect.

Sevik brushed his lips over hers. "You feel so good. So fucking good, Mina."

She tipped her face toward his, but he held her trapped as he slammed into her welcoming body again and again.

"Sevik," Mina rasped. "More."

"You want more?"

"Yes."

"Do you want my mouth?" Sevik pressed kisses to her forehead, her nose, the corners of her lips, and finally, crushed his mouth over hers in a quick, harsh kiss.

"My tongue?" He flicked it over her kiss-swollen lips. "My cocks?" Drawing back his hips, he drove into her even harder, forcing a cry from her throat.

Panting, Mina slipped a hand between their bodies. "I want" —she curled her fingers around his upper cock and squeezed— "everything."

"Fuck," he growled, releasing her neck to plant his other arm on the bed as a shudder blasted through him. His hips bucked, disrupting his rhythm, forcing her hand to pump along his shaft.

Sevik gritted his teeth. "You want everything, *val'syra?*"

Her fingers glided along his cock, exploring him, and when her thumb swiped over the slit at its tip—through the seed gathered there—he nearly came right then.

"I want you." She spread her thighs farther and undulated her hips. "Don't hold back, Sevik. I want you as you are."

Those words pierced Sevik to his center. Arousing, commanding, liberating; they sliced through his self-control and left it in tatters, immediately forgotten.

He rose on his knees, dropped both hands to her hips, and angled her pelvis up off the bed. She looked up at him with her cheeks flushed, her lips parted, her eyes gleaming, and her short curls in disarray.

So. Fucking. Beautiful.

"I will give you everything, Mina. But you must give all of yourself to me." Sevik drove his cock into her, pulling her hard toward him at the same instant.

Before she could even catch her breath, he pounded into her again, and again, and again, his pace more frantic with each thrust.

The pleasure surged in him, pushing him ever faster, ever harder, ever deeper, but none of it was enough. He wanted everything too. He would take everything. Would mark her with his scent, his seed, his fangs and claws.

"Yes! I'm yours, Sevik." Mina arched her back, her hands going over her head to grasp the bedding. "Yours! You have all of me."

Her small breasts bounced with his every powerful thrust, and her cunt clenched around his cock, growing wetter as her cries escalated in pitch.

She whispered his name again and again as a plea, a benediction, a cry of pleasure. And the only word that chanted in his mind was *mine*.

Mine.

Mine.

Mine.

With each ragged breath, the pressure in Sevik grew stronger, coalescing in his cocks. Every slide of flesh on flesh, every twitch of muscle and flicker of their pulses, everything propelled him closer to the peak, closer to climax.

His gaze shifted to the flawless skin where Mina's neck met

her shoulder. His fangs itched, and heat thrummed in his venom glands. Instinct roared inside him. He couldn't ignore it, didn't want to.

"Mine," Sevik snarled as he dropped over her with hands braced on the bed and sank his fangs into that sweet, soft flesh.

Mina gasped, throwing her arms around his neck and stiffening beneath him. Her fingers gripped his hair. She screamed, and her cunt convulsed, clenching his cock, as a gush of liquid heat flooded her.

The feel of her pussy clamping down on him was too much. Everything in Sevik seized for an instant, and the pressure became so great that it would tear him apart, unmake him. Then ecstasy surged through him, and seed erupted from both cocks. He growled against her skin, forcing his hips to keep moving, keep pumping, even as mating venom flowed into her through his fangs.

With Mina's sweet, passionate cries in his ear, Sevik finally buried himself deep and stayed there, reveling in the feel of his mate's lovely body coming undone around him.

Only when she began to settle did he ease his jaw and withdraw his fangs. He could detect a faint metallic tang through the sweetness of the mating venom—Mina's blood. Gently, he licked the wounds, which had already stopped bleeding thanks to the venom.

Sevik lifted his head and settled his forehead against hers. Their ragged breaths mingled as he laid atop her, panting, the ache of exertion only making the lingering pulses of pleasure all the more enjoyable.

"Sevik," Mina whispered, her voice so soft, so reverent.

Had anyone ever said his name that way? Had anyone ever infused it with such care, such meaning, such...adoration? Just those two syllables from her lips were enough to rekindle the fire in him. He grinded his hips against hers, pushing himself deeper still and drawing another breathy moan from her.

"Mina," he rumbled.

He didn't want to leave the heat of her body, the welcoming cradle of her thighs, the caress of her breath. Right here, right now, everything was blissful, perfect. Mina's delicious fragrance lingered in his nose, combined with the scent of their mating. Every inhalation was flavored by it, and he would never tire of the smell. Chest to chest, he could feel her heart pounding, matching the pace of his own. Their bodies simply fit. Being here with her, inside her, it felt like...

Home.

Mina felt like home.

And that was an unfamiliar feeling for Sevik. He'd lived in several places on Vabos, but had any of them ever been home to him? There'd never been a time in his life, not even as a youngling, when he'd been able to let his guard down. There'd never been a place where he could just...be.

He'd already shared more with Mina than he had with anyone, and he longed to share more still. To share everything.

That was strange too. Wanting to own everything was normal, but wanting to give everything? The concept was almost alien to him.

Yet for her...

A pang of protectiveness pierced his heart, but something gentle, warm, and pure was at its core. Mina was undeniably his. But at the same time...he'd become hers.

This was all so new, so fresh, so jarring and exciting. But it was also delicate. The things he'd endured, the injuries he'd survived, the danger that had defined his life, it was too much for his Mina. She deserved better.

And he would do everything in his power to shield her from pain. If anyone so much as thought about doing her harm, he would eviscerate them. He would fill this world's expansive oceans with blood before he let her suffer so much as a scratch.

Mina's gentle fingers combed through his hair, trailed over his horns, and traced his ears to their tips. She raised her knees, which only allowed him to sink deeper into her, and hummed contently.

"I don't want this to end," she said, wrapping her arms and legs around him again.

Sevik groaned, nearly losing himself in her hot, welcoming embrace.

"It doesn't have to." He pressed his lips to hers. This time, the kiss lacked urgency. He didn't ravage her mouth—he coaxed and caressed, savoring her feel, her taste, thrilling in the way her body shivered with desire and her cunt clenched his cock with each stroke of his tongue.

Sevik pumped his hips slowly, shallowly, keeping himself buried inside her. Her pussy was slick with their combined essences, and fuck, she felt blissful. His upper cock, pinned between their bodies, glided over her clit and through the mess he'd made on her belly. Mina tangled her fingers in his hair and held him close as she rolled her hips in time with his.

He swallowed her breathy pants and little moans, answering them with his own grunts and growls as heat and ecstasy built in him again, layer upon layer. His instinct demanded he move faster, harder, but it wasn't about instinct now. It was about Sevik and Mina. About this...foreign closeness. This intimacy that would never have been possible in his old life, that he would've avoided at all costs.

Mina broke their kiss when her breath quickened and her thighs began to quiver. But he chased her mouth with his own, unwilling to relinquish her lips. She grasped his back and shoulders, clawing at him with her blunt nails, as he continued pumping into her body and grinding against her clit. Each scratch blazed through him, stoking the fire in his core.

And when she shattered, he took her cries of pleasure into himself and fell apart along with her. As their bodies quaked, he wrapped an arm around her, holding her as close as was physically possible.

His mate.

His.

Mine.

Only after their breathing had calmed and their bodies had settled did Sevik raise his head and look down at her. Her cheeks were flushed, her lips red from his kisses, her hair damp with sweat, and her eyes luminous.

She was radiant.

Breaking her hold on him, he pushed himself up onto his knees to gaze upon her. His eyes roved from her lovely face down her elegant neck, pausing on the mark he'd left. His mark. The bite wounds had scabbed over, and soon, only scars would remain. He grinned with possessive satisfaction.

Sevik's eyes dipped lower, past her collarbone and over the small mounds of her breasts, to her belly, where his seed glistened on her skin.

Something primal stirred within him. A need to have her covered in his scent, covered in him. He pressed his palm over the cum and rubbed it into her skin, spreading it, wanting her coated in it. Wanting it to seep into her. Every male who came close to Mina would smell nothing but Sevik, and they would know his claim upon her.

"Sevik..." Mina said, drawing his attention to the bashful expression on her face. "What are you doing?"

He smoothed his hand higher. Cupping Mina's breast, he squeezed the soft flesh and pinched her nipple, eliciting a gasp from her. "Marking what is mine."

She gave him a cheeky grin. "Am I yours?"

Sevik bared his fangs with a snarl as he leaned over her, capturing her jaw. "You made your choice." He stroked her bottom lip with the seed covered fingers of his other hand. "You belong to me, *val'syra*."

Her eyes flared as he pushed two of his fingers past her lips. With a delighted moan, Mina closed her mouth around them, licking his claws and sucking his fingers clean. He groaned and pumped them in and out of her hot mouth.

Soon, he vowed. Soon, he would have her drink from him, and she'd swallow every drop and more.

Sevik withdrew his fingers and planted that hand on the bed, bending lower until he was all she could see. "I will not let you go, Mina. You are *mine*."

He slammed his mouth over hers, and he didn't hold back the savagery of that kiss. It was meant to bruise. He would mark her in any way he could so everyone knew—especially Mina—that she was his.

She succumbed to his forceful kiss, opening to him. He tasted himself on her lips, and that only intensified his need to claim her in every way.

He broke the punishing kiss with a growl. Mina gasped and opened her eyes. Shoulders heaving with his ragged breaths, Sevik grasped her hair close to her scalp and tipped her head back, forcing her to keep her eyes locked with this. Her palms flattened against his chest, but she didn't push him away.

"Say it," he demanded.

"I'm yours," she rasped.

"Again." Sevik thrust hard into her body, making her jolt and cry out. "Louder."

"Yours!" Mina cradled his jaw and brushed her thumbs over his cheeks. "I'm yours, Sevik."

The tenderness in her deep, dark eyes and the gentleness of her touch combined with the vehemence and passion of her words to make Sevik's heart constrict. It was the sweetest, warmest, most maddening ache, unlike anything he'd ever experienced. And he was utterly undone.

Since Brekker's betrayal, the whole universe had been askew. Nothing had been as it should have, and though he'd had direction, Sevik had been lost. But she made everything right, put everything back into place.

Mina was his. All was as it should've been.

"Fucking mine," he grated, driving into her again and again, using her, claiming what was his, until rapture once more clutched at his entire being.

Sevik held himself over Mina, teeth bared, cocks twitching, as the pleasure slowly ebbed. His heart thundered inside his chest. With each beat, that word echoed in his mind.

Mine.

Mine.

Mine.

She'd told him to fuck her. He'd fucked a lot of females in a lot of ways, but this... This had been something else entirely. Though he'd taken possession of her body, she'd taken possession of something more—part of him that he'd never known existed, a part that she'd awakened.

Or maybe it hadn't existed at all before Mina.

Without a doubt, Sevik knew he wouldn't hesitate to claw his own heart out of his chest if it was necessary to keep her safe. There'd been very few people in his life for whom he had killed to protect.

Mina was the first person he would've died to protect.

That was...terrifying.

Sevik couldn't remember a time when he'd feared his own death. He'd been bold, had taken risks others wouldn't have taken, had seized what he'd wanted for himself. But the thought of Mina's death was more than he could bear. Nothing was more frightening—not even his mother's death when he was a youngling.

That made Mina a weakness. His weakness. A vulnerability to be exploited by his enemies, because he valued her above all else. Money, weapons, vehicles, residences; all those material things could be replaced. But there was only one Mina.

And Sevik would protect her at all costs.

Those heavy thoughts dulled the last ripples of pleasure in him. Though still reluctant to do so, he finally withdrew from his mate. She made a soft sound of disappointment as her hands fell away from his face. Between that sound and the chill of the open air on his shaft, it was a struggle for him not to push his cock right back into her heat. To push *both* of his cocks into her.

Leaning back, he grasped her knees, spread her thighs wide, and lowered his gaze to her pretty pink slit. The swollen folds glistened with her slick and his seed, which was seeping from her. Instinct stirred in him again; he didn't resist.

Sevik dropped his hand to her cunt, dipped his thumb low,

and gathered his seed. He swept it up and pressed it into her entrance, returning his cum to where it belonged.

Inside her.

Mina's breath hitched, and her pussy clenched. Sevik looked up at her. She remained still, hands resting on either side of her head, watching him curiously with her bottom lip caught between her teeth. Her gaze flicked down to his hand.

He held his thumb there, allowing nothing else to escape, and only then did he realize what he was doing. Only then did he realize why he was doing it.

An image flashed in his mind—Mina, her belly round with his youngling.

A low growl rumbled from deep within Sevik, and the sweet ache of his venom rekindled in his fangs. He moved his hands to her waist, splaying his fingers over her flat stomach and through his seed.

He was korasi; she was human. The likelihood that she could bear his offspring was incredibly low. Yet now that the thought was there, it wouldn't leave. What would it be like to watch her belly swell with their growing child, to watch new life take shape within her? Would it make her even more vibrant than she already was?

It didn't matter if they were compatible or not. He would plant his seed in her no matter how many times it took. He would fill her cunt again and again, would ensure she was flooded with his seed, with him.

And what danger would I bring upon that youngling?

Sevik clenched his jaw, and his muscles tensed. His return to Vabos would be a bloody, violent affair, and it would end with either himself or Brekker dead. Even if he succeeded and had his revenge, even if he reclaimed his empire, what life could he provide for a mate and child? There'd always be danger. There'd always be threats and attempts upon their lives.

It would certainly be more comfortable than the childhood he'd had, but no less dangerous for the comfort. Going back to

Vabos with his mate and youngling would be no better than bringing them into a den of wild, ravenous beasts.

His brow knitted.

And if I don't return to Vabos?

The thought gave him pause.

His life, his world—even the organization he'd worked so hard to build—seethed with brutality and corruption. The people were ruthless, cold, calculating. They did whatever it took to survive. Did he truly want to return to that?

Did he want to bring his mate, his sweet, soft, kind-hearted Mina, into that world?

Earth wasn't free of struggle, wasn't free of suffering and pain, but what he'd seen here was nothing compared to his home world. What if...

What if he stayed on Earth?

This part of it, at least... This little piece of Earth was quiet. Peaceful. Removed from the hardships he'd endured throughout his life.

Sevik could choose to stay here. This could be a chance to start a new life, one without violence and betrayal. This was a place where he and Mina could be safe. Where they could be...happy.

All this time, he'd been planning revenge against Brekker. He'd intended to return to Vabos and take back what belonged to him.

But what exactly would he be reclaiming? Power, wealth, influence? Luxury and excess? Anything he'd wanted had been his. And ultimately, that life had been...empty.

All those things had formed the walls of his fortress, a shell, hollow and cold and lonely. They'd kept him from making honest, meaningful connections with anyone, from truly knowing anyone. From truly being known by anyone. Despite his success, despite his riches, he'd merely been surviving. He'd been fulfilling an instinctual drive to hoard more than his rivals, to possess everything so he wouldn't have to worry about how he'd get his next meal, about where he'd sleep at night.

But surviving and living were two very different things. Though he'd survived for a long, long time...did he even know how to live?

What did he know about making a life on this planet, with a mate? About making a human happy, making her feel cared for and safe? What did he know about any of this?

Mina settled her hands over his.

Sevik looked up and met her concerned gaze.

"Are you okay?" she asked softly.

The corners of his mouth curled into a smile—the sort of smile he'd give to no one but her—as he turned his hands over to take hold of hers. "Better than ever, *val'syra*."

Mina smiled wide. "I could say the same. That was, well... That was the best sex of my life."

He arched a brow. "Didn't you say you've never had sex before?"

She chuckled. "Yep. Doesn't make me wrong."

Sevik's expression sobered. "Best of my life too."

"Oh." Her cheeks pinkened as she brushed her thumbs over his hand. "We could...do it again?"

Sevik's cocks were already throbbing with need as he grasped her hips, ready to flip her over and prepare his little mate to take both his shafts from behind. To fill her completely.

Mina's stomach made a pathetic little rumble.

Brows falling, he stared at her stomach before looking at her questioningly.

She smiled sheepishly. "Or, uh, maybe we should eat? Actually, I could really go for a shower first. You kind of..." Clearing her throat, she gestured to her belly, where his seed was drying.

He laughed. Though he was loath to have his seed cleaned from her skin, her comfort was more important. And no matter how much she washed herself, Sevik's scent—his *true* scent— would never leave her. "We will shower first. Then I will feed my female."

NINETEEN

The sound of sizzling meat, paired with the aroma of pan-fried chicken, almost made Mina's mouth water. She hadn't felt hungry until that unfortunately timed growl from her stomach, which had informed her that she was, in fact, famished. But she couldn't decide what was more tempting—the chicken or the man cooking it.

Definitely the man.

Or rather...the alien.

Mina sat at the dining table, wearing clothing Sevik had lent her, all of it too big for her—a button-down flannel shirt, boxer-briefs, and socks. She had her chin propped on one hand, with the other curled around the glass of water he'd set in before her with a single-word command—*drink*. Apparently, she wasn't very good at following orders, because she'd only taken a couple sips before she'd forgotten the water and turned all her attention to him.

He stood in front of the stove. His long, damp hair was pulled up into a messy bun atop his head, and his sweatpants were slung low on his hips. The muscles of his shoulders and back flexed with every movement. Mina dragged her gaze along the black markings on his spine, following them down to the spot where they flared out to enwrap his waist, down to where they disappeared under his pants.

A slow smile spread across her lips. She'd seen his tattoos in their entirety while she and Sevik had showered. They dipped into the cleft of his ass.

If only it was her tongue instead of her eyes tracing those markings right now.

But Sevik had insisted upon tending to her needs first. His struggle had been clear since they'd left the bedroom—he'd been battling lust. She'd seen his pupils dilating and shrinking, his nostrils flaring, had seen his muscles flex with hard-won restraint and his fangs bared in silent snarls.

Their shower had been torture.

Not just for him, but for Mina.

Sevik had bathed her himself. His big hands, the hands of a fighter, a killer, had almost been trembling as he cleaned her, yet he'd done so with a gentleness she'd never thought possible. He'd washed her hair, massaged her scalp, and then had caressed her body with soapy hands, cupping her breasts and tenderly cleaning between her thighs. Mina had leaned back against him with her eyes closed as soft sighs escaped her.

He'd done nothing more than bathe her, but it had been a seduction all on its own, leaving her quivering with need when he finished.

And then he'd washed himself. Mina had stood there under the hot water, watching him, and he'd held her gaze as he'd stroked his hand along his erect cocks.

Two cocks.

She still couldn't get over the fact that Sevik was an alien... with *two* cocks.

Both her pussy and her ass clenched at the thought.

Mina squirmed on her chair. More and more, she wondered what it would feel like to have both shafts inside her. One had been divine. It had stretched her so deliciously, and she'd felt so full of him. No matter how deep he'd pushed into her, she'd only wanted him deeper, deeper, deeper.

She could only imagine the delicious fullness of having both cocks buried within her, could only imagine the feel of him pushing them deeper, and God, she wanted to feel it now.

What is wrong *with me?*

Sevik had made her come so many times since last night, had fucked her so hard and so sweetly, that her desire should've been sated at least a little. But it wasn't. She still wanted him. She wanted more.

However, her pussy was sore, and she needed a break.

So, Mina was complying—begrudgingly. Not that Sevik was giving her a choice. He'd known from her subtle sounds and winces in the shower that she was in discomfort, and he refused to cause her more.

For now.

Those had been his words.

Mina bit down on her bottom lip and again wriggled upon the chair. Having sex was supposed to curb her arousal, not make it worse. She was turning into a sex fiend.

Not that anything was wrong with that...

This was only the beginning. Sevik had explored her body, and Mina was eager to do some exploring of her own. She wanted to run her fingers over his slit, wanted to coax it open, to wrap her fingers around his cocks and feel their ridges, their slickness. Wanted to get down on her knees and—

Mina sat back, pressing her fists on her lap as she squeezed her thighs together. She barely held in a groan.

Distraction. I need a distraction.

"So...do your tattoos mean anything?" she asked.

Sevik glanced at her over his shoulder. "Tattoos?"

"Those black markings?"

"Ah." He flipped the chicken breasts he was frying, briefly intensifying their sizzling. "They mean I'm korasi."

Mina's brow furrowed. "But wouldn't people know that from looking at you?"

He chuckled and turned to face her, leaning a hand on the counter beside the stove. "All korasi are born with markings.

They're called *lyros*. My mother told me that our people believed the markings predicted one's fate. She always seemed sad when she said it. That's stuck with me, because she didn't show emotion very often."

A sorrowful pang struck Mina's heart. "Why do you think she was sad about it?"

Sevik's eyes dropped, taking on a far-off, wistful gleam. "Can only guess. When I was young, I thought it was because she'd been told that her *lyros* marked her for greatness. For some grand destiny. But she ended up on Vabos, raising two sons alone, struggling through poverty and sickness until she died far too young.

"Maybe she believed that. Our people did, a long, long time ago. But..." His shoulders rose with a deep inhalation that he released as a heavy sigh. "They're just genetics. Hereditary markings shaped by our lineage, a blend of our parents' *lyros*. I think that's why it made her sad. Whenever she saw our markings, she was reminded of the world and people she'd left behind, of whatever had driven her away in the first place. She was reminded of a past she was trying to escape.

"Maybe she thought that pain was her destiny. That it was written on her from the beginning." He lifted his hands, splaying those clawed fingers. "Even as a child, I thought that was bullshit. We make our own fate. Some fucking markings on our skin don't affect that."

It hurt knowing how much Sevik had suffered as a child. To have struggled every day just to survive while also caring for his ailing mother... How could such a life inspire hope?

And she understood it all too well. She'd endured loss, poverty, and bullying through her childhood and into her adult years, though it had been nowhere near as harsh as what Sevik had experienced. There'd been times when she couldn't see any chance of things improving. When she couldn't believe life was anything but suffering.

But as a teenager, she'd discovered romance novels. Those stories helped get Mina through some of those dark times, had provided an escape from the pain, had given her hope when her world was at its bleakest. And they'd made her wonder.

Was there really such a thing as a soul mate? A...fated mate?

How could she not wonder that now, when an alien was standing right in front of her?

"You don't believe in fate?" she asked.

Sevik met her gaze. His expression was hard to read; his mouth was a flat line, his brows low over those ethereal eyes, which were far too piercing to betray what lay behind them. "You do?"

Though his tone hadn't been at all judgmental, her cheeks heated, and she looked down at the table. "I...I want to. I want to believe that there is something out there for each of us, something that is ours from before we even exist." *That there's that one true, destined love for us to claim.* "But if I accept that, then it means..."

"Means that all the pain and suffering is already planned for us too," Sevik said quietly.

Mina offered a shallow nod. How could she not think about her parents? How could she so badly want to believe in fate when it came to love, knowing it meant she'd also have to accept that fate had killed her parents when they should've had decades of life ahead of them?

Knowing it meant that every tragedy, every bit of suffering, was necessary just so a person could meet their fated one.

Tears stung her eyes, and she fought them back.

Distraction queen right here.

The silence in the room was long and thick, broken only by the hissing and spitting of grease in the pan. At the upper edge of her vision, Mina saw Sevik turn back to the stove and tend to the meat, the muscles of his back defined more harshly than before.

"Both things don't have to be true," he said, his voice low, gravelly, strained.

She lifted her eyes to him. "What do you mean?"

He stood with his head slightly bowed and his hands braced to either side of the stove, motionless but for his breathing. Mina's heartbeat marked the passing time. Finally, he turned off the burner and lifted the pan. She watched as he put the fried, breaded chicken breasts onto two plates, which he carried to the table. He placed one before her and the other in front of his chair before sitting down.

Her gaze didn't leave him as he slid the chair in and propped his forearms on the edge of the table.

"I mean..." His eyes searched the tabletop like there were answers written there that only he could see. "I mean that maybe there are moments. Moments that are fated, that we can't escape. But that doesn't mean the time between isn't random. Maybe existence is chaos, but there are moments of order within it. I...don't know how to say it better. I don't usually think about things like this."

"I get it," Mina said softly.

He looked at her. The vulnerability she'd glimpsed in his eyes only a few times was back, warm and gleaming.

"A week ago, I would've thought it was fucking laughable," he said with a dry chuckle. "But looking at you, *val'syra...*" Sevik lifted a hand, tucking a few loose strands of hair back behind his pointed ear. "The chances of us meeting were so small, so fucking unlikely, that betting on it happening would've won me all the money in the universe. Yet here we are. So yeah, it could be chance. But this? Us?"

Sevik shook his head. "You tell me our meeting was fate, and I'll believe it. Because that's how it feels. And I've never felt anything like it before. Not even close."

Mina picked up her fork and smiled as she sliced off a piece of chicken. "Then our meeting was fate." Stabbing the prongs into the small chunk, she brought it to her mouth. "Either that, or I actually hit my head when I fell from that shelf in Cornerstone, and this is my coma-dream about a sexy alien."

He laughed, and his eyes smoldered as he looked at her through those beautiful white lashes. "This is no dream, Mina."

Considering how her pussy currently felt—and the sudden spike of desire piercing her—Mina's body agreed that this was definitely not a dream.

Mina stuffed the chicken into her mouth.

You're not supposed to be thinking about sex!

Then maybe Sevik shouldn't be looking at me with those fuck-me eyes.

As Mina chewed, she watched him pick up his utensils and cut into his chicken. She let her eyes roam over those long, black-tipped, clawed fingers, those defined knuckles, and the tendons on the back of his hand.

He had such sexy hands...

And they'd been all over her body, making her feel the most wondrous things.

Once again, she shifted uncomfortably on her seat, sure that the boxer briefs she wore were embarrassingly wet from her arousal. She'd needed to turn her thoughts away, but she couldn't take her mind off him. Everything was a reminder of him. Even over the aroma of the chicken, she smelled him, like his scent was branded into her senses. And the exquisite soreness of her pussy provided no distraction either; she could almost still feel him inside her.

Picking up the glass of water, she took a long drink.

Her eyes met his over the rim of the glass. The heat in his gaze hadn't faded at all, and it was now paired with a sultry, knowing smirk.

"Such a tempting fragrance," he said.

Something told her he wasn't talking about the chicken.

Those haunting, alien eyes did not release her. "You can't help yourself, can you, Mina?"

Mina's brow pinched as she set her cup down. "Wait. Can you... Can you seriously smell me? From over there? You can smell..." Her eyes widened when she suddenly realized what he meant.

"That's right. *All* of you." He tilted his head to the side. "Nothing can mask your scent from me, *val'syra.*"

Cheeks blazing, Mina hid her face in her hands. "Oh God."

Every time she'd been turned on around him since they'd met, *every time*, he'd known. He'd known!

"That embarrasses you?" he asked.

"You're basically a walking arousal detector," she said into her palms.

He chuckled. "Even if I couldn't smell your arousal, Mina, I'd know. You don't hide it well."

She lowered her hands to look at him, her skin burning all the hotter. "What do you mean?"

His lips stretched into a wide grin. "I knew you wanted to fuck me from the first time we spoke in the store. When you said you don't normally make a habit of falling for men...or was it *onto* men?"

Mina gaped at him. "I...I kind of hoped you would forget that."

Sevik set his utensils down. "When it comes to you, I remember everything. Every glance. Every word. Every touch, scent, and taste. All of it." Reaching across the table, he caught her chin. "You're imprinted upon my very soul, Mina."

Her heart quickened, and her breaths became shallow. There was a pressure in her chest, growing and growing, and all she could do was stare into his eyes as her own stung with a flood of emotion.

This...wasn't an *I love you*. It couldn't have been. It'd only been a week since they'd met, so it wasn't possible...right? Affection, sure, but love?

Yet what he'd said felt like *I love you* and so much more.

Don't read into it too deeply, Mina. They're...they're just words. He wasn't professing love.

But after being alone for so long, after yearning for that connection, for that only-found-in-fiction love, she wanted this to be more. It didn't matter that Sevik was an alien, or what he'd done in his past.

Mina still wanted him.

Sevik searched her gaze. His eyes burned with passion, but there was a graveness in them now, wrapped around that glimmer of vulnerability. She sensed that he wasn't only searching for something in her, but in himself.

The right words? The answer to her unspoken question?

Slowly, he stroked her bottom lip with his thumb. Sevik's eyes dipped, settling upon her mouth, and the heat in them intensified, making his pupils dilate before he dropped his hand and sat back in his chair. Acting as though he hadn't been about to kiss her, Sevik picked up his fork and took a large bite of chicken.

Ooookay then. I guess we're pretending that didn't happen.

Good luck with that, Mina.

She set her utensils back to work on her own food. But as she ate, something niggled at the back of her mind.

You're imprinted upon my very soul, Mina.

Imprinted. Sevik had used that word when he'd talked about Brekker and Enthi, and the way he'd said it just now implied deeper meaning.

"Sevik, what do you mean when you say imprinted?"

He swallowed his mouthful, washed it down with a drink of water from his glass, and leveled his gaze on her. "It's a biological process for korasi. Changes our...chemical makeup or some shit. Alters our instincts, strengthens them. Basically, it's...a mating bond. The start of one, anyway."

"The start of one?"

"Imprinting can be triggered by a strong, lustful attraction. Sets off our glands to produce a chemical, and that chemical makes that attraction singular and endless. Enthi knew all the scientific terms for it. She was more connected to korasi culture than me and Brekker. It's a leftover from our ancient past, I guess. Something our kind learned to control as we became civilized.

"Modern korasi do not imprint without consent. It's one of the biggest taboos. But sometimes, when the attraction is so powerful, when the lust is so overwhelming..."

"Is that what happened with Brekker?"

Sevik nodded, darkness flickering across his face. "And me."

Mina's eyes widened. "You mean you...imprinted on me?"

"I resisted it several times since that night at Cornerstone. But last night, there was no stopping it."

Her fork slipped from her suddenly numb fingers and clanked atop the plate as her heart stuttered. "Does that mean..."

"It means I'm yours, Mina."

Oh God. Oh God, oh God, oh God.

Her heart accelerated to a frantic beat, spurred by her rapid breathing, as Mina shook her head. "No. No, this is wrong." She pressed a hand to her chest. "When I came here, I never meant to... I didn't want to force you to..."

Sevik shoved his chair back and rose. He was beside her in an instant. Dragging her chair out, he turned her to face him and loomed over her. The light behind him cast shadows on his face that made his white eyes gleam and look even more otherworldly than ever.

Bending over Mina, Sevik caught her jaw, keeping her head tipped back and her eyes locked with his. "*Nobody* forces me to do anything."

His other hand rose, and with a tenderness in stark contrast to his grip, he brushed the loose strands of hair out of her face. "This was inevitable, Mina. I knew you long before we first spoke. From the moment I saw you through the café window, I wanted you. I'd watch you through that glass, knowing that for all my talk of taking what I desired, I couldn't fucking take you. Whenever I saw you walking down the street or shopping in the store, I fought the urge to go to you.

"But that was always a losing fight. I was always going to give in. I thought I couldn't have you, and now that I do...I will never let you go."

He lowered his hand to her shoulder, claws tracing the bite mark he'd left there with just enough force to make her shiver. "This morning, my venom sealed the bond. It flows through your veins. I'm part of you now."

Sevik dipped his head and pressed his forehead against hers, his lips a whisper away from her mouth. His voice fell into a thrilling rasp. "I wasn't lying when I said there was no going back. You belong to me, Mina, irrevocably. You. Are. *Mine.*"

Tears stung her eyes, and she closed them.

He's mated to me.

Just like Mina had read in so many of her alien romance books. She never would have imagined such a thing was possible, not until Sevik entered her life.

And he wanted her. Not just for a single night, not just for sex. He wanted all of her, and he had for far longer than she'd known.

She waited for the shock, for the panic, to set in. For some mental alarm over what had been done and could not be undone. For...regret. But all she felt was joy.

I want him.

That had been her birthday wish. She'd yearned for it to come true with all of herself, heart and soul. And it had.

Closing her eyes, Mina smiled and cradled his jaw between her hands. "And you're mine?"

"Every fucking part of me."

Happy birthday to me.

TWENTY

LEANING her shoulder against the doorframe, Mina crossed her arms over her chest and watched Sevik through the front door window.

Haloed by the carport light, he shoveled the snow from around her car in huge scoops. Yet as fast as the snow was coming down, it wouldn't be long before his work was undone.

He was dressed in a pair of snug jeans, big black boots, and a tank top. Yesterday, she would've tried to stop him from going out in the blizzard dressed like that. But that was when she'd thought he was human.

And it did grant her quite the view...

The way his muscles flexed, the way they played on his powerful arms and chest and stretched his shirt, was hot as hell. She could happily watch that *all* day. But she couldn't shake the feeling that this sight was wrong.

Because he'd reactivated his disguise before going out.

He was no longer Sevik. He was Viktor again.

His long, raven hair was tied back to keep it out of his face. There were no devilish horns or alabaster skin, no intriguing black markings on his neck, no claws or fangs. Just that human mask. A wildly attractive mask, but now that she knew it was an illusion—

now that she'd seen the real him—it would forever seem wrong to her.

He'd insisted on it. Had said that he couldn't risk anyone else seeing him, even though this was a secluded cabin.

What was it like to live behind a mask like that? To have to hide so much of who and what you were?

Don't you know how it feels at least a little, Mina?

Put on a friendly smile and pretend you're not hurting. Laugh politely at the veiled insults and insinuations. Keep the peace at the cost of your dignity.

Mina wrinkled her nose and glanced down at her cellphone. It was after two o'clock in the afternoon, and she hadn't even thought about her café since she'd awoken that morning. Not that there was much to worry about. During a storm like this, most of the businesses in town would be closed, their owners and employees hunkered down to ride out the weather just like the rest of the townsfolk.

Bet I'm the only one who gets to ride it out with a sexy alien.

Get it? Ride?

Blushing at her own corny joke, Mina unlocked her phone and tapped on the news app. It loaded extremely slowly, but it did eventually load. She was frankly surprised it worked at all out here.

She skimmed through local news reports. The blizzard was expected to continue for another day or two, and apart from the main roads, most routes were impassable right now. Town officials had stated that they had crews working to keep the main roads clear, but that their resources were limited, and it would likely be a couple more days before everything would be opened up.

Well, it looked like she'd be here for a few more days at least.

After posting a quick announcement on the Bookish Bean social media letting everyone know she was safe but not at home, she locked her phone and looked back at Sevik.

She tilted her head. The cold didn't seem to affect him, which only made her realize that she'd seen him out in freezing weather without a coat several times. At most, he sometimes wore a light jacket. How cold was the planet his people originated from?

For her, even this planet was too cold, and Sevik knew it. He'd commanded her to remain inside while he dug out her car. She'd wanted to help, had pressed him on it, and he'd first stated that he only had one snow shovel. When she'd changed tactics and said she could just keep him company, he'd glared at her and revealed his true concern.

"It's fucking freezing, Mina," he'd growled. "Keep your ass inside or I *will* tie you to a chair."

There was no way she could feel cold when he talked to her like that. But she still would rather have been out there with him.

Folding her arms, Mina huffed, absently tapping her foot on the floor. She muttered, "Could've just put on pants."

Outside, Sevik bent over, and Mina's gaze dropped to admire his taut backside. She smirked.

That's mine.

She knew pants wouldn't have made a difference. She hadn't exactly shown up to his house dressed for a winter storm, and she felt the intense chill radiating through the door, flowing off the glass, slowly sapping the warmth from her skin. It would be a hundred times colder outside.

Now, she was stuck watching, plagued by restless energy that came from wanting to help but being unable to do so.

So much had happened since yesterday that she couldn't believe she hadn't even been here for twenty-four hours. From an innocent drinking game to being eaten out on the couch, from waking up and discovering a demon on the floor to losing her virginity and becoming an alien's mate, it felt like a lifetime had passed since Mina made the impulsive decision to come here.

Mate. I'm Sevik's mate.

Mina touched her fingertips to the healing bite marks on her shoulder, near the base of her neck. What exactly was a mate to him? He'd imprinted upon her, injected her with his venom. And the way he made it sound...

It was binding.

Did korasi take one mate, or...did they take several?

Jealousy flared in her heart even as dread pooled in her belly.

She hugged herself, clenched her jaw, and narrowed her eyes, staring at the floor. No. Mina couldn't stand the thought of him taking another mate. That was not something she'd be able to stomach. She could not, would not, share him.

The slam of a car door jarred Mina from her thoughts, calling her attention back to the window. Sevik walked toward the door, snow shovel in one hand, the emergency bag from Mina's car in the other. Snowflakes had gathered on his hair and shoulders, dusting him with white.

She shifted aside and opened the door for him. A blast of frigid air swept in, making her shudder as her skin prickled.

Sevik propped the shovel against the exterior wall, stomped off his boots, and stepped inside. His spicy scent flooded Mina's senses, calming her anxiety while also making her very, very aware of him. Warmth pooled in her core. A rush of desire hit her so suddenly that it almost stole her breath. She squeezed her thighs together, toes turning inward, trying to fight back that surge.

Had that always been her reaction to his scent, or was it related to the mating bond? To those...chemical changes Sevik had mentioned?

Mina took the duffle bag from him when he held it out. "Oh, thank you, thank you, thank you."

She hauled it into the kitchen and set it atop the dining table. She heard him kick off his boots before he entered the room. His shroud had already fallen; the melting snow was difficult to discern from his white hair, but it was clearly visible on his black horns.

Mina laughed as she pointed at them. "Does the snow vanish when it lands on your horns?"

"It enters the field of the holoshroud," he replied. "It's adaptive, accounting for changes like that. Would look pretty fucking suspicious to have piles of snow hovering over my head."

Rising on the tips of her toes, she brushed the snow off his horns. "I'd love to see you explain that to someone."

He hooked her chin with a finger before she could turn away. Leaning down, he brushed his nose along the side of her neck and breathed in. "Mmm. You're happy to see me, aren't you?"

Mina shivered and sucked in a breath when his tongue flicked over the bite marks, and more delicious heat bloomed between her thighs. It was so unfair that he could smell it anytime she was aroused.

She gently pushed him away before jabbing his chest with her finger. "It's all your crazy alien venom's fault."

"Ah, *val'syra*," he purred, "you lusted for me long before I bit you."

"Okay, so maybe you're right."

He was absolutely right.

Damn it.

His lips slowly stretched into a grin that showed off his fangs. Mina turned back to her bag and unzipped it, unable to hold back her own smile.

"It's still your fault for smelling and looking so good," she said.

Sevik chuckled darkly. "Not the first thing I'm guilty of."

Shaking her head, Mina took out her plastic bag of toiletries and opened it, setting a few of the items on the table—a stick of deodorant, a toothbrush, a hairbrush, and some hair product to help tame her unruly curls. If she remembered correctly, there were at least four pairs of pants and shirts folded neatly within the duffle bag, along with a bra and several pairs of socks and underwear. She dug out the latter, relieved.

Moving closer, Sevik peered into the bag. "Don't see how this counts as emergency supplies."

Mina shifted aside some of the clothing to reveal what was hidden beneath. A few military rations—MREs—and some other non-perishable food, road flares, a hatchet, gel handwarmer packs, a thermal blanket, a metal lighter, and a knitted wool hat and big winter gloves.

"All just in case," she said, smoothing the clothes back into place.

"In case of what?"

Raising her eyebrows, she gestured to the window. The rapidly darkening sky was still dumping snow on little Sullford, Alaska. The news she'd read earlier said there'd already been two feet of snowfall since yesterday.

"Ah." He reached in the duffle bag and almost daintily plucked out one of the objects—an old, dog-eared historical romance from Mina's teens. "And this?"

"You can get bored when your car gets stuck in the middle of nowhere." Mina snatched the book back and carefully returned it to its place.

"And that's happened to you?"

"My old car broke down once. Thankfully, it was in the summer, and I had cell service, so I didn't need any of this. But Randy got stranded during an ice fishing trip one winter. His car wouldn't start, so he had no heater and no phone service to call for help. He was out there for hours. It wasn't until late into the night that my mom and I got worried because he hadn't come home, and we couldn't get a hold of him.

"It was midnight when we took the two hour drive out there to look for him. We found him huddled in his car, wrapped in a thermal blanket. Had he not had that, and had we not known he was out there, he could've frozen to death."

Mina ran her fingers over the top of the bag. "When I got my first car, Randy made sure I always had a bag like this in there because you never know when you might need it."

Sevik caught her hand with his and curled his fingers around it. His warmth chased away the chill. "You miss him."

She nodded. "He was basically like a...surrogate grandparent to me after my dad died. We still call each other from time to time, but... It's not the same as talking with him face-to-face or seeing his eyes light up when he laughs." Mina looked up at Sevik. "But he's happy. That's what matters."

Expression sober, gaze heavy, Sevik searched her face. Tenderly, he brushed the backs of his fingers over her cheek and tucked her hair behind her ear. "Are you happy, Mina?"

Mina closed her eyes, turned her face into his palm, and

covered his hand with her own. "I wasn't. Not for a long, long time." Opening her eyes, she smiled. "Until the day you caught me."

Turning to face him, she drew his hand down and held it between both of hers as she lowered her gaze. She ran her thumbs over his callused palm and fingers, down to the tips of his claws. His hands were so unlike her own. Big, strong, inhuman. Capable of such cruelty, stained with blood, but they'd only ever protected her, soothed her, pleasured her.

"It's still hard to believe that I'm not dreaming," she said. "That you're not something I conjured from my imagination after reading so many romance books. I'm scared that I'll wake up one morning and you'll be gone. But this isn't a dream, and this isn't fiction. This—*you*—are real. An alien. I still know so little about you, and what I...what I mean to you."

Sevik grasped her chin with his other hand and tipped her face up, forcing her to meet his narrowed gaze. "You know more about me than anyone, Mina. I told you things about myself today that I've never said aloud." His hold on her chin tightened slightly, and something fierce sparked in his eyes. "I've never let anyone get so close."

Mina believed him, and that meant so much to her.

"What...exactly is a mate to you, Sevik?" she asked.

A crease formed between his eyebrows, and those sinfully sculpted lips fell. The tip of his thumb claw grazed just beneath her bottom lip. His voice was low and raspy when he finally spoke.

"Before, I would've said a mate is a weakness. A treasure to be locked away, a trophy too precious to be displayed."

"And now?"

"Now I see a mate as...possibility. As a new beginning. As my salvation." Sevik lowered his face, resting his forehead against Mina's. Their breath mingled, luring her mouth toward his, but he held her chin in place. "I see *you*, Mina. As mine in every way. Mine to hold, to enjoy, to fuck. Mine to protect and please. My future.

"And because of you, I see a chance at a new life. A different life. One where the only thing I'll ever want is you, where the only thing I'll ever need is you."

Mina clutched his hand to her belly. Her heart was beating so fast that she feared it might sprout wings and fly right out of her chest.

"Can you...imprint upon someone else? Take another mate besides me?" she asked, voice unsteady and near a whisper.

Please say no. Please, please say no.

"No," he growled, "and I wouldn't want to. You're it for me, Mina."

The tension that had built inside her dissipated, and she closed her eyes in relief. There was some part of her, a part she hadn't known existed, that had only awoken and bared its teeth after she'd met Sevik. Mina had never been a violent person, but she knew her own claws would come out if anyone ever touched him.

Mine. He's mine.

"I don't want you to take another either." She curled her fingers into his shirt. "I won't share you."

He released her chin, moving his hand to the back of her head and sliding his fingers into her curls. "Much as that jealous fire in your eyes thrills me, *val'syra*, I swear you will never have to."

Grasping her hair, Sevik slanted his mouth over hers, sealing his words with a kiss.

TWENTY-ONE

Night had turned the world outside the bedroom window into one of contrasts. Pale snow, glittering with ice crystals, against the deep, consuming shadows beneath the trees. The vast, overcast sky, the gateway to the boundless universe, over a dense fir forest that barely had enough space between the boughs for air to flow.

The cabin held its share of contrasts.

Mina's soft, lithe body tucked against Sevik's hard, rough form as they lay in his bed. Her innocence and passion against his remorseless savagery. Human against korasi.

His mate slept with her head upon his shoulder and her warm breath fanning across his skin.

Sevik smiled. She'd crawled right into bed with him, cuddled close, and had fallen asleep within moments of closing her eyes. No hesitation. Only trust.

Ornyr valaas duun, that felt good.

Holding her a little tighter, Sevik looked up at the ceiling. Firelight from downstairs danced along the log beams, deepening the shadows between them and highlighting the imperfections in the wood. Highlighting the natural features.

Natural...

That's what this is.

Lying here with Mina after a long day together, languid and vulnerable, felt natural. This ease, this serenity, this rightness, all came so naturally with her. Money and power had never gained him any of those things. Only at his lowest point had he found them, had he discovered what he'd been missing.

What he hadn't known he needed.

He brushed his fingers along her upper arm, just beneath the cuff of her T-shirt sleeve. Nothing could compare to the softness of her skin beneath his fingertips.

When Sevik had first come to Earth, the calm and quiet had been a welcome change from Hestryn's noise and bustling activity. But over the months, restlessness had unfurled within him. The once soothing calm and quiet had seemed increasingly vast and empty, and he'd felt powerless to change it. He'd felt... trapped. Stuck.

And then Mina had fallen into his life.

She'd shattered the monotony, the silence, the solitude. She'd been like the sun breaking through bleak gray clouds after a long storm, bathing the warmth-starved land in its radiance.

Years of struggle for survival, success, and status had formed an icy barrier around Sevik's heart. A shield against life's pains and regrets; a prison for all his emotions. Nothing penetrated that wall, whether in or out. And no aspect of his life had been left unscathed by its frigid touch.

Because it had been best to show nothing. To feel nothing.

No pain, no sorrow, no weakness.

No love.

The first cracks in that shield had formed when Brekker murdered Enthi and attempted to kill Sevik. But they'd allowed only fury to escape.

It was the female beside Sevik now who'd truly penetrated his defenses. She'd pierced him more deeply than any bolt or blade ever could have. The great icy barrier that had been thickening around his heart for twenty years had been melted into a puddle by Mina in a week.

He turned his head toward her, brushed his cheek against her hair, and breathed her in. Her scent, forever altered by their mating bond, poured heat into his veins.

Sevik gritted his teeth against the resurging ache in his groin. He'd resisted since this morning; he would resist now. His mate was sore, and she needed to recover. He would not cause her more discomfort.

No matter how much discomfort it caused him.

She moaned softly, stretching her arm more securely across his chest. Her voice was thick with weariness when she asked, "You're still awake?"

"Mmhmm."

She let out a long, sleepy sigh as she rubbed her thumb over his skin. Such a simple touch, but its tenderness and affection soothed him, easing that pervading ache, lulling that ravenous need.

"Sevik?"

"Hmm?"

"What if you couldn't go back to your home planet?" she murmured against him. "What if...you couldn't take back your empire from Brekker? What would you do instead?"

He glanced down at her. Those dark curls were another contrast, this time against his pale skin. Her eyes were closed, and her cheek was smushed against his shoulder in the most endearing fashion, but her lips were downturned in a little frown.

Sevik shut his eyes and ran his tongue over his fangs. He tasted a hint of sweetness from his venom. Despite the grogginess with which she'd asked it, the question had weight, and he felt every bit of it settling over him, pressing down.

He hadn't lied to her earlier; he believed a mate represented possibility. His circumstances on Vabos hadn't been ideal for taking a mate, not that he'd cared about such things. All that had been important to him was power—the power to ensure he was never helpless again.

Mina had awoken him to a universe of possibilities. He understood now that he could have something different, that he could make something new. Something with her.

"Not sure," he said softly. "My old life was all I knew. Didn't realize there could be anything else. Not until you."

Her breath, slow and steady, caressed Sevik's skin as he awaited her response. Time crept along, second by second, falling away to the past.

He opened his eyes and looked at his mate.

Mina's features were relaxed, lips slightly parted, and her hand was motionless upon his chest.

She'd fallen asleep.

Sevik's mouth curled into a smile as warmth wrapped around his heart and squeezed. His *val'syra* looked so peaceful, so beautiful. Protectiveness swelled alongside possessiveness in his chest, making his heart flutter and compelling him to hold her just a little more closely.

She is mine. All mine, only mine.

My always. My everything.

Settling his head on the pillow, he closed his eyes and slowed his own breathing. With Mina snuggled against him, sleep should've come easily. Nowhere in the universe could've been more comfortable.

But sleep eluded him, chased away by a question echoing in his head, no louder than a whisper yet nearly deafening in the otherwise quiet cabin.

What would you do instead?

What would he do if he couldn't take his revenge and reclaim his place?

What would he do, if given a choice?

His eyes opened, staring unfocused toward the ceiling.

If given a choice?

Since when had he ever waited to be given something? The choice had always been his—he only had to make it.

Sevik clenched his jaw and exhaled slowly through his nostrils. Carefully as he could, he slid Mina's arm off his chest. With even greater care, he withdrew from her, not lowering her head until he'd shifted a pillow beneath to cradle it.

She stirred as he did so, reaching for him in a reflexive way that made his heart ache anew, but she eased when he draped the blanket over her.

Before he could think further about what he was doing, he rose from the bed and strode to the stairs. Without looking back, he descended into the living room, retrieved the aetherkey from its hiding place under the floorboards, and set it on the coffee table.

He paced before the fire, and its heat skittered across his skin. The aetherkey was his only true link to Vabos, to his old life, and it was a necessity. It was his only means of remaining informed. One of his only lines of defense.

And his urge to break the ice on the lake and drop the damned thing into the dark, frigid water was absolutely fucking foolish.

But part of him longed for the severance of this last connection, longed for the final tether to be cut, longed for him to be truly unbound from the past.

He glanced at the aetherkey. Such a simple, unassuming thing. He knew it wasn't truly holding him back, but it was always easier to have something to blame, wasn't it? Because he refused to be held back anymore.

He'd told Mina that he had spent his life taking what he wanted. Living the way he chose, on his terms, until death inevitably came for him. Why stop that now?

Since arriving on Earth a year ago, he'd wanted to go back to kill Brekker and reclaim his life. But that had changed.

Sevik halted and faced the fire, watching the low flames dance around blackened logs and white-hot ash. What had he read during his time here? That some humans saw fire as a cleansing force? He understood the desire to burn everything down and start over.

Because in this moment, with absolute, unflinching certainty, he knew what he wanted.

Mina.

What would he do instead of seeking revenge? Have her. Protect her. Hold her. Fuck her. Worship her. Be with her. Live with her, live for her. *Zekt'al*, the rest didn't fucking matter.

Fuck Vabos. Fuck the Syndicate, fuck his old life, fuck

Brekker. Nothing on Vabos—nothing in the entire universe—was more precious than Mina. Money, power, revenge…he didn't need any of it. All he needed was his mate, safe and happy.

The only choice to make was Mina. The only choice he would ever make was her.

And he would sooner see the universe collapse upon itself than bring her anywhere near his homeworld.

He leaned forward and snatched the aetherkey off the table, curling his fingers around it. His arm trembled.

It would've been so easy to crush the thing in his hand and be done with it. But reason prevailed. For now, he needed the aetherkey. To protect himself—and to protect his mate.

He returned the device to its hiding place. As he walked back toward the stairs, he glanced at the window overlooking the lake. The snow was piled high on the deck, but he could see all the way to the far shore. The storm had dwindled to a flurry. Big, slow flakes tumbled lazily on the breeze, and the clouds had broken on the horizon, revealing a sliver of the starry night sky.

He'd not stopped to think about it before, but the stars looked lovely from this planet. Why hadn't he taken the time to appreciate them?

Sevik returned to the loft, taking the steps carefully to avoid making them creak. The answer to his question was lying in his bed, visible only as a mess of dark, curly hair poking out from the top of the blanket.

Life before had been about the tangible, the material. But Mina was teaching him just how much he'd missed. Just how much else there was to experience, to enjoy, to appreciate, to dream.

Just how much beauty was in the universe, and how fulfilling it was to admire it.

But the beauty in his bed was just for him.

He chose to have Mina's smiles, her voice, her laughter, her bright eyes and bouncy curls in his life every day. Chose to have her—here, on Earth, where they had a chance at peace and quiet.

Where they could be themselves and enjoy one another for who they were. No hiding, no pretending. Just being.

Because he wanted her, and he would not be denied what he wanted.

Rounding the bed, he slipped back into it and joined Mina beneath the covers. When he slipped his arm under her head and drew her close, she murmured an unintelligible question, clutching at him in confusion.

"I'm here, *val'syra*. Sleep," he soothed.

She settled, melting against him with a sigh. He kissed the top of her head and held her tight, burying his nose in her hair and filling his lungs with her sweet, thrilling scent again and again.

With no regrets, no hesitation, Mina was his choice. His only, his always.

And anyone who tried to get in his way would pay very fucking dearly for it.

TWENTY-TWO

Mina awoke cocooned in warmth. The blanket was drawn
up around her shoulders, her arms were tucked against Sevik's
side, and she had one leg hiked up over his. It seemed they had
barely moved from the position they'd been in when she'd fallen
asleep, though his hold on her had slackened. She snuggled a little
more firmly against him.

He was her own cuddly, toasty warm teddy bear.

She almost snorted at the thought, but she held it in for fear of
waking him. Sevik, a teddy bear? He was anything but soft. And
she doubted anyone would ever consider him cuddly. Dangerous,
lethal, beautiful, but not cuddly.

Smiling, Mina opened her eyes, and she was surprised to find
gloomy daylight spilling in through the windows. That meant it
had to be at least eleven o'clock. Had they really slept that long?
She couldn't remember ever sleeping this late, not even on her
birthday. But lying here with Sevik, in his embrace... She'd never
felt so safe and secure, so comforted and cared for in her life.

She tipped her head back and looked up at him. His face was
turned toward her, features relaxed in repose, eyes closed. Mina
ran her gaze down to his chest. It rose and fell in a steady rhythm
with his deep breaths.

Mina's smile faded as her eyes stopped upon a scar near his shoulder. Moving carefully to avoid disturbing him, she eased the blanket down.

His body was a mapwork of scars. It wasn't her first time seeing them, but it was her first chance to study them closely. They told the story of a violent, dangerous life. Gunshots, stab wounds, cuts, burns...the variety was as startling as it was heartbreaking. Many were faded, paler than his white skin, but one—the one left by Brekker—was tinged gray, making it stand out from the rest.

She lightly touched her fingertips to it. This was the scar that had brought him here. The scar that had brought him to her.

If Sevik hadn't been betrayed by Brekker, he would never have come to Earth. Mina would never have met him, would never have fallen into his arms, would never have known the feel of his kiss or his touch. She wouldn't be lying beside him now.

It was a what-if she didn't want to contemplate. She didn't need to. Because he *was* here with her.

Mina caressed each of his scars, wishing she could make them disappear and erase their hurt from his memory, wishing she could ensure he never received another.

It wasn't until her fingers traced a thin scar low on his belly that she realized how far down her hand had traversed. But she also realized that she'd never actually had a chance to explore his body, especially down *there*. And oh, how curious she was about a particular part of him...

Or rather *parts* of him.

She peeked up at his face. His eyes were still closed.

A wicked thought came to mind, and Mina bit her bottom lip.

Could she be so bold?

Turning her attention to her hand, Mina drew the blanket farther down. Sevik's sweatpants were low, revealing his toned adonis belt and his black markings, both of which pointed toward the top of his slit that was just visible above his waistband.

She glanced at his face before she slipped her finger under his waistband and slowly, soooo slowly, peeled it down, exposing more of his slit. It was dark along the seam and bulged slightly.

Carefully releasing the waistband, Mina hesitated. Was this wrong? Here he was sleeping, and Mina was about to touch him so intimately. Of course it was wrong. But more than anything, she wanted to explore this alien part of his body and wake him with pleasure.

She caressed his slit with her fingers.

Sevik's hand caught her wrist in an iron grip and forced her hand away. Mina started with a gasp, looking up at his face.

His eyes were open, alert, showing no signs of grogginess despite him having been sound asleep an instant ago. His pupils were narrowed to razor-thin slits.

"I'm sorry!" she said quickly, propping herself up on her elbow. "I'm so sorry. I shouldn't have done that. I should've waited, should've asked. I—"

"Mina," he rumbled, pupils expanding. His grip loosened, and the pad of his thumb brushed along her inner wrist, its soothing motion in harsh contrast to the speed and strength he'd just exhibited.

She turned her face away, ashamed, and frizzy curls fell over her brow. "I shouldn't have done that. You were sleeping. It was wrong."

"Ah, *val'syra*." Gently, he brought her arm up and placed a kiss on her palm. "I'm not used to...this. Sleeping with someone. Being vulnerable."

Sevik had reacted similarly yesterday morning, when her failed attempt at sneaking out had startled him awake. He'd instantly had her on the floor, a hand around her throat and claws poised to kill, as though anything that had awoken him must've been a threat. But as soon as he'd realized it was her, he'd released her.

Mina looked back at him. "I'd never hurt you."

"I know, Mina." Sevik guided her hand to his chest. "Touch me. However you desire. I want it." He smoothed her palm down his abdomen, letting it glide over the ridges of muscle, until her fingers once more rested over his slit. "I crave it."

Mina's breath stuttered, and warmth bloomed inside her at the sound of his husky voice. Her fingers twitched.

His pupils expanded into inky, gleaming pools of lust, and he released her wrist. "I'm yours, *val'syra*."

Sevik was giving her free reign. Anticipation and excitement swept through her.

She sat up on her knees, and with a blush, gave his sweatpants a tug. "Could you, umm...remove these?"

His lips spread in a sultry grin, and he hooked the hem of her shirt with a claw. "Will you remove this?"

"I guess it's only fair."

"Are you still sore?"

Mina shook her head.

He hummed, released her shirt, and ran his big palm over her thigh and down to her knee. "Good. Now take it off, female. Let me see you."

Liquid heat pooled between her thighs at his touch, his voice, his command. When Sevik took control, whether by word or action, it aroused her. Were she not so eager to explore his body, to touch him, she would've begged him to shove her face into the bed and fuck her from behind right then and there. She wanted him to dominate her.

The flare of his nostrils and the darkening of his eyes as he watched her told Mina that he was well aware of his effect on her.

Grasping the hem, she drew the T-shirt up and over her head and tossed it aside. The chilly air made her skin break out in goosebumps and her nipples harden into tight little nubs.

Sevik brushed the back of a finger across her nipple. Mina drew in a sharp breath as pleasure whispered through her body.

"You are beautiful." He skimmed his claw over the soft skin of her breast, then turned that finger to trail it down the center of her chest, toward her belly. "So fucking beautiful..."

Mina caught his finger, halting its descent. As much as she wanted him to continue, as much as she wanted to part her thighs and let his clever fingers delve between them, it was her turn to touch him. "Your pants are still on."

Sevik smirked. "So they are."

She raised her eyebrows as though to say, *Well?*

He laughed, grasped his waistband, and lifted his hips, shoving his pants and boxer briefs down. He used his feet to kick them off the rest of the way. With a grin, he gestured at his body before interlocking his hands behind his head. "Do with me as you please, *val'syra*."

Mina narrowed her eyes. Sevik was toying with her, playing up his arrogance and pretending that he wasn't just as affected as her, that he wasn't consumed with desire. He was acting like he was giving her the reins, but he remained in control. Like he'd make her beg for what she wanted.

But his eyes—and the glistening moisture of his slightly parted slit—said otherwise.

And Mina intended to have *him* begging.

She smiled and settled her left hand on his hip as she shifted to kneel between his legs. He widened them to accommodate her.

Bending close, Mina flicked her eyes up to his and lightly touched the tip of her middle finger to the top of his slit. "Is it sensitive?"

He held her gaze. "It is."

"So if I stroke it like this"—she slid her finger along his seam, through the moisture, and back up again—"like I do my pussy, it feels good?"

His body tensed, and his slit parted just a tiny bit more as the bulge beneath grew. "It does."

Mina lifted her other hand from his hip and placed it over his mound from the bottom, positioning her fingers to either side of his slit to pinch it closed. She was met with a surprising amount of resistance.

"Mina..."

"Hmm?" She slowly brushed her fingers along his slit again and again; they glided easily due to the oils seeping from his seam. Sevik's gaze didn't waver, even when the cadence of his breathing changed, even when the force pushing against her hand increased.

His arrogant smile had faded. His jaw was tight, its muscles ticking, and his lips twitched erratically as though on the verge of peeling back in a snarl.

Responding to his reactions—and the pleasure she was giving him—Mina's core clenched. She caught her lip between her teeth, dipped her fingers into his slit, and stroked what was inside it.

"*Vazk*," he growled, baring his fangs. Sevik's entire body flexed, back arching and knees rising on either side of Mina. His arms trembled, undoubtedly against the strain of keeping them in place behind his head.

Keeping a firm hold on his mound, she thrust her fingers in and out. His hot slick coated her fingers, and its heady fragrance filled her senses, flooding her with need.

Sevik's toes dug into the bedding. With a breathless chuckle, he said, "I underestimated you, *val'syra*."

"Mmm..." She continued pumping her fingers, curling them to stroke the rigid head of one of his cocks. "What did you think I'd do?"

"Submit to me." He shuddered, and his fangs caught his lip.

Mina smiled. "I will always submit to you, Sevik." Withdrawing her fingers, she ran his slick over his slit. "But I want you to submit to me also."

"Haven't I already?"

"Beg."

"I don't beg."

Keeping the hand on his mound firmly in place and his cocks trapped, Mina lifted her fingers from his slit.

Sevik snarled.

"Beg me." She brought her oil-coated fingers to her mouth and slipped them between her lips.

She'd tasted Sevik's cum from his fingers, and it had been a shock. She'd expected saltiness, perhaps even bitterness. Instead, its spicy flavor was reminiscent of cinnamon and cloves, with just a hint of sweetness, and oh, was it delicious.

She craved more.

His eyes were fixated on her hand and mouth as she sucked on her fingers and slowly pulled them free.

"Release my cocks, Mina," he grated.

"That's a command, not a plea." She coated her fingers with his slick again and slipped them between her thighs, stroking her clit, mingling their essences. A pleasure-filled moan spilled past her lips, and her words were breathy when she said, "Beg me, Sevik. Beg your mate."

The cords of his neck stood out, and the strain in his arms left their every muscle sculpted in perfect definition. Ragged breaths sawed in and out of his lungs. When he spoke again, his voice was hoarse, bestial, desperate. "Please, Mina. Please, fucking release me."

Removing her hand from her sex, she braced it on his hip. "Good boy," she said sweetly before lifting her other hand from his mound.

His cocks emerged, thick and erect, throbbing and glistening.

"Fuck," Sevik rasped.

Mina ran her gaze over them. Such a deep, pure black, ringed with prominent ridges. Alien. But God, they were beautiful. Curling her fingers around the bottom one, she stroked it, and those ridges slid along her palm. This was exactly what she'd felt when it'd been inside her, what had brought her so much pleasure. And she yearned to feel that again.

Soon.

Sevik slapped his hands on the bed, sinking his claws into the bedding as he lifted his hips to force more friction along his shaft. A groan sounded from deep within him.

"Do you want more?" Mina asked, squeezing his cock.

"Need more."

She smoothed her other hand toward the base of his upper shaft, caressing the inside of his slit along the way. Seeing him like this—his long hair in disarray, his composure shattered, completely at her mercy—was more arousing and empowering than she could ever have imagined.

Mina wrapped her hand around his upper cock and stroked, slowly, leisurely. Her core ached. She wanted him inside her, needed him. But not yet.

"Tell me, Sevik," she said. "How much do you need me?"

"So much it hurts," he growled through his fangs. Only the thinnest rings of white remained in his eyes, and the black held blazing, hungry fires that threatened to consume both him and Mina at any moment.

"It hurts me too." She dropped her head, wrapped her mouth around the head of his bottom cock, and sucked.

"*Fuck!*" Sevik snarled. His fingers delved into her hair, grasping her head as his hips bucked, pushing his shaft deeper into her mouth.

Mina made a sound of surprise and tightened her grip on his cocks, holding him down so he couldn't force himself too far. Her jaw was stretched wide around his girth. She swallowed, and he moaned.

"Your mouth feels so fucking good, *val'syra*."

The praise and pleasure in his voice spurred her on.

Though he held her hair, he didn't restrain her movements. She lifted her head, relaxing her jaw as she moved her mouth to the head of his cock, her tongue gliding over his ridges. When she reached the tip, she flicked her tongue over the slit there and sucked.

As her mouth worked his length, she pumped her fist up and down his other shaft, strengthening and easing her grip, matching the unhurried pace of her mouth and the shallow thrusts of his hips.

Sevik groaned low and deep, the sound reverberating through his body. His fingers flexed, and his claws grazed her scalp, sending tingles through her. The sensation added to the arousal thrumming within Mina. Her clit throbbed with need, and her pussy was so wet that her slick was trickling down her inner thighs.

But this? This brought her pleasure too. Feeling the strain in his body, hearing the hoarse sounds from his throat, tasting his delicious oils on her tongue.

Quickening her hand, Mina moaned around his cock and took him deeper, sucking hard.

"*Zekt'al*, Mina!" Sevik's hips bucked faster and more erratically, and his harsh breaths faltered. Tension gripped his whole body. "Fuck, fuck, fuck!"

His cocks thickened and pulsed, and a flood of heat filled her mouth. Mina's eyes rounded, and she squeaked, but she swallowed his cum as quickly as she could. Sevik's other shaft twitched in her grasp, and warm wetness coated her hand, but she didn't stop stroking as jet after jet of seed shot from it.

Sevik grunted and growled, clutching her hair until his body eased. Slowly, Mina lifted her head, dragging her tongue along the underside of his shaft, licking away cum that had spilled from her mouth. A shudder racked him.

Straightening, she looked down at what she had wrought. Seed covered both his cocks and her hands, which still gripped the bases of his shafts, and had pooled within his slit. Her eyes followed a trail of it over his abdomen and chest, where it glistened on his pale skin.

Mina met his gaze.

He stared at her with a fervent, possessive gleam in his eyes. If she had expected to see him sated and languid after what she'd just done, she would've been wrong; he looked only hungrier now. His cocks continued throbbing in her hold, remaining just as hard.

Sevik's lips curled into a devilish smirk. "I smell your desire, Mina. Your cunt's fucking dripping, isn't it?"

Her core clenched, achy and hollow. Lust burned hot and bright inside her; it was a craving she could no longer deny.

A whimper escaped her. "I need you."

"I won't make you beg." Sevik's hands caught Mina beneath her arms, and he pulled her atop himself with no apparent effort. "This time."

Mina yelped and flailed her hands, uncertain of what to grab hold of. Her struggles sent her tipping forward. She grabbed his horns and stared down at him with wide eyes. Her belly was flush with Sevik's, covering her in his cum.

"Sevik! You're... My hands..." Her hands, sticky with his seed, were now curled around his horns. "We're a mess! *I'm* a mess."

He thrust his fingers into her hair, grasped the back of her head, and tilted it back.

"I don't fucking care." That long tongue of his dragged up her throat and over her chin before he captured her mouth in a crushing kiss. When he broke the kiss, he grinned up at her. "I want you covered in my cum. Covered in me."

He was right. Why did she care if they were messy? Sex was messy. It was messy, dirty, and raw. And...she actually loved that she was covered in him. That she bore his scent.

"Now"—Sevik dropped his hands to her hips and scooted her down his abdomen until she felt his cock against her ass—"take what you want. What is yours."

Releasing his horns, Mina sat up. Sunlight was now streaming through the window, brightening the room and setting his alabaster skin aglow. The black *lyros* on his neck and hips stood out in stark contrast, as sleek and alluring as ever.

Take what you want. What is yours.

Because he *was* hers.

Placing her hands on his chest, she lifted herself, easing back farther until his cocks stood beneath her. Grasping his lower shaft, she poised its tip at her entrance and lowered herself upon it. The head parted her, stretched her, and she felt each and every ridge as they entered her body. Mina moaned.

"*Ornyr valaas duun,* you feel so good," Sevik said. "Take my cock into that pretty pussy."

Rising slightly, she pushed back down, taking him deeper.

His fingers flexed on her hips, pricking her with his claws and gripping her tight enough that she was sure they'd leave bruises. And Mina wanted those marks. She wanted everything, every reminder of the pleasure they shared.

He bared his fangs, focusing his gaze between her thighs, where his cock was entering her.

Not wanting to endure this torture any longer, Mina rose again and slammed down. She gasped his name as his full, thick length filled her. Her pussy clenched. The sting of being stretched so quickly, so completely, was chased by a hot ache of pleasure.

Sevik groaned and grinded her upon him, burrowing even deeper. "I would burn a thousand worlds for just one more second inside you, Mina. Let the whole fucking universe come apart. You are my everything."

Mina's chest constricted. Part of her still couldn't believe that this was real, that he was real. Couldn't believe this wasn't a dream. But if it was a dream, she never wanted to wake up. She never wanted to lose this. Never wanted to lose him.

"Sevik..." Locking her eyes locked with his, she began to move. A slow, steady glide, up and down, up and down. The ridges of his upper shaft stroked Mina's clit, while those of his lower rubbed her inner walls, sending electric currents through her, each stronger than the last. They pushed her to take him faster, harder, deeper. And she did.

Her movements were wild, unrestrained, selfish. All she wanted was to take—to take every bit of sensation Sevik offered, to take every bit of him. She wanted everything. Her breath came in quick bursts, and she curled her fingers, digging her nails into his chest.

"Yes, female, just like that," Sevik growled. He raised his knees, making Mina moan as the position forced him deeper. "Use Me. Fuck me. Take your pleasure, *val'syra*. Make me yours."

"You are mine," she rasped. "Mine. My mate. Mine, mine, mine."

The words came with every drop of her pelvis, with every thrust of his cock. A low, whimpering cry built in the back of her throat, and her legs trembled, threatening to give out. The pleasure coiled inside her, growing hotter and hotter, like a star about to burst, about to consume her.

Close. She was so...so...

Mina's body went taut. Rapture seized her, stealing her thoughts, her sight, her breath. She fell upon Sevik, burying her face against his neck as her sex contracted. He wrapped his arms around her and held her tight, his hips thrusting with bestial urgency.

"That's it, Mina," he said as throaty cries tore from her. "Let me hear you. Let me feel you."

She shuddered through the spasms, lost to ecstasy, lost to the feel of Sevik. As Mina clung to him, something visceral took over. She clamped her teeth down on his neck.

Sevik roared, slamming into her harder than ever, seating himself impossibly deep. One of his hands slapped onto her ass, pinning her in place as his body convulsed and hot seed erupted from his cocks. It filled her and sent her over the edge once more.

Their voices blended in ragged, animalistic cries of pleasure as they rode the waves of ecstasy. For those moments, Mina felt as if she were one with him, felt the sort of connection that wasn't supposed to exist outside of stories.

He held her as their bodies eased, as the pleasure faded, as her pounding heart gradually slowed. She closed her eyes. There was no other place she wanted to be. Were it possible, this was where she'd stay for the rest of her life, safe in his embrace, feeling wanted, feeling...loved.

Breath still ragged, Sevik pressed a kiss to her forehead. The kiss lingered until he tipped his head and rested it against hers. "Never letting you go, *val'syra*."

TWENTY-THREE

Mina sat on the sofa with her legs curled to the side, a blanket draped over her lap, and her tablet in her hands. All was quiet except for the crackling of the fire in the hearth. With the windows blacked out by alien technology Sevik had installed to protect his privacy, shutting out the world beyond, the cabin felt cozier than ever. This was the perfect reading environment.

But she wasn't really reading.

Her eyes moved over the words on the screen, but her mind drifted elsewhere. To Sevik.

Mina smiled. She'd been doing that a lot since coming here four days ago. Well, smiling and thinking of Sevik. When had she ever been this happy?

Never.

There were some wonderful people in Sullford. Most of the townsfolk had never said an unkind word about Mina or her mother. But a lot of them had also stood by, silent, as others made their hateful comments. They'd turned their heads and pretended not to see anything. They'd ignored years of harassment, simply because it hadn't involved them.

And while doing nothing wasn't nearly as bad as bullying, all those bystanders carried some of the guilt. Because the silence had told Mina's tormentors that they'd been justified in their actions, that there were no consequences for their behavior. That the world didn't give a shit.

Despite the good that was here, this town was tainted in Mina's eyes...and in her heart. She couldn't look upon those long-time residents without remembering the terrible things they'd done and said—or that they'd allowed to happen.

Every single day, she'd had those memories, that pain, stirred up. And every single day, she'd put on her false smile and acted like she wasn't hurting inside. Like she was above letting them affect her. At least while Randy had been around, she'd had some-one. Someone who spoke up for her, someone who consoled her, who helped carry the burden of those memories.

She'd had to face all of it alone for more years than she cared to count.

Until Sevik.

It wasn't just that he'd spoken up for her, that he'd protected her. He saw her. When he looked upon her, she felt like the most important person in the world.

She looked forward to waking up beside him every morning, to talking with him, to spending time with him. These days she'd spent in his cabin, snowed in, had been...magical. Her hometown, with all its emotional baggage, was only fifteen minutes away, but it felt like this cabin was its own universe, removed from every-thing else. A sanctuary. A paradise.

Here, she had no reason to rush, had no responsibilities. There was no need for false smiles and empty niceties. Mina's smiles, laughter, and joy were all very, very real. Every moment with Sevik was a balm for her wounded soul. Even yesterday, when they'd spent hours cuddled in bed while Mina read to him, had been *perfect*.

Of course, that reading session had grown pretty steamy during certain parts of the book, because Sevik, with his super-human sense of smell, had picked up on her arousal immediately. More than once, he'd snatched the tablet from her, tossed it aside, and showed her that there was truth to the spicy scenes in romance novels.

Mina's cheeks heated as she recalled the many times they'd come together physically. Sevik was insatiable, but her hunger matched his. She couldn't wait to feel both his cocks inside her, to feel that fullness. She wanted all of him in every way.

Desire blossomed in her core, and she pressed her thighs together.

He'd been incredibly patient as he had continued preparing her body for the time when he'd finally claim her fully. He wanted to ensure that she'd feel no pain, that she'd take as much pleasure from the act as he would. The sensation of him thrusting a finger in her ass, slowly stretching her, had been so strange... And yet, it had felt amazing.

A door opening jolted Mina from her thoughts. She looked up to see Sevik stepping into the living room from the back door.

Mina smiled wide, her heart fluttering at the sight of him. As soon as he closed the door, his holoshroud fell away. His long, white hair was loose, hanging around his shoulders and down his back, and he wore a snug, long-sleeved black shirt and dark blue jeans that hugged his thick, muscular thighs.

He kicked off his boots onto the mat beside the door, glanced at her with a smirk, and strode into the kitchen.

Curious, she sat up and craned her neck to look toward the kitchen entryway.

Sevik returned quickly, arms laden with her coat, hat, gloves, and boots. He placed the latter on the floor in front of her and the rest on the couch beside her.

Mina tilted her head. "What's going on?"

He knelt before her and drew the blanket off her lap. "I have something to show you."

She shifted her legs forward as she set her tablet on the end table. "Something to show me?"

Lifting her foot, he slipped one of her boots on, repeating the process for the other.

Mina furrowed her brow and pointed toward the back door. "Outside?"

He chuckled. "Why else would I put on your boots?"

"But there's like three feet of snow out there. It's also night-time and freezing!"

Sevik caught her chin and stroked it with his thumb, his eyes growing heated. "I'll keep you warm, *val'syra*."

That warmth in her belly spread.

I bet you will.

She poked his chest. "I am not taking off my pants in the snow."

Sevik's thumb claw grazed her lower lip as the corner of his mouth quirked. "Won't be in the snow. And we'll see."

"I'm serious. Do you realize how cold Alaskan winters are? No, of course you don't, because you don't feel the cold. My pussy is staying all cozy and warm *inside* my pants."

He just laughed, released her chin, and took hold of her hands to guide her onto her feet. Picking up her coat, he reached around Mina and helped slip it over her arms.

"I could've done this," she said, smiling.

"I know," he replied, drawing the sides of her coat together before zipping it up.

Meaning he was content to do this for her. It was incredibly sweet, and just another thing that made her feel so cared for.

"Are you going to finally show me your spaceship?" she asked, trying to ignore how wildly her heart was beating.

"No."

Mina stuck her bottom lip out in a pout as he put on her hat. "Will you ever show me your spaceship?"

"It really isn't as exciting as you seem to think, Mina."

She gave him a droll look. "It's exciting when you've never seen one."

"I'll show you eventually."

Mina grinned as she pumped her fists in victory. "Yes!"

Sevik held up her gloves. "But not tonight."

She opened her hands for him. "That's okay. The promise to show me is good enough for now. Will you take me flying?"

He slipped her gloves on, taking the time to ensure each finger fit snugly. "We'll see."

"Thaaaaat's not a no."

"Not a yes, either."

"But there's still a chance."

One of his brows arched. "Ready?"

"Yep. I'm all toasty warm."

Sevik took her hand and led her to the door. His holoshroud shimmered into place as he moved. He stepped back into his boots without letting her go, stomping to get them on. Just as he was reaching for the handle, he paused.

"*Leskahn tor lesk,* almost fucking ruined it," he muttered, turning to face her.

Mina raised her brows. "Ruined what?"

He released his hold on her and dropped his hand into her pocket, taking out the scarf she'd stuffed into it the day she'd arrived. He moved behind her and raised the scarf over her head. But instead of wrapping it around her neck, he brought it over her eyes.

Mina started and looked at him over her shoulder. "What are you doing?"

"Covering your eyes," he said flatly.

"Oh! Is it a surprise? I love— Wait..." She narrowed her eyes at him. "In every mobster movie I've seen, anyone who gets blindfolded is about to"—she brought her hands up and made finger quotes in the air—"sleep with the fishes."

Sevik stared at her long and hard. "What the fuck is that supposed to mean?"

"Means they get whacked."

"Whacked."

"Killed. Dead. Come on, shouldn't you know this stuff?"

He wrapped an arm around her middle, but rather than hug her, he yanked her hips back and forced her to bend over his forearm. A sharp crack sounded an instant before pain flared on her ass cheek. Even through the material of her jeans, she felt the sting from his palm. Mina cried out in pain and in shock.

He'd spanked her. *Spanked* her.

And she would've been lying if she said she hadn't actually liked it.

His hand came down again, this time on her other ass cheek, and her sex clenched with arousal.

Mina gasped and gripped his forearm. "Sevik!"

"That's for even thinking I'd make you sleep with the fucking fishes," he said sternly as he rubbed his palm over her backside, soothing the warmth blooming across her flesh.

"Okay! Okay! Bad joke. I won't do it again. I'm sorry."

"Good girl." Sevik gave her ass a little pat before standing her upright. He caught her jaw in a firm grip and tipped her head back. His pupils had expanded, flooding his irises with black. "I would *never* fucking hurt you."

Well, beyond a spanking.

Mina touched a hand to his chest. "I know. I'm sorry."

Sevik pulled her closer as he bent down, pressing a hard, searing kiss to her mouth that sent a wave of heat through Mina and made her toes curl in her boots.

When he pulled back, he flicked his tongue over her lips. "Never again. Not even a thought."

"Never," Mina promised. "But I...wouldn't mind you spanking me again."

A low chuckle rumbled from him before he nipped her bottom lip with a fang. "Oh, I will, *val'syra*." Releasing her, he grasped the scarf in both hands again and raised it. "Now turn around."

"Yes, sir." With a grin, she gave him her back. The friction of her jeans as she moved enhanced the warm sensation on her ass. She was sure she wouldn't forget this *punishment* anytime soon.

Who knew I'd be into spanking?

After covering Mina's eyes with the scarf and tying it into place, Sevik stepped in front of her. "No peeking."

"I won't."

He took her hand, opened the door, and led her outside. Though she was bundled up and knew it was coming, nothing could ever have prepared Mina for that blast of frigid air. A deep shiver ran through her, and her first breath stung her nostrils and throat. She tucked her nose behind the collar of her coat.

Sevik reached around her and tugged the door closed. No sooner had it shut than he scooped Mina off her feet, cradling her against his chest with one arm under her back and the other behind her knees. Grinning, she wrapped her arms around his neck and turned her face against it. She drew warmth from his skin as she breathed in his spicy scent.

His boots thumped over the deck's wooden boards until he descended a small set of stairs and stepped onto snow.

"So where are you taking me?" she asked.

"You'll see. No more questions."

Mina chuckled.

Snow crunched beneath his boots as he walked, his gait deliberate and seemingly unhindered. How much snow had he shoveled? He'd spent a lot of time outside over the last couple days clearing the driveway, but she hadn't realized he'd also made a path out back.

She could tell that they were steadily moving downhill, toward the lake. Yet when his footsteps again became hollow thuds on wood planks, her brows rose in surprise.

"Are we on a dock?"

"Mmhmm." Sevik finally drew to a halt. Gently, he lowered Mina onto her feet, keeping an arm around her until she found her balance. Then he pulled the knot of the scarf loose.

She reached up to catch the scarf, opened her eyes, and froze.

The sky was aglow with waves of dancing green light that flowed from the horizon like ribbons of magic. Their luminescence reflected on the lake below, where the wind had left patches of ice bare of snow, making everything radiant and surreal.

Mina had seen the aurora borealis many times in her life, but never like this. Never without the town's lights interfering. Never with the heavens stretching out to infinity overhead, with countless stars twinkling against a backdrop of purples and blues.

"Sevik," Mina whispered, her breath coming out in a small cloud, "this is beautiful."

"Between the city lights and the pollution, you never see the sky on Vabos," he said, drawing her attention to him. He too was looking up. "Never see much of anything beautiful. But this planet... This planet has many beautiful things."

Sevik's eyes met Mina's, their light rivaling the display overhead—but burning just for her. "And none of those things can compare to you."

Warmth blossomed in her, chasing away the cold, and her heart thumped a frantic rhythm.

How could she have come to feel so much for him in such a short amount of time? A single look from Sevik sparked a fire in her belly, a single touch stoked it to a blazing flame. And his words... They stole her breath. Though it had been less than two weeks since they'd met, Mina couldn't think of living even a day without him in her life. Just the thought of it flooded her with dread and panic.

Was this...love? Could it be?

Sevik smiled and curled his fingers, beckoning her. "Come. Sit."

It was only then that Mina realized the entire end of the dock had been cleared of snow, and she was standing on a large, beige blanket that had been spread out over the planks.

He'd done all this for her.

Tears stung her eyes. She held them back as best as she could, not only because she didn't want to cry in front of him, but because crying out here in the cold freaking hurt. Yet they came despite her efforts, blurring her vision.

Sevik scowled, a deep crease forming between his eyebrows. "What's wrong?"

Mina shook her head and wiped her eyes with the back of her gloved hand. "Nothing. I'm just...happy."

"Crying can be happy?"

She nodded. "A lot of emotions can make you cry. Even good ones." She slipped her fingers into his. "Thank you."

His gaze lingered upon her, still skeptical, before he guided her to sit with him. He rested his back on a dock piling, and she settled between his bent legs, reclining against his chest. He picked up a second blanket from beside him, unfolded it, and drew it over Mina before wrapping his arms around her. Though it was cold at first, she was soon enveloped in the sweet, blissful warmth generated by their bodies.

In comfortable silence, they stared skyward, appreciating the beauty gifted to them by nature, relishing each other's closeness. Mina didn't even mind that her cheeks and nose were numb from the freezing air. Being here with him, in this moment, made everything worth it.

She wanted more moments like this. Wanted a lifetime full of them.

"I've lived here all my life," she said quietly. "I've always known that there's a whole world out there to explore, that there's so much to discover, but...I stayed here. Even when Randy invited me to move to Arizona with him, where there'd be so many more opportunities for me, I stayed."

"Why?"

"Because of ghosts." Mina laid her head back against Sevik's shoulder. "My parents are buried here, and this...this place is where all my memories of them are."

Sevik shook his head and gently touched a finger to her temple. "All your memories of them are here, Mina. You carry them."

"I know. It's more that the places are reminders. Like...sometimes, when I walk into the café, I can almost see my mom working behind the counter. Can almost see her smiling and hear her asking me to give her a hand with something. Or when I go to the diner, I can picture all of us—me when I was little, my mom, and my dad—all sitting together, laughing as my dad arranges our breakfast into some silly cartoon face."

Tears brimmed in her eyes again. "For years, I've been stuck in the past. Been haunted by it. Memories of my parents, memories of the cruel things people said about me and my mom, of the way we struggled… And I stayed because I didn't want to feel even further away from my parents. These memories, these places, were all I had left. But the good and the bad are so intertwined, so tangled…"

Mina tugged off a glove and lifted one of Sevik's hands, lacing their fingers together. She needed to feel him, skin to skin, with nothing between them.

"I don't want to let the past hold me back anymore," she said.

"Then don't." He squeezed her hand. "Live in the present with me, and we'll make whatever future we want."

Mina's chest constricted. She wanted that so, so much. But he'd said he saw her as a *chance* at a new life.

That didn't mean he was going to forget his past, didn't mean he would just let it go. How could he, after everything he'd been through? Why would he forsake everything he'd had before he met Mina?

"What about getting back what you lost?" she asked. "What about your…revenge?"

The final word came out small and strained. Sevik had said he wouldn't let her go, but if he went back to Vabos, wouldn't he be breaking his word? Because going back meant that she could…

Lose him.

Mina couldn't bear the thought of Sevik getting killed. She'd lost everyone else in her life that had mattered. She couldn't lose him too.

"Fuck what I've lost," he growled. "My revenge will be living, mated and content. Full in a way I never knew was real."

"What?"

Sevik caught her chin and turned her face up toward his. Even with his features changed by the holoshroud, even with his eyes so strangely human, it was still him. It was his intensity, his inner fire, blazing in his gaze.

"I'm not going back, *val'syra*. The only thing I want, the only thing I *need*, is right here, in my arms."

TWENTY-FOUR

Sevik turned his truck onto Main Street, following Mina's SUV. The harsh red of her taillights glinted off flecks of ice in the otherwise dirty snow the snowplows had left on the sides of the road.

Not for the first time during the drive from the cabin, he wished she were beside him. These twenty minutes without her felt longer than the six days they'd spent together at his place; it was torturous.

The choice to take separate vehicles had been a surprisingly difficult one for him. He wanted her close, and didn't want her driving on potentially dangerous roads. But at least he was right behind her if anything happened.

Had they just taken her car, she would've eventually had to drive him back to the cabin, which meant her making the return trip to town alone. And Sevik would've been driven mad not knowing if she'd made it safely.

Maybe it's finally time to get one of those phones the humans always use...

She brought her vehicle to a stop in front of The Bookish Bean, reverse lights flashing for an instant as she shifted into park. Sevik did the same. Her driveway hadn't been cleared at all, and the snow piled at its entrance was even higher than everywhere else thanks to the plows.

Mina's car door opened, and she hopped out, slinging her bag over her shoulder as she shut the door behind her.

Sevik exited his truck, reached into the bed, and took out the snow shovel he'd brought along. He strode to the snowbank at the driveway entrance.

"You don't have to clear all that," Mina said. "It'd be a lot less work to just go in through the front."

"You park in the back."

"Yeah, but I don't have to."

Eyebrows falling low, he glanced at her. "If I don't do this now, you'll do it later. That's not acceptable."

"Sevik, you really don't have to."

He jabbed the shovel into the mound. "Go back in your car, Mina. Stay warm."

Snow crunched softly under her boots as she approached. "I'm staying with you."

The swell of pride in his chest came with a hint of frustration. As much as he wanted her near, he did not want her to suffer—and there was no way she wasn't already feeling the bite of the cold. But how could he not be touched by her willingness to choose him over her own comfort?

"Get back in the car." He tossed aside the shovelful of snow and scooped up another.

"I'll go get my shovel to help," she said from behind him. "It's, um... Well, it's by the back door. Maybe if you just give me a boost over this mountain, I can swim over to it."

"No." Sevik continued shoveling.

"But—"

"No."

Even the shallower snow would be past her mid-thigh. He wouldn't have her straining to move it, and her proposed trek around the back would've had her shivering with cold before she ever reached her destination.

Mina huffed. "Stubborn male. You expect me to just stand here and stare at your ass while you do all the work?"

Sevik smirked as he heaved aside a pile snow that might've weighed half as much as Mina. "Yes."

"Okay. I can do that."

He felt a sharp sting as her palm struck his ass.

"You do have a nice butt, so I won't complain," Mina said happily.

Sevik chuckled. Whirling around, he caught her by her waist and yanked her body against his. "That will be repaid, female."

She grinned at him. "I look forward to it."

Leaning down, he slanted his mouth over hers. He allowed himself a moment to thrill in her taste. Such a sweet, playful, seductive mate... If he gave in now, he didn't doubt the heat of their passion would melt the snow around them.

But too soon, he released her and resumed his work, sped on by his desire to get his mate out of the cold. Heat was thrumming in his muscles by the time he'd cleared a path large enough for Mina's car, making wisps of steam rise from him in the frigid air. Mina's breath came out in large puffs, sometimes through chattering teeth, and her nose and cheeks were red.

Should've forced her to wait in her vehicle.

Like she can be forced to do anything.

He snickered to himself.

Stubborn female.

Once the way was clear, Mina rushed to the back door, unlocked it, and held it open for him. Sevik stomped snow off his boots and pants before entering. Two scents struck him immediately—Mina and coffee. The small entry room had hooks on the wall, upon which a couple coats and hats hung, with a pair of boots standing on a mat beneath them. Straight ahead was an open door and a hallway that led into the café, and to the left was a wooden staircase going up to the second floor.

Mina closed the door, toed off her boots, and removed her gloves.

"Do you want anything to drink?" she asked. "Coffee? Tea? Cocoa? Water?"

"Water," he replied. It was the safest option if he didn't want to be overwhelmed by sweetness or kept awake all night.

She unzipped her coat and removed it, hanging it on one of the hooks before she raced up the stairs. As Sevik removed his boots, he heard her keys jingling, then the sound of the door opening and Mina darting through.

The stairs creaked softly beneath Sevik as he walked up. With each step higher, his heart beat a little faster, and his chest felt a little tighter.

He was about to enter his mate's home, where she was the most herself, the most comfortable, the most vulnerable. This moment was far more significant than he could've guessed, far more meaningful.

Mina met Sevik at the door, holding out a glass of water to him. "Here."

"Thanks." He took the glass, and under her oddly expectant gaze, sipped the water.

She put her hands on her hips and narrowed her eyes. "All of it. You just shoveled all that snow by yourself."

Sevik chuckled. "If it pleases you, female."

He gulped down the rest of the water without looking away from her. The cold liquid was admittedly refreshing, battling the heat that had built in him while he'd worked.

He returned the empty glass to Mina, and she stepped aside.

"You can come in," she said, a little shyly.

That hint of shyness squeezed his heart. After what they'd done together, what they'd shared, there should've been no room left for it, and yet he found it endearing.

Sevik moved past Mina, somehow managing to take his eyes off her so he could study her apartment. Her scent, fresh, sweet, and heady, permeated the air.

Sheer white curtains allowed ample daylight into the room, which was filled with light colors—whites, beiges, gentle grays, pale greens and browns. It made the space, which seemed to be a combined kitchen and living area, feel much larger and more open.

Plants hung from the ceiling and sat upon wall mounted shelves, adding vibrant greens to the mix. They were accented in many places by delicate strings of tiny, hanging lights and small lamps basking the leaves in their glows. Framed art on the walls contributed more varied color, but it all seemed...balanced. Harmonious.

Comfortable.

"I've...never invited anyone in here before," Mina said softly, calling his attention to her. "You're the first."

She stood with her hands folded against her belly. The sadness that had been evident in her voice was also present on her face, and it made him want to burn this whole town to the ground. To punish all the people who'd made her feel so small, so alone, to make them fucking beg for mercy and to offer them none.

But he wasn't going to focus on them. This was about Mina, about being in her place, learning about her. She wasn't alone anymore, and she knew it.

Sevik stepped toward the couch, running his gaze over the décor. A tiny artificial fir tree, decorated with white and red glass balls and miniature books and teacups, stood on one of the end tables.

He'd seen such trees through the front windows of other homes, though those had been much larger and more elaborately decorated. He'd wondered if they were some sort of status symbol. Why else would so many humans leave the insides of their homes so visible to anyone who passed by? But having seen the decorations in the stores and the live trees being sold from a corner lot down the street, he knew now that the trees had something to do with an approaching holiday.

Sevik tapped one of the red ornaments with a claw. "What is this for?"

"The tree?" Mina moved to stand beside him. "People put them up and decorate them for Christmas. Usually there'd be wrapped presents under them, waiting to be opened on Christmas day."

Sevik tilted his head. There were no gifts under hers.

"I, um, put this one up just for decoration," she said. "I haven't really celebrated Christmas in years."

"What is Christmas about?"

She chuckled to herself. "Depends on who you ask."

"I'm asking you."

"For me, it was about family. Spending time with your loved ones, eating yummy food, and as a kid, of course the presents. But even when I was young, my favorite part about the presents wasn't what I got. It was when my parents opened whatever little thing I'd made for them. No matter what it was, whether a silly pasta ornament or a picture frame made of popsicle sticks that I'd painted, they'd always smile and hug me tight. I...always loved that."

Mina brushed her fingers over a bristly branch, making it rustle. "They kept all that stuff. I found the box in my mom's room after she died. Every single card I drew for their birthdays, every craft I made for them in school, and all the gifts I made for Christmas."

Sevik looked back at the little tree. For a long, long time, his life had been about taking. Even a couple weeks ago, he would've laughed at the foolishness of a holiday like she'd described. Would've dismissed the possibility of deriving pleasure from giving anything to other people.

But his time with Mina had reminded him that he knew better. That he'd always known better.

All those years ago, nothing had made him feel prouder or more accomplished than presenting his mother with the medicine he'd worked so hard to obtain. And he'd been motivated not by selfishness, but by the desire to see his mother get better, to see her happy.

In all his life, he'd never felt as good as he had in that single, fleeting moment. Not until he found his mate. Not until he found Mina.

Now nothing was as fulfilling to him as Mina's pleasure. If he was greedy, he was greedy for her happiness. And every moment with her was a new high.

Sevik vowed to shower his mate with as many gifts as he could, with whatever her heart desired, just to see her smile.

"It's coming soon?" he asked, looking back at Mina.

She smiled at him. "Christmas is in thirteen days. December twenty-fifth."

That didn't give him much time, but he would make it work. Even in this tiny town, on an alien planet, he would make it work.

Sevik resumed his perusal of Mina's décor. Everything seemed simple, and he suspected that many of her belongings had been handmade based on their small irregularities and imperfections, but that lent a charm to the place that made it only more welcoming.

His attention shifted to the photographs, which were scattered everywhere—between potted plants, hanging on the walls, standing on shelves and any other flat surface. The greatest concentration of pictures was on a tall shelf cabinet against one wall.

He walked to the cabinet. The images were displayed alongside little vases, sculptures, trinkets, and a few more plants.

Based solely on their clarity and vibrancy, he guessed that most of the photos were older. Some had a faded look, like they'd seen too much sunlight, while others had dulled, washed-out colors. Carefully, he picked up one of the framed pictures and angled it to cut the glare on the glass.

It depicted a human child in a yellow sunflower dress standing in front of a pair of adult humans, a male and a female. Behind them was an abstract, cloudy smear of blue. He knew immediately who he was looking at.

The child was Mina, complete with that dark, curly hair and those unmistakable big brown eyes, and the people with her must've been her parents. The resemblance was undeniable. While Mina favored her mother's tiny frame and dark hair, she didn't have the same blue eyes; she shared the warmth and shade of her father's.

Sevik smirked. Little Mina was smiling wide, revealing a gap where her two front teeth should have been. She was...adorable.

She was still adorable.

He looked at his mate to find her smiling at the picture.

She's beautiful.

"That's one of my favorite pictures with them," she said.

Sevik returned the frame to its place. "You looked happy."

"We were."

Though the pictures didn't seem to be arranged in any particular order, there was a story in them, one that hit Sevik much harder than he would've expected. Hearing about the loss she'd endured had been difficult enough. Seeing it through the images only added another layer to the emotions.

He could see little Mina growing up through the pictures. After a certain point, her father no longer appeared in them. Some of the light was gone from Mina's eyes after that; almost all of it vanished from her mother's.

An older man appeared in a few of the following pictures. Randy. He seemed to bring a bit of joy back to the two females. The happiness and pride in Mina's expression in the picture where she stood beside Randy on the shore of a lake, each of them holding up a large, shimmery-scaled fish, was heartwarming.

And then it was her mother's turn to disappear.

All the pictures of Mina as an adult were of either her alone or with Randy, and there were very few of them. Her smile didn't reach her eyes in any of those.

Sevik's gaze rose to the top shelf, where a larger picture in a more elaborate frame stood prominently at the center. Mina's parents. They looked younger than they had in the other images and were dressed in formal attire—a black suit for her father, an intricate white dress for her mother. The two were looking into each other's eyes, their gazes holding far more meaning than should've been possible.

Sevik recognized that look. That was how he looked at Mina, and how she looked back at him.

He gestured to the image. "What's that one?"

"Their wedding picture."

Sevik turned his gaze back to Mina. "Wedding? That's...a human ceremony?"

She chuckled. "It's when people get married. When they officially...become mates."

"Explain."

"Well..." Mina touched the bite mark on her neck. "It's different than imprinting by scent or, uh, marking with a bite."

Primal satisfaction filled him at the sight of that mark, and a slow grin stretched across his lips. "Tell me of your mating customs."

"I guess I should start from the beginning. When people decide they're ready to find a partner, or when they find somebody they like, they'll go on dates. It's like a getting-to-know-you stage. If they feel chemistry or still really like that person after a date, they'll go on more. Some people will go on tons of dates with different people until they find the one they like most. And eventually they might decide that they're together, in a relationship. A couple. Of course, some people are polyamorous, which means they're in a relationship with more than one person, but—"

"Mina," he intoned. "How do we become mates? I don't care about anyone else."

Her cheeks pinkened. "Oh. Okay, well, if it were us, the first step would be dating, then deciding we're boyfriend and girlfriend. And then, when we're ready, you'd buy a ring and ask me to marry you. If I say yes—"

His brows fell. "*If?*"

She grinned. "I would say yes. Then we'd be engaged. An engagement can last for a short period of time, or years. It really depends on the couple. But eventually, we'd have a wedding ceremony. There'd be an officiant who would make it official after we exchange vows, declaring us man and wife, and then we'd kiss."

Sevik grasped her jaw with one hand and leaned closer to her. "You are my wife, Mina."

She laughed and settled her hands on his chest. "That's not how it works here. There's usually a document that we'd sign, a marriage certificate, which would declare us legally bound, so it's recognized by the government."

"Fuck that," he growled, baring his fangs. "Nobody tells me who I can mate with. Nobody tells me what's mine. I decide." His other arm banded around her middle, tugging her against his body. "This is between us and no one else, *val'syra*."

Sevik lowered his head until his lips were a breath away from hers. "Say the vows, Mina."

She stared up at him with wide eyes and shivered. He felt her warm, shuddering breath as she curled her fingers against his chest. Her voice was soft when she spoke.

"I, Mina Anastasia Walker, take you, Sevik kol Talris, to be my husband. To have and to hold from this day forward, for better or worse, for richer or poorer, in sickness and in health, to love and cherish, till death do us part."

Heat stirred in his chest, and his fangs ached. He'd never felt the mix of emotions brimming in him now—pride, devotion, adoration...love.

Mina was his. His all, his everything, his forever, and it went so much further than imprinting, so much deeper than venom and biology. He adored everything about this female, and the more he learned about her, the more he wanted her.

"I, Sevik kol Talris, take you, Mina Anastasia Walker, to be my wife. You are my heart, you are my world, you are my reason. I will possess and protect you, pleasure and provide for you, and give you everything I have and more. Nothing will tear us apart. Not even death." He moved his hand from her chin to cup the nape of her neck, tilting her head back farther. "And now I'm kissing my *wife*."

He captured her mouth with his. She closed her eyes and gave in to the slow seduction, to the consuming, searing kiss, the claim, returning it in kind and sealing their vows.

They kissed until their hunger roared to life, until their need could no longer be denied, and their clothes could no longer act as barriers between their bodies. And then they sealed their vows in a different way, again and again and again.

TWENTY-FIVE

Mina smoothed her hands down her thigh-length, off-white sweater dress as she stared at her reflection in the standing mirror. Her matching knee-high leg warmers made the outfit both cute and sexy. The material's light color complemented her dark hair, which she'd taken extra care with to ensure her curls were perfect. Her makeup—black winged eyeliner, mascara, and a matte sepia lip gloss—rounded out the look.

We're going on a date!

Mina brought her hands to her chest and stamped her feet excitedly, grinning so wide that her cheeks hurt.

She was going on a date with Sevik. A date! They'd finally be out in public as an official couple. It'd been five days since they'd returned to town, five days since Sevik had declared Mina his wife, since they'd performed their private marriage in her living room, and Mina couldn't wait to show off her mate.

Her *husband*.

She squealed into her sweater cuffs, muffling the sound.

Okay, so maybe they were doing things backwards, but who cared? As Sevik had said, what they decided to do was between them. It was their choice. She didn't need a piece of paper to tell her that Sevik was hers.

Turning, Mina grabbed her knitted boots and walked to the door. Her hand paused on the knob as anxiety washed through her.

She hadn't been on a date in six years, and the few she'd gone on before that had all been horrible.

But this was Sevik. Her mate. He wasn't some guy from town who knew about Mina and her mother's past, who expected something from her because of it, who would use it to hurt and demean her if she didn't give him what he wanted.

And he was on the other side of this door, waiting for her.

Smiling, Mina turned the knob, pulled open the door, and stepped out of her bedroom, making her way down the short hall and into the living room.

Sevik stood before the bookcase that held most of Mina's photos. He'd studied the pictures often, sometimes looking almost perplexed, other times wistful. Knowing his past, she could guess how he must've felt.

He turned toward her, and a slow smile spread across his lips as those white-hot eyes raked over her from head to toe. He was dressed in a black button-down shirt—with the top couple buttons left undone to offer a tantalizing glimpse of his chest—and black jeans. The snug clothing accentuated his tall, athletic frame. His white hair, which would turn black before they stepped outside, was pulled back into a thick, messy bun.

"*Zekt'al, val'syra,*" he growled as he moved in front of her, "maybe we'll stay here instead."

Sevik skimmed his fingers up her bare thigh and teasingly traced the hem of her dress before easing it upward. Mina shivered, rocked by a jolt of arousal despite the lightness of his touch.

"Mmm." He dipped his head, positioning his mouth near her ear, and whispered, "I could just bend you over the sofa and feast on your sweet cunt right now. Could listen to your pretty cries as I thrust my cock into you and fill your belly with my seed."

Mina's breath quickened as she rubbed her thighs together, her pussy swelling with the mental image his words created.

Liquid heat gathered in her core, and she knew Sevik could smell her want. He knew exactly what he was doing to her.

He raised the hem of her dress higher, over her hips, and palmed her ass. A low chuckle rumbled from him. "Ah, Mina..."

Oops. Did I forget my underwear? How forgetful of me.

With a laugh, Mina danced away from his arms and faced him, tugging her dress back down. "Since you've gotten us both quite worked up"—she glanced pointedly at his crotch, where his jeans bulged—"I will hold you to those words when we get back from our date."

His eyes were dark with lust, and though his smirk remained in place, it was strained. "So determined to make us wait."

"Mmhmm." She bent down and tugged her boots on. Once she straightened, she walked toward the door, running her fingers across his chest as she passed him. "And the entire time we're out, you can think of just how wet my bare pussy is for you."

Three, two—

Sevik growled and snatched her up into his arms. Mina squealed with delight, throwing her arms around his neck.

He grunted and opened the door. "Let's get this date over with so I can show my mate what happens when she taunts a beast."

Mina was thoroughly looking forward to it.

She giggled against his neck before nipping it. He hissed.

RIVERSIDE SALOON WAS LIVELY when Mina and Sevik entered. She wasn't surprised; this was the only bar in town. It was busy most nights it was open. A buzz of conversation overlaid the music from the jukebox, all accented by the clacking of pool balls and the clinking of glasses.

Mina hadn't come here since Randy moved away. She'd never been much of a drinker, had never cared for the noise, and certainly wasn't a fan of some of the locals who frequented the place. But Sullford wasn't exactly overflowing with options for entertainment, and Riverside had pool tables, dart boards, and even a few old pinball machines, making it the obvious—and only—choice.

The lighting was dim but warm, with the usual neon signs on the walls accompanied by strings of colorful Christmas lights and shimmery garland. The wood of the floors, tables, and bar top were polished to a reflective gleam. The décor was just as cluttered and random as Mina remembered—old photos of Sullford and the surrounding area, expired license plates from Alaska and other states, a smattering of bigfoot memorabilia, the heads and racks of deer, elk, and moose, and various tools that must've dated back to the town's founding.

The red Santa hats flopped atop a few of the mounted animal heads were likely a seasonal addition. And of course, the high definition, flatscreen televisions broadcasting several sports games were all brand new.

As Mina hung her coat at the entrance, many patrons turned their eyes toward her and Sevik. Her skin itched under such scrutiny. Maybe coming here wasn't a good idea?

She dashed that thought aside. *No.* She was done hiding. She needed to show them that their judgment didn't matter, that they could no longer affect her happiness. Plus, she wanted to show Sevik off.

Mina slipped her hand into his and looked up at him. "Come on. Let me show you how to play pool."

She led him toward the only vacant table, slipping through the small crowd of laughing men clustered at the neighboring one. Releasing his hand, she retrieved two cues from the rack against the wall, handing him one.

"I haven't played in years, so I'm probably rusty," she said. "Randy and I used to come here on occasion. He taught me how to play."

Sevik studied the stick, running a hand along its length, before glancing at one of the nearby tables. If he was uncomfortable being in a new place, an alien hiding amongst humans about to try an unfamiliar game, he didn't show it. He stood tall and confident. Like he belonged here.

When he returned his attention to Mina, he smirked and gestured to their table. "Show me, *val'syra*."

Thankfully, the previous players had been courteous enough to rack up the balls. Mina pulled the triangle closer, rearranged the balls so the eight ball was at the center, and moved it back into place.

"Okay, so, the goal is to get the balls in the holes. You do that by hitting the cue ball"—she pointed to the solid white ball left outside the triangle—"into them with the stick. Easy, right?"

Mina removed the triangle and set it aside. "The first person to go breaks, and if they get a ball into a hole, they claim that type, which is either the stripes or solid colors. If they get a ball of each in the hole, they choose which they want to go for. If they miss, the next person goes. To win, you need to get all the balls of your type into the holes, except the black one."

Sevik cocked a brow. "Why not the black one?"

Mina gave him a serious look. "It's a bad, bad ball."

He laughed. "Why's that?"

She shrugged. "I don't know. It's just the rules. If you get it in before you get the rest of your balls in, you lose. But once you have the rest in, you can go after the black one. You have to call it, though."

"Call it?"

"Yeah. Call which pocket you're going to hit it into. So, do you want to break?"

Sevik shook his head. "Let me observe you first."

Oh, she'd give him something to observe all right.

Moving into position, Mina bit down on her bottom lip to suppress a grin as she spread her legs and bent over the table, lining up her cue. She felt the immediate draft on her pussy and knew her dress had ridden up quite a bit.

Before she could take her shot, Sevik's hands clamped on her hips. His pelvis pressed against her ass as he leaned over her. His voice was gravelly, with a hint of menace in his tone, when he spoke into her ear. "You're playing a dangerous game, female."

The knitting of her dress provided no protection from the prick of his claws when he flexed his fingers. "If another male so much as glimpses what belongs to me, I will delight in gouging out his eyes."

Then he withdrew, leaving her breathless and aflame. His threat of violence shouldn't have turned her on, but it did. The evidence was in the tightness of her nipples and the needy ache growing between her thighs.

What was wrong with her?

Nothing. It had everything to do with Sevik. The idea that her body was his and his alone, that he'd go to such lengths for her, was arousing as hell.

Mina released a shaky breath, focused on the cue ball, and struck.

The balls scattered, and one with stripes made it into a corner pocket.

She straightened and tugged her skirt down, casting a quick glance around. As arousing as Sevik's jealousy was, she didn't really want someone's eyes gouged out.

"Looks like the stripes are mine!" she declared with a smile.

Sevik's unwavering stare told Mina that she could have the stripes. *She* was his.

He walked toward her, taking his place next to the table just as a waitress approached. Mina immediately recognized her.

Angela Maitlin.

They'd gone to high school together, though they'd never interacted back then. Now, Angela often came into Mina's café for her morning coffee, where she complained about her husband's laziness around the house, his inability—or unwilling-ness—to care for their kids, and even her suspicions that he was cheating on her.

Mina knew much, much more about Angela's marriage and intimate life than she'd ever wanted to, but her heart went out to the woman. Angela deserved better.

"Hi Mina!" Angela said with a grin. "I can't believe I'm seeing you here." Her gaze turned to Sevik. "Oh my gosh, you're Viktor, right?"

Sevik dipped his chin in a shallow nod.

She playfully slapped his shoulder. "You're such a hottie up close!"

The change to his expression was subtle, all in the way his jaw slowly bulged. Mina tensed as what she could only identify as possessiveness twisted in her belly.

"You have *no* idea how much people have been wondering about you," Angela said, shifting her body toward him fully. "No one's going to believe you came in here tonight. I have at least a thousand questions I could ask, and all my friends are dying to know the answers."

"Could I get a chocolate White Russian?" Mina interjected before Angela could scratch any of those questions off her lengthy list.

She couldn't fault the woman's curiosity—Mina had been curious about Sevik since he'd arrived in Sullford too—but that possessive side of her was baring its fangs at the sight of another woman touching him.

"Oh! Right." Angela offered Mina a smile and looked back at Sevik. "What about you, hun?"

"Water."

"You got it. I'll be right back with those."

Mina watched her walk away before returning her attention to Sevik. One side of his mouth was slanted up in a smirk.

"I like seeing that fire in your eyes, *val'syra*."

She blushed and stood her stick up on the floor. "You're not the only one who can get jealous."

"Good." Tucking his cue in the crook of his arm, he rolled up his sleeves one at a time, revealing those powerful, toned forearms, letting her see the muscles moving under his skin. "Shall we resume our game?"

Mina stared at those arms.

Oh, that is so unfair.

With a huff, Mina turned back to the table, struggling to focus on the game. But her next shot came up short, making it Sevik's turn. And he must have watched her very, *very* carefully, because he leaned forward, lined up his cue, and sunk his first ball almost effortlessly.

He straightened and circled the table like a predator sizing up its prey, tilting his head and narrowing his eyes. He took his second shot, sinking a second ball.

"You've played this before!" Mina said.

"I haven't. I just have a talented, beautiful instructor."

Angela returned with their drinks, setting them on a small round table nearby. "I opened a tab for you two. Just wave me down if you want anything else."

Thankfully, she hurried off to take care of the men at the neighboring billiards table without further conversation.

Sevik didn't even look at Angela; he was too busy studying the table with an intensity that only made Mina more excited for later. She picked up her glass and took a drink, savoring the sweet, creamy, chocolatey concoction.

On his next shot, he sank yet another ball—but the cue ball also rolled into a pocket.

"That's a scratch," Mina declared.

He glanced at the felt tabletop with a brow arched.

"Not literally," she said, retrieving the cue ball. "When this goes into a pocket, it's called a scratch, and it's a foul."

"Meaning?"

She grinned at him, set down her glass, and strutted around the table. "Meaning it's my turn."

Their game went back and forth, with neither more than a ball or two ahead of the other. Sevik was a fast learner who seemed to have a natural aptitude for the game, forcing Mina to shake off the rust quickly. The playful competitiveness between them was a little thrill all its own, but it was nothing compared to seeing him laughing, smiling, and teasing her without a hint of self-consciousness or hesitance. For Sevik, the rest of the bar might as well not have existed.

Of course, she wasn't above a little gloating when she clinched victory in their first round. Wicked promise gleamed in his eyes as he racked the balls for a rematch.

After a hard-fought battle, he took the win, but he didn't rub it in her face. Instead, he moved close, caged her in against the pool table with his arms, and growled against her neck, making her giggle.

She ordered another White Russian as they began their third round. Yet as much fun as Mina was having, she was eager to return home, to feel his hands and mouth on her body. To hold him to his threat of teaching her a lesson. She loved it when the beast came out to play.

Halfway through the match, Mina held out her hand. "Could I have a dollar?"

He looked up from the table, eyes narrowed as though he were trying to determine her ploy. "For what?"

She laughed. "Don't look at me so suspiciously! I just want to pick a couple songs on the jukebox. They can be my victory songs."

Sevik chuckled and shook his head, reaching into his pocket. He held out a dollar bill. "You haven't won yet, Mina."

She playfully snatched it out of his grasp. "I will though. Just you wait and see." As she walked away, she called over her shoulder, "No cheating while I'm gone!"

Mina stood in front of the jukebox's glowing neon lights, hands braced on either side of it, as she skimmed through the playlist. So many of the songs had changed in the years since she'd last come here with Randy. All his favorites were by The Beatles.

God, she missed him.

What would he think of Sevik? Would they be able to tell him who and what Sevik really was, or would it be better if he never knew? Either way, it would be Sevik's choice. All Mina knew was that she wanted them to meet. Eventually.

A man appeared beside Mina and rested his arm atop the jukebox. He grinned, his eyes dipping along her body before meeting her gaze. "Well, hello beautiful."

Mina frowned. She'd seen him around town maybe once or twice, but she didn't know his name.

The stranger was tall and looked to be around her age, though his short, thick beard made him appear a little older. His stocky frame, combined with his height, made Mina feel small and uncomfortable given his closeness. It wasn't anything like what Sevik made her feel.

And she didn't like the way he was looking at her. It made her skin crawl.

Ignoring him, she inserted the dollar into the machine. Once it had processed, she picked her first song—*Twist And Shout* by The Beatles.

For Randy.

"Hey." The man shifted closer. "I'm talking to you."

"I'm married," Mina said as she continued skimming through songs.

"I don't see a ring."

"Doesn't mean I'm not married."

"Now, why do you have to be like that?" he asked, lowering his arm from the jukebox and settling his hand over the song labels in front of her, forcing her to take a step back. "I'm just trying to be nice."

Forget the other song. She just wanted to get back to Sevik.

Without responding, Mina turned away.

His hand caught her forearm, halting her.

Mina glared at him, giving her arm a tug. In a firm, controlled voice, she said, "Let me go. I'm not interested, so leave me alone."

Instead of releasing her, he drew her closer. "I was just trying to talk to you. What is it with you women? Why do you have to be such a bitch abo—"

A large hand clamped on the man's wrist and twisted his arm, breaking his hold on Mina. She stumbled backward, eyes wide as Sevik slammed the man into the jukebox with a snarl. The song it was playing skipped, and the machine struck the wall with a bang, remaining tipped up on its hind legs as Sevik pinned the man against it.

Glowing white flashed in Sevik's eyes—a slip of the mask, a glimpse of the real him. And Mina knew what was going to happen. What he was about to do.

She'd wanted the beast uncaged, but not here, not like this.

The bar had fallen silent but for the jukebox now. Mina glanced around quickly; every eye in the place was on Sevik. She felt true fear in that moment. Fear for him.

Not simply for the repercussions of potential murder, but because if his shroud slipped, if they saw the real him, they would...

She didn't want to think of it. Didn't have time.

Mina threw herself forward, forcing her way between Sevik and the stranger and wrapping her arms around him tightly just as he was about to swing his fist. "No!"

He halted, entire body tense and stiff, and looked down at her. His lips were peeled back, and his expression was feral, fierce, bloodthirsty. Fortunately, his shroud seemed to have recovered, but his eyes were pools of bottomless, impenetrable black, utterly inhuman despite his disguise.

The stranger spat a curse and shifted behind her. Sevik's body jolted as he slammed the man back again, causing another skip in the music and drawing a pained grunt from the man.

"Sevik, please." She caught his face between her hands, forcing his attention to remain on her, as tears flooded her eyes. "Please don't. He's... He's not worth it. Let's just go, okay? Take me home. Please? I want to go home."

Please don't kill him.

TWENTY-SIX

MOLTEN FURY BLAZED through Sevik's veins. It suffused him, consumed him, and flooded his muscles with raw, wrathful strength.

He touched my mate.

My mate.

Mine.

His every instinct demanded he attack. His claws yearned to shred flesh, his skin craved the splash of warm blood, and his ears longed for the music of desperate pleas and agonized screams.

The male human reeked of sourness—sweat, alcohol, and fear.

He needed to die.

Sevik would tear the male apart and piss on the pieces.

Everything in him thrashed, snarled, and roared at his stillness. Why wasn't this male dead? Why wasn't Sevik bathed up to his elbows in blood?

The reason the male needed to die was the same reason he was still sucking air into that soft, hairy face.

Mina.

Sevik felt her touch. He felt her warmth, wholly distinct from the firestorm raging within. Her quick, ragged breaths teased his chest through the opening of his shirt, and her gaze weighed upon him.

Ornyr valaas duun, she was so fucking beautiful, but he hated seeing fear in those big, dark eyes. It made his rage flare and his instincts more volatile. Made him want to kill this male with more savagery than this world had ever seen.

Tremors rippled through Sevik's limbs as he strained to resist that urge, as his mind clawed at the words Mina had just said, struggling to hold onto her plea, to respect it. To honor her wishes despite this rage.

Please don't.

He's not worth it.

I want to go home.

Sevik's hand tightened on the man's wrist, which he held firm against the man's chest. A pained gasp escaped the human as Sevik's claws pressed into his flesh through his long sleeve shirt.

This male had disrespected Mina. He'd frightened her, touched her, hurt her.

Any one of those things was enough to warrant death. All three?

One death was not fucking enough.

"Please." Mina's voice, a nearly broken whisper, drew Sevik's focus back to her.

His next inhalation was laden with her scent. It eased the heat in him like a cool breeze, and he suddenly understood the fear in her eyes.

It wasn't fear of this man, not anymore. Nor was it fear of Sevik or what he was about to do. No, this was something different, something he'd never encountered.

This was selfless. She was afraid *for* him.

Clarity pierced the fiery haze in Sevik's mind.

They were in a bar filled with witnesses, and everyone was staring. Chief Harrigan would have testimony from at least twenty people describing how Sevik had beaten this man to death.

He released a harsh breath through his fangs and lifted his gaze to the male's. Voice low and venomous, he grated, "You even look in her direction again, and your last meal will be your own fucking cock."

Sevik carefully shifted Mina aside before thrusting the male away. The man cried out as he fought for balance with frantic, stumbling steps that carried him across the room. A few of the patrons at the bar scrambled off their seats and out of the way just before the bearded human crashed into the counter, knocking over the now empty stools along with several glasses and bottles. The sounds of objects falling were thunderous.

Angela appeared beside them and reached out toward Mina. Sevik moved to shield his mate, a low growl building in his chest. The woman quickly withdrew her hand, but Sevik saw the concern and understanding in her eyes as she looked at Mina.

Angela's voice was just loud enough for Sevik to hear over the music when she spoke. "You guys go on. I'll take care of your bill."

"Thank you," Mina said.

"Can't have this kind of shit going on in here," said the older male human behind the bar, his eyebrows set in anger as he stared at Sevik.

Fighting back a surge of fury and resentment, Sevik turned toward the man.

When a male twice Mina's size had grabbed her, no one in the bar had spoken a fucking word. Not a single whisper of protest, not a single person coming forward to defend her until Sevik stepped in himself. It'd been no different when Sevik had been poised to kill the bearded man—not one word until Mina, the very female the man had accosted, stepped in to save his life. They were all going to stand and fucking watch.

But now that the immediate threat had passed, they had something to say?

After what Mina had told him about the people of this town, could Sevik have expected anything different?

The song on the music machine changed to something upbeat. A gravelly-voiced man sang about shaking things up.

Mina stepped forward to face the bartender, but Sevik banded an arm around her waist, pulling her back against him.

Pointing at the bearded male, Mina raised her voice, clear and cold, over the music. "That guy harassed and grabbed me. Was that part okay? Was it just a problem when someone stood up for me?"

Many of the onlookers, including the man behind the bar, averted their gazes, some with their faces visibly reddening.

Neither their shame nor their silence assuaged Sevik's fury. He gritted his teeth, and his claws dug painfully into his palms. The inferno at his core could not be contained for long. All the energy in his limbs would demand action, and he would not be able to resist. Already, it was making his skin itch, making his bones pulse with maddening heat.

Mina had been right. It was time to go.

Now.

Before he did something that would destroy any chance he and Mina had at a life together.

Sevik stalked toward the exit and snatched Mina's coat off its hook. He swept it over her shoulders, shoved the door open, and took her by the hand to lead her out into the brisk night air. The cold only made the fire inside him seem all the hotter in contrast.

He stormed along the sidewalk, heading toward Mina's building.

Aggaan sin thar, those humans should've been grateful his mate had such a kind, tender heart, because he would have carved all theirs out and laid them at her feet.

Mina gave his hand a tug. "Sevik? Could you...slow down? Just a little?"

Halting abruptly, he spun to face her. She walked into his arms, and he lifted her off her feet, drawing her against his chest. Her arms and legs wrapped around him, and he planted a hand on her ass, preventing her skirt from riding any higher.

The tip of his middle finger encountered the hot, slick flesh of her pussy. Mina's breath hitched, and her hold tightened as she whispered his name against his ear.

No underwear. No fucking underwear.

He felt the heat from her cunt through the fabric of his shirt.

Radiating into him, fucking taunting him, pouring fresh fuel into the blaze at his core.

His fury twisted and reformed, shaping all that fire into a consuming, undeniable need that had his cocks instantly straining for freedom from his slit.

"Fuck," Sevik grated through his teeth.

He turned and ran, sliding his hand lower so the pad of his finger rubbed against Mina's folds and teased her entrance with every slam of his boots on the concrete.

By the time they reached her home, she was panting and whimpering, moving urgently against his hand. Her fragrance was suffused with the perfume of her arousal, and it was all he could smell, filling his mind with a lustful fog, making his heart pound harder and faster, making his blood flow hotter and thicker.

It took tremendous willpower to avoid breaking down the door. He forced his hand into his pocket, took out the key she'd given him, and unlocked the door. He slammed it shut the instant they were inside.

His holoshroud melted away. He kicked his boots off, pulled her coat away from her shoulders, and tugged off her footwear as he walked to the stairs, not caring where any of it fell. When his hand returned to her ass, it found bare skin. Her skirt had ridden up with their movements. It took everything inside him to keep from rutting her right there on the stairs. His clothing was abrasive against his skin, restrictive, keeping it from touching Mina's, and heat was consuming him from the tips of his toes to the points of his horns.

She kissed his neck and flicked her tongue over his earlobe an instant before she nipped it with her teeth.

He growled and slapped his hand back down on her ass as he carried her upstairs.

"Sevik!" she gasped, her thighs tightening around his waist.

Fuck, he needed to be inside her. Needed to claim her.

Sevik flung open the door to her apartment and brought her in. He kicked it closed; before it had even finished its journey, he had his mate against the wall.

He caught her mouth in a hungry, bruising kiss, lifting a hand to cup the nape of her neck and keep her head angled just how he wanted. She returned the kiss with equal fervor, her hands delving into his hair and catching fistfuls of it.

When his tongue demanded entry, she offered no resistance, allowing him to explore her mouth and declare his ownership of every bit of it. His groin pulsed with that deep, needful ache. Mingled with her taste was that of his venom, adding to her sweetness, enhancing his desire.

Bracing a thigh under Mina's ass to keep her in place, he slid his lower hand between their bodies. Her wet, dripping cunt radiated maddening heat, and he slipped his fingers between her folds, gathering her slick before stroking her swollen clit.

Mina whimpered. Sevik swallowed the sound, finding it just as delectable as the rest of her. She ground against his palm, riding his finger with uninhibited passion, her whimpers turning into panting moans.

"Did you enjoy taunting me?" Sevik rasped against her mouth before pressing his forehead to hers. "Did you enjoy teasing me?"

She opened her eyes with a strained, whispered, "Yes."

Staring into her eyes, he stroked her clit in a frantic rhythm until she released a strangled cry and came undone in his arms. Her clit thrummed, and essence spilled from her, coating his hand; he reveled in it all.

He slanted his mouth over hers, kissing her hard, relishing her muffled sounds of pleasure. When he broke the kiss, he said, "Game's over, *val'syra*."

Sevik carried her to the bedroom, dipping his head so he could graze his fangs over the mark he'd left on her shoulder. She shivered.

Setting her down on the floor at the foot of the bed, he took a step back. Mina moved as though to reach for him.

"Stay there," he commanded.

She lowered her arms. Her lips were red from his kisses, her cheeks were flushed, her dress was hiked up around her hips, and her inner thighs were wet with her slick. She looked sexy as fuck.

Sevik raised his hands to his shirt and began unbuttoning it. "Strip."

The speed with which Mina grasped the bottom of her dress and pulled it off over her head made Sevik's lips curl into a grin.

Eager little thing.

She tossed the dress aside and reached for one of her leg warmers.

"No." Tugging open his shirt, Sevik shrugged it off. "Leave those."

"Yes, sir," Mina said with a smile. Keeping her eyes on him, she sat on the bed and scooted back until she reached its center, propping herself up with her hands behind her.

Sevik unbuttoned his jeans and shoved them down his hips so quickly it was a wonder he didn't tear them. His cocks extruded fully, no longer confined by the restrictive garment, and he groaned, wrapping the fingers of one hand around them.

Mina's eyes dipped down his body, and her lips parted with a shuddering exhalation. "I want you."

"And I need you." Sevik crawled onto the bed. "All of you, Mina."

She met his gaze. The spark in her eyes told him she understood what he meant.

Mina sat up and tucked a lock of his hair behind his ear before caressing his cheek. "I'm yours, in any way you need me. In *every* way."

Sevik caught her hand as she withdrew it and pressed a kiss to the center of her palm, his eyes never leaving hers. "As I am yours." He lightly raked his fangs along her finger, flicked his tongue over her fingertip, and released her. "Turn over."

She got onto her hands and knees, thighs parted.

Sevik stared at her backside—at her cunt, swollen and slick with her arousal, and the hole above it, which he'd toyed with but had not yet taken.

Until now. Now, there would be no part of her left unclaimed.

He moved closer, settling his hands on her hips. He smoothed a palm over the rounded globe of her ass before raising it and bringing it back down with a sharp crack. Mina gasped, flinching, but she didn't withdraw.

"Again," she said softly.

Sevik chuckled as he soothed where he'd struck her. His cocks were so hard they fucking hurt, pulsing with lust, so close to what they wanted. But he couldn't resist this opportunity. Raising his palm, he brought it down on her other cheek.

She cried out, and her fingers curled into the bedding. "Again."

His sweet little mate wasn't quite as innocent as she'd once seemed.

This time, he spanked her in quick succession, back and forth, back and forth, snaking an arm around her waist and flattening his hand on her belly when her trembling limbs nearly gave out beneath her.

When he stopped, she was writhing and undulating, voicing a mix of cries and pleas. Bright red handprints stood out on her pale skin. He lightly trailed his fingers over her flesh and dragged them through her cunt.

Sevik groaned. "You're so fucking wet, Mina." He carefully slipped a finger inside her. Her inner walls clamped down on it. "Your pussy is so needy."

"Yes," she rasped, pushing back against his finger, making it sink deeper. "Oh God. Please, Sevik."

As he slowly withdrew his finger, her cunt squeezed, attempting to draw him back in, and his cocks twitched. He couldn't wait to feel her body clutching them. Sevik slipped his finger through her folds, moved it up to her ass, and circled her rosette, smearing her essence over it.

Vazk, the pressure built up within him was already beyond what he could handle. The slightest touch from her might've sent him over the edge, triggering an explosion well before he was ready. He couldn't allow this to end too soon, wouldn't allow it to.

He wrapped his hand around his upper cock and stroked it, gathering as much of his oil as he could. Returning that hand to her ass, he rubbed the natural lubricant over her rosette, teasing it and dipping his finger in and out shallowly, going just a little deeper each time.

"Sevik," Mina breathed, rocking against his finger as she looked at him over her shoulder. "I need you inside me. Now."

"And I need to feel you."

Placing a hand between her shoulders, Sevik pushed her down so only her ass was in the air. She turned her face to rest on her cheek, planted her hands on either side of her head, and clutched the bedding. With one hand on her hip, Sevik grasped his lower cock and brought it to her cunt. The head slipped into her with ease.

Mina moaned, closing her eyes as she pushed back, attempting to take more of him.

Gritting his teeth, Sevik tightened his hold on her hip, halting her. "Not yet."

"But—"

"Not. Yet."

Her heat beckoned him to thrust deeper, but he resisted the urge. Taking hold of his upper cock, he notched the tip to her rosette, and with a flex of his hips, breached the tight hole. Mina gasped, her anus clutching him.

Sevik slapped her ass. She cried out.

"Do not resist me, Mina," he said, rubbing the spot he'd struck.

"I'm not. I swear I'm not," Mina rasped. She wriggled her hips. "More."

Gripping both of her ass cheeks, he parted them and looked down at his cocks, which glistened with oils, looked down at the place he and Mina were connected. He pushed deeper, watching as her rosette stretched to take him ridge by ridge. She whimpered and panted.

"Good girl. That's it, my wife," he rumbled, barely keeping a tremor from his voice as her holes squeezed his shafts hungrily. "You're doing so well."

He eased back and pushed forward, again and again, and her body took him deeper and deeper.

"You're so fucking beautiful, Mina. Just look at how you're taking your mate inside you."

Mina moaned and bore back against him, pushing him farther in.

It was all the sign he needed. With a quick thrust, he sheathed both cocks completely inside Mina, pressing his slit flush against her.

She gasped.

"Fuck," he growled, curling his fingers and digging his claws into her flesh. "You feel so fucking good, *val'syra*. So fucking *good*."

"I feel you. All of you. I feel so full, but I...I..." Her cunt and ass clenched as she undulated her hips. "Oh God, Sevik, I need more."

A ragged exhalation escaped Sevik as her movements jolted him with pleasure, but he held her in place. This moment went beyond the feel of her body enveloping him so completely, beyond the heat, the friction.

Finally, he was inside his mate fully, connected to her fully. And it was fucking perfect.

She was perfect.

Sevik breathed in her scent, filling his lungs with it, with her, and slowly drew his hips back. When he pushed in, she cried out and he groaned. But he didn't stop. He pumped in and out, gradually faster, gradually deeper, and the blood flowed hotter and hotter through his veins, the pressure built higher and higher in his cocks.

Each time he pulled back, her body clutched at him, desperate to draw him in again. But he was in control. He set the pace. He continued quickening his thrusts, pushing ever harder, until each was punctuated by the slap of his thighs against hers.

"Don't stop," she rasped between her breathy cries. She turned her face down and clutched the bedding tighter. "Please don't stop."

He bared his fangs in a snarl. Each thrust was more powerful than the last, driving him even deeper. Her cunt was so wet it was weeping around his cock, and her essence combined with his oils to ease the glide of flesh on flesh. Ragged breaths clawed their way in and out of his chest, but he did not slow, did not relent.

Mina whimpered and moaned, her sounds escalating as she writhed and scratched at the bed. His thrusts were merciless; he wanted to consume her as wholly as she consumed him.

"That's it, *val'syra*. Let me hear you. Let me hear you sing as you come around my cocks."

"Sevik, I...I can't..."

"You can."

"It's too much, it's, it's..."

"Come for me, Mina!"

"Oh, God! *Sevik!*"

Her body locked up, and her pussy and ass clamped around his cocks. Her cunt convulsed, its walls fluttering, and threatened to push him out, but he was unrelenting. He slammed into her harder, snapped his hips faster.

And she sang.

"You're so fucking beautiful. And all fucking mine." The pleasure in his core coiled tight, and his cocks expanded despite the viselike grip of her body. It was too much to withstand, too much to contain. "My mate, my wife, my Mina."

Sevik surged forward one more time, burying himself deep inside her. Fire blasted through him, a supernova of ecstasy that raced along every nerve, leaving no part of him unaffected. His every muscle flexed, and all he could do was hold on to his mate as he growled and flooded her with seed.

Giving into the euphoria, Sevik curled over Mina, catching himself on an arm. He banded the other around her middle, holding her close as a second wave swept through him, followed by another, and another. His body twitched and spasmed with every release from his cocks, prolonging the pleasure quaking through them.

When that pleasure faded, leaving only languorous contentment, Sevik nuzzled her neck. Their heavy, rasping breaths mingled, and their hearts pounded in unison. Her scent and heat were indistinguishable from his, and their bodies remained blissfully connected.

Never in his life had he felt so...complete.

"Mina." He kissed her shoulder, kissed her neck, kissed the scar where he'd marked her.

"I love you," she whispered.

Sevik froze. For a moment, he wondered if he'd imagined those soft words.

"I-I'm not just saying that in the heat of the moment," she said. "After we've... After..."

As loath as he was to do so, Sevik carefully withdrew from her body and flipped her onto her back. He lowered himself over her, hips between her thighs, and his hair fell onto her chest, covering her breasts.

Catching her jaw, he forced her eyes to his. "What did you say?"

She searched his gaze as she wrapped her fingers around his wrist. "That I love you."

Sevik closed his eyes. "Again."

"I love you." She slipped her hands up his chest and into his hair. "I love you, Sevik."

It felt like she'd reached right into his chest and taken hold of his heart. Everything in him was hot and tight, and he felt so full. Too many emotions swirled within him, too many for any one person to hold.

What the fuck did he know about love? His mother had loved him, but her love hadn't been affectionate. She'd hidden all of herself away from him, and she'd never really let him love her back.

But this...this was entirely different. Entirely new. A foreign love, something he never would've expected, never would've deserved, of which he never would've dreamed.

No. Not foreign. Not new.

He'd felt this for a while now, hadn't he? It had dwelled in him, expanding day by day, ever since they'd first spoken in

Cornerstone. It had been there all this time; he simply hadn't recognized it for what it was.

And now that she'd said it, he knew. He knew what that feeling was.

His heart was pounding again, and his breath was shaky.

Some part of him had known all along, he'd just been too blind to realize. The first time he'd called her *val'syra*, he hadn't meant to do so; the word had simply come out. He hadn't understood the weight of it then. Hadn't understood how deeply he meant it.

Sevik opened his eyes and stared down into hers. In those dark, enthralling pools, he saw the reflection of everything he felt for her.

"I never answered your question," he said, voice low. "Didn't know how to before."

Her brow furrowed. "What question?"

"*Val'syra* doesn't translate directly into English. It's two korasi words put together. *Ostval*, which is the piece that completes a thing and holds it together. The piece that is the key. And *syra*... which means heart."

Mina's expression softened, and moisture welled in her eyes. "So *val'syra* means..."

"It means that you are the key to my heart. That you are the piece I've always been missing." He leaned down, stopping only when his mouth was a hair's breadth away from hers. "I love you, Mina."

Sevik pressed his lips to hers, giving life to his words with a long, tender, heated kiss.

TWENTY-SEVEN

Mina glanced at the clock as she waited for the coffee to brew.

Only three more minutes had passed. Three measly, excruciating minutes. It was still an hour before three o'clock. An hour before Sevik was due to pick her up.

Why can't time just go faster?

Tomorrow was Christmas Eve, and Mina and Sevik had made plans to spend the holiday at his cabin. He'd only been back there once since they'd returned to town after the big storm, just to grab clothing and essentials. He'd been living with her this whole time. Working with her, spending time with her.

And Mina loved every second of it.

Even knowing that their time apart today would be temporary, Sevik had been reluctant to leave this morning. She knew his protective instincts must've been railing at the thought of her being alone. But he'd needed to buy groceries so his kitchen would be stocked with something more than meat for her stay, and he'd said he wanted to clean the place up—not that she recalled it being messy when they'd left.

She was excited for their little getaway, excited to be secluded from the rest of the world. To spend Christmas with...her husband.

Grinning, Mina picked up the decanter and filled a paper cup with fresh coffee. The strong aroma permeated the air as steam rose from the hot liquid.

"That's quite a smile," Chief Harrigan said from the front counter. "Thinking about your man?"

Heat flooded Mina's cheeks as she glanced at him, expecting a judgmental stare, but thankfully there was only good humor in his teasing grin.

"I am." She plucked up a lid and pressed it onto the cup, making sure it was secure.

The bell over the door tinkled. Mina turned her head to see two men enter. Both were big and broad-shouldered, standing around Sevik's height. They were dressed in dark winter coats and sunglasses. One wore a knitted hat, while the other had his long black hair pulled back into a ponytail.

They were definitely new to the area. At least, Mina thought they were. She'd never seen them, and word usually traveled fast when someone new moved to town. Maybe they were visiting family for the holidays?

"Hello! I'll be with you in a moment," she said to them with a smile.

"He treating you good?" Harrigan asked as he eyed the newcomers.

It took Mina a moment to recall their conversation. When she did, the thought of Sevik filled her chest with something fuzzy and warm, widening her smile.

"He does. He really, really does." Slipping a coffee sleeve onto the cup, she turned and offered it to him. "One large medium roast."

Harrigan accepted it with a gruff thanks. "So, you're closing early today?"

"Yep."

"Got plans then?"

"Viktor and I are spending the holiday at his cabin."

Harrigan chuckled. "Well, forecast isn't showing any storms, so you shouldn't get stuck out there this time."

Mina blushed, but her grin endured. She could think of many, many reasons to get stuck at Sevik's cabin that had nothing to do with the weather...

Did she and Sevik even *need* a reason if they wanted to stay?

Nope. They could spend as much time as they wanted doing whatever they wanted—like having wild, freaky sex—and it was no one else's business.

The chief sipped his drink and let out a satisfied sigh. "Good coffee as always, Mina."

He raised the cup in a mock salute, turned, and walked over to the newcomers, eyeing them up and down. "Don't often see new faces in our little paradise. What brings you boys to town?"

The black-haired stranger said something to his companion in a low, deep voice, speaking a language Mina didn't recognize.

After a brief reply in the same language, the man in the hat smiled at the chief. Something about that smile seemed a bit too wide. There was a hint of an unidentifiable accent on his words when he said, "We're just passing through. Touring the Alaskan wilderness with my friend."

He tipped his head toward his companion.

Though the long-haired man's eyes were hidden behind the dark lenses of his sunglasses, Mina could feel his gaze upon her.

"Where you from?" Harrigan asked before taking another sip of his coffee.

Mina couldn't help but wince at his line of questioning. It wasn't surprising though.

"Seattle," the man in the hat replied.

"Huh. Didn't realize Washingtonians had accents like that."

"We have many accents in Seattle"—the man lowered his glasses briefly to glance at the chief's chest—"Chief Harrigan. But our scenery is lacking in comparison."

Nodding, Harrigan turned his attention to the black-haired stranger. "Where you two staying?"

"We have a camper," the man in the hat said. "Our other friends are with it now, outside town."

"Other friends? And how many of you are there?"

The man in the hat chuckled. "Do you suspect us of a crime, or do you ask the same questions to everyone who comes through this town?"

Chief Harrigan offered a smile of his own that was devoid of warmth and humor. "I'm just a naturally curious person is all. Love meeting new people and learning all about them. You two have names?"

"I'm Laszlo, and he is—"

"I heard him talk before," Harrigan said, gesturing to the silent man. "Can't he speak for himself?"

"I am called Ivan," the dark-haired man replied, his accent much thicker than his companion's. There was something familiar about that accent, and that familiarity niggled at the back of her mind, but a few words wasn't enough to identify it.

The chief stared at the man. Mina understood the tension in the air; Harrigan seemed to have that effect on a lot of people, especially when he treated them like they were criminals simply because he didn't know them.

"Well, Laszlo and Ivan, I hope you enjoy our little town while you pass through." He lifted his cup and nodded to them. "And it should go without saying, but don't cause any trouble while you're here."

He strode to the door, pushed it open, and turned back toward the newcomers. "Mina's got great coffee and pastries. Just don't let her talk you into buying any of those smutty books of hers."

Mina wrinkled her nose and pursed her lips as Harrigan stepped outside.

He just had to go there.

The men looked at her, and she offered them another smile. "To answer your question, yes, the Chief does interrogate everyone new that comes into town. Don't take it too personally."

"We know his type," Laszlo said with a dismissive wave. "He thinks himself...what's the saying? A big fish in a little pond? But we aren't concerned with him."

The two men moved to the counter. Only as they neared did

Mina get a true sense of their size; they definitely rivaled Sevik in height and build. It was...a bit intimidating.

"Well, welcome to Sullford!" she said. "It's really a lovely area, especially if you like the outdoors. Though this time of year, daylight is pretty scarce. Enjoy it while it lasts."

Laszlo's lips stretched into an unsettling grin. "Oh, we don't shy away from the dark, Mina."

Mina's skin prickled with unease.

Okay... That isn't a creepy thing to say.

"So, what can I get you?" she asked, keeping her smile in place.

Ivan braced a hand on the counter and leaned closer to her, nostrils flaring as he inhaled. A growl rumbled from his chest. "She reeks of him."

Reeks of...him?

Of...Sevik?

Mina's brow creased, and she took a step back. "What?"

"Fucking police," Laszlo muttered as he walked to the front door. He peered out the window, casually turning the hanging sign to *CLOSED* and locking the deadbolt.

Terror crashed through Mina as her eyes flicked between the two men. Their strange mannerisms, their size, their accents.... She knew with chilling certainty that these men weren't human, and that they were after Sevik.

And they knew she was his mate.

She needed to go. Now.

Mina spun and ran down the hallway toward the back door.

Heavy, rapid steps followed her. When she reached the door, she wrapped her fingers around the knob and tugged it open.

A hand struck the door above her head, slamming it shut.

No. No! No, no, no!

Ivan's thick, powerful arm banded around her middle and pulled her against him. She shrieked, kicking her legs and swinging her arms, striking him with feet, hands, and nails anywhere she could reach.

With a growl, he clamped his other hand under her jaw,

forcing her head back against his chest. "So lively. I will enjoy breaking you in front of Sevik."

Her already cold blood turned to ice. She breathed, "Brekker."

He snarled and spun around. "I see he spoke of me."

Mina's eyes widened; Laszlo strode toward her with a small gun in his hand. Brekker jerked her head aside, exposing her neck, and Laszlo pressed the tip of the gun to her skin. It clicked and hissed. She felt a prick, and a new cold flowed into her body, spreading outward from her neck. Her limbs grew heavy, and black spots clouded her vision.

"No..." she rasped, trying to fight the sensation, to fight Brekker. But no matter how hard she tried, she couldn't stop what was happening.

Her body sagged in Brekker's hold.

"Sleep, female," he said. "It is the final peace you will ever have."

Those words were the last thing she heard before darkness enveloped her.

TWENTY-EIGHT

Sevik climbed into the bed of his truck and swept out the snow, twigs, and pinecones from within with a broom.

Almost done, Mina.

Though he willed that thought out to his mate, he knew it was more for himself than her. Since he'd left her apartment early this morning, Sevik had battled temptation. He'd longed to return to Mina, make her close the café even earlier than planned, and take her all for himself immediately.

He hopped down, shut the tailgate, and scattered the fallen twigs and needles into the deeper snow outside the carport's shelter using his boot.

He'd almost allowed himself to skip the cleanup. It would've brought him to Mina a minute or two sooner—which felt like an eternity while they were apart. But old habits had compelled him.

Destroy all the evidence you could, obscure what you couldn't. Those rules from his former life apparently applied to preparing a surprise for his mate.

After purchasing nearly every Christmas decoration he could find in Sullford between the grocery store, the hardware store, and the thrift shop, and spending hours putting them up, he wasn't about to let a few stray pine needles give everything away.

Sevik strode to the cabin door. When he opened it, a wave of warm air, redolent of cinnamon and spices, flowed over him. The wreath he'd hung on the door and the baskets of scented pinecones he'd placed on the tables had filled the place with their fragrances. He'd seen Mina's smile when she'd paused to smell them at Cornerstone a few days ago, and knew she'd appreciate them now.

He returned the broom to its place in the laundry room and flipped the switch for the exterior power outlets before stepping outside and locking up. A warm, golden glow filled the carport thanks to the strings of Christmas lights he'd hung.

But he paid those lights no attention as he entered the truck and started it. There was a tightness in his chest, a restlessness in his limbs, and an impossible-to-scratch itch just beneath his skin. He'd felt them all day...because he was apart from her.

Did Mina feel the same? Was this as difficult for her as it was for him?

As he drove along the driveway, he glimpsed the cabin in the rearview mirror. Red-orange light from the setting sun diluted the brightness of the lights he'd hung, but he still got a taste of the effect—the building seemed friendlier, more inviting.

By the time Sevik returned with Mina, it would be dark. He couldn't wait to see the Christmas lights shining beneath the night sky, couldn't wait for her to see them. Her smile would be even brighter.

Excitement carried him along the roads leading to town. His mate was waiting for him, with no idea of what awaited her.

Heat stirred low in Sevik's belly, and his cocks pressed against his slit, aching dully. He smirked.

Well, she knows some of what awaits her.

But that would come later. Unless... Unless he took her before they left her apartment, just to satiate their hunger for a little while...

Though some of the lights were off inside the café when he arrived, and the door sign was already flipped to *CLOSED*, the chairs hadn't yet been put up on the tables. Why would she turn off the lights when she still had work to do?

She's probably just as eager as me to start the holiday and wanted to make sure no more customers came in.

A simple, likely explanation, but it didn't quite quell the whisper of misgiving in the back of his mind.

He turned into her driveway and pulled around back, parking beside her vehicle. A single floodlight, mounted high on the exterior wall, shone down on the parking area, bathing it in orange-tinted light.

As Sevik strode to the back door, he was stricken by just how different everything was. How different he was. It wasn't a new realization—he'd been aware of it for a couple weeks, at least—but each time it hit him, it did so with surprising power.

Nothing was the same anymore, and he never wanted it to be again. For the first time in his life, he had a positive, hopeful future to look forward to.

Sevik unlocked the door and entered the building. Familiar scents filled his nose, including coffee, books, and pastries, but as always, Mina's fragrance commanded all his attention.

He glanced down the hall toward the café. Light spilled from the doorway on the left side of the hall, which led into the kitchen, but the front of the shop was dark.

"Ready to go, *val'syra?*" he called.

When Mina didn't answer, he wiped his boots on the mat and walked toward the front. "Mina?"

Sevik peered into the kitchen. No Mina, but there were unwashed dishes and utensils in the sink. Frowning, he continued to the front. The counters hadn't been wiped down, the coffee machines were running, the display case still held pastries, and the florescent lights over the bookshelves had been left on. All that in addition to the chairs having not been put up.

That unease prickled at the back of Sevik's mind. In the days he'd spent here with Mina, he hadn't seen her deviate from her closing routine. She'd been consistent in cleaning everything up before leaving the shop.

He called her name again, directing his voice toward the bookshelves. Still no answer.

As he turned to head back to the stairs, something at the corner of his eye gave him pause. He moved to the register and picked up the book lying beside it—the book Mina was currently reading. Her bookmark was nestled between the pages two-thirds of the way through.

She always had a book nearby to fill in the slow parts of her day, when nothing needed her immediate attention. But every evening, she'd brought her book upstairs after closing.

She's just excited. Closing early, disrupting her routine.

He'd go upstairs to let her know he'd arrived, and then he would start cleaning down here. He didn't want anything left undone that would worry her even a little during the holiday.

After removing his boots at the back door and leaving them on the mat beside Mina's, he climbed the stairs. Another twinge of unease hit him when he realized the apartment door was ajar.

Mina always kept that door closed and locked, whether she was inside or not. She'd once mentioned—while Sevik waited a few steps down for her to unlock the door—that some of the townsfolk had criticized her for it. They'd insisted that Sullford was such a safe little community that no one had any need to lock anything.

Mina had maintained that she was a single woman living by herself, so the door would stay locked. Her recent experiences in town had only solidified her stance.

Sevik agreed with her. Anything left unlocked was as good as an invitation.

Calling for her again, he pushed the door open. None of the lights were on. No sound came from inside the apartment but for the ticking of the wall-mounted clock in the kitchen.

Sevik's unease shifted, twisted, and expanded into a leaden chunk of dread. Instinctively, he reached back to grasp the plasma pistol holstered under his belt, though he didn't draw it yet.

Overreacting. She's fine. Lying down for a nap, or...she ran down to the store for something she remembered at the last moment.

But her boots were downstairs, her coats had been hanging on the hooks, and her car was parked in its usual spot. Unless she'd walked coatless to Cornerstone, where could she be?

She wasn't on the couch, wasn't in the bathroom, wasn't in the spare room she used as a reading room.

"Napping, then," he muttered as he moved to the bedroom. "You're supposed to be ready to go, *val'syra*. Are you so eager for a punishment that—"

Sevik froze in the doorway. That dread sank in his belly, pulling everything down, wrenching his insides into knots.

The floodlight's orange glow spilled in through the window, casting a skewed rectangle of light across the bed. Mina was not there, but two objects lay in the center of the light, atop the neatly spread comforter.

Mina's phone, its screen dark, and a small, disc-shaped device that could only have been a holographic projector.

No.

No, no, no.

The word sounded in his head again and again, losing meaning with each repetition until it was a hollow, incessant echo. Unbidden, his suddenly numb legs carried him toward the bed. An agonizing eternity passed over the course of those few steps.

All he could smell was himself and Mina—both their individual scents and the blended scent of their joining. But someone else had been here. Someone else had invaded and violated this intimate space, and the complete lack of alien smells meant a scent mask had been used. The intruder knew what Sevik was...

And Sevik knew who the intruder had been. There was only one possibility.

Under any other circumstances, he wouldn't have touched either of the devices on the bed. Both could've been rigged with explosive charges. But this...this was no simple assassination, or he would've been dead already.

Leskahn tor lesk, he'd let his guard down often enough lately to have given any would-be assassins hundreds of opportunities.

Gritting his teeth, he touched the front of Mina's phone. The lock screen came on. Its background had been changed to a picture of Mina lying on the floor, seemingly unconscious, with her arms bound together at her wrists. The mat beneath her was the same one by the back door downstairs.

Sevik's heart thumped. A surge of fear, icy and insidious, coursed through his body. A roiling, fiery blast of fury followed. That fire and ice raced through him, one after another, with each heartbeat, and every new wave added to the terrible pressure building at his core.

My mate, my wife, my Mina.

Taken.

Ragged breaths escaped through his nostrils as strength poured into his muscles. A bloody haze gathered at the edges of his vision, and his jaw clenched tighter still.

With a trembling finger, he activated the projector.

A holographic screen appeared over the device, displaying words written in the native language of his people. He recognized it as one of the ancient warrior mantras Brekker had found so fascinating.

Speak and give name to your death, that you may face it with honor.

Honor? That piece of shit really had the nerve to bring up *honor?*

The pressure nearly burst as he spoke with all the seething rage of a firestorm and the frigid wrath of a blizzard.

"Brekker arn Urgen."

He curled his hands into fists and squeezed. His claws bit into his palms.

The words vanished, and the projection changed to a horizontal, three-dimensional map of Sullford. Its focus zoomed out to show more of the surrounding area before shifting to the northwest, focusing on a point off an old, secluded road several miles outside of town.

It was a large clearing in the thick of the forest, connected to the road system by what appeared to be a tiny access road. The perfect spot to hide a spacecraft.

A new message, also in Korasi, appeared over the location.

Come, Sevik kol Talris, and meet your fate.

Sevik snatched up the projector and hurled it against the wall with a roar. It dented the drywall before falling, its projection flickering and glitching. He spun on his heel and raced out of the apartment, limbs quaking with the need to kill.

Meet his fate? He'd already fucking seized his fate, and *nothing* would keep him from it. Nothing would keep him from Mina. Whether Brekker had come alone or with an entire fucking army, Sevik would kill them all and reclaim his mate.

I'm coming, Mina. Hold on.

TWENTY-NINE

*B*REKKER IS HERE.

Brekker has my mate.

He touched her. Took her.

Those thoughts tore Sevik apart, devoured him, and spat him back out again and again as he sped out of Sullford. Nothing could silence them—not the thunderous pounding of his heart, not the groaning of the steering wheel in his ever-tightening grip. Not the engine's rumbling growls, nor the rattling, creaking, and snow crunching under the tires as miles of driving brought him to the narrow access road leading to the location on the holo.

He needed to lash out, to rend and destroy, to violently dismantle everything in his path until he had Mina back. He needed to spill so much blood that the snow would weep crimson beneath his boots.

He needed to see Mina, to smell her, to hold her and kiss her and swear to her that he would never let anything like this happen again.

Brekker is here.

He has her.

Sevik struck the steering wheel with a snarl. *"Fuck!"*

This was why he'd tried to stay away from Mina in the beginning, this was what he'd sought to protect her from.

But he never would've been able to stay away from her forever. She'd been his from the moment he first saw her.

Sevik didn't slow the truck as it neared the clearing. There was no time to case the area and assess what he was up against; he already knew. This was a trap, and if he refused to walk into it, Brekker would make Mina suffer.

He raked his gaze over the clearing when he entered it. The few structures it contained were made of weathered, rotting gray wood, and were in varying states of disrepair and collapse. A black SUV was parked near the clearing's center. The tire tracks worn into the snow looped back to the access road, meaning the SUV— or other vehicles—had come and gone numerous times over the recent days.

The headlights revealed two large males in heavy coats standing between the SUV and Sevik's approaching truck. One wore a black hat and dark sunglasses despite the gloom. The other was bald with a bushy beard. Though their faces appeared human, the plasma rifle in the bearded male's hands certainly hadn't come from Earth. Both stood with the practiced confidence and performative indifference of seasoned thugs.

Neither of the males raised a weapon.

And neither of them was Brekker.

"Fucking coward," Sevik growled, bringing the truck to a stop.

They were just another obstacle between Sevik and Mina. Another thing in his way, another thing to fucking destroy.

He threw open the door and leapt out of the cab, pistol in hand.

The male in the hat grinned; the expression seemed to have too many teeth to be human. "You finally arrive. We—"

"Where is she?" Sevik demanded. He could smell neither Mina nor Brekker here, and he felt time slipping away with each heartbeat. Every moment apart from her was one during which she could come to harm.

The male in the hat chuckled. "You korasi, always so direct."

Sevik raised his pistol, aiming it at the male. "Where?"

Now the bearded male turned his rifle toward Sevik. "Weapon on the ground."

Sevik knew that voice. Jakalg, a burly navat who served as one of Brekker's enforcers. Another fucking traitor. Another obstacle to be destroyed.

Fury boiled in Sevik, tensing his muscles and making his teeth grind. ... "Where. Is. My. Mate?"

Jakalg braced the rifle's stock against his shoulder. "Drop the gun."

The other male shook his head. "He won't do anything. He—"

Sevik shifted the angle of his pistol and fired. With a high, whining thump, the weapon spat a bolt of plasma that passed within inches of the male's cheek.

The male in the hat hissed an ilventyrian curse and ducked, while Jakalg swayed aside.

"Where the fuck is Mina?" Sevik roared, recentering his aim on the male in the hat and advancing toward him.

"Drop the fucking weapon!" shouted Jakalg once he recovered.

"Answer me *esklaat*, or the next one won't fucking miss."

Sevik's heartbeat pounded in his ears, but his hand was steady. He didn't pry his attention from the male with the hat—the unknown. He knew Jakalg had orders from Brekker, or else the navat would've fired already.

Again, the male in the hat chuckled. He braced a hand on the SUV and righted himself. "From what your associate told me, Sevik, you know how this works. You understand the consequences, yes?"

Sevik stared at the stranger, barely managing to keep his trigger finger still. Every bit of him, down to the tiniest sliver of his being, was driving him to get to Mina at all costs. To attack without mercy, without hesitation, to destroy this world piece by fucking piece until she was back in his arms. To let his rage seize control and turn him into a vengeful engine of death.

His rage only intensified now because this fucking stranger, this ilventyr, was right. Sevik knew very fucking well how this worked.

Giving in to his fury would only bring Mina suffering.

A torrent of curses swirled in his mind as he forced his arm to move, first pointing the pistol skyward and then stiffly, reluctantly, tossing it aside. It landed in the snow with an insignificant *pff.*

"Very good," the ilventyr said. "You will get to see the female, and I will collect the remainder of my fee. Everyone wins."

"Tell that coward to come out," Sevik said.

"Shut the fuck up," Jakalg commanded, neither his glare nor his rifle wavering. "Laszlo, restrain this *jattosh.*"

"Hands behind your back," Laszlo said as he approached.

Sevik's jaw ticked, and his every instinct screamed in protest as he complied. Laszlo stepped around him. Warm metal clamped around Sevik's wrists before the thrum of a magnetic seal forced them together. The cuffs struck each other with a dull *clank* and locked in place.

Reflexively, he strained against the bindings. His muscles bulged, the hard metal bit into his skin, and a harsh exhalation escaped through his nose.

The cuffs did not give.

Chuckling again, Laszlo frisked Sevik with rough hands. He took Sevik's wallet, pistol and holster, boot knife, and the little case containing his injector and the remaining serum cartridges, dropping them all into the deep pockets of his coat.

"Good," Laszlo called.

Finally lowering his rifle, Jakalg walked over, crunching snow beneath his heavy boots. He took position behind Sevik.

A low, barely perceptible hum vibrated the air, followed by the muffled hiss of an airlock releasing. On the other side of the SUV, reality rippled, warping the trees seen through it in fleeting waves. A horizontal line of light appeared at least ten feet off the ground.

That light stretched downward as the ramp of a cloaked spacecraft lowered. The opening stood like a tear in the universe, a gateway to another world—a world to which Sevik never wanted to return.

A world to which he'd never wanted Mina dragged.

"All this fucking trouble," Brekker said as he emerged from the cargo hold to stand at the top of the ramp. He wasn't shrouded; those sharp features, piercing, malicious blue eyes, and backswept black horns were all his. One of his arms was banded around Mina's middle, holding her against him.

Sevik's heart stilled, and the heat and pressure inside him swelled, making it impossible to breathe.

Mina's head lolled, and her eyelids fluttered, giving him a glimpse of dark, glossy eyes. Her arms hung before her, bound at the wrists with the same sort of magnetic cuffs Laszlo had put onto Sevik.

No one could touch Mina but Sevik.

No one could touch her and live to do so a second time.

"Release her!" The words erupted from Sevik's chest, raw and ragged, as he ran forward on a surge of fury.

Astyr, another korasi who'd been Brekker's lieutenant for the last few years, rushed around Brekker and descended the ramp to intercept Sevik. He too had a plasma rifle hanging from his shoulder on a sling.

But Sevik hadn't made it even three steps before the back of his leg was hit by Jakalg's boot. Sevik's leg buckled, and he dropped onto his knee.

Jakalg and Astyr allowed him no chance to rise; they were on either side of him in an instant, clamping their hands on his shoulders and pressing their weight onto Sevik to lock him in place.

He growled and pushed against them. His leg muscles quivered with strain, and the enforcers grunted with exertion.

"Let her go, you honorless *rheveshk!*" Sevik shouted. His clenched fists buried his claws into his palms, and the wounds oozed blood. His boot slipped on the snow as he threw himself forward.

His captors dragged him back, one of them grabbing a fistful of his hair. He snarled.

"Sevik?" Mina's eyes flared and sought him, unfocused and filled with confusion.

"I'm here, Mina," he replied. "I'll keep you safe. Bring you home."

"You talk to me, not her," Brekker commanded. He walked down the ramp, half dragging and half carrying Mina, who he kept in front of him. "Even now, you think you're in control. Fucking blind."

Laszlo strolled through Sevik's peripheral vision, returning to the SUV to lean against it with his elbows on the hood. "You said yourself that he was stubborn."

"Take your fucking hands off her," Sevik ordered in a low voice.

Keeping their hands on his shoulders, the enforcers grasped Sevik's upper arms, wrenching back in their attempt to keep him in place. He barely felt the strain in his joints as his arms were pulled past their normal range of motion.

"You must've hit your head in the fall." Brekker halted several paces away from Sevik. "Could've spared her all this if you'd just spilled your fucking brains in that alley."

Mina's head was drooped forward, and her messy curls dangled in her face, but her gaze met Sevik's through those locks. Her bottom lip quivered erratically as shallow breaths escaped her in little clouds.

She was still dressed in the clothing she'd worn for work—a loose, knitted cardigan over a thin shirt, denim jeans, and tennis shoes, which were covered in snow.

She must've been freezing.

Sevik's muscles bulged, flooded with fresh rage. He stilled himself as it built, as heat gathered under his skin, as electricity crackled through his bones. "It's going to be all right, Mina."

Brekker growled and tugged Mina closer as he stalked toward Sevik. "*Zekt'al,* you fucking talk to *me* or I will rip out your tongue."

Sevik lifted his gaze to Brekker's. "You shouldn't have come here."

"You shouldn't have taken my mate," Brekker grated through bared fangs.

Mina was so close. Her scent filled Sevik's nose, obliterating all others. She was right there, and he couldn't reach for her, couldn't free her. His arms strained against the cuffs.

"Enthi was never yours," he said.

With a snarl, Brekker hammered his fist into the side of Sevik's face. The impact snapped Sevik's head aside and sent a blast of pain across his cheek.

Mina gasped his name. The fear and concern in her voice hurt far more than any blow Brekker could ever have landed.

"She was always mine," Brekker said, "and you—"

"Enthi belonged to herself. She came to me by her choice. And you killed her."

Brekker struck Sevik again with a ragged growl. "You made me kill her! You drove me to it! You tried to fucking take her from me, tried to take everything."

"Please stop," Mina breathed, her shoes scraping the snow as she struggled to reach for Sevik. Brekker's iron hold kept her at his side.

"Equals," Brekker spat. "That's what you told me, Sevik. That we would rise to the top together."

"We did," Sevik replied. "I brought you with me."

Brekker answered with another punch, intensifying the pain in Sevik's cheek and filling his mouth with the taste of blood. "You brought me? *You* brought *me*? You betrayed me over and over, Sevik. Fucking chose that organization over me every time you could."

Sevik's lips peeled back. "That what you think?"

"I know. All you do is take"—another blow to the face—"and take"—and another—"and fucking take!" Brekker put emphasis on those words with a final strike that nearly knocked Sevik out of the enforcers' holds.

"You took opportunities from me," Brekker continued. "Took favor. Took control. And then you took *her*. I could've forgotten everything else, but you. Took. Her."

Sevik squared his jaw and looked at the male who had been his only friend for most of his life. "*Aggaan sin thar*, you've fucking twisted this in your head, haven't you? I built the Syndicate with you. The three of us were equal partners. I gave you everything, and you betrayed us to walk the coward's path, yet you dare to fucking question my honor?"

"No." Brekker stepped back, taking Mina with him. "You are not in control anymore. You're nothing. Less than nothing. Now, everything that belonged to you is *mine*." He unwound his arm from Mina's middle to grasp her hair at the back of her head.

Mina cried out in pain. Moisture gathered in her eyes as Brekker forced her to face him.

"Don't fucking touch her!" Holoshroud dropping, Sevik shoved himself up, propelled by fire.

Jakalg and Astyr swayed, but they quickly forced him back down.

"You took my mate, Sevik." Brekker stared down at Mina with a malevolent gleam in his eyes. "And before I kill you, you're going to watch me take yours."

Brekker slammed his mouth down over Mina's.

Her eyes rounded, and she released a muffled cry. She pushed against Brekker's chest, digging her feet into the snow in a vain attempt to free herself.

A roar burst from the depths of Sevik's soul, from the most primal, bestial part of him, and tore across the heavens with enough force to split them open.

Sevik flung himself forward with fangs poised to sink into flesh. His boots gouged the ground as he kicked his legs for purchase. He was only distantly aware of hands pulling him backward, of a rifle's barrel being braced across his neck, crushing his throat.

My mate!

My Mina!

She's fucking mine!

Brekker snarled in pain and pulled away from Mina. For an instant, his lower lip stretched outward, caught between her teeth.

Dark blue blood ran down his chin. He yanked her hair, making her gasp, and her teeth lost their hold. As soon as Brekker broke free, he backhanded Mina across the face. The dull *thwap* of the impact resonated in Sevik down to his bones.

Mina crumpled into the snow, landing on her side.

"Mina!" Sevik fought harder still to escape the enforcers as his mate groaned.

"*Hruta*." Brekker ran the back of his hand across his mouth and glanced down at the blood smeared upon it. His lips curled into a grin. "She marked me. Can't wait to return that bite and leave a mark of my own. I will enjoy her, Sevik. She's not as meek as she appears."

"As I said earlier," Laszlo said from his place at the SUV, "I know buyers who will pay very well for a female like her."

"No." Brekker met Sevik's gaze. "I'm keeping her. Give my friend something to make him more manageable. Just make sure he's still aware enough to watch."

THIRTY

Frigid air stung Mina's throat and burned her lungs. One cheek throbbed with agonizing heat, while the other pulsed with the freezing, abrasive scrape of snow. Darkness encroached on the edges of her vision.

No. No, you have to stay awake, Mina.

It didn't matter that she'd only just regained consciousness, that she still hadn't shaken off the grogginess of whatever drug she'd been injected with. Nor did it matter that Brekker's blow had felt like being hit by a freight train.

She needed to keep her eyes open. She needed to help Sevik. Somehow.

Nothing else mattered.

Mina drew in a deep breath; the air felt like shards of glass slicing her throat. Brekker's blood was on her tongue, and she tasted her own from where her teeth had cut into her cheek. Her stomach churned. She spat onto the snow, staining it dark. Trying to ignore the metallic tang, she pressed her lips together and rolled onto her belly. Every muscle in her body ached, and she was so, so cold.

She never would've guessed that she'd miss the numbness brought on by being drugged.

"Our contract may be fulfilled, but I'm feeling generous," Laszlo said. The sound of his slow approach was barely audible over Sevik's animalistic growls and snarls.

Shivering, Mina gritted her teeth and got her elbows and knees beneath her. Her clothes were wet, only enhancing the chill against her skin—but the cold sharpened her focus. She lifted her head and stilled. There was something ahead of her, a dark object only just breaking the surface of the snow. What little of it she could see was contoured, textured…familiar.

It was the grip of a gun.

Laszlo continued, "Perhaps we may consider this the start of a longer partnership."

Mina glanced at the males. None of them were looking her way. Scooting forward, she took hold of the grip.

"Just take care of him," Brekker said. "I will make it worthwhile."

Rising on her knees, Mina dragged the gun out of the snow.

Her already frantic heart quickened. She knew this weapon, even with the snow clinging to it. This was the alien handgun Sevik carried whenever he went out.

Struggling to slow her breathing, she adjusted her hold on the pistol. The metal restraints digging into her wrists made it difficult to get a firm, comfortable grip, and the gun felt so heavy, so unwieldy.

She'd never used a firearm. They were almost a way of life for many people in Sullford, especially anyone who spent time outdoors. Even in town, moose and bears could sometimes pose a threat. But she'd never had the desire to arm herself—had never felt the need to.

She squeezed her eyes shut. In her mind's eye, she saw Brekker's sneering face, saw his fist striking Sevik over and over, saw her husband, her mate, wild with rage but utterly helpless.

Never again.

Mina would never again give up without a fight. She wouldn't remain idle while someone she loved was hurt.

The anger she'd so long carried tore wide open, crashing into the new rage Brekker had ignited in her today. It overtook her fear, swallowed it, redirected it, repurposed it.

Mina spun on her knee to face the males.

Sevik thrashed in the big men's hold. Brekker watched with a fanged grin. He didn't appear as he had in the café, before kidnapping Mina. His skin was an ashy gray, contrasted by his raven hair, horns, and claws. He'd removed his coat; his crimson shirt was molded to the powerful frame the bulkier garment had obscured. The black markings on his cheeks only enhanced the alienness of his features.

Laszlo was beside him, nonchalantly changing the cartridge out of a small injector. Likely the same one he'd used on Mina.

She raised the gun with wobbly arms.

Don't hit Sevik. Please.

"Take your fucking hands off my mate!" she shouted.

All five males turned their heads toward Mina.

Sevik's eyes rounded, and he rasped her name.

Brekker laughed, shifting his body to face her. "You are no killer, little female. I see it in your eyes. Put that thing down before you hurt yourself."

Her finger twitched on the trigger. Everything inside her was taut, thrumming with tension.

Laszlo snickered and snapped the injector's cartridge compartment closed. "Did he call your bluff, human?"

When it came to Sevik, Mina never bluffed.

Laszlo's stepped toward her mate.

Mina pulled the trigger.

The barrel flashed. A bolt of fire shot out of it with a high, piercing sound, so bright that it left an afterimage in her vision.

She reflexively flinched away from the flash, but not before she saw the bolt strike Laszlo's shoulder. He yelled something she didn't understand as the injector fell from his fingers.

Everything that followed happened impossibly fast. Laszlo staggered, fell, and ducked down with his face in the snow. Brekker reached for something at his waist. The men holding Sevik swung their alien machine guns toward her.

Mina pulled the trigger again and again. The weapon bucked not because of any recoil, but the frenzied motion of her finger. Heated bolts of energy lit up the snow like fireworks in the night sky.

Brekker growled a curse and fled toward the SUV. His gait faltered as one of the shots struck his thigh, but he dove out of sight behind the vehicle.

Sevik roared and shifted his weight, throwing the males holding him off balance before either could aim at Mina. With his arms bound behind his back, he used his torso and legs to tangle himself with his captors.

"Run, Mina!" he commanded.

Some part of her almost refused. She couldn't leave him behind, couldn't abandon the man she loved. But she wasn't a fighter—and she couldn't keep relying on surprise and blind luck. As long as she was here, she was vulnerable, and her vulnerability would distract and endanger Sevik.

Her legs protested as she struggled onto her feet. She couldn't tell if her limbs were so shaky and weak because of the drugs, the cold, or the adrenaline, but it made no difference.

Sevik's eyes caught hers. Their gazes held for only an instant, but that instant conveyed everything—fury, fear, concern, desperation, love. So much love.

But more than anything, Sevik's eyes held promise.

This would not be the last glance they shared.

Mina hoped her eyes told him the same.

She turned and ran for the trees.

THIRTY-ONE

Sevik didn't want to take his eyes off his mate. He had to watch her, had to see her reach the cover of the forest. But he couldn't.

Astyr broke free from Sevik's legs, grasped the front of his shirt, and dragged him off Jakalg. "You fucking—"

Sevik snapped his head forward, hammering the thick bases of his horns into Astyr's face. The other korasi stumbled backward with blue blood pouring from his crushed nose.

Run, Mina. Run.

Jakalg wrapped a thick arm around Sevik's neck from behind, almost entirely cutting off his airflow. Righting himself, Astyr lunged, driving his knee into Sevik's gut. Sevik grunted, but the pain was far away. Jakalg drew back, forcing Sevik more upright and keeping his abdomen exposed for Astyr's subsequent strikes.

"Fucking *hruta!*" Brekker shouted as he emerged from behind the SUV.

"Let's finish him." Astyr spat blood onto the snow. "The female won't get far." He swayed back when Sevik kicked at him, avoiding the boot and answering with another knee to Sevik's stomach.

"No." Favoring one leg, Brekker took a few halting steps

forward. Tendrils of smoke curled from a long, deep plasma burn on his left thigh. "He doesn't get to have a quick death. Knock him the fuck out and secure him in the hold."

He continued in the direction Mina had gone, speeding up to an uneven lope.

"Don't you fucking run from me, you coward!" Sevik choked out, straining toward Brekker.

But Brekker continued onward without response, slowed by his wound but undeterred.

"*Zekt'al*, ilventyr, get up and stick him already," Jakalg said, shifting his weight to hold Sevik back.

Laszlo sat up, clamped a hand over his shoulder, and shook his head. "*Kregvahk.* I'm not getting paid to be shot. My job is fucking done."

With a curse of his own, Astyr turned to scan the ground for the fallen injector.

Out of sight, Brekker's footfalls moved closer and closer to the trees.

"Hurry the fuck up, Astyr!" Jakalg leaned farther back, putting yet more pressure on Sevik's throat.

Hurry.

Mina needs me.

Sevik pressed his claws against Jakalg's belly, planted his heels in the snow, and shoved himself backward.

Jakalg grunted as he lost his balance and fell onto his back. Sevik came down atop him, his weight driving his claws into the navat's abdomen.

With an agonized cry, Jakalg released Sevik's neck and pushed as though to dislodge him. Sevik hooked his fingers, sinking his claws deeper.

Astyr spun toward them. He grasped Sevik's shirt with both hands again, hauling him up, but Sevik locked his arms, using Jakalg as an anchor.

"Get him the fuck off me!" Jakalg shouted raggedly.

Astyr widened his legs and bent down farther. Before he could pull again, Sevik darted his head forward and buried his teeth in the other korasi's throat. Warm blood flowed into his mouth, over his lips, and down his chin.

Astry screamed and pushed away from Sevik, who wrenched his head back, tearing out a chunk of Astyr's flesh as he fell atop Jakalg once more. The tips of his horns struck flesh and bone.

Jakalg struggled to get his hands up in defense as Sevik drove the points of his horns down repeatedly. Bone crunched, flesh squelched, and rattling breaths escaped from mashed lips until Jakalg stilled.

Growling, Sevik sat up and spat the tattered flesh from his mouth.

Astyr lay on his back with both hands clasped over his neck, weakly kicking his legs on the snow. Frothy blood bubbled through his fingers, and his chest heaved with gurgling breaths.

Sevik shifted his gaze to Laszlo, who remained sitting on the snow, stunned as he watched.

"Felyrog bor gethuk." Still clutching his shoulder, the ilventyr scrambled to his feet.

Crimson pulsed at the edges of Sevik's consciousness as he got up and gave chase to the fleeing ilventyr, who ran for the SUV. Sevik's long, rapid strides quickly closed the distance between them.

"I'm not part of this!" Laszlo called. "He hired me as...as a guide!"

Laszlo glanced over his shoulder and uttered another curse. He stumbled, nearly tripping over his own feet, before turning to face Sevik. He plunged his left hand into his right coat pocket and tried to pull something out.

The object caught on the pocket's lining.

Sevik lowered his head and rammed Laszlo with his horns, striking the ilventyr's sternum.

Bones snapped, and air exploded from Laszlo. He fell onto his back.

Sevik skidded to a halt over the dazed, squirming ilventyr. Somewhere in the woods, a plasma weapon fired, its high report muffled by the trees.

Sevik's heart quickened.

Mina!

No time. No more time.

He pinned Lazlo's hands beneath his boots and sat hard on the ilventyr's chest, ignoring the breathless pleas as he forced his bound hands into Laszlo's pocket. Finally, he found what he sought, buried under the pistol Laszlo had attempted to draw—a small, rounded control. He pressed the button.

The maglock cuffs separated from one another before unsealing and falling from Sevik's wrists.

The primal fury at his core roared in triumph, at last freed from all restrictions, at last uncaged.

Laszlo shook his head. "I was...just... Please..."

Sevik drew the pistol from Laszlo's pocket and fired three bolts into the ilventyr's face. The sounds of the shots hadn't finished echoing across the clearing before Sevik was on his feet and sprinting after Mina.

Hold on, val'syra. *I'm coming.*

THIRTY-TWO

MINA FOUGHT to bring her panting breaths under control as she scanned the trees, slowly backing up. The alien gun swung along with her eyes, shaking with the tremors running through her extended arms. The forest was little more than shadows, black on darker black, against which the snow seemed white only in comparison.

Her heel bumped something solid. Her racing heart leapt into her throat, and she spun, turning the gun toward the threat—a large rock, partially buried in the snow. Apart from the rock, there was nothing behind her but more trees, the nearest of which stood several feet away.

Mina carefully moved around the obstacle, returning her aim to the direction she'd come from. Snow crunched under her feet, trees creaked in the wind, and soft *thumps* marked clumps of powder falling from the branches.

She'd heard Brekker behind her. She swore she'd seen him only moments ago, darting between the trees like a phantom.

Her teeth chattered, and a chill coursed up her spine, flowing to the tips of her fingers and toes.

It was too dark for her to see. Her feet were numb, and her

shivering had worsened. The gun—and her eyelids—only grew heavier with her every broken, stinging breath.

Mina forced her legs into motion, continuing onward in a clumsy jog hampered by her own weariness and the deep snow.

She'd heard the echoes of shouts and gunfire from the clearing. Each sound had tightened the icy vise around her heart. Now the clearing was silent, and her fear for her mate was almost paralyzing. Sevik might've been hurt or...or...

No. He's alive. He is alive.

I'm still alive too.

And they would both stay that way. They would be reuni—

A branch snapped somewhere behind Mina. She turned around and pulled the trigger. The traveling projectile's light was almost as fleeting as a flash of lightning, though nowhere near as bright.

Snow crunched elsewhere. She turned again, her arms now dragging well behind her darting eyes.

What if I'm shooting at Sevik?

Just the thought made her stomach twist into a knot. What if she hit him? What if she...

No, Mina! You need to keep moving.

Clouds of her breath obscured her vision further as she trudged on. Moving was the only thing that would keep her away from Brekker, and it was her only means of generating any warmth. The angry heat at her core certainly wasn't doing anything to battle the chill pervading her limbs. Her face, hands, and feet had already lost feeling, and she was losing sensation in her arms and calves. The metal of her cuffs was so cold it burned as it rubbed against her skin.

Another chill crept up her back. The fear clutching her chest strengthened its grip, making her breaths falter. With impossible, instinctual certainty, she felt eyes upon her—the cold, intent eyes of a predator.

Mina spun around again, braced her shoulder against a tree trunk, and raised the gun.

Though he couldn't have been more than twenty feet away,

the night had transformed Brekker into a demon formed of living shadow, with faintly glowing blue eyes, inky markings on his neck and face, and curved horns. But it wasn't his imposing size or otherworldly features that held Mina's attention—it was the gun in his hand, pointed directly at her.

"Chase is over, little female," he said in thickly accented English.

Mina struggled to keep her gun raised, to keep the barrel aimed at him. Rough bark dug into her shoulder, which received scant padding from her cardigan, but that solid wood was the only thing keeping her upright. "S-stay back."

Those words might've sounded confident if not for her shivering.

Brekker took a step forward.

Mina fired. The shot passed over his head by several feet, drawing not even the slightest flinch from him.

"Put the gun down," he said through his teeth.

"No."

Good job, Mina. You managed to keep that to one syllable. That'll definitely make him think twice.

His jaw ticked, and he stretched his arm further to empha-size his weapon. "I will not miss, human. Can you say the same?"

Mina's mind flashed to the scar on Sevik's chest, the mark Brekker had left. That wound had almost stolen Sevik from her before she ever knew he existed. Fury swelled inside her, finally spreading fire through her body.

Brekker's mouth curled into a perverse blend of a smirk and a sneer as he advanced another step. "You are small. Weak. Keep fighting, and you will only hurt yourse—"

Mina squeezed the trigger again.

Faster than she could comprehend, the glowing projectile crossed the empty air and struck Brekker's abdomen. His gun went off so quickly in response that its sound blended with that of her own.

Something small and bright darted toward her. Mina threw

herself down reflexively, bringing her arms up to shield her face. She came down on her side, the snow cushioning her fall.

Something sizzled and hissed above her. The smell of burned wood hit the air. As rapidly as her heart was beating, she wouldn't have been surprised if it had begun smoking too.

A furious growl and heavy footfalls across the snow startled her into lowering her arms. Brekker rushed across the much-too-short distance between them.

Every curse she knew—along with a few she'd heard from Sevik that she didn't understand—tried to come out of her mouth simultaneously, resulting in only a choked, meaningless sound. She propped her elbow on the ground and aimed at the charging alien.

Brekker's boot struck her hands. The pain was explosive, her flesh still in the hypersensitive state that preceded numbness. She cried out as the gun flew from her grasp to land in the snow somewhere.

He came to a stumbling halt a few feet past Mina, clutching at his wounded leg and abdomen and snarling in pain.

Mina drew her throbbing hands against her chest. The burn of tears in her eyes only added to the pain.

Need to get up, Mina.

Breathing through the agony, she braced her trembling hands on the ground. The ache in her bones sapped all the strength from her arms. She had to get up, had to keep moving, keep running, had to survi—

A large, strong hand grasped her hair. Tears spilled down her cheeks as Brekker dragged her up onto her knees.

"*Zekt'al.* I should kill you right here." He pressed the barrel of his gun to Mina's cheek. Compared to the winter air, the metal was scalding.

She blinked away her tears and looked up at him. His eyes, glowing blue in the darkness, were cold, remorseless, and filled with contempt.

Mina had never been so terrified. She refused to show it,

refused to give this monster the satisfaction, but she couldn't stop her traitorous body from trembling.

Somehow, she held his gaze.

Please be all right, Sevik.

Please...come soon.

"No words now, *hruta?*" Brekker pushed harder on the gun, pinching Mina's cheek against her teeth. His firm hold on her hair prevented her from moving her head to alleviate the pressure and pain.

"L-let me g-go," she rasped.

He laughed, though the glint in his eyes held no amusement. Using the barrel of the gun, he forced her head to tip, adding to the sting on her scalp. His eyes blazed down at her. "You will learn how fragile you are, *Mina.*"

Her eyes itched with the urge to look away. It was an almost instinctual impulse; submission to a bigger, stronger, faster, more aggressive beast. Because fear was a survival mechanism, wasn't it? Fear was your subconscious trying to protect you.

But this wasn't only about her survival.

She didn't avert her gaze. She didn't try to pull away. Despite her body shaking with cold and terror, she kept her eyes on Brekker.

Some of the heroines in her books might've said something snarky, bold, or defiant in this situation.

Yet you're the one who needs a human shield.

We'll see who's fragile when my mate catches up to you.

Put down the gun, and let's see which of us is weak.

But no such words came out of her. Holding his gaze...that was enough in that moment. Facing the monster who wanted to hurt her and kill Sevik, that was enough.

After several ragged breaths, Brekker growled. He pushed the gun so hard against her cheek that Mina swore it would punch through her flesh and shatter her teeth. She tasted fresh blood on her tongue.

"*Zekt'al!*" He abruptly withdrew the weapon, slamming it into the holster on his belt.

The ache in Mina's cheek just became another on a long list of pains, but all those pains were fading as the cold chased away all feeling.

Brekker yanked up on Mina's hair, pulling her onto her feet. Her legs refused to take her weight. She caught herself by slapping her hands against his stomach. The flaring agony in her fingers remained bone deep.

At best, they were badly bruised from his kick, but she wouldn't have been surprised if bones had been fractured or broken. Of course, none of that would matter if they succumbed to frostbite...

Or if he killed her.

His free hand wrapped around her throat, and his claws pricked her flesh. "You will pay, Mina, for every wound. For every difficulty. I will enjoy your screams."

Brekker lowered his face closer to hers. Her gaze flicked to the bite mark on his lip. Mina shuddered at the memory of his mouth on her, at the sense of wrongness, of violation.

He inhaled deeply through his nose. "I already enjoy the smell of your fear. But it does not always have to be this way. Be good to me. Be my obedient little mate, and I will grant you my favor. Sevik will not survive this, human, but you can."

Sevik will not survive this.

Mina shifted her cuffed hands, attempting to stand straight on her own two legs. Her fingertips brushed the edge of the scorched fabric around his wound. Despite the tremors wracking her, despite her chattering teeth and stuttering breaths, her voice held steady as she said, "I will not let you hurt him."

Chuckling, Brekker flashed his fangs in a devilish grin. "You will not let me? You are nothing, female. You are—"

Baring her teeth, Mina stabbed her finger into his open wound.

His body tensed, and a pained grunt rumbled in his chest. He dropped his hand from her neck to grasp her forearms in a crushing grip.

Mina threw all her weight behind her hands. Brekker pulled

her arms and hair, bringing fresh, burning tears to her eyes, but she curled her finger, hooking it in. He snarled and staggered, limbs trembling.

You will not take my mate away from me!

She dug her feet into the snow and pushed with all her strength.

Brekker roared. His grip tightened, making his claws break skin on her forearms and scalp, and she let out an agonized, furious cry of her own.

He jerked her head aside. Her temple struck the tree trunk with a *thunk* she felt through her whole skull. A bright flash filled her vision, her head spun, and her knees wobbled.

Can't pass out.

Have to fight, Mina!

Brekker tore her hands away from his wound and forced her body back against the tree. He raised a fist, growled something in an alien language, and swung.

As Mina's eyes widened, another roar—this one more guttural, raw, and bestial—ripped through the night air. Brekker's fist faltered as he snapped his head toward the sound.

The breath seized in Mina's lungs and her heart stuttered as overwhelming relief and love flooded her chest, crashing into the fear she'd been battling to create a maelstrom.

Sevik.

A large form moving much too fast for its size collided with Brekker. She glimpsed glowing white eyes and silvery hair.

Sevik knocked Brekker aside. Mina cried out as Brekker's fingers, tangled in her curls, tore free. Her feet scrambled on the ground for purchase, but her tennis shoes found no traction on the snow. The bark scraped her back as she slid down onto her backside.

The males crashed to the ground nearby.

"She's mine!" Sevik snarled, straddling Brekker.

Strands of hair that had escaped Sevik's bun dangled down his back, which was toward Mina now. She watched those strands sway as his arms moved in blurs of speed, raining blows upon

Brekker. His body blocked the other alien from her view; she could see only Brekker's legs, kicking and thrashing on the ground.

Though the males' snarls, growls, and grunts were much louder, it was the sounds of flesh hammering flesh and bones cracking that were the clearest to Mina.

Something splattered on the snow around the men, made black by the darkness. Mina couldn't pretend it was anything other than blood; even with her eyesight impaired, she could see the stain spreading with each punishing strike.

Brekker's struggles weakened and slowed. The sounds he made did the same, until they diminished to only choked, broken exhalations and shallow, labored gasps.

Even after Brekker fell still and silent, Sevik didn't relent. His attacks only gained ferocity, each punctuated by a sickening squelching. His shoulders heaved with his harsh breaths.

"S-S-Sevik," Mina said, her voice little more than a ragged whisper.

Sevik froze but for the rise and fall of his shoulders. The twilight turned his breath into fleeting, shadowy clouds. He braced a hand on the ground beside himself and, moving as slowly as someone waking from a dream, twisted to look back at her.

His eyes were orbs of white fire, blazing beacons in the dark. She barely felt the fresh, scalding tears running down her cheeks.

She'd never seen anything more beautiful.

"Mina." He crawled toward her only to stop short. "Fuck."

She drew her arms against her chest. As much as she yearned to go to him, that was all the movement she could manage.

The pain's mostly gone, at least.

Just need him to hold me, and everything else will be okay...

Sevik knelt just beyond her reach. He tore off his shirt, turned it inside out, and used it—along with handfuls of snow—to frantically scrub his hands and face. The snow came away darker.

He doesn't want to get blood on me.

More blood, anyway.

Her heart warmed at the gesture.

But the rest of her... God, she was so *cold*.

The instant he finished, the space between them vanished, and he banded his arms around Mina to draw her against his chest. Even though he'd just taken a snow bath, he radiated heat. She felt his heart pounding, felt its echo in his pulse all around her.

"I'm sorry," he rasped, his voice uncharacteristically thick and strained, as he smoothed a hand over her hair. "Sorry, *val'syra*. Sorry."

"D-Don't ap-pologize," Mina stammered, managing a tiny smile.

"*Zekt'al*, Mina." Sevik drew back, moving his hand to cradle the nape of her neck. He gently angled her head up as he ran those glowing eyes over her. "That fucking *rheveshk* coward."

Mina felt the tension in him, which only intensified when he turned her head aside to look at her temple. He growled.

"Doesn't even hurt," she said. That shouldn't have been a comforting truth.

"Quiet," he said, not ungently. Releasing her, he removed something from his pocket and pressed a button in it. The cuffs around her wrists separated and clicked open. He pulled them away.

Without the weight of the metal bindings, her arms felt so light they were in danger of floating away on the wind.

Before she could so much as flex her fingers, Sevik scooped her off the ground, cradling her in his arms. She curled against his chest and closed her eyes.

"My brave wife," he rumbled. "You fought so fiercely."

Mina could tell by the sound of his boots on the snow that he was moving fast, but his hold was so solid and steady that she barely felt any movement. He was so warm it almost hurt, yet the cold had penetrated her so wholly, so deeply, that none of his heat seemed to make a difference.

"For you," she whispered.

"Ah, female... My sweet, strong mate."

She opened her eyes to the sound of a car door opening. The

light from the cab of Sevik's truck was like the first sunrise after an eon of night.

Sevik sat her on the driver's seat, reached around the wheel, and pressed the ignition. The engine roared to life. He muttered another curse and tugged off her shoes, followed immediately by her socks.

"Sevik, w-what are y-you—"

"Shh." Sevik's hands, despite a noticeable trembling that had nothing to do with the cold, moved quickly, tearing her blouse down the middle.

Her eyes widened in alarm. "Sevik?"

"Your clothes are soaked." He pulled her cardigan and shirt off her arms, then removed her pants and panties in one fell swoop, lifting her ass off the seat like she weighed nothing.

"N-Not how I imagined being naked in your t-truck," she stuttered as frosty air swept over her bare skin.

"*Ornyr valaas duun*, female, you are shameless."

She didn't miss the quivering in his voice, didn't miss its rawness and emotion.

Sevik threw open the back door and leaned over the back seat. Mina hugged herself, seeking any shelter she could find from the cold.

His arms were full when he straightened. He draped one of his coats over her lap, tucking it around her legs and feet, then one of hers over her shoulders.

"Should've packed one of those fucking car bags," Sevik growled as he swept a thick, heavy blanket behind her and wrapped her in it.

"S-s-see? T-told you."

Mina huddled beneath the coverings as he again reached past her, this time to adjust the heater and turn on the seat warmer. Then he cupped her cheek in one big, warm hand. Mina leaned into his touch and let her eyes fall shut.

"This might hurt," he whispered.

Something small, hard, and circular pressed to the side of her neck.

Behind her eyelids, Mina saw Brekker and Laszlo—saw the injector in Laszlo's hand.

The device clicked, and she felt the pinch of a needle on her neck. Her eyes flew open, and her racing heart hammered against her ribs. "No!"

She tried to throw off the blanket, tried to fight, to run, but strong hands stilled her arms.

"*Val'syra.*" Sevik's voice broke through that rush of panic. He was there with her. Not Laszlo or Brekker. It was her mate, her husband, her Sevik. "It's to help you heal. Nothing more. I swear it."

Swallowing lungfuls of chilled air and willing herself to calm, Mina nodded.

Sevik carefully separated her coverings, took hold of her right wrist, and guided it free. She looked down as he placed one of those alien pistols on her palm, grip first.

Brow furrowing, Mina lifted her gaze to his.

His otherworldly features were somehow grim and gentle at once. "Anyone other than me approaches the truck, you shoot."

"What?" She shook her head, pushing the gun back toward him. "N-no. Don't leave me! Let's go. Please, Sevik. Let's go home."

He didn't take gun back as he bowed his head and touched his forehead to hers. "The last fucking thing I want to do is leave you alone, Mina. Don't want to ever let you out of reach again, much less out of sight. But if I don't clean this up..."

They risked someone coming across this scene—dead aliens, sci-fi weaponry, a functioning spaceship. And considering that the local police chief, who was already suspicious of Sevik, had spoken with two of those dead aliens face-to-face in Mina's shop...

Shitshow wouldn't be anywhere near adequate enough a term to describe what would unfold.

Mina curled her stiff fingers around the pistol grip. "Then I'll come with you. I...I can keep watch."

Sevik pressed his mouth first to her forehead, then to her lips. The kiss was tender, almost delicate, and she recognized it as a thin layer to mask the desperate, thrumming emotions belied by his ragged breaths and thumping pulse. When he broke the kiss, he hooked his hands behind her knees, turned her atop the seat to face the windshield, and tucked the blanket more snugly around her.

"What are you going to do?" she asked.

"Launch them into the fucking sun." He slipped strands of her hair behind her ear, caressing its shell. "I'll be careful and quick, *val'syra*."

She could only manage a small nod.

"You are safe now." He locked the door, stepped back, and hesitated. "*We* are safe. Because of you."

Sevik closed the door, and his form shimmered as his holoshroud activated. Mina watched him stride away to finally put his past to rest. She had no doubt that he would come back to her.

Neither of them would accept anything less.

THIRTY-THREE

THE DRIVE to the cabin was quiet except for the sounds of the heater and snow being compacted under the truck's tires. Mina sat nestled against Sevik's side. His arm was around her in a tight hold, keeping her close, and his body was tense. He hadn't let her go since he'd returned to the truck. She was just as unwilling to break contact with him.

I almost lost him.

The thought brought tears to her eyes, and she closed them, turning her face and burying it against his bare chest. His skin was warm. Alive.

He was alive.

She drew in a deep breath, taking in his scent. The spicy aroma of teakwood mingled with that of snow and sweat...and blood.

Mina pressed her lips together to hold in a sob. She was trying so hard to keep it together. It was over. They were safe, and they were going home.

But those thoughts, those feelings, those memories, wouldn't leave. Even with the blanket and coats wrapped around her, the heater blasting hot air into the cab, and the seat warmer toasting her ass, she couldn't stop the tremors racking her.

Because it wasn't the cold bothering her anymore.

She'd been drugged and kidnapped by brutal aliens, had been forced to watch her mate get beaten, had been assaulted, chased through the snowy forest in the dark, and shot at...

Sevik moved his hand up, threaded his fingers in her hair, and cradled her head against him. "I have you, *val'syra*."

"I know," she whispered.

He pressed a firm kiss atop her head.

Mina kept her eyes closed. Though her body continued to shake, weariness was setting in, draping her with an inescapable heaviness. The rocking of the truck as it drove over the snowy, bumpy backroads lulled her toward sleep.

But before she'd completely succumbed to exhaustion, Sevik's voice pulled her back.

"We're here, Mina."

He withdrew his hand from her hair and repositioned it on her arm.

Mina opened her tired eyes and lifted her head, turning it to look out the windshield. Her breath caught.

Sevik's cabin stood ahead, glowing brilliantly. Golden icicle lights wrapped the eaves, and strings of gold lights wound around the pillars of the carport and framed the windows. With the quiet, snowy countryside surrounding it, the place looked...magical.

As they drove closer, Mina noticed the glowing candy canes standing between the carport posts, forming a festive, waist-high fence.

Mina sat up a little straighter. Sevik didn't release her.

"You did this?" she asked.

"Yes." The word rumbled from his chest with an unhappy growl. "Should've stayed with you instead."

She worked her arm out from under the blanket and embraced him. She didn't look away from the beautiful lights as they approached the cabin.

Sevik pulled in under the carport and shut off the truck. When he opened the door, freezing night air swept in, battling back the warmth that had filled in the cab. He slid out, drawing

Mina alongside him, and took her into his arms once he was standing, keeping the coat and blanket wrapped around her.

She clung to him desperately, gratefully, lovingly.

He nudged the truck closed and carried her to the cabin's entrance. The wreath hanging in the front door window was new —one of the decorative scented wreaths from Cornerstone, with cinnamon pinecones, red berries, and a gold-trimmed red ribbon.

Mina stared at the wreath. She hadn't made a secret of how much she loved the smell of those pinecones at Cornerstone, and he'd bought it for her. Tears gathered in her eyes; she blinked them away.

That cinnamon fragrance struck her the instant he opened the door. She breathed deep as he brought her into the cabin's warmth, and the tightness in her chest eased, just a little, when he kicked the door closed behind them and locked the deadbolt. His holoshroud melted away immediately.

We're safe. We're safe.

Without setting her down, Sevik toed off his boots, stepped out of the laundry room, and passed through the kitchen. Mina barely had time to notice the bowl of pinecones and the red and white mistletoe tablecloth on the table before he continued into the living room.

Which had been completely transformed.

It was only her rasping his name that halted Sevik on his trajectory toward the bathroom. He turned so she faced the living room.

The seven-foot-tall Christmas tree in the corner drew her eye first. It was real, perfuming the air with its pine fragrance, and he'd decorated it with lights, red, gold, and green balls, and shimmering gold garland. Several wrapped gifts lay beneath it, their rumpled paper and uneven folds at odds with the neatness and precision of the tree's decorations.

Nearby, the fireplace had been adorned with pine garland and more lights, and two stockings hung from the mantel. More garland ran along the tops of the walls, connected with big red ribbons. A decorative centerpiece on the coffee table had even more of those scented pinecones, and the backs of the sofas were draped with red and green blankets.

This was what Sevik had been working on today. He'd done all this for her, for their first Christmas together.

The multi-hued lights blurred as her eyes again filled with tears. The sob she'd been holding in since Sevik had appeared in the forest, alive, to save her from Brekker burst free. She wrapped her arms around him and buried her face against his neck as that sob was followed by another and another, each more ragged than the last. Tears spilled down her cheeks, dripping onto Sevik.

"Mina..." He held her tight, sliding one hand up to cup the back of her head.

"I was so scared. I almost lost you!"

"You didn't."

But she could have, and that knowledge kept her tears flowing. It had been so close. Too close.

"If...If I hadn't..." she whispered. "If that gun hadn't been there..."

Sevik rested his cheek atop her head. "You did, and it was. And we're here, Mina."

She released a shuddering exhalation and tightened her embrace. "I don't want to lose you."

His chest vibrated with a deep growl, and he strengthened his hold on her. "You won't. And I will *never* let you be taken from me again."

He ran his fingers through her hair, petting her, soothing her, until her cries diminished to soft hiccups.

"You brought me Christmas," she said quietly.

He strode toward the bathroom. "And it will fucking wait until I've tended to my mate."

Mina's lips curled into a small smile, and she pressed a light kiss upon his neck. He shuddered, his fingers flexing with a hint of possessiveness.

When they entered the bathroom, Sevik switched on the light and sat her on the counter next to the sink. Though she was reluctant to release him, she dropped her arms, looking up at him.

A lance of pain struck her heart at the sight of his face.

Navy blue blood and a darkening bruise marred the pale skin of his cheek and jaw, and his lip was split, leaving a dried trail of blue down his chin. And his eyes...

She'd seen intensity in Sevik's gaze before, had seen it blazing with desire, with passion, with anger. This was all that and more. This was a glimpse into his very soul, bared to her and only her, with all its strengths and vulnerabilities in the open. She saw the lingering fear in his eyes, saw the unbridled fury, saw the pain as he studied the wounds on her face, saw the deep, consuming love and the overwhelming relief.

He lifted his hands and brushed her hair back. His fingers, trembling slightly, stroked her skin again and again. His jaw tightened, and his nostrils flared.

Then Sevik took her face between his hands and slanted his mouth over hers in a breathless kiss.

Her eyes fell shut as she kissed him back, his desperation piercing right to her heart. She slipped her arms around his neck and leaned into him as more tears trickled down her cheeks. The blanket and coat fell away from her shoulders, and her skin broke out in goosebumps as the cold settled over her. It didn't take long before she was shivering again.

But she didn't care. All that mattered was right here. All that mattered was Sevik, her mate, her husband.

His breath was ragged when he broke the kiss and rested his forehead against hers.

"I've lived most of my life without fear. Knew from a young age that death was inevitable, and I refused to be afraid of it." Sevik's hands slid higher, and his fingers delved into her hair. "But when I went to pick you up, and you weren't there... I was terrified, Mina. Just the thought of losing you was more than I could bear. If he had killed you..."

He bared his teeth with a growl. "I would've torn my own heart out of my chest and shoved it down Brekker's throat. Would've made him fucking choke on it. Because without you... My heart would never have beat again once yours stopped."

"I love you so much," Mina rasped against his lips before she kissed him again.

"You're my fucking heart, Mina."

The conviction with which he said those words—and the way his voice nearly broke with the depth of his emotions—made her chest constrict. She'd never heard him like this before. She couldn't have imagined she ever would. He'd always been so powerful, and he had endured such terrible hardships without showing fear, discomfort, or pain.

But because of her, he was breaking.

"We're okay," she said gently. "We're okay."

Sevik lifted his head and searched her eyes. His expression softened until his gaze dipped, and then his brows fell. "Fuck."

He withdrew from her suddenly, though he placed a hand upon her thigh as he reached over and slid open the glass shower door. He cranked the knob all the way to hot. Water sprayed from the nozzle, creating a familiar, soothing drone.

As the water warmed, Sevik returned his attention to Mina, dampened a washcloth, and gently cleaned the wounds on her face. Mina winced when he touched the tender spot on her forehead, and his frown only deepened.

"*Zekt'al*, I'd kill him a hundred more fucking times if I could," he muttered.

"I think you did?" she offered with a little smile.

Sevik paused, met her gaze, and said in a grave tone, "A thousand more fucking times, then."

Mina didn't miss the slight upward curl at the corner of his mouth before he lowered his gaze.

When he looked down at her hands, which she'd settled atop her lap, his lips peeled back into a snarl. He slid his hands beneath hers with such delicacy and lifted them. Despite his care, she hissed and flinched, nearly pulling away out of reflex.

Blood was caked beneath and around her fingernails, and it stained her skin dark blue. A deep, blue-purple bruise spanned across several fingers on both her hands and the back of the right one.

Sevik scowled, but his touch remained gentle as he lowered his head and placed a light kiss upon her knuckles. "The serum will take away the pain soon."

"What about you?" she asked, her gaze flicking over him. More bruises of various sizes mottled his torso. His wrists were raw and dark gray from the restraints they'd put on him, looking far worse than hers.

"I'll be fine."

She met his gaze. "You used one of those serums on yourself too, right?"

"No."

"Sevik—"

He cradled her cheek with one hand, brushing the fingers of the other across her wrist and up her arm. "I have survived much, much worse than this. Brekker and his enforcers had more serum with them, but our supply is limited. I will not waste any on minor wounds."

"Minor? Those are not minor! Why suffer if you can heal quickly?"

Sevik sighed and shook his head before pressing a kiss to her forehead. "My bruises will heal fast enough on their own. Maybe you haven't noticed, but I'm not human."

Mina gave him a droll look.

"And as long as you are safe, *val'syra*, I will know no suffering."

She frowned at him, brow knitting.

He chuckled softly. "I will be sore tomorrow. But by then, my mate will be healed...and I look forward to her tending to me."

Mina smiled. "Then you'll have to call me *Nurse* Mina. And you'll have to do everything I say."

"Gladly, Nurse Mina." He leaned aside, reaching into the shower to feel the water. He jerked his hand out of the stream, adjusted the knob, and checked again. "But for now, you're in *my* care."

"Yes, Nurse Sevik."

Shaking his head, Sevik drew his pistol and placed it on the counter beside Mina before he unbuckled his belt, shoved his pants down, and kicked them aside. As he straightened, she surveyed his body. Though she hated seeing him hurt at all, she was relieved that he hadn't sustained more serious wounds.

None that she could see, anyway. Despite his reassurances, she would always worry about him, and planned to keep doing so for a long, long time.

For the rest of her life.

He stepped between her thighs and bent toward her. "Arms around my neck, *val'syra*."

When she did as instructed, Sevik slipped his hands beneath her ass, lifted her against him, and carried her into the shower.

Mina's breath caught; the hot water was a shock to her chilled body. It spread tingles across her skin, making her only more aware of how incredibly cold she'd been. But the warmth suffusing her soon became bliss. She leaned her forehead against his and closed her eyes.

For a time, Sevik simply stood there, holding her beneath the hot water, his thumbs stroking her soothingly. It was as though he was as loath to put her down as she was to let him go. But exhaustion was catching up to her, and she knew Sevik would need rest too. They couldn't stay here all night.

"I can stand," she said softly.

"Mmhmm." He didn't move.

Mina chuckled and opened her eyes, meeting his inhuman, white-on-black gaze. "You can put me down."

He grunted unhappily and lowered her feet to the floor, letting her slide down his body. Her hardened nipples dragged over his torso, and pleasure rippled through her despite her pain. Mina released a shuddering breath and settled her palms on Sevik's chest.

Unbidden, her gaze dipped to his slit. It bulged, slightly parted, but his cocks remained hidden within.

Sevik caught her chin, tipping her face back toward his. Both his smile and his words were strained. "I am trying very hard to control myself, wife. You staring at my slit isn't helping."

Mina's eyes widened, and heat flooded her cheeks. "Sorry! I didn't mean to stare."

He chuckled and reached for the shampoo. "I want you, Mina, but I will wait."

She couldn't help her disappointment, but she understood. Now wasn't the time. Both of them were hurt and tired. But God, after everything they'd gone through, she wanted nothing more than to be as close to him as possible. To feel him inside her, moving within her, virile and alive, their bodies and souls interconnected.

Keeping her in the water, Sevik turned Mina and worked his hands into her hair, his touch firm but gentle as he massaged her scalp and brought the shampoo to a lather. Mina closed her eyes with a sigh. Those large, callused hands moved on to caress her body, washing her with soap. He took great care when it came to her hands. Though her fingers hurt, the delicacy with which he used the tip of a claw to remove the blood from beneath her fingernails made her smile.

Once she'd been cleaned, Sevik briskly scrubbed himself from head to toe. Rivulets of diluted blue trickled down his skin and stained the soap clinging to it. He rinsed, turned off the water, and dried Mina with a soft, fluffy towel before seeing to himself.

She'd only taken one step toward the door when he swept her into his arms and carried her out of the bathroom.

"I can walk," she protested, slipping her arms around his neck.

He cradled her against his chest. "I like carrying you."

Mina smiled and pressed a kiss to the corner of his mouth. "And I like being carried by you."

When they reached the bed, he drew back the covers, laid her down, and climbed up beside her. She rolled onto her side to face him, and he did the same, putting his arms around her and drawing her body against his. She rested her head on his arm as he pulled the blanket over them.

The loft was dark but for the warm glow of the Christmas lights downstairs—and the softer but far more intimate glow of his eyes.

"Go to sleep, *val'syra*," he rumbled.

"You need sleep too."

"I'm not ready to close my eyes. I...don't want to open them again and find you gone."

Mina's heart clenched, and tears pricked her eyes. This time, she didn't let them fall.

She took one of his hands and placed it between her breasts as she settled a palm over his chest. "Our hearts are still beating, Sevik. We're here, together, safe and whole. I'm not going to disappear."

Sevik pressed his lips to her head and held her tight.

"I'll never let anyone hurt you again," he vowed, his voice low and grave.

THIRTY-FOUR

Six Months *Later*

The graveyard was quiet as Sevik walked alongside Mina, hand in hand. The lush green grass whispered beneath their feet, having been recently trimmed based on the sweet fragrance lingering in the air. The expansive sky overhead was a pure, soft blue, and cottony tufts of cloud lazily drifted across it. Flowers of all sorts that had been left at some of the stone grave markers added splashes of color everywhere.

Mina turned and led Sevik along a row of gravestones, some of which were weathered and faded from years of exposure to the elements. With each step, her grip on his hand tightened, and her tension became more apparent.

Sevik's chest ached for her.

Compared to the hardships she'd endured, this should've been trivial. She'd suffered loss at a young age, had been impoverished, demeaned, insulted, and isolated. She'd faced her own death, risking everything by looking Brekker directly in his hateful eyes and choosing to fight back for the male she loved. She'd shown courage and strength when most other people would've crumbled.

There was no threat here, and their lives weren't at risk. But Sevik knew his mate. He knew that, in some ways, this was more difficult for Mina than the ordeal they'd survived six months ago. And he wished he could do something, *anything*, to make this easier for her. Wished he could take away all her pain no matter its nature.

Halting in the middle of the row, Mina tipped her head back, closed her eyes, and took a deep breath.

The sunlight played upon her skin and set off subtle highlights in her dark hair. *Ornyr valaas duun*, there was never a moment when she didn't look more beautiful than the last.

A bird called from the trees beyond the graveyard's boundary, its notes high, musical, hopeful. It seemed improper for a place like this, and yet...fitting.

Sevik did the only thing he could—he squeezed her hand, letting her know he was still right there, still with her, that he would be at her side no matter the trials ahead, no matter the danger.

Mina looked at him and gave him a warm, genuine smile despite the sorrow in her eyes.

He dipped his chin. She returned the nod and faced forward, taking the last few steps to reach their destination. Together, Mina and Sevik turned toward a pair of small stones, the flat faces of which were flush with the ground. Both were etched with writing.

Zachary Peter Walker
Devoted Husband and Father

Hannah Grace Walker
Beloved Mother, Cherished Wife, Truest of Hearts.

Releasing Sevik's hand, Mina knelt on the grass and placed a bouquet of wildflowers between the two stones. She'd picked the flowers in an open field on their way here, tying the stems off with a length of twine.

She had told Sevik that her father used to bring bouquets just like that home to her mother all the time—always hand-picked, always colorful. And when he'd died, Mina and her mother had picked flowers to lay upon his grave together as often as they could.

"Hi Mom and Dad," she said, sitting back on her heels and resting her hands on her thighs. "I...I know it's been a while since I last visited, and I'm sorry for that. There was never a day where I felt like I couldn't talk to you, Mom. You were just always there for me, no matter what. But coming here...is always hard for me."

Her voice had grown huskier; Sevik knew by the sound of it that she was fighting back tears.

"Talking to you," Mina continued, "knowing that I'll never hear your voices again... It hurts. Coming here is just a reminder that you're not standing in the next room, that I'll never be able to pick up the phone and call you. You're just...gone. I was alone for so long, and I miss you both so much."

Mina sniffled and brushed the back of her hand across her cheek. "But I'm not alone anymore. Today, I brought someone I wanted you to meet. He's not from around here. He's actually pretty...out of this world! Get it? Out of this world?" She winced. "Okay, bad joke."

Bending forward, she cupped a hand to the side of her mouth and whispered, "Don't let his glamour fool you. He's an alien. But that's a secret between us, okay? No one else can know."

Sevik snorted.

"Anyway..." Mina straightened, looked at up Sevik, and held her hand to him. "I would like you to meet Sevik."

Sevik's brows rose, and his eyes shifted to the stones before returning to Mina. This was new to him, and strange—not only the situation, but the place. There were no graveyards on Vabos. Too many people, too little space. There was no place to go visit the remains of friends and loved ones, whose bodies were inevitably burned to ash.

Death had always been a simple fact to him. There was no mystery to it, no questions to unravel. A person was alive until suddenly they weren't. Then they no longer existed, and the living moved on.

Part of him looked upon Mina now and saw a grieving female speaking to two cold, inanimate stones laid on the ground. But he'd learned. He knew better now, and even if it was strange, he understood.

Death was not an end to existence. When you loved someone, truly loved them, they lived inside of you forever. Mina would always exist in his heart, and nothing in this universe would ever be able to take that from him.

But he found himself wanting more—more than memories. He wanted something to come after, wanted to exist beyond death, so he could find Mina again. So he could claim her again. She would always be his.

Sevik took her hand and knelt beside her. He cleared his throat. "Hello...Mina's parents."

Mina beamed at him. Her lashes were spiked with moisture, the whites of her eyes were tinted red, and her cheeks were wet from fallen tears, but fuck was she beautiful. And when she smiled at him like that? She took his breath away and made his thundering heart feel like it would burst from his chest.

"We'll have to work on making that less awkward sometime." She faced the gravestones again. "Mom, Dad, Sevik is my husband."

It didn't matter that her parents weren't here. Hearing her claim him like that, with such confidence and that hint of possessiveness, flooded Sevik with pride.

"We, uh, got married kind of suddenly," Mina said, "and it wasn't really in the traditional way. Technically, it's not even legally recognized...but..."

She cleared her throat, shooting him a shy little glance that made him want to sweep her into his arms and kiss her. But he wouldn't interrupt. This was important to her, which meant it was just as important to him.

"He's my husband in every way that matters. He takes great care of me, and he's protective. And I do mean *protective*. But in a good way. I think you'd be happy to know that he'd never hurt me or let anyone else hurt me either. He might seem broody, but he really does have a wonderful sense of humor. He's also a bit flirty." Her cheeks pinkened. "Okay, maybe a lot flirty."

A smirk curled Sevik's lips.

Mina cleared her throat. "I don't think you'd approve of some of the things he's done, but...but he's come a long way from his past, and I think you'd both love him. Eventually. Like, once you really got to know him?"

"High praise, wife," Sevik said with a chuckle. "Don't talk me up too much, or they won't believe you."

She laughed, and that light in her eyes was so damn brilliant that he'd gladly stare until that radiance blinded him.

Mina laced her fingers with his, and her expression softened. "Even with the whole universe between us, with all the odds against us ever coming within a billion lightyears of each other, we were brought together, and we've enriched each other's lives. But what matters is that I love him, and he loves me."

"I do," Sevik said, his voice thick. "She is my heart, and I will protect her until there's nothing left of me."

"I promise he means that. I know firsthand. I'm definitely not going to go into any details, so just...trust me."

He couldn't hold back a flicker of rage in his gut. Months later, it hadn't died down. Even with Brekker dead and gone, the scars hadn't completely healed. He hated that his oldest friend—his fiercest enemy—still cast a shadow over their lives, even if it was so faint.

But Sevik and Mina would get there in time. They would heal. Together.

"For the first time since I lost you, Mom, I feel like a whole person again. I'm *happy*. And that's because of Sevik. I can be myself with him. No more hiding, no more pretending. Just me... and he loves me for myself."

"Always and forever, *val'syra*. Whatever comes."

"Which, um, brings me to the next thing." Mina bowed her head and settled her other hand over his, squeezing it between her palms. "I'm...I'm leaving Sullford."

She drew in a shuddering breath and tipped her head back, blinking quickly as her eyes filled with tears. She laughed with little amusement. "I thought this would be easier to say out loud, but it's so much harder than saying it in my head."

"Take your time, Mina," Sevik said gently. "The words will come."

She sniffled and nodded. Tears spilled down her cheeks. Reaching forward, she grazed her fingers over her mother's stone. "This town holds so many wonderful memories of both of you. Staying here made me feel like I was still close to you, because everywhere I looked, you were there. But there are also a lot of painful memories here...and most of the people who caused them are still here too.

"For a long time, I let that pain keep me from truly living. I clung to the past, clung to you, and it was the only thing that kept me from suffocating...but it also left me stuck. I never really let myself think about what I truly wanted and what would make me happy because I was so scared it would mean losing you guys all over again."

Mina flattened her palm on her father's stone. Her voice was thick with emotion when she said, "It's time for me to let go. To... to live."

She sat back, and more tears fell. Sevik carefully wiped them away. Her eyes met his. Fuck, he could gladly lose himself in their warm brown depths.

Mina smiled, brought his hand up, and kissed the back of it before returning her gaze to the stones. "I sold the café. I thought it would've been such a hard decision to make, but it wasn't. I'm excited. I'm excited for the life Sevik and I will build together."

She brought their laced hands to her chest and held them there. Sevik could feel the steady, rhythmic beat of her heart.

"It's time for me to move on," she continued. "Sevik and I bought a camper, and we plan to travel all over. Randy's excited to see me and meet Sevik. But we want to see the world. And maybe, someday"—she peeked up at Sevik—"the universe?"

Sevik scowled. "Fuck no."

Mina chuckled. "I'm still working on convincing him. He'll warm up to the idea eventually."

"I won't."

Earth had dangers enough. He absolutely would not bring his mate out into a universe that was even more fraught with them, especially when her species wasn't officially part of the intergalactic community. He knew more than enough about the universe's underbelly to keep her as far away as possible.

Mina looked back at the stones, and her smile faded. She was silent as a breeze drifted past, tousling her curls and tugging at her blouse.

"It's time for us to go," she said softly. "And this...this is my goodbye. I love you both so very, very much."

Sevik stared down at those stones, at those names, feeling every ounce of love and sorrow and hope in Mina's voice. "Mina is my everything. And I swear to both of you that I will do every-thing in my power to keep her safe, happy, and loved. So...you may rest peacefully."

He bowed his head briefly before rising and helping Mina to her feet. She wrapped her arms around his waist, and Sevik banded his arms around her, holding her close. Her body shook as she cried quietly, her face buried against his chest.

"This isn't losing them again, Mina," he whispered, smoothing a hand over her hair. "You're not leaving them behind. You're carrying them forward."

"I know." She sniffled and tipped her head back, resting her chin against him as she met his gaze. "Thank you for being here with me."

"I'll always be by your side." He leaned down and kissed her forehead.

Keeping an arm around her, he led her back toward the truck, walking at an unhurried pace. He couldn't help but notice the graveyard's serenity. A place of death, but still so vibrant with life. He understood now what humans meant when they said to rest in peace.

Sevik wished he could've laid his mother to rest in a place like this.

EPILOGUE

One Year Later

A GENTLE BREEZE flowed over Mina, cooling the skin left bare by her baby blue bikini. She lay atop a blanket with the summer sunshine bathing her in warmth. Grass, flowers, and trees rustled around her, adding to the soothing, natural music created by the lake's gently lapping waters and the songs of nearby birds.

Tall trees with full, lush leaves surrounded the lakeside meadow, which abounded with colorful wildflowers—pure white daisies, pink musk mallows, and stalks of violet-petaled blue lupin. Smiling, Mina set down her book and ran a finger over the delicate petals of a daisy that stood beside the blanket.

The Catskill mountains were beautiful. Whenever she'd heard about New York in the past, she'd always pictured a massive, congested city with intimidating skyscrapers and indifferent people. But the last year had definitely reshaped her impressions of many places across the country and had put into perspective just how big the US really was.

Sevik and Mina had traveled extensively since leaving Sullford. They'd explored British Columbia, Canada, on their way south, and had followed the Pacific Coast nearly down to Mexico, taking in all the sights along the way. They'd seen the southwestern deserts—Sevik had enjoyed the scenery but hated the heat—and stopped in Arizona to visit Randy and his girlfriend, Katy.

Mina grinned as she recalled when they'd met the older couple at a restaurant for dinner. She'd never seen Randy's eyes go so wide as they had when she'd introduced Sevik. Throughout the meal, Randy had kept glancing suspiciously between Sevik and Mina, and at the first chance he'd found, he'd pulled her aside and asked if she was okay.

With no need to hide from Brekker, Sevik had altered his shroud. Though he still wore a human face as Viktor Novak, he did so with his white hair and black *lyros* unhidden.

Despite his politeness toward the older man, Sevik's appearance had apparently set off alarms for Randy. That grandfatherly concern had come through, and he hadn't quite believed Mina when she said she was okay until he'd really looked at her.

She remembered how his expression had sobered, and how a slow smile had spread across his face before he'd told her that he had never seen her eyes shine so bright. That he'd never seen her so happy.

And he'd looked happy too. Though he was almost seventy years old, Randy seemed more energetic and youthful than ever, and it was clear where that spark had come from. He and Katy were so sweet together. The woman was kind, warm, and funloving. After that first dinner, Mina had felt like she'd known Katy for years.

Mina and Sevik had spent a week in Arizona, seeing Randy every day. The man had really come to life when they went fishing together and Mina still nailed the cast he'd taught her. His excitement had only grown when he learned that Sevik had never fished before.

Nothing seemed to make Randy happier than taking the role

of teacher, especially when it came to his two great loves—baking and fishing.

When Mina and Sevik had moved on, they'd done so with the promise that they would visit again soon, and she meant to keep it.

Their course had meandered across multiple states from there, with stops wherever and whenever they'd felt like. They'd visited more silly roadside attractions than she could count, had gazed upon some of the most beautiful landscapes in the country, had met all sorts of people and eaten all sorts of food.

Sevik still preferred meat, but she'd find something sweet that he enjoyed eventually.

Mina loved every moment of it, even when they'd faced the challenges of travel. But her favorite times were still the times like this—when it was just her and Sevik, somewhere secluded. When it was just the two of them.

A splash drew her attention toward the lake, and she propped herself up on her elbows to look. The sight before Mina made her heart flutter and her core clench.

Sevik rose from the lake like a seductive sea god. The water cascading over him caught the golden sunlight and set him aglow. Mina's eyes followed its course from the tips of his horns, down past his sharp-featured face and broad, powerful shoulders, and over the sculpted muscles of his chest and abdomen. The water line hid his lower half.

Lifting her sunglasses to rest atop her head, she caught her bottom lip between her teeth and watched Sevik walk toward shore. Desire kindled low in her belly, growing hotter with every inch of his body that rose above the water's surface—the seductive V of his adonis belt, his hips, and finally his slit.

Mine.

This gorgeous male was *all* hers.

Mina curled her fingers into the blanket as unadulterated lust speared her.

Her gaze trekked over his body, following the rivulets of water streaming down his skin as he approached.

God, she wanted to lick every inch of that delectable skin. Her nipples hardened into achy points, and her pussy clenched with the sudden, visceral need to have him inside her.

As she stared at his slit, it parted, revealing a sliver of the glistening black flesh within.

Only then did she truly register his appearance.

Mina gasped, her wide eyes shooting up to meet his. "Sevik! Your holoshroud!"

He displayed his fangs in a sultry, wicked grin. "We're in the middle of nowhere, *val'syra*."

"But—"

"The birds will keep our secret. And I've been watching you, craving you, this whole time. Only fair that I get to see you look at me with the same hunger."

Sevik settled on the blanket beside Mina. Twisting his fingers in her hair, he tipped her head back. His white eyes were bright against his black sclera, fiery with possessiveness and carnal need. "Hello, my beautiful wife."

His mouth captured hers in a hard, claiming kiss.

Mina's lust surged back to the forefront. Bold flicks of his tongue coaxed her mouth open, and he deepened the kiss with a ferocity that she returned in kind. Pleasure spiraled through her, and heat pooled between her thighs.

Her breasts felt heavy and achy, her skin tingled for his touch, and her clit thrummed with need.

"More," Mina rasped, flattening her palms against his chest. "I need more."

Sevik chuckled. "As my mate commands."

He braced his hand on the blanket and moved over her, caging her in with his body. She loved how small he made her feel, how easily he could overpower her, restrain her. Conquer her.

And that was exactly what she wanted him to do right now.

She smoothed her hands up his chest to his shoulders.

Long, sopping wet strands of his hair fell onto her, followed by several drops of cold water.

Mina squealed with laughter as more droplets trickled onto

her neck. She pushed against his chest and wriggled beneath him. "You're getting me all wet!"

He lowered his head, pressed his face to her neck, and inhaled deeply. "Mmm. I know, *val'syra*. I smell it." He growled against her throat. The sound reverberated through Mina, making her giggle.

"Sevik!"

He lifted his head with a chuckle. "Should we see just how wet you are for your male?"

His free hand moved to her face, and he trailed the backs of his claws down her cheek, her jaw, and her neck, past her collarbone and between her breasts until he'd reached the string holding the cups of her bikini top together. A delightful shiver coursed over her skin in the wake of his touch. Those white eyes blazed, holding hers captive as he hooked the string with a claw.

A flick of his finger sliced it apart. Mina's eyes flared. The material fell away, baring her chest to the sun-kissed air.

Sevik cupped one of her breasts. His big, rough palm kneaded her flesh, and she arched her back to press her nipple more firmly against it with a soft moan.

"Ah, my needy wife." He caught her nipple and pinched, making her gasp and buck her hips. "I fucking love how responsive you are. Love the little sounds you make."

Keeping his eyes locked with hers, he dropped his head and kissed the hardened peak of her other breast. Just that light touch sent a bolt of pleasure straight to her pulsing clit.

Mina's breath caught, and her hands flew to his horns, gripping them tight.

His lips and tongue caressed and teased her nipple and the surrounding flesh while his fingers continued pinching, plucking, and twisting the other.

"Sevik," she breathed. "Please."

He hummed against her nipple. The vibration made her tremble and squirm. He moved his mouth toward her other breast, placing tender, tormenting kisses along the way, each of them scalding compared to the cold water still trickling off him.

"I could make you come just by toying with these rosy little buds," Sevik said, his warm breath flowing over her flesh. "Should I try?"

Then he closed his mouth around her nipple and sucked.

Mina cried out, squeezing her eyes shut as pleasure shot through her. And Sevik didn't relent. The flat of his tongue rubbed her nipple in quick, firm strokes; he might as well have been lashing her clit.

Her thighs trembled as Sevik continued his maddening sucking. Liquid heat flooded her core, soaking her bikini bottoms, and a whimper escaped her throat. Mina held Sevik to her. She was on the verge of coming. She could feel it as that pleasure coiled tight, as tingles spread through her body, and she never wanted him to stop.

Sevik pulled his mouth away. The sensation was both painful and blissful as the air, frigid compared the heat of his mouth, touched her nipple.

Mina tensed and tried to pull his head back down. "No!"

Sevik chuckled, low and dark. "No no, little wife." He blew upon the throbbing bud. "Not yet. Not until I say."

"Not fair," she whispered, glaring at him.

He just smiled and kissed the center of her chest before sliding his body down along hers. His kisses trailed lower, to her belly, which he cradled between his hands.

"One day I will see you round with my child," he rasped. When he lowered his lips again, their touch was delicate, reverent, and lingering, and a whole new sort of heat ignited within Mina.

She smiled, releasing his horn to caress his damp hair, and let that warmth spread through the entirety of her being. "One day."

Mina wanted that too. Wanted children, wanted a family with him. She knew Sevik would make a wonderful, protective father.

They weren't even sure if it was possible. Aliens weren't supposed to be on Earth at all, so it wasn't like there were published studies about reproduction between humans and nonhuman species. That didn't stop them from yearning, from hoping.

But they weren't ready for that yet. For now, Mina and Sevik simply wanted to enjoy one another, and neither of them were quite willing to share the other. That was why she'd started taking birth control just to be safe.

Sevik kissed her belly again and again, each time more affectionately than the last, but when his eyes rose to meet hers again, they were just as ravenous as before. He stared at her as he slid lower still, until his face was above her pelvis.

With torturous slowness, he undid the knots at her hips that held her bikini bottom together. The tickle of the strings made her skin break out in goosebumps, especially when accompanied by the brush of his fingers.

She ached for him, God did she ache.

He slid a finger under the waistband of her bikini and peeled the fabric away. "Mmm. Just look at how wet you are, *val'syra*."

Curling his hands around her inner thighs, he parted them, gaze fixated on her pussy. "Fucking beautiful."

Sevik dropped a searing kiss right at her center.

"Ah!" Mina cried, threading her fingers into his hair and closing her eyes.

He lapped at Mina from her entrance to her clit, and she moaned his name as pleasure shuddered through her.

"*Ornyr valaas duun*, you taste divine."

His voice rumbled into her, making her hips undulate, and he drove his tongue into her pussy to slide and twist along her inner walls. When it curled, it stroked the sensitive flesh of her G-spot.

"Oh fuck!" she gasped, catching his horns again and bearing down on his tongue to ride it shamelessly.

He stroked that spot repeatedly, greedily, relentlessly.

"Yes! Don't stop. Oh please, don't stop!" Mina panted and writhed, her thighs quivering as the sensations within her built. But he didn't let her escape. He kept her legs pinned and spread wide, his claws pricking her flesh.

Heat curled in her core, stoking the flames of her pleasure higher and higher, threatening to engulf her in a fiery blaze. And she was a willing sacrifice. Let her burn. She'd revel in the inferno.

It was always like this with Sevik. Intense, all-consuming, passionate. His every kiss, his every touch, his every caress made her come alive.

Sevik withdrew his tongue. Before Mina could plead, he latched his lips around her clit and sucked.

Stars burst behind her eyelids, and ecstasy poured into her veins. Mina's head craned back, her back bowed, and ragged, breathy cries tore from her throat. Her pussy contracted, and a gush of essence flowed from her as her entire body seized.

But Sevik didn't stop. His tongue lashed her clit, prolonging her pleasure, making her come again and again until she was a trembling mess whispering his name like a benediction.

He released her with a growl and ran the flat of his long tongue over her pussy before placing a soft kiss on her sensitive clit—as he always did after pleasuring her with his mouth. Mina smiled. It was like he thought of her clit as a treasure, a gift, even though it was her that benefitted from his attentions.

Sevik lifted his head, gently pulling his horns out of her lax hold. Panting, she met his gaze. The searing white of his eyes revealed how desperately he wanted her. He crawled up her body, the muscles in his shoulders and arms flexing, his long hair trailing across her heated skin, and when his head dipped, he pressed his mouth to hers.

He kissed her slowly, sensually, tenderly, but no less passionately despite the sweetness. Mina reciprocated, cupping his face between her hands. She tasted herself on his lips as much as she tasted him; the combination was intoxicating.

Sevik broke the kiss and smoothed Mina's damp curls from her face. "My heart."

Her eyes stung with the threat of tears as she stared up into his. "And you are mine." Mina stroked her thumbs along where the black markings on his neck met his jaw. "I need you inside me."

His pupils expanded into lustful pools of black, and he slipped a hand between their bodies. "And I need to be inside you."

The head of one of his cocks settled against her rosette, and with a nudge of his hips, the tip of his other cock slipped into her pussy. Mina's breath hitched, but she forced herself to breathe as he slowly pushed into her. His natural oils eased his entrance, but it didn't diminish the pressure or the brief flickers of pain as her ass stretched around his girth.

"That's it, my love," Sevik crooned as he sank deeper.

Mina held his gaze, keeping her body relaxed and her thighs spread around him. That minor pain quickly gave way to satisfying fullness, to pleasure, and she arched, wanting him only deeper still.

"Sevik," she whispered, lifting her head and brushing her mouth across his.

He nipped at her lips as he shifted onto his elbows and moved his hands under her head to cradle it. With his body curled over Mina like this, sheltering her, it always made her feel so safe and cherished. It always made her feel like the two of them were the only ones in the whole world.

Sevik pulled back his hips slightly only to thrust deeper, little by little. Mina moaned. She could feel each ridge as they slipped in and out of her, as they grazed her inner walls.

"Fuck, you feel so good," he groaned. "Just a little more, my wife, my mate. You were made for this. For pleasure. You were made for *me*."

With a final thrust, Sevik sank fully inside her, nestling deep. Mina's head tipped back with a soft gasp, but her eyes did not leave his.

If they could've stayed like this forever, Mina would've been sorely tempted to do so. She was one with him, intertwined body, heart, and soul; she was enveloped in love, filled with it.

He stroked his thumbs through her hair as he gazed down at her. Despite his dilated pupils having nearly swallowed his irises, there was no darkness in his eyes. The hurt and anger that used to smolder in them was gone. She saw herself reflected in them—and in that reflection, she saw happiness, hope, light, and love. A bottomless well of warm, free-flowing love.

And it was all hers.

She slipped her fingers into his hair. "I love you."

"My Mina." Sevik smiled and kissed her forehead. "My love." His lips grazed her nose. "My *val'syra*."

And just before his lips met hers, he whispered, "My home."

AUTHOR'S NOTE

We hope you enjoyed Saved by the Alien Crime Boss! We always love returning to the Aliens Among Us world, and hope you had as much fun reading as we did writing this book.

To keep up on current news from us, be sure to join our newsletter. We always share monthly updates on what we're working on as well as art, book recommendations, and more. Also consider joining our Facebook Reader Group!

Are you new to our books and wondering what else to dive into? If you love aliens, action, playful banter, found family, and plenty of spice in a cyberpunk setting, consider checking out our Infinite City Series! Turn the page for

SILENT LUCIDITY

THE INFINITE CITY #1

He's an alien assassin who has never known a female's touch—until hers.

Abella hasn't allowed four years of slavery to break her spirit, but after numerous failed escape attempts, the chances of making it home to her family seem bleak. That is until she shares a passionate, forbidden dance with a silent stranger. His piercing silvery eyes haunt her with a taste of hope.

Intense, mysterious, and deadly, Tenthil may be the key to Abella's freedom. But as she finds herself increasingly drawn to him, she realizes the truth—Tenthil has no intention of taking her home.

Get it on Amazon!

THE CURSED ONES

His Darkest Craving

His Darkest Desire

ALIENS AMONG US

Taken by the Alien Next Door

Stalked by the Alien Assassin

Claimed by the Alien Bodyguard

Saved by the Alien Crime Boss

STANDALONE TITLES

Claimed by an Alien Warrior

Dustwalker

Escaping Wonderland

Yearning For Her

The Warlock's Kiss

Ice Bound: Short Story

ISLE OF THE FORGOTTEN

Make Me Burn

Make Me Hunger

Make Me Whole

Make Me Yours

VALOS OF SONHADRA COLLABORATION

Tiffany Roberts - Undying

Tiffany Roberts - Unleashed

VENYS NEEDS MEN COLLABORATION

Tiffany Roberts - To Tame a Dragon

Tiffany Roberts – To Love a Dragon

ABOUT THE AUTHOR

Tiffany Roberts is the pseudonym for Tiffany and Robert Freund, a husband and wife writing duo. The two have always shared a passion for reading and writing, and it was their dream to combine their mighty powers to create the sorts of books they want to read. They write character driven sci-fi and fantasy romance, creating happily-ever-afters for the alien and unknown.

Sign up for our Newsletter!
Check out our social media sites and more!
http://www.authortiffanyroberts.com

9 781961 376236